T0271529

THE FATES

THE

FATES

ROSIE GARLAND

QUERCUS

First published in Great Britain in 2024 by

QUERCUS

Quercus Editions Ltd
Carmelite House
50 Victoria Embankment
London EC4Y 0DZ

An Hachette UK company

A CIP catalogue record for this book is available
from the British Library

HB ISBN 978 1 52942 812 4
TPB ISBN 978 1 52942 813 1
EBOOK ISBN 978 1 52942 814 8

10 9 8 7 6 5 4 3 2

Typeset by CC Book Production
Printed and bound in Great Britain by Clays Ltd, Elcograf S.p.A.

Papers used by Quercus are from well-managed forests and other responsible sources.

For my father, who forged his own destiny

'Of The Fates, there are no stories'

Pausanias, *Description of Greece*

THE FATES

Olympos

A Time out of Time

Cruel Fates, malevolent Fates, haggard and heartless.

So say the storytellers, when speaking of us. You have heard the legends wherein we are vicious crones, three weird sisters who cackle over the meagre span of years we allot to men, smug in our own boundless aeons. You have seen the sculptures portraying us foul-featured, our breasts dry folds of skin draping our ribs. There is bent-backed Clotho, gnarled fingers grasping the distaff as she spins the thread of mortal destiny. There is beak-nosed Lachesis, squinting a rheumy eye as she measures how long a single life will last. Last and most terrifying of all is Atropos the Inflexible, who severs the thread of life and allows not one instant longer.

Since the first tale was told around the first hearthside, we have been silenced and slandered. We have held our peace for too long. Draw close. For the first time, we shall speak in our own voices, and tell the plain truth.

Before the Gods were, we are.

We exist outside the mortal reckoning of Time, with its tidy parcelling into Time Was, Time Is, and Time To Come. We are as far beyond such distinctions as a shooting star and the child who looks up in wonder.

When the Gods are not yet born, our mother Nyx claps her hands in the deeps of the abyss and brings forth light. She sets her shoulder to the Wheel of Time and sets it rolling. Grabs a handful of dust and names it Earth, weeps tears and names them Ocean; squeezes three daughters from her fathomless body and names us Clotho, Lachesis and Atropos.

While the world burns and cools, Nyx teaches us how all life springs from stardust, and to stardust all life returns.

We watch as Nyx brings forth the Titans, and then the Gods. She scoops river clay and fashions the mortals. Male and female she creates them, and they dance in the garden of their infancy. Foolish and fragile, they make easy prey for beasts of land and air and water. Before they are half-begun, their numbers dwindle into danger.

It is then our mother Nyx teaches us our essential place in the pattern: to craft, shape and seal mortal destiny. To do this, we spin the thread of existence, measure out each flicker and then sever the link with life and breath. We tighten a cord of protection around their fleeting lives so they may multiply.

Sister Clotho reaches into the heavens and wraps a skein of stars around her distaff. She swings the spindle and teases out a glimmering thread, entwined with the tenacity at the heart of creation, for mortals need its dogged persistence in order to thrive.

Sister Lachesis hefts her measuring rod, a beam of divine light true as a comet's tail. She measures each according to their fate, stretching mortal lives long enough for learning. Finally, sister Atropos swishes her shears and cuts the thread. Each creature needs an ending so it might lay down its aching years and sleep.

In the beginning we spin lives without struggle. Mortals eat and breed and die, over and over, with no more significance than limpets suckling rocks that string the shore. But all life must have meaning, from the smallest ant to the tallest forest pine, and Mother Nyx does not intend for humankind to live like limpets. There is much in store for this most wonderful of Nyx's creations.

So we twist hunger into the thread; fear as well as desire; struggle and hardship as well as satisfaction. A little here, a little there. To each, we measure fairly, mixing good luck and bad. We shepherd their curious natures, weave caution, and watch the aching slowness of their increase. For ages beyond reckoning, we shape ordered lives, coaxing and nudging mortals to shine bright as the stars from which they are made. They are our progeny; toddling babes who stumble and fall, stumble and fall again. We pick them up, shush their weeping, and urge them to go on.

Mortals face our challenges, push against them, and grow. As well-reared children, they blossom. They venture out of Eden, planting anxious footsteps through forest and tundra, desert and ice. With strict destinies, we hone their intellect. They learn quickly because they have to.

We do not goad alone. There are gifts also. They discover the pharmacopoeia Nyx has planted in every tree and leaf; the wisdom to track a bird to its nest, a scatter of saplings to a spring. They weave songs so enchanting the very birds fall silent, paint their caves with beasts so wondrous we can hear panting breath. They learn love, such a sweet discovery they dive in and out of it a hundred times in one lifespan.

They learn to sow and reap, and for the first time fill their bellies to bursting. We wonder if they will grow lazy, but they confound all expectation. They build: first wood, then clay, then stone; each generation impelled by the destinies we weave to outshine the last. And always, they gaze into the heavens and feel the echo of stardust in their bones.

In the heavens meanwhile, the squabbles of Gods and Titans overspill into violence and war. The victorious Gods wreak vengeance on the vanquished. When done with punishment, they turn their attention to the mortal creatures far below, taking some as playthings and breaking them with their ungentle touch.

We blink and human empires rise and fall, rise and fall again. Through it all, we spin and measure and snip. We are The Fates and nothing can change us. We shall be here when the world crumbles into final dust; shall be here when Nyx breathes out new stars for Clotho to wind around her distaff, and the cycle of life begins once more.

We are endless. For us, there is no death. Neither is there growth. We spin the radiant thread of life yet can only watch as mortals revel in its urgent and tantalising joy. Not for us the leaping of the heart with new love, nor the agony of grief. Not for us the singing of the blood when running a race, nor the exhilaration of diving into a lake's frigid depths.

We gaze down at Earth and sigh. We hear the lies. We are blamed for bad luck and bad judgement, accident and happenstance, envy and betrayal, for every sly knife in the back. We shrug it off, keep our own counsel, and we spin and measure and snip.

And now, we are forsworn to a special task: to keep a vigil over the lives and destinies of two mortals. We watch the huntress Atalanta: Fleet-of-Foot, Equal-in-Weight, beloved of Artemis. We watch Meleager, hero of the Argonauts. He left his home a dozen years ago and the desertion weighs heavy on his conscience. We peer into his heart: snarled up in hatred for The Fates. And why? He blames us for laying a curse upon his life. Meleager is angry, desperate and lost, a dangerous combination.

Follow the line of our intention, from Olympos down to the middle sea. Atalanta stands at the prow of her ship, peering ahead, eagle-eyed and eager. Wind tangles her hair; her bow is slung across her breast, arrows tipped and ready. She is bound for Calydon and her friend Meleager.

Ah, Calydon! Famed for its temples heaped with gold, its olives groves and vineyards; famed for its fields bursting with wheat, as though Demeter upended her cornucopia and spilled out the entire bounty of her harvest.

Look again.

A pall of misery stretches over the kingdom. Famine has trampled the cow pastures to slurry. The cornfields are churned into empty dust; fruit trees display bare ribs of branches. The land shrivels. The people cower. They hear the thunder of a monster rumbling through the earth: the boar that has laid waste to their home. No one can rid them of this curse. A legion of brave men have lost their lives trying.

We spin, we measure, we snip. Across the gem-green sea, Atalanta and Meleager are hastening toward their fates and we must follow. On their frail mortal shoulders rests the future hope and destiny of all humanity. More than Achilles, Agamemnon, Theseus and Helen combined, this man and woman will change the course of history for ever. At what dreadful cost, we shall reveal.

ATALANTA

Calydon, Aetolia

As the ship rounds the headland into the bay, a sharp breeze swoops in and stings my cheek. I'm happier when my feet are on solid ground, so have been brooding. The wind catches me unawares, forcing a gasp of surprise.

Nimble as squirrels up a tree, sailors scramble the rigging. The sail ripples and swells; the ship tacks to the left, the deck tilts and I hang onto the gunwale. As we head into harbour, the peaked prow slices the water, waves foaming and falling away to each side. In the distance, the quayside beckons. Men tiny as manikins stand ready with ropes and gangplanks, waving their arms. The ship's captain barks a command. I expect the sail to be gathered up in readiness for mooring. Instead, there's a plummeting splash.

'We're dropping anchor right here,' he snarls, in answer to a question I haven't asked. He tugs the amulet of Poseidon tied about his wrist and raises it to his lips. 'I'm not having my lovely ship brush a single stone of their city. It's been cursed by Artemis. Good luck to anyone foolhardy enough to oppose the will of the Gods.' He spits, muttering a prayer against the evil eye. 'And good riddance,' he adds.

Sailors are a suspicious crew at the best of times, and I am a woman, unlucky at any time and on any boat. They'll be relieved to offload their female cargo. Out of respect as much as self-preservation, I've kept myself bundled in my cloak the whole journey. An imp of doubt calls me coward for the compromise: if I were a true sister of Artemis I would stroll above decks, right breast uncovered for the world to see. I hear the criticism, but choose not to listen.

'*We* honour the Gods!' shouts the captain, to a chorus of agreement from his men. He kisses the amulet again. 'All of them!'

I'm not the only passenger drawn to Aetolia seeking adventure. The ship is loaded with eager hunters. From the roughest tavern in Macedon to the finest goldsmith in Athens, the talk is of the monstrous boar and how no man has been able to destroy it. In the way of hearthside tales, the beast has grown in the telling until it's become more fantastical than the Hydra: its hide throws off arrows, its glance is more deadly than a basilisk and on its head it wears a crown worth a king's ransom.

I shall believe it when I see it.

Above, the sail groans and strains against the pull of the anchor. Ancaeus joins me, shading his eyes and watching a small craft row out to meet us. He's a sturdy and neat-mannered youth, full of shy questions about the strings I favour for my bow and whether it's true I was raised by a bear. Others are less respectful of a woman who can outrun, outshoot and outhunt them. I don't trouble myself with learning their names.

We shin down a rope cast over the side and jump into the jolly-boat. It requires a feat of acrobatic skill, because the sailors keep shoving the little craft away with pikes so it doesn't touch their precious ship. At last, all are aboard and only a few take an early bath.

The rowers bend to their task, wrestling the oars with arms thin as wheat-stalks. When I turn to cry a farewell, the ship is already weighing anchor. Released from the drag of the rope, the vessel turns swiftly, sails catching the wind. By the time I've climbed the steps up the harbour wall, it has rounded the cove and is gone.

I stride along the dockside, trailed by my fellow-hunters. Strangers attract attention, myself in particular. I'm gawped at by men and women alike, elbowing each other as they try to decide whether I am male or female or something other. Their mouths are flopped open so wide, they'll find themselves catching flies if they're not careful. Children hop about my ankles, curious as puppies. A boy grabs the hem of my tunic and peers up into the shadows. I kick him halfway across the harbour.

'Its legs are hairy like a man's,' he squeaks, rubbing his aching backside. 'But it's got no pizzle!'

A steward scurries to meet us, brandishing his staff and chasing the lads away.

'Welcome, welcome,' he pants, flushed with embarrassment at my first brush with his fellow-citizens.

He bustles about, shepherding us forwards, bobbing and smiling the whole way. Calydon is as fine a city as I ever saw. The houses are freshly plastered, the streets swept so clean I could eat my supper off the cobbles.

For all its splendour, Calydon is a haunted place; a city weighed down by terrible misfortune, heavy as the shackle of a galley slave. A smear of oily fog hovers over the rooftops, oppressive as a swarm of flies over a carcase. The shops stand empty, shelves picked clean. Amphorae loll on their sides, the last drop licked away long ago. Pinched faces surface from shadowed doorways. Skeletal infants drag at their mothers' withered breasts, their bellies bloated with the cruel emptiness that mimics fullness. With a shudder, it occurs to me I've not seen a single cat slink past, nor heard one dog bark.

I recollect how only this morning, I shared rough wine and grilled fish with the sailors. Our leftovers were tossed into the waters. It was sport brought me here: the prospect of a challenge to my prowess, a bracing hunt followed by carousing around the fire, boasting and laughter. I did not consider the fate of the Calydonians and how they have been brought to their knees. I itch with shame, and make a vow: I will not leave until I have slain the boar.

We arrive at the public square, a broad space paved with russet-hued sandstone and ringed with tall buildings of remarkable elegance. A crowd of gentlemen approach, and a fellow wearing a hefty gold chain gets onto one knee, puffing with the effort. The skin of his belly hangs in a wrinkled apron over the belt of his kilt. A man who loves feasting, yet since the boar plundered his land, he has starved along with his people.

'Welcome, honoured gentlemen,' he says. 'Oh, most courageous company! Hear the greeting of Kleitos, elder of Calydon!' The hunters smile and look very pleased with themselves. He turns to me and raises his hand in a salute. 'Gracious and renowned Atalanta!' he cries. 'Our grateful city flings open its doors to you. Fleet-of-Foot! Beloved of Artemis!'

The city elders nod furiously; each man in his finest robes, yet stooped with hunger. Their hands tremble, greenish shadows around their eyes. Wealth counts as nothing when a lord would trade his riches for a crust of day-old bread. As the proverb says, *A man cannot eat money.* I shift from foot to foot, mumbling thanks.

'Enough of greetings,' cries one of the hunters, waving a short spear. 'The boar! Lead us to it!'

Kleitos twists his beard nervously. 'The rumour is about that we did not honour Artemis.' He glances over his shoulder in case she is eavesdropping on our conversation, an arrow aimed at a spot between his ribs. 'A vile rumour. We honour the Goddess!'

'All good men offer Artemis honour and praise!' I reply as loudly, so my words reach her ears.

'And surely,' he continues anxiously, 'if one so favoured by the Goddess has come, it proves we committed no sacrilege?'

I place my hand over my heart. 'I entreat her to strengthen my bow-arm,' I reply, 'and to guide my arrows true.'

Kleitos and the elders break into a chorus of hopeful blessings. I begin to wonder if we'll stand here all morning when a shout goes up; my name called clear across the square.

'Atalanta! My friend!'

'Meleager!' I cry.

Of all men, the one I most desire to meet. We fall upon each other, embracing as closest kin. One of my more scornful companions watches in amazement as it dawns on him that I, a mere female, count the revered warrior Meleager as a comrade. I permit myself a frisson of gloating. Not altogether praiseworthy, but gratifying all the same.

'Atalanta!' Meleager declares again, grasping my shoulders and jiggling me like a poppet. 'It fills my heart with joy to see you.'

The man I saw a scant few moons ago has added a fresh crop of scrapes and scratches to his butcher's block of a face. He could not be more welcome in my sight. I laugh with delight, merry as a pampered child.

'It fills my heart also, Meleager,' I say. 'It has been far too long.'

Oh, that I had words to capture the spirit of this man: dearer than brother, closer than breath on breath. Our connection is that of a hand hovering above the strings of a harp, teasing the air with a secret sound.

As we hug, a youth saunters towards us with a Kushite slave scurrying in his wake. I've never seen a man so . . . the word that comes to mind is *beautiful*. He looks for the world as though he just stepped from a bathhouse. He unfastens his cloak – a costly garment trimmed with the pelt of a spotted cat – and tosses it to the Kushite. The lad catches it with a skill born of long practice.

Beneath his cape, the grand gentleman is clad in a kilt of supple red leather and nothing else. I'll wager the nakedness is for our benefit, the better to admire his shaven chest and the bunched muscles of his stomach. His skin is smooth as an apricot and exudes a waft of sandalwood; his hair is styled in the Persian fashion and not a curl is out of place.

His thighs ripple, his arms also. At first I think the flexing of his limbs is by chance until I see he is posing carefully to display this or that part of his athlete's body to best advantage. One moment he looks to the left, chin lifted like a statue of Hermes. The next, he turns to the right, curving his lips in the smile of Dionysus. I wonder if he spends a lot of time studying sculptor's models for inspiration.

When satisfied he's been admired sufficiently, he glances at me along the bridge of his pretty nose. He wears the expression of a man holding in a sneeze. Unlike the city elders who are prostrating themselves at his feet, I do not bow obeisance. Nor does Meleager.

'So you are the famous Atalanta,' he drawls, veering just this side of rudeness.

'I am,' I say mildly.

He examines me as you might a bolt of unrolled cloth, checking it for slubs in the weave. 'There are some who call you She-Bear,' he says with a smirk. 'Coarse and uncouth men of course.'

I smile to show I do not give a Corinthian fig for such trifles as vulgar names. Besides, it is true. I am tall as a temple door and as broad. My hands are the size of shovels, biceps firm as altar-stones. I am a woman, plain and simple. Well, plain, certainly. Minstrels will never sing of my beauty, ships will never be launched to preserve my virtue, nor will heroes be called upon to save me from peril.

'I have also heard such a thing,' I say cheerfully. 'But never to my face.' He scowls. 'And you, my lord, are . . . ?' I ask.

He flaps a hand with an air of fatigue at having to explain himself to lower beings. Meleager guffaws, turns it into a cough.

'I am Toxeus,' he announces with a flourish, as though expecting Helios to rein in his horses and gaze down in awe. He jerks a thumb at Meleager. 'I am his *half*-brother.'

Meleager raises an eyebrow. I've heard the sorry tale and am able to keep a straight face.

'Well met, Toxeus,' I say and extend my hand.

He glances at it briefly, weighing his options. I am a fearsome adversary, and no man willingly makes an enemy of me. After the length of time it takes to drink a small cup of wine, he clasps my hand and shakes it.

'So, Meleager,' he says. 'Are you not grateful for the strong spear-arm of your beloved kinsman?'

'Indeed, brother Toxeus,' replies Meleager courteously,

and indicates Kleitos, who is wringing his hands in a frenzy. 'I present to you our host, Kleitos of Calydon.'

'Yes, yes,' says Toxeus, snapping his fingers at the Kushite, who twirls a flywhisk.

I sigh, and counsel myself to patience: if we are going to defeat the boar, we shall need every man, even popinjays. More and more men join the throng, their names flooding in one ear and out of the other. After the introductions are done, Kleitos leads us to the riverside, where we board a fleet of barges waiting to carry us to the sanctuary of Artemis.

As we are rowed upriver, I stand transfixed, gazing in disbelief at the ruined land. I heard the gossip but had no idea things were this bad. Calydon is famed for producing enough grain to feed half of Aetolia. Its soil is so fertile there's an old wives' tale about two farmers meeting in a field: the moment they lean on their walking sticks to pass the time of day, the sticks sprout roots and leaves.

What I see is a nightmarish perversion of that story. The earth is grey with mildew, vineyards torn up as though a horde of barbarians charged through on war-horses. What remains rots where it stands. Meadows and pastures are piled with the swollen carcases of sheep and cows. The stink of decay hovers like a fog. No bird sings, no insects buzz. The air itself is dead, spreading across the afternoon as heavy as a funeral pall. Meleager and Kleitos join me, staring at the wreckage.

'We have offered everything we have to appease the Goddess, but in vain,' says Kleitos.

'Could a single boar do this?' I ask Meleager.

He passes me a sprig of rosemary. I mumble thanks, crush the leaves and inhale their fragrance.

'What the beast did not trample, the people were too afraid to harvest,' he says. 'And now it is too late.'

Kleitos nods. 'A farmer went out one morning with his sickle. He was never seen again.'

'The Goddess struck him down,' whispers another of the elders, tiptoeing close. 'Dragged him into the underworld.'

'At night he screams,' adds a third. 'We can all hear him.'

Despite the sweltering air, I hug my cloak tight. Some great wrong has been wrought here. I cannot – will not – believe it is the work of Artemis. It does not bear her mark. *My* Artemis gathers her women at the full of every moon. We clothe ourselves in stars, raise our cups, and kiss the nights away. We sing hymns of praise and she shakes the trees with the roar of her approval. Fierce queen of the wild places, she reserves her wrath for those who despoil her forests. She does not quibble over a slip of the tongue at a sacrifice.

Kleitos and the elders plough me with their eyes. For the first time I can recall, I'm looked upon without disgust, or fear, or lust. Their gaze is frantic with hope. I am sticky with their desperation, and itch to dive into the river and wash myself clean. I take a breath and check myself. Unkind thoughts are beneath me.

After a pause that becomes more uncomfortable with every passing moment, Kleitos and his men shuffle away to the stern. Meleager and I observe the destruction in silence, each league worse than the one previous.

'I am sorry,' I say. 'This sight steals away my skills at conversation, and they are meagre to begin with.'

'I too am more skilled in action than small talk,' says Meleager.

A sluggish breeze carries the sound of harps and flutes from the boat leading the flotilla.

'Can I hear laughter?' I ask in disbelief.

Meleager sucks his teeth. 'Toxeus commandeered the grandest boat. He and our uncle Plexippus are men much given to pleasure.'

The rattle of tambourines drifts to our ears. On the riverbank stands a mob of people spindly as bulrushes, holding out empty hands. Their cries are too feeble to carry over the music.

'Toxeus is . . .' I begin.

Meleager nods stiffly, gazing across the scarred land towards the mountains, their jagged peaks spearing the clouds like the teeth of a leviathan. 'You need not play at politeness in my company, Atalanta. Toxeus is not easy to love. But he is kin, and I endeavour to do my fraternal duty.'

Below decks, the drum beats time; the oarsmen grunt and strain. The flow of the river is listless, as though it too has surrendered to despair. In the shallows, a boy is thrashing the surface of the water with a flail, hoping to scare up a few fish. His companion perches on a skiff of bundled reeds, gripping a net and ready to pounce. The only thing stirred up is silt.

Although a long way off, I can count their ribs. They turn and watch us pass. When they see the glint of spears and shields they cry out, *Health and strength to our redeemers! Health and strength to the hunters! The Gods smile upon you!*

'These people truly are at the end of their tether,' I say. 'Boys usually bend over and show their bare backsides when a boat sails by.'

Meleager is kind enough to smile, although there is little to smile about. 'Dear friend, I am weighed down with guilt. I am a son of this blighted land. When I left, it was beautiful.' A muscle ticks in his cheek. 'I have been away too long. I should have returned the moment I heard of this disaster. I am here to make restitution.'

'You are not alone,' I say. 'I too have sworn an oath to rid Calydon of this curse. You need feel no shame. Not in my company.'

He shudders, as a horse shakes off flies. 'You are good to me. And I am veering dangerously into the maudlin,' he says with forced merriment. 'If I carry on like this, you'll hurl yourself over the side to get away.'

'Meleager . . .' I begin.

Meleager holds up a hand. 'Let me have my false cheer, dear friend,' he whispers, voice a husk. 'I have need of it this day.'

MELEAGER

Calydon, Aetolia

I am Meleager: son of Lord Oeneus of Calydon, born of the Lady Althea. So begin warrior's tales. I suppose it is how mine ought to commence. I should rattle off a list of illustrious ancestors and sing hymns praising my own achievements: damsels rescued, armies routed, enemies slain. I should boast of how I held the front line single-handed, wiping sweat and blood from my eyes and bellowing, *None shall pass! I am Meleager! Hear my name and tremble!*

If these are the stirring tales you desire, there are plenty to be had and very rousing they are too. I have a handful of brave exploits to my name, it is true, but it is not my way to puff myself up. If I dissemble, it is out of respect rather than excessive modesty. I have seen a legion of brothers-in-arms die, more than I thought possible. I have leant on my spear and wept for the fallen. These are matters for solemnity, not swaggering celebration.

A captain's life is lived for others, not for himself. Early each morning, before I thrust open the tent-flap, I put on a brave appearance and wear it closer than skin. It is for the sake of my comrades' resolve, for the chance of them returning from a skirmish with nothing more grievous than scratches, for the sake of them returning at all. They are thirsty for the bluff reassurances in which martial men trade. I do not disappoint. I display courage and they drink me dry.

There are times – a very few – when I almost believe it myself: Meleager, the leader in whom all men place their trust; Meleager, first to scale the siege ladder; Meleager, first through the rampart's breach.

The Gods forbid anyone should glimpse what lies behind my own fortifications. At the heart of my citadel huddles a small boy beleaguered with night terrors, aye, and day terrors too. A boy born to a woman mired in treacherous superstitions, a boy whose childhood was bare survival rather than growth, whose body grew around a shrivelled core.

That boy cowers within me still. Each day I buckle on the gleaming façade. Each day my companions cry, *It is Meleager! All is well!* What they cannot guess is that I need this vision of Meleager as much, if not more than they.

I am older than any soldier dreams of. There are times I wonder if I've lived too long. I have dark days, when the curse laid upon me by The Fates casts a long shadow. The shades of kith and kin draw close and the hours stretch a deep and dangerous valley. Then I tip my battered face to the sky, and remember the sustaining affection shared by Atalanta and myself.

Atalanta: a friendship more precious than pearls, more radiant than the sun itself. I never thought to meet a creature for whom I would open my gates a hairsbreadth, let alone fling them wide. I thought myself resigned to live out the adage: *Children have friends; women have lovers; men have enemies.*

All men are good for is to jibe and parry in games of one-upmanship. We show off our wealth, our bravery, our possessions, spending upwards of an hour in a passionate rapture over a new sword. By all the Gods, there is nothing to match a man for tedium. We call it sport and joshing, but there is loneliness at its core.

When it comes to matters of the heart, we are useless. We squeeze out a blunt word, two at a stretch. We are creatures of surfaces. The life within is an unknown country. I used to think it was because soldiers lead brief lives and shrink from intimacy with fellows who will, as like as not, perish in the next battle. I believe it is more profound.

While my drinking companions brag and boast, rattling like dried peas in a jar, I watch women strolling past. Arm in arm, they inhabit a private world of sharing, low-voiced and intimate. I don't know how they do it. All I know is I am envious.

Or used to be. Words lack the power to fully express the change Atalanta has wrought: the lonely boy and the cynical, wary youth transformed by simple friendship into a happy man.

If you would know why Atalanta means so much to me, call for wine, rest awhile and I shall unravel the tangled cat's cradle. Oh, Atalanta, Fleet-of-Foot; Atalanta, Equal-in-Weight;

Atalanta of the Golden Hair! Well, that particular detail is exaggerated, as her tangled locks lend her the appearance of a gorgon, but to my eye she radiates beauty. I could go on, in a rhapsody to rival the poets.

Of course I burn for her. It is more than lust, however, a connection so deep I have yet to plumb its depth. I have often asked myself when I first knew. The answer is clear. My world is turned upside down the day I clap eyes on her, a wild girl wrestling a bear-cub on a lonely mountainside. A sighting that works healing magick on a broken boy.

A subsequent meeting is not so auspicious. It is many years later, at a feast given in her honour. She is scowling like a thundercloud, having discovered her father Iasus plans to marry her off to the highest bidder. I am dazzled. My heart quickens and I sweep in, proposing marriage on the spot, vowing to rescue her from the ghastly suitors paraded by her father. I think I bestow an honour and she'll be grateful. Think she needs protection and rescue, and I can give her what she lacks. As if Atalanta could want for anything.

Of course she refuses me.

I look back on that Meleager, and cringe. What a green and tender creature. What a fool.

Fool I may be, but at least I am not wicked, in the limited and tedious ways men are wicked when it comes to their dealings with women. Men who grasp what is not theirs to grasp, convinced anything they take a fancy to is theirs by right. Men as greedy as toddling boys, who push everything into the red and sticky hole of their mouths yet are never satisfied. Men

22

who treat the world in the same fashion: a possession to be grabbed, pawed and devoured. Men with never a *please* or *thank you*, imagining the sun rises for them and them alone.

If I display scant affection for those exemplars of my own sex, well, you may come to your own conclusion. As a tribe, we are selfish and could improve ourselves a good deal if we took a moment to notice those who stand hungry at the gate.

Enough. I said I am a fool and mean it. I shall not fall into the error of holding myself up as a shining example of virtue. Even now, I blush when I recall my pride and stupidity.

And yet.

Despite our shaky beginning, Atalanta chooses to be my friend. Not out of pity, but of her own free will. A greater gift I cannot imagine. Oh, lucky Meleager, most fortunate of men! Oh, Atalanta, sister of my heart!

I would follow you to Hades and back.

ATALANTA

Calydon, Aetolia

We disembark at an abandoned mooring. As soon as we put up oars, the insects discover us. Kleitos guides us along the rocky track winding up into the hills. He walks backwards a lot of the way, clucking like a hen and fluttering his hands in a panic of gratitude. Towering over the forest where our monstrous quarry awaits, a cloud stretches to the heavens, hooded and black as an anvil. Lighting pulses and twitches in its belly.

'Mighty Zeus sends his thunderbolts to frighten the boar!' cries one fellow.

'The Gods are smiling!'

Or are mocking us, I think, biting back a snarl.

Meleager brushes my elbow, a finger to his lips. I hold my tongue, contenting myself with a muttered invocation to the Goddess. We climb to the sanctuary at the peak of the sacred mountain. Hewn from the rock, it is squat and unadorned, a place of squared-off corners and blank walls devoid of the fussy furbelows of city temples. It was built by the Titans when the world was young. I think of those ancient giants, stacking huge stones on top of the other as easily as children make castles out of pebbles.

Kleitos points to the Holy of Holies, a rugged shrine perched on the topmost tier of the sanctuary. 'Tomorrow, the elders shall make a fitting sacrifice to Artemis,' he says. 'Tonight, we shall feast you all. A hunter cannot run down his quarry on an empty stomach.' He blinks. '*Her* stomach, begging your pardon, Lady Atalanta,' he adds, on the verge of frightened tears.

'All is well, Lord Kleitos,' I say gently. 'No offence is taken.'

'Bless you, honoured guest,' he says. 'Bless you.'

The apologies go on some time, but at last I'm left to my own devices. In the precinct surrounding the temple, a makeshift camp has been set up. It is the size of a town and as busy. A host of youths are unpacking the gear and tending to the mules and horses. A man stirs a pot, squinting against the steam. I hear the clangour of a smithy, the snapping and barking of hounds. Cressets are spiked into the ground and have already been set alight, draping the sky with a greasy fug that shrouds the encampment. My nostrils sting with the scent of boiling pine resin, the stink of hastily scooped field latrines, the brackish odour of sweat and the general belching and farting of soldiers.

Heroes from the uttermost ends of the earth have answered Calydon's plea for deliverance. A brace of Libyans are whetting spearheads hammered into the characteristic leaf-shape of their clan. Three Egyptians, dressed finely as princes, bend and test the longbows of their people. Rasping a whetstone along the blade of a double-headed axe is a colossal fellow with a beard so red I could warm my hands at the fire.

To my right, a man is polishing a breastplate chased with a design of eagles and surely too fine to get dented. It belongs in a victory parade. To my left, another man is knapping arrowheads, a heap of flakes gathering about his ankles. His companion fixes them to arrow-shafts, dabbing pitch around the knot.

I never realised so much fuss attached itself to a hunt. There is enough here for a winter campaign rather than a day's sport, even if it is to kill a monster. When I hunt with my sisters, we tread lightly upon the earth, a quiver over one shoulder and a bow over the other. Streams quench our thirst, and any game we bring down is to slake our hunger, rather than providing trophies for display.

I sigh. If it makes people feel they are helping, it is to the good. However, I can't help wondering if the commotion will act as a warning and send every boar, sow and piglet scampering into the next kingdom.

I come upon Toxeus ordering folk about and complaining about his sleeping appointments. His tent is sumptuous enough to satisfy a Persian satrap. His Kushite slave and I catch each other's eye. His expression does not alter by a whisker, but in the silence we speak plain.

A kindly lad shows me to a tent set aside for my sole use. He gazes at me with undisguised awe and I'm far too courteous to say I'll probably end up sleeping under a tree. I thank him graciously and he skips away. I imagine him telling his friends that Atalanta does not have snakes for hair, nor the paws of a bear.

The clanking of metal on metal proclaims the feast. My stomach growls with approval. To the accompaniment of more bowing and smiling, we are ushered into the sanctuary hall. Trestle tables line the room, long benches to each side. The place is scented with cedar. Everything is of the finest quality: walls hung with cloth that might have been spun by divine hands, lamp-stands of polished bronze so beautifully worked they would not look out of place in a palace. I notice the flames burn low, guttering in a tiny puddle of fat. Even lamp-oil is in short supply.

Kleitos thumps his staff. Servants scuttle from the shadows, bearing silver tureens decorated in the Cretan style. They arrange the dishes along the tables, sufficient plates and platters to feed everyone twice over. They are almost empty.

I tear off a scrap of bread. It is studded with weevils. I have no doubt the loaves, barely sufficient for one bite for each man here, are baked from the last scrapings from the last barley bin. A scrawny suckling pig sits forlorn on a trencher, mouth agape and lacking even a crab apple to ram between its little teeth.

I think of King Minos: each mouthful of meat turned to gold, each gulp of wine also. Calydon is a twisted version of that tale. These people have everything, and at the same time, nothing. A golden plate is worthless when there is no food to place upon it. I thought I felt shame before. It is as nothing compared to the guilt now rising up my gorge. These folk are offering us the little they have.

Toxeus sniffs and pulls a face.

Don't, I beg the Gods, hoping against hope that his tongue might be transformed into a clapper of wood. My prayer goes unanswered.

He shoves away a bowl, which rattles to the edge of the table. 'We were promised a feast,' he says, voice carrying from one end of the hall to the other. He folds his arms, face sullen. 'The broth is water. The bread smells mouldy. How am I supposed to hunt if I am famished?'

'Come now, Nephew,' coos Plexippus, patting Toxeus on the arm.

It's as much use as wafting a feather at a war-charger. Toxeus throws his uncle a look of contempt and opens his mouth again. Before he has a chance to disgrace himself further, Meleager springs to his feet and claps his hands.

'My lord Kleitos,' he says. 'With your kind permission, I beg leave to offer a humble gift.'

There's a commotion from the direction of the kitchens. A slave scuttles along the ranked tables and bends to Kleitos's ear. Serving-men reappear and take the empty dishes away. The guests look at each other. Something is going on, but none of us have an inkling what it might be.

Meleager claps his hands again. 'When the poets sing of this night,' he cries. 'They *will* call it a feast!'

With much banging and shouting, the platters are carried in for the second time. By some magick, they are heaped with bread, olives, figs and slabs of cheese the size of roof tiles. Flagons of wine are lugged in and our cups filled to the brim. The aroma of meat grilling upon charcoal drifts in upon a wonderful cloud and we are presented with hunks of lamb and venison steaming in their own juices. The lamps are charged with oil and the room grows bright.

I raise my cup to Meleager, who toasts me in return. It is too much for Kleitos. His face is awash with tears, weeping as a child lost in the marketplace who turns to find his mother, arms open and calling his name. Even Toxeus cracks a smile. Perhaps he has a good side and all it needs is a jug of wine to be teased out from its hiding place. Everyone falls upon the food, gorging not for the sake of gluttony but hunger, pure and simple. We slather our fingers in the sauces up to the knuckle, sop up rich gravies with crusts of fresh bread.

I wipe grease from my chin and clap Meleager on the shoulder. 'You are a generous man,' I say, indicating the crowd feasting and toasting each other. 'The food and wine must have cost you dear.'

'I thought they might need some help,' he says. 'I have money. Enough to gladden the night before a hunt. Besides, a man carries only his bones into the Underworld. What finer way to enjoy the wealth I cannot take with me?'

I nod agreement and return to the serious business of eating. When I cannot cram in another morsel, I lean back and pick at my teeth with the point of my knife. The full length of the table, men are discussing the coming hunt.

'I shall take my first prize tomorrow!' says Ancaeus eagerly, voice cracking.

'And the cloud,' adds his companion, to a ragbag of agreement. 'Do not forget the cloud!'

Once again, I restrain myself from snarling. It is unfair. Anxiety shows itself in many guises: they cling to omens, I am snappish as a dog. Many of the company are little more than boys: upper lips barely shadowed with hair, cheeks blotchy with pimples. There will be plenty of time tomorrow for the grim realities of a hunt to teach them lessons. I hope for their sake the lessons are not too brutal. They are not bad lads, merely untried.

As I was once.

I grunt an excuse about a woman's needs and they blush and mumble *of course, go.* I slip from my seat and slink from the hall. Cloak wrapped tight, I take myself to the forest edge and watch the last glimmer of twilight leave the sky. As the day surrenders to night, I offer a silent prayer to Artemis, curl up and close my eyes. Sleep dances out of reach. Just when I need the nourishment of rest, my mind gallops in untidy circles, unable to settle.

I think about my mother, Arktos the bear, teaching me survival on our mountain: how to sniff out the winter stores buried by foxes, how to stomach stringy roots and filthy puddles, how to track a deer for three days and run it to exhaustion. I could do with her wisdom now.

I think of Iasus, my human father, and the suitors with which he still hopes to saddle me, now I'm famous enough to bring wealth and prestige to his house. I think of Toxeus and what he'd look like if I punched him. I think of the kindness offered by the beleaguered folk of Calydon. I think of my loving friendship with Meleager. I think a hundred rambling thoughts and a hundred more. My body pleads for slumber; my unruly mind will not comply.

In the end, I give up. I watch the moon lift herself from the earth, face red as though dipped in blood. As she climbs, the stain rinses away, revealing silvery features bright as a temple lantern. I taste the warm scents of a camp at evening, hear the buzzing music of insects. The sound of the feast is as the rushing of distant waters.

Just when I think I will burst from exhaustion, a sparkling shimmer begins to knit itself together in the darkness beneath the trees. Little by little it grows, taking on the appearance of a door, one I know well. Through it step my beloved guardian spirits, reaching out their arms and smiling. At once I feel strength return.

'Thank you, blessed Artemis,' I murmur.

Once, I feared I had a sickness of the mind that engendered visions. Nothing could be further from the truth. For as long as I can remember, the Goddess has blessed me with divine protectors: two lasses who shower me with an affection that fills my being with hope and courage. They appear when I am in greatest need of help.

He is coming, they say. *Watch over him.*

At the edge of earshot: the padding of footsteps. One of tomorrow's hunters and a good one, judging by his careful

31

tread. As he approaches I sigh, ungraciously. I would rather be alone with my otherworldly maidens than endure more chatter.

'I will go, if you wish it,' says Meleager, and the spirits melt away.

I smile with genuine pleasure. 'No, Meleager. Your company is always welcome.'

We sit shoulder to shoulder, admiring the moon in all her beauty. Both of us are too animated to sleep. From the feasting-hall comes the sound of drinking songs and the whinnying of excited men. On the morrow, we will pit every ounce of brain and brawn against a ferocious enemy. Meleager and I shall enter the lists as equals. Here, tonight, we also meet on level ground.

As though he is peering into my mind, Meleager clears his throat. 'There is something I would say before the hunt,' he says, soft and shy.

I am suddenly alert, the tone of his voice prickling my skin with wakefulness.

'If I die tomorrow – no, let me finish – I am glad of our friendship. I shall enter the Underworld with head held high, in the knowledge that I loved and was loved.'

'Ah, yes!' I say. 'Be assured there is affection between us. And more.'

'I have need of a friend this night.'

'I am by your side, Meleager. This night and any other.'

His eyes sparkle. 'And if by some twist of fate you *did* change your mind one day and settled upon marriage, we would bear the most wondrous of children, would we not?' He nudges me with his elbow to reassure me he is jesting.

'You'll have to catch me first.' I laugh, and shove him playfully.

He rolls like a puppy. 'Then all is lost.' He chuckles. 'Our marvellous children shall remain unborn. Alas and alack!'

Laughter is a great reliever of worry, and ours works its magick.

'Meleager,' I say, wiping my eyes. 'You are as close to me as kin, as dear as my sisters in Artemis.'

His expression shifts, serious once more. 'Artemis,' he muses. 'They say she sent the boar.'

'I think not. The wreck of Calydon bears the mark of a vengeful God.'

He chews a leaf of wild mint. 'Which means tomorrow will be no simple chase and capture. We may sacrifice all life and breath.'

'We may. I call upon the Goddess for protection.'

I cock my ear, hoping for the murmur of her consent. It does not come: only the burr of crickets and the rustling of nocturnal creatures. As I gaze into the shadows, the door between worlds opens once more. Rather than my protectors, I see into a tangled future, and not for the first time: two funeral pyres ablaze, mourning cries lifting themselves to the heavens. A ship with black sails.

'Atalanta?' Meleager peers into my face as though seeing danger there.

I swallow. 'I am well. I dreamed . . . nothing.'

I shake my head to rid myself of the disquieting image. Meleager is right; tomorrow there will be death, and it may be our own. Those pyres may be mine and Meleager's. I am seized by a powerful yearning, thrumming through my blood and bone. A desire to drink the cup of life to its depth, to touch and be touched.

My breath is ragged, his also. *Oh blessed Artemis*, I think. Or perhaps I speak aloud; I am unsure. Some sweet spirit of the woods takes my hand and guides it to Meleager's cheek. Stubble grazes the calloused skin of my palm.

'Atalanta?' he whispers.

I press my forefinger to his lips. 'I am she,' I say. 'We have this night, this hour, this moment. Let us taste love, in all its variety.'

I smell the pungency of his sweat, trace the curls crisping over his ears. I touch the length and breadth of him, hear the sharp inhalation as I plumb his most tender and private places. The inky pool in the centre of his eye blooms with delight.

Bashful as a maid, he touches me also. His fingertips discover every inch of my flesh and relish in the discovery. When he happens upon a spot that kindles bliss, I murmur encouragement. I wish him to know what pleases me, and guide him as a teacher guides an eager pupil. He guides me also, knowing I am a traveller in the unknown land of a man's body. He tells me what thrills him and together we map the delicious contours of our geography.

All my life it has been dinned into me that women and men are irredeemably separate beings. I wonder if it is truly so.

Certainly, I cannot grow a beard. I have a cave between my legs and he carries a torch to light the way into my darkness. But we share arms and legs, belly and back, teeth and tongue. We are not so far apart after all. I wonder why such a fuss is made over our small differences, which seem to amount to a few scraps of skin; wonder why men and women are thrust far apart and told there is no bridge wide enough to span the chasm. Tonight, Meleager and I seem to be bridging that gulf well enough.

Before he enters me, he searches my face and asks, *are you sure?*

Yes, I tell him. *I am sure*, and enclose his flesh in mine. We roll in the dust, pine needles sticking to our skin, fragrant with the tang of fir. An owl hoots. For an instant, I wonder if Athena has sent a spy. But the Gods take little interest in a man and a woman enjoying each other for the first time.

I could describe our delectable hour in the manner of a poet; could sing of roses opening their petals, the crashing of waves and all manner of picturesque nonsense. We are simply two bodies finding shelter in each other. It is not better than making love with my beloved Antiklea, it is not worse. I do not suddenly ache with the notion to trade one for the other. Nor do I wish to toss aside bow and arrow and swaddle myself in a wife's robes. It feels – I flounder, always seeking the best word – different. It is thrilling, certainly. I understand why Artemis demands chastity, for it is distracting, dangerously so.

Perhaps the Goddess will punish us. Perhaps she is as cruel as Zeus. Somehow, I doubt it. Love is love, in whatever body it finds itself. I believe – I hope – the Goddess will look down and smile at two little mortals treading the wilder shores of love, crying out their surprise and ecstasy into the endless skies.

ZEUS

Mount Olympos

The Throne of the Gods

Every night, a feast. Every night, we revel in our divinity. We dine on peacock's tongues, fricassee of basilisk, pastries flavoured with attar of roses and seasoned with the breath of nightingales. The nectar flows in rivers. The sirens sing so sweetly the stars hang their heads in shame. Harpists pluck their instruments, dancers skirl and loop to pipes and tambours, bards weave enticing webs of words. Every instant is a vindication of our absolute dominion: over the earth, the heavens, and chiefly over death.

I survey the luxurious surroundings. Gloomy Goddesses Eris and Nemesis are not invited to pour their strident sourness upon our merriment. Let them skulk and sniffle into their sleeves. Beauty and charm alone are welcome.

The plunder of empires is piled in heaps: walls hung with silken tapestries that glisten like water without being wet; the floor strewn with the pelts of exotic beasts from Ethiopia to Uttermost Thule. We are cooled with fans fletched with the rainbow plumes of birds captured in the paradise east of the sunrise.

It is all so very fatiguing.

'Junk!' I cry, and kick over an alabaster jar in the shape of an ibex. It shatters, oozing a puddle of perfumed oil. 'I am bored of feasting!'

Joyous expressions fall from dewlapped faces. Gods and Goddesses toss their goblets aside, spring from their couches and fight to be the first to prostrate themselves.

'Oh, we hate feasting too!' they twitter.

A flood of greater and lesser divinities abase themselves at my toe-tips: naiads, dryads, hamadryads, nereids, nymphs, tree-spirits, river-spirits. I watch them wring their fingers into knots, wetting themselves with eagerness and fear.

'Command us, mighty Zeus!' they squeak.

'Radiant Zeus, one word and we are yours!'

'Shall we foment a war between the Thracians and the Scythians?'

'Pour down fire and raze a city?'

'Sink an island beneath the waves and drown its sons and sciences, for your amusement?'

'Hold your tongues, you measly grovellers!' I bellow. 'Is this all you have to offer?' As though in response, a sound rises from the earth below: a thin, reedy wail, chilling and unpleasant. 'By all that is sacred, what is that infernal keening?'

'It is humanity, my lord Zeus,' says Hermes with an exasperating simper.

'What are they complaining about now?'

Hermes sweeps the clouds aside with the blade of his hand. 'I see Calydon, my lord. You laid waste to the land, you recall?'

'So?'

'Famine, my lord,' he replies, screwing up his eyes for a closer look. 'The people are dying.'

'Why should I care? They are grubs, without feeling.'

Hermes tips his head on one side, golden curls tumbling over his brow. 'Men, women and – oh yes, children in particular. Of slow starvation.'

'Well, someone silence them.'

I cross my arms and scowl. Laying waste to Calydon had its moments. I snapped my fingers and the land was seared to ash. Sending a gigantic boar to trample the wheat fields to gruel and laying the blame on my unruly daughter Artemis quirked a smile or two. It was over so quickly. I sigh. All I ask is for my pleasure to last. And for that piercing clamour to cease.

'Musicians!' I roar. 'Strike up a merry tune and drown out that blasted caterwauling. It is souring the wine.'

They do as commanded. Hera tosses an olive, catches it in her pretty mouth.

'You have not toyed with a mortal female for an age,' she says, chewing idly.

'They break too easily,' I grumble.

'True, true,' she muses. 'Their bodies are annoyingly fragile. And my husband is indomitable in all his ways.'

'I am,' I say, flexing my biceps.

Hera flicks the olive stone and it takes out a cyclops's single eye. We giggle as the blinded oaf stumbles away, bumping into walls and tipping over tables. My wife has an unerring knack for restoring me to a fine temper. I rub my palms together and toss a thunderbolt, which sets a wood-nymph ablaze. I glower at the assembled company until everyone joins in our mirth.

Hera stretches and yawns. 'Now, despoiling a mortal's entire life rather than merely breaking her body,' she says. 'That would provide years of fun. A diverting pastime where you could cut and come again.' She nibbles at the roasted heart of a newborn unicorn. 'Just a passing notion. But I daresay better than the dreary ideas spouted by these syco-phantic duck-quackers.'

'Intriguing,' I say. 'You are a clever wife.' I glare at the company. 'Far more ingenious than these fools. It is why we are so well suited.'

'Oh my lord is too kind,' she coos. 'I am yours to serve.' She licks a fingertip and pokes a hole in the clouds surrounding Olympos. 'Oh look,' she says, peeping through the gap. 'I believe I've found the very woman. A new mother, Althea by name. So happy. Why, I do believe she loves her child more than she adores mighty Zeus. Tsk tsk.'

I peer down at earth. The female is easy to spot, sticky with contemptible human happiness.

'She is no different to any other breeding cow,' I scoff.

Hera shifts and her chiton slides open, revealing the cleft between the ample treasures of her breasts.

40

'Perhaps, my lord,' she says lightly. 'You know, I listen in on The Fates and the silly destinies they foist on mortals. Turgid stuff, for the most part. This one is different. About an enchanted log and the son dying when the last scrap is consumed by fire. It is so deliciously . . . cruel.'

'So?'

'I was thinking. The Moirai hide their work from mortals.' She sighs. 'Such a waste! They weave a strikingly unpleasant destiny for this boy – what is his name? Oh yes. Meleager. So much nastiness, yet they do not tarry to watch it take root and fester.'

'Go on,' I say, fascinated despite myself.

Hera takes a long draft of ambrosia and wipes her mouth on the back of her hand. 'It seems an awful shame not to have some sport in it. Oh, if only Althea were to discover the ghastly truth! It would blight her entire life, not to mention the boy's.'

'The Moirai aren't going to tell her in a hurry,' I snort.

'No, they aren't,' says Hera. 'But someone should. Misery is so enduring, is it not? And you *are* seeking a tasty morsel that lasts longer.'

'I am.'

'Not to mention the added twist of The Fates being hated into the bargain. We could have such fun.'

The female Althea and her brat Meleager: two ruined lives for the price of one. The Fates accursed. A fine game indeed. A plan begins to form. It is decided.

THE FATES

Olympos

A Time out of Time

We have begun our tale at the end, or close to it. For that, we apologise. To us, existing outside the flow of Time, there is neither end nor beginning. We stand dry-shod on the bank of the river, watching mortal epochs sweep past.

We reach in and pluck an instant. Here: in our hands we hold the night shared by Atalanta and Meleager. Fleeting, and yet treasured as the rarest pearl. We rejoice in their rejoicing. Mortals have so few moments in their lives, let alone ones so delectable. We wish we could pause the onward rush of hours and let them lie in each other's arms a hundred years.

They are happy now. It was not always so. Both Meleager and Atalanta have travelled paths fraught with difficulty and danger to reach this hard-won haven. To understand the significance of this encounter, and why it is vital as sweet water in the desert, we must turn our attention to the past. Every ending needs a beginning, and every mystery an explanation.

We have hesitated from telling all.

To explain, we must return to the infancy of humankind. The world turns, and the long, slow ages of innocence slip by. Like all doting parents, we are unprepared for our mortal babes to grow so fast. One morning in eternal time they are crawling and puking; at the stroke of noon they are standing tall.

Suddenly, they are no longer children, yet we continue to treat them so. We mean well, but keep them in the cradle, even when they overspill its confines. Once a place of safety, it becomes a prison. Our safeguards stunt their growth; the destinies we weave keep them in thrall. We have fulfilled our purpose, too well perhaps. By nursing them as sucklings when they have grown, we hinder and hobble.

It is time for change. We must let them leave the nursery. No more coddling and coaxing, no more guiding every step with our woven destinies. But we are The Moirai. We have always shaped the fate of mortals. We have no other purpose.

What can we do?

The centuries unroll as we cudgel our wits. Fate is the unbreakable law of the cosmos. Through all the ages, there has been no deviation, not by a whisper. No mortal can alter its course, no God. When the thread of Fate is severed, death comes at the predestined hour. Neither prayer nor pleading can add a single breath.

What if the law of Fate was broken? What if a man eluded his appointment with death? Why, our power would be broken. The reign of The Moirai would come to an end. For good. Aye, for the good of humankind. Mortals would live free of our interference, and that of all immortals.

Our solution is simple, and yet we have never done anything more difficult. We shall break the unbreakable rule of Fate, surrender our power and step down from immortality. We shall place destiny into the hands of our grown children and give free will to mortals. It shall be their birthright.

To do this, we must create a destiny for a single mortal, and then prevent it from coming to fruition. All it needs is for the moment of death to be hindered: one hour's delay, one moment, even an instant will be enough.

And so we shape the fate of a man. Of all the million million destinies we have spun and measured and severed, this one is the most important. A small and niggling fate is insufficient. We fashion an unfair destiny, so that when it is thwarted the ripples will surge through the cosmos, stretching it to breaking point and further. Knowing it is the only way does not make it easy.

We choose an honourable man, a clear-eyed and clear-hearted soul. His name: Meleager. We weep when we shape his fate. The wool hangs heavy on the distaff, and Clotho sears her fingertips when she tugs out the malicious thread. Lachesis burns her hands when she measures out the days. Cruelty blunts the shears and Atropos has to sharpen them a dozen times to sever the wicked cord.

Everything must be done in secret. For our stratagem will not only wipe out our power, but that of the Gods also. The Gods had their chance to be wise and gentle. They could have made the earth a paradise. They chose to be vicious and conniving, lazy and petty. It is imperative they do not

44

discover what we are doing. If they uncover our plan, we are undone.

Now, we turn to Meleager's birth, and reveal the moment our strategy was set in motion. We shall also recount Atalanta's strange birth and stranger childhood, a misfortune she forged into victory by sheer force of will. They can tell their story far better than we are able, for our skill is in spinning and not in words. We shall step back and leave the telling to them.

Time Was

MELEAGER

Calydon

Every man is assigned a portion of bad luck and I have had more than my share, for my birth was cursed by The Fates. It is a horrid tale, the sort told to frighten children into submission. Certainly, it frightened me. My mother told it at every opportunity, and never tired of the retelling. Yet, I have striven hard. Any good fortune in my life has been forged and hammered by myself.

Ah, but I am dashing towards the end when I have not even explained the start. The one cannot be understood without the other. It is not a long tale. A one-flagon story, if you will. I shall begin at the beginning, where all tales should.

My mother is Althea.

In many ways, that is the whole of it. There are men for whom the name Althea is its own explanation; men who clap my shoulder and say, *dear Meleager. We understand. Unlucky fellow, to be the son of such a mother.*

Before Althea is given in marriage to Oeneus, she asks her own mother what a bride must do on her wedding night.

Her mother purses her lips and says, *a lady does nothing*. She is instructed to lie still as a temple statue and stretch her eyes wide in admiration, whatever her husband looks like when he drops his tunic to the floor.

Chiefly, Althea is tutored in silence. How never to display signs of pleasure. Only women paid to service men make those sorts of noises, and are pretending in any case. *No lady enjoys what men do to them*, her mother tells her. The talk is of duty and the distasteful congress of the body she must endure in order to birth sons.

Sons, says her mother over and over, like the chorus in a badly written play. *The more sons, the greater your security. Make sure there are plenty of them and that they live.*

My mother Althea does as she is bidden. Four times she catches the seed of her husband and plants it in her womb. Four times she ripens. Four times she loses a full-born child at the last moment, bringing forth blue and breathless girls, their eyes sealed shut against a world they hadn't survived to see.

Four times she grieves in private desolation. Barely out of girlhood, her entry gate to womanhood is marked with graves. Oeneus grows restless. Then, by some rare and blessed chance, my father's seed takes root and I spark into life. I seize hold and do not let go.

Althea's mother promises agony, and a mother does not lie.

The birthing-chamber is lit by flickering torches that throw strange shadows upon the wall. In the far corner, a wise woman is shaking a sistrum and kissing a statuette of Eileithyia. She offers prayers and libations to the Goddess,

50

intoning spells to scare off the demons who prowl about. Demons with teeth long as skinner's knives, poised to pounce and devour a mother and baby in a single gulp.

My almost-mother crouches on the birthing-bricks, borne up by the midwife and her attendants. The air is humid, thick with the reek of bitter herbs. The midwife slips her hand between Althea's thighs and slides in up to the wrist, murmuring, *Good, very good*. She nods to her closest attendant, leans close to Althea's ear.

'My lady, your babe is hurrying to be born, and all is well.'

The midwife smiles. My almost-mother reads honesty in her expression and smiles also. The sun of their shared hope illuminates the room far brighter than the guttering lamps.

'Blessings be upon you,' she hisses, gritting her teeth for the final struggle.

A son has been foretold. When her aunt dangled a mouse by its tail over the mountain of Althea's stomach it swung back and forth. A boy-child, beyond any doubt. She rejoices: a son will put the seal on their marriage. The previous four stillbirths shall be forgotten and her husband will love her, at last.

There is pushing, there is puffing. There is screaming, there is blood. There is the slithering of a baby from his mother's womb and into the harsh, parched world without. The midwife places me in Althea's arms. My eyelids are closed tight against her, my lips clamped in an angry scowl. Terror squeezes its fist around her heart. Why won't I look at her? Do I know about my dead sisters, and hate her for losing them?

'Please,' she croaks. 'Please.'

The Gods hear her prayer. I open my eyes and love rushes in. I latch onto her teat fast as a dog on a rabbit, and do not unfasten my gaze from hers, not for an instant. I suck so lustily Althea thinks I intend to swallow her whole breast into my little mouth. She laughs at the keen, wild joy of this moment and thinks she will never be done laughing.

Her belly trembles with emptiness. The midwife cuts the cord, clucking, *All is well, and barely any tearing, you lucky lass.* It is no lie: the midwife has seen girls Althea's age split in half like a tree struck by lightning when bringing forth a baby as large as me.

The attendants cook the afterbirth on a little griddle shaped like a woman's nether parts, and divide it between them, being careful to offer Eileithyia a generous portion. The delicious scent of roasting meat fragrances the air. The wise woman croaks, *The Goddess accepts her offering. It is a good omen.*

They drink the birthing-brew of wine mixed with herbs and honey. An attendant builds up the fire. The room swelters. My mother is finding it hard to breathe. The air is dense as soup.

'Can you not open the shutters, Sister?' she begs.

The midwife frowns. She does not want to speak of malicious spirits, and conjure them with the speaking thereof. An open shutter is an invitation for wandering demons to do mischief. But it has been an easy birth, with a mother barely out of childhood herself. Surely there is no harm to be done.

'A hair's breadth, my dear,' she coos. 'Not enough to slide a finger.'

Her assistant raises an eyebrow, but obeys. A gust of air dashes in and Althea gulps it like wine. The fire crackles merrily in the hearth. The wise woman takes her leave, along with the assistants. The midwife remains, propping my mother against a heap of cushions.

'I will stay and do your bidding until the morrow,' she says. 'Call upon me, if there is need.'

She curls under her cloak and is snoring within the minute. Althea clutches me, a prize won at the cost of a day of torture. Through the window, she hears the sounds of night as it surrenders to the dawn: the stirring of the house-slaves, the rustle of chickens. Any moment now, the cock will clear its throat of sand and commence crowing. She has heard these noises a hundred times and a hundred more, but never listened with such attention. Her senses sparkle with new light, kindled deep within. She gazes upon her perfect son: the huge dark eyes, the wavering fists.

'I am here, beloved,' she murmurs.

My pudgy fingers splay, pressing the air, a strange new element after my nine-month sojourn swimming in her inner ocean. For the first time, Althea understands the meaning of adoration. No wonder the Gods demand it. She smiles, decides there and then that she will never stop. Her son deserves every scrap of her worship. She'll spend her whole life lavishing him with love and praise.

What Althea does not know is that The Fates are leaning close, measuring out the baby's thread. They hear my mother's disobedient intention and suck in shocked breath.

How dare this woman adore her child! Veneration belongs to the Gods, especially to the Lord of Olympos, potent and powerful Zeus. Yes, Zeus is whom she ought to be worshipping. This is blasphemy.

As Althea drowses, it seems she can hear voices drifting through the breach in the window-shutters. It must be a house-slave drawing water from the well, she tells herself. No, it is too close, buzzing like a wasp trapped in the next room. More than one voice. She strains to pick out the words, for there are words, to be sure. If only the speakers would come a little closer.

Sensing her distraction from its rightful place, I mew for attention. She kisses my soft scalp, inhales my luscious aroma. The whispering is forgotten. The fire burns, the midwife sniffles and snorts, and my mother drifts into a half-dream once more.

As soon as she lets slip the reins of wakefulness, the voices return and she jerks upright. The murmuring is closer now, louder, easier to hear. The speakers are not in the courtyard outside the window, however. They are standing at the inner door. Althea grips me tight, wondering who has been granted access to her birth-chamber. Her husband would not dare, not until the bloody linens are carried away and burnt. Not until she is primped and preened, her hair oiled and curled.

She pricks her ears: there are two of them. She listens as they bat questions back and forth. I grizzle, and she pokes a nipple between my lips. I get back to the serious business of suckling, she to the task of eavesdropping.

What say you, Sisters? says one.

I say we play a game, replies the other.

A game! The Fates love games.

We have not played with a mortal for so long.

Yes! Let us have good sport with this one!

The voices are of a man and woman, yet The Moirai are a trinity of sisters. Althea creases her brow at the riddle. She glides on the tide of their chirruping conversation, bobbing like a scrap of cork. Until she hears a name.

Meleager.

Only she and her husband know the name intended for me. Not the midwife, not the wise woman, not even her own mother. It is bad luck of the worst kind. Only a fool would dream of incurring the wrath of spirits by speaking a son's name before his rightful naming at the temple of Apollo on his eighth morning. She must be hearing things.

There it is again, *Meleager.*

Althea hugs me and I let out a kittenish mewl. She sets her teeth. No one is going to take me from her, neither man nor God. The lingering pain in her bowels is as nothing. If these chatterers try to hurt her little boy, she'll flatten them with a birthing-brick. Pain shoots a spear into her innards and she winces. The voices carry clear through the agony.

See that log? giggles the man.

Yes, I do, Sister! giggles the woman.

When it burns away, the boy will die.

What a fine game! Let us watch it crumble into ash.

Althea is fully alert now. She stares at the hearth where a

single brand remains, blazing its life away. Crying out against the arrow-bolt of anguish between her legs, she rolls onto her side and hauls herself towards the fire with me squalling in her arms. Yesterday, she'd have covered the distance in one pace, perhaps two. Now, the fire seems as far away as Iberia.

'Help me,' she croaks.

The midwife snores on. Althea drags herself along, clutching me to her breast. Pain drenches her in a chilly wave.

'For the love of the Gods, help me!' she cries. 'The fire!'

It is no use. The midwife is gripped in a sluggish glamour, as though she drank poppy-juice. Inch by terrible inch, Althea approaches the hearth. Between her knees, her robe is sopping wet. She knows it for blood without needing to look. The voices taunt.

The fire, they say, gloating and vindictive, taking pleasure from Althea's frenzied misery. She does not care. Nothing will prevent her from getting to the hearth. Nothing will stop her from saving the life of her child.

She is within reach. She grasps the end of the log and yanks it from the devouring flames, scattering sparks. But the timber is still burning, and halfway gone to cinders. She looks about. The water pot is standing beside the door. By the time she crawls to it and crawls back the log will be finished, that's if she can manage the pot, the babe and the journey from one side of the room to the other.

'Help!' she wails.

The midwife may as well be river-clay for all the good she's doing. I am sobbing in earnest now. Althea understands:

she'd weep too if she had any liquid left in her body. There is no more time. I must not die. Her marriage must be saved. Her husband must love her. Nothing else matters.

She kisses my brow and lays me at arm's length, swallowing a yelp of distress. She gets to her knees. Crying, *my beloved son!*, she throws herself onto the log, smothering the embers with her body.

Remember, hisses the deeper voice, throaty and resonant. *This is the curse of The Fates. They have wrought this prophecy: When the log burns away, the boy will die.*

Remember, cheeps the other. *Blame The Fates. Hate them.*

And then they are gone.

This is what the story says, and what my mother swears to, my entire childhood and beyond.

They tell Althea she is lucky not to be dead. Tell her she is doubly blessed that the wounds do not fester. Thrice blessed that her face is undamaged, and she may still show herself to visitors.

Althea has the midwife flogged until the bones show white through the flesh. She watches until her fury is quenched, deaf to the woman's pleading screams that she heard nothing, saw nothing, and must have been put under a sleeping spell.

It is a quarter-year before my mother's scars scab over. Another quarter before the skin on her breasts and belly grows shining and new. Oeneus does not divorce her. In public, he speaks long and loud about matters of decency. In private, he knows Althea is not a woman to go anywhere quietly, and has fierce brothers, poised for the snap of her fingers to initiate a blood-feud. At night, Oeneus takes her like an animal, commanding her to face away from him so he does not soil his eyes with the sight of her ruined flesh.

Althea bears it all, because I am safe. I take my first tottering step. I lisp my first word, which is *Mama*, although she follows the custom for a boy and declares I say *Papa*. She guards the hunk of wood, for it is more precious than gold. Each evening, she unlocks the iron-bound casket and gazes upon it, caressing it as a miser his riches. When sure I am protected for another day, she closes the lid and turns the key.

An hour afterward finds her opening the box again.

And again.

And again. Every hour, at the calling of the night-watch, she rises from her tangled couch and checks the box is guarding its contents safe and sound. Night after night, year after year, I watch my mother perform her ritual of fear. The scars of her body knit themselves together. The scars of her mind bloat, and remain open and suppurating.

All because of The Fates.

The summers give way to winter and to summer again. There are no more births, despite Oeneus's sterling efforts, the finer details of which I am not spared. Labouring under the buffeting storms of her failure to conceive and the curse laid upon her only son, Althea grows stunted and superstitious. My memories are of her forever clutching amulets and jumping at shadows.

The chorus to my childhood is, *Mother, this is making you ill.*

Althea becomes a woman devoured by delusions. Tricksters rub their hands together whenever her shadow falls across their threshold. Quacks and false prophets use her as a never-empty coffer, palming off gewgaws and swearing a hundred oaths they will grant protection. They laugh behind her back, as do cousins, friends, and even my father Oeneus. The Gods laugh at her, or would do if they could be bothered.

Mother, I say, over and over. *This is making you ill.*

I cannot recall a time when Althea is not teetering on the brink of terror, clutching at my sleeve and whispering, *Do not speak ill of The Fates, for they are vicious and quick to anger.* Her hands fumble in the folds of her gown, grabbing for one of the many charms she wears about her body. I wonder how she manages to sleep, what with all the signets and papyri and seals and scraps of leather digging into her.

She reminds me of the Mother Tree on the road leading out of the town. Older than my grandfather's grandfather, it dangles with waxen poppets, each inscribed with the prayer of a barren woman, aching for a child to plant itself in an empty belly. Althea is a frightened tree, hung about with leaden weights that poison the earth around her roots. Their deadweight drags her this way and that, till she is rendered unsteady in life's storms. I swear, if she had a chance to grow unencumbered of false magick and fear, she might have grown straight and noble as a pine.

I nurture rage against The Fates. At my birth, those viragos poured poison into Althea's ear. Their prophecy laid a blight upon a blameless woman and her blameless son. They despoiled my life with a spiteful destiny and reduced my mother to a snivelling half-wit: half-alive, half-dead and wholly ruined. I hate them with all my heart. I curse them for their spite. There can be no other reason for their cruel interference. I do not know how, but one day I shall be avenged.

When I am six years old, my father Oeneus dies.

I think things might get better. With the reasoning of a child, I reckon they can hardly get any worse. Children are creatures of unquenchable hope, and I have not yet learnt that hope is worse than its absence. When one is without any hope at all, at least one is in the dead place where one feels nothing.

For a while, I see my mother happy. We live in a blissful squeeze of weeks where she is mistress of her own little kingdom. While the two families wrangle over the estate, she sleeps late, eats honey buns dipped in melted butter, drinks neat wine. When a steward brings news that one of Oeneus's trading vessels has been commandeered and all its goods carried off, she shrugs. The steward wipes his brow and adds that the foul deed has been done by cousins and not pirates. Althea shrugs again. Her esteemed husband never vouchsafed the size of his fleet, so why should she care if one is gone missing, or ten?

Even better, she stops her wheedling and cajoling. I go where the fancy takes me and no one bars the gate, not even when I spend all day at the quayside, guzzling fish-head stew, swigging rotgut wine and drinking my fill of sailor's fables. It is the brief Arcadia of my life. If the drinking-halls of Hades are half so sweet I shall be satisfied.

However, families only bicker a short while when money is at stake. One mid-afternoon, Althea yawns and opens her eyes to find an unfamiliar troop of body-slaves at the foot of her bed, clearing their throats politely and displaying a bridal robe and wreath. I am bustled away and instructed to be merry, for I have a fine new father, who will teach me to shake off the mother-milky ways in which I've been steeped.

Smile, I am commanded. *For the love of the Gods, boy. Smile.*

Obediently, I stretch the corners of my mouth and make courteous obeisance to my new father Therios, who inspects me with the air of a fishwife who's been short-changed an obol. I am half-a-son. Within a year, Toxeus is born and I become half-a-brother. I am half of everything: half-nuisance, half-useful; half-tolerated, half-despised; half-loved, half-hated.

Althea lavishes her adoration, hopes and attention upon my little brother. With Toxeus in her arms, she stops wittering about the prophecy and my never-to-be-paid debt of gratitude. I ought to feel relief at the respite from nagging. Instead, I feel a lonely vacancy I do not understand.

I love Toxeus. This I swear by all that is sacred. From his stubby toes to his ebony curls, he is the prettiest thing I ever saw. He is also the craftiest. Perhaps he imbibes the art of manipulation with our mother's milk. Before he's fully weaned, he wails if I so much as stroll past his cradle. Before he can crawl, he sobs when I'm in the same room. I'm chastised for scaring him, and my pleas of innocence go unheeded. All the while, Toxeus peers at me from wine-dark eyes, wearing a smile partway between nymph and satyr.

61

I grow fast, Toxeus faster. Even in this, Althea finds a new stick with which to beat me. She brandishes comparisons: Toxeus possesses noble height and bearing; I am stocky as a Sogdian horse with barrel chest and short legs. Toxeus displays filial piety; I am thankless, full of churlish disregard for her dreadful sacrifice.

There are lights in the darkness. Alone of Althea's dour kindred, I look forward to visits from my Uncle Plexippus. A colourful mixture of foppish dandy and sturdy campaigner, he is the only man with the wit and subtlety to see through Toxeus's malevolent games.

I choose from one of a myriad instances.

At Althea's request, Plexippus agrees to stand witness for Toxeus at the festival of Dionysus, when boys are given their first sips of wine. When he arrives on the morning of the ceremony, the women's quarters are in uproar.

Althea's body-slaves are huddled behind a couch, weeping into their sleeves. Althea is on her knees, begging Toxeus to calm himself. In vain, for the little monster has screwed himself into one of his freakish rages. He sprawls prostrate, kicking his heels and banging his fists on the floor, rolling left and right, purple-faced and squawking. The sound he makes is as shrill as the whistling used by shepherds to call their dogs from two valleys away.

He is surrounded by a wasteland of broken toys, torn linens, and upturned breakfast bowls. The tiled floor is a slither of bread-sops and the smeared contents of my mother's cosmetic pots. Her finest, of Egyptian alabaster so translucent I can see my hand through it, is a scatter of shards and puddled cassia oil. A dockside tavern brawl would not come close for wreckage. The fracas can be heard from that distance too, I'll wager.

'Toxeus!'

My uncle's voice rings through the house, shaking the rafters. Toxeus hiccups into a startled silence. The room holds its breath.

'Toxeus!' roars Plexippus. 'Now! Come and greet your uncle!'

Toxeus scrambles to his feet, skids through the debris, down the stairs and into the courtyard. I follow at the safe distance I have calculated as too far for my brother to hit me with a missile, and skulk in a doorway where I can observe without being observed.

'Uncle!' squeaks Toxeus, bowling into Plexippus.

Rather than gathering Toxeus into his arms for the usual welcome of tickling and kissing, Plexippus thrusts out a hand, palm forward. Toxeus totters to a halt.

'No, boy,' says Plexippus, not harshly but not gently either. 'What's all this to-do?'

'Nothing,' replies Toxeus, forever incapable of honesty.

Plexippus frowns. 'Doesn't sound like nothing to these ears,' he says, flicking a neat curl with his forefinger.

Toxeus pouts. No one ever rebukes him; no one dares suffer the enraged consequences. A storm builds in his face. His lower lip trembles. He screws up his eyes, sucks in a ragged breath and stretches his lips for a scream.

'Don't you try any of that nonsense on me, boy,' growls Plexippus, once again dancing between anger and mellowness.

A wondrous thing happens. Toxeus gulps, closes his mouth, and blinks.

'It's the feast of Dionysus,' says Plexippus. 'I've travelled here to see a brave lad take his first manly draught of wine, not a bleating, whimpering piss-the-bed.' He crosses his arms and taps an elegantly sandaled foot. 'Which one are you?'

Every doorway in the house glitters with the eyes of curious onlookers, every upper window also. I wouldn't be surprised if the neighbours are stretching their ears and hanging onto Plexippus's words. The wonder becomes a miracle. Toxeus wipes his snotty nose along his arm, and stands up straight.

'I am a brave lad, Uncle,' he says, voice clear as a lark. 'I am sorry for my bad behaviour.'

'I should think so too. Now you must go to your mother and apologise.'

Surely, I think, Plexippus has pushed it a step too far. Surely, Toxeus will stamp his foot in refusal. However, he smiles gaily, bows to Plexippus and springs up the stairs two at a time. I dive into a corner and he leaps past me, unseeing. While he's surrounded by clucking, coddling women, I step out of my shadow and into light.

'Thank you, Uncle,' I say.

Plexippus tousles my hair and calls me a good lad, but he is distracted. His mind is upstairs with his ungovernable nephew, whom he has governed with no effort at all. The truce lasts until Plexippus departs, and things go back to their titanic clashing.

As a boy, I think Toxeus merely spoilt and wilful, satisfied to see me flogged for something he has done. I have no idea his taste is growing for stronger meat. He has another trick to play, the most dangerous of all.

ATALANTA

Mount Parthenion

Where to begin?

Those of us who are different are often lonely. Those of us who are lonely are often different. I am lonelier and more different than most.

There are scores of tales about me, each wilder than the last. One tells how I struck a rock with my spear and a spring gushed forth; another that I wrestled the hero Peleus and tossed him high as the moon; another that I – the only female Argonaut – was the one to seize the Golden Fleece from the jaws of the Hydra and spread it at Jason's feet. Good stories, every one.

Wait. There are others, less succulent. They also say I was duped by the toss of three golden apples and thereby lost the footrace against Melanion; that I was turned into a lion because my husband offended Artemis. That's the funniest of them all. Not the part about the lion. No, the husband.

These tales are taller than me, and that is saying something. They are the invention of storytellers, not one of

66

whom bothered to meet the woman herself. Here is my story, plain and unadorned. I have little skill with words, so you can expect no flowery turns of phrase. If you choose to hear me out, be welcome and let us call each other friend. If you choose to close your ears and leave, I bear no ill-will. Go in peace, and may Artemis bless and keep you.

In any case, does it matter overmuch which tales are true and which false? They are fine diversions to while away an evening over a goblet of wine, the arms of one's beloved wrapped round one's waist.

Besides, what is truth?

A good question. One story I swear is true. The most fantastical of all, perhaps. My mother was a bear.

My fate is to be born into the tribe of daughters. My father he does not want me; my mother she does not fight to keep me. At my birth, I am bundled up and tossed onto the side of a mountain. My first battle is the primal struggle to live and not perish. How many girls begin and end the same way? Too many to count. Some of us are lucky. Shepherds are drawn to our bleating cries and find a little naked lamb, which they take in, showing more fondness and care than a hundred perfumed lords and ladies. Some of us are found by slavers who sell us for a tumble of copper coins. Some of us do not last the night, and make a grisly supper for carrion crows.

I am one of the luckiest.

I am found by a mother both wonderful and strange. A mother with four legs instead of two, a mother with fur thicker than the densest thicket, a mother with teeth sharp as butcher's hooks, a mother who stinks fit to raise the dead.

My mother is Arktos: the honey-eater, the shaggy one.

She finds me yowling, the cord still pulsing crimson. I waggle my frail limbs, half-frozen and more than partway gone into the greater darkness. She sniffs me from top to tiny toe and licks her chops, her tongue rough and sodden as an anchor rope.

She knows the cruelty of men. She seethes with wrath. Only that day, her two cubs have been killed by hunters, who sawed off their paws for medicine and left the bodies to rot. Only that day, she has clawed graves for her children and drowned the earth with her tears. The sky rings with her keening grief, for she has called on the Gods of retribution to send a sign.

Here is her sign. A human babe. One life for two. It is a start. She opens her great jaws, and pauses.

Later, she tells me she sees two shining spirits, pleading for compassion. She looks me in the eye, and sees my cruel beginning. I've been thrown out like a soiled breechclout to starve, a slow and terrible ending. She sniffs me again, and smells brutality. Today, Arktos has seen too much death. Tonight, there will be mercy. She licks me, rubbing warmth into my flesh and reawakening my lagging blood into a rushing sparkle.

Not once do I cry out, she tells me.

When I am pink again, she nips away the cord and bathes the wound with healing spittle. She gathers me gentle as a housewife a new egg, and cradles me to her teat. My lips can barely stretch wide enough, but I latch on.

Her milk bursts from the nipple: richer than the heaviest cream, ranker than week-old goat's milk. I drink and I drink, greedy as a glutton. Gulp by shuddering gulp, the tide of death turns. With each mouthful, she fills me with life: laced with rage and sorrow, heady as unmixed wine. I suckle on her anger and anguish, draw it into my blood and bone and I grow strong. Strong as a bear. I clutch the soft fur of her belly. Never will I let her go. We are mother and daughter, she and I.

In the estimation of humans, my father is Iasus, my mother is Klymene. They throw me onto a hillside because I am not a boy. As a girl, I lack that all-important dangle of skin and gristle between my legs.

My true mother is the Lady Arktos. My mother is a bear.

I live in a paradise, and fatten on her heady milk. Arktos teaches me to walk, to run, then run faster. She shows me how to sniff out the ripest berries, how to flip fish from a stream, how to climb a tree and swipe a piece of honeycomb, how to count the bee-stings and laugh at them.

The days slide into months and the months slide into years, smooth as water over a rock. Every winter Arktos climbs to the mountain peak to seek her mate and the following spring, brings forth a new brother or sister. We roll and play, and my hide grows tough with the raking of their claws and playful nipping of their teeth.

Knowing no other, I learn the language of bears. Arktos teaches me how the stars reveal the time to mate, when to gorge ourselves in autumn and sleep through the times of ice and snow. I learn the wisest lessons of Mother Gaia: how all life is indivisible and interdependent, how every creature depends on the other, from the humblest blade of grass, to the smallest beetle, to the greatest oak and mightiest lion.

I learn to kill, but only for food or in the extremity of self-defence. I learn the difference between the honourable way beasts kill, and the dishonourable way of men. Most of all, I learn to beware the wolves who walk upright.

Childhood is brief for a human child, even briefer for a cub. Spring comes round again and again. The years pass, and I grow. When I rear up on my hind legs I am the same height as my mother Arktos, eye to eye and crown to crown. I can outrun a buck, swim a raging river. Tufts of hair sprout under my arms and between my legs, and I am seized with joy that I become more like a bear with every passing day. I study the hopeful growth, praying it will spread along my arms and legs, but it remains stubbornly sparse and un-bearlike.

Then comes the winter when, for the first time, my mother does not go into the wilderness to mate. The odour of untapped desire hums around her, putting her into a foul mood. We snap and snarl, and I earn fresh scrapes if I fail to leap out of her way sufficiently swiftly. They are not deep enough to fester, only enough to hurt.

'You are my daughter,' says Arktos, licking me in apology after a particularly vicious swipe. 'I have never hidden the truth of how I came upon you, a wriggling cub tossed onto the mountain to die. I am only your foster mother.'

'You are my true mother!' I cry, burying my nose in her chest.

'You are a child of Man. Soon, you shall have to leave this mountaintop and go to them.'

'Why would you make me do such a terrible thing?' I wail. 'Have I wronged you?'

'No. You are, and always have been my beloved child. There are things I cannot give you. You shall have to live amongst your own kind, as I live amongst mine.'

'Never.'

Very gently, Arktos pushes me away and scratches her belly with long, dangerous claws. 'The day is coming. It is the way of beasts and men. You cannot live with me forever.'

Leaving me to bawl my broken heart out, Arktos quits the den and ambles down the mountain. She does not look back. For the waxing and waning of six moons, I'm wary. I startle at every growl in case it is the one commanding me to leave. Spring comes and gives way to summer. The year ripens past the full, and Helios steers the chariot of the sun across the heavens for a few moments less each day. I tell myself Arktos has forgotten her threat. I tell myself all is well.

One morning, as the air is sharpening into autumn, Arktos pokes me with her snout, shoving me from the den and ignoring my grumbles that I haven't had enough sleep.

'Today,' she says tersely.

'What of it?' I yawn, rubbing my eyes.

'You know full well.' She tosses her head. 'Go. Away. To the human village.'

I turn my back on her. I will not dignify this conversation with the word *No*. I shall sit right here and not budge, not ever. She cups my face, claws grazing the flesh of my cheek. Not sufficient to draw blood, but a message nonetheless.

'Now, Daughter,' she growls. 'I command you.'

Despite my squawked complaints and furious tears, she chases me down the mountain before I have a chance to gather any breakfast. What she does not know is that, in secret, I have made a plan. I will go, stay a little while, and creep back. In my absence, Arktos will grieve so piteously she won't find it in her heart to send me away again. There'll be no more foolish talk of sending me to live with men.

Their stench alerts me before I get first sight of them. They smell appalling, an unhealthy sourness that is a mixture of trapped sweat and unhappy bowels. Any creature downwind will be slapping its paws over its nose.

Their offspring dash about squealing and cuffing each other happily enough, but the adults behave very oddly. In the kingdom of the bears, males keep to themselves. Human males gather in droves, and yet no fights break out over the females. They drift back and forth, seemingly without purpose, calling out to each other in grating tongues. Not one of them – male or female – rolls in the dust or rubs their belly.

Everything about them is bizarre. Rather than being excavated safely beneath the earth, their dens are hovels of dried mud, topped with a thicket of straw. Rows and rows of them are clustered together. They must be forever falling over each other. Young or old, they cover their bodies. This is sufficiently outlandish, but for some reason I cannot fathom the females are swaddled completely, with only their faces and hands showing. I have no idea how they manage to run. It seems a very dangerous way to go about things.

I'm about to flee the stinking midden and return to Arktos, when I hear voices raised in song. It is far gentler than the discordant noises they make when speaking. I follow the sound to the river, where I find a group of women, legs and arms bare. They have removed some of their bothersome wrappings and are dunking them in the stream, swirling and sloshing before beating them lustily with wooden sticks.

I crouch behind a tree and listen, swaying my head in time to the tune. All my life, wild creatures have provided my music: the birds' morning chorus tempting the sun out of night's cavern; the liquid trill of the lark as she rises from her nest. I know the twilight lamentations of wolves; the rowdy hymns of bears in celebration of a fine scratching post. The women's melody surpasses them all and throws me into an enchantment. That should act as a warning, but I am held in its thrall. I hug the tree so passionately I'm surprised I don't pull it up by the roots.

Their chanting matches the thumping rhythm of their paddles. One woman sings a scrap, another picks up the thread and passes it to her sister, who passes it to her sister in turn. Voices weave in and out, creating an intricate pattern that holds the forest under its spell: trees silence their leaves from continual rustling; bees lay off buzzing. Even the pigeons snap their beaks shut. I am in such a daze of wonderment it takes me a long while to realise I am being watched.

She is a girl about my height and from the look of her, one who's lived a similar number of summers. In every other way, we are different. Her hair is sleek as an otter's and flops in a shining tumble over her breasts. Her cheeks are the texture of crocus petals, her fingernails unbroken. She approaches me cautiously, as if to a skittish colt. I cower in the shadows. Now she will pierce me with a spear, cut off my paws and sling my hide over her shoulder, as humans do to beasts.

She glances towards the women, but does not call for them to come and look at the monster. Very slowly, she lifts a finger to her lips. For the length of time it takes to eat a pawful of pine nuts, we stare at each other. A smile blooms on her face and two tiny dimples appear in her cheeks. I've never seen anything so exquisite. I reach out to touch them and she giggles. Just as cautiously, she stretches out her hand and pats my hair, which is rough as a furze bush.

There are no bows, no arrows, no killing. She murmurs something I cannot understand, but I know kindness when I hear it, whether spoken by beast, bird or human. I murmur kindness in return and her smile is renewed in all its blossoming loveliness. She says a word. I wrinkle my brow. She repeats it, drawing out the sounds.

'Ah,' she says.

That part is simple. I let my mouth fall open. 'Ah,' I say.

She nods encouragement. 'Te,' she says.

Far more difficult. Eventually, I work out I must tap my

tongue against the back of my teeth. 'Te,' I say after a lot of mangling mistakes.

She nods again, delighted. 'Miss,' she says.

This is easy. I begin with a hum, end with a hiss. Little by little, I wrap my coarse bear's tongue about all three sounds.

'Ah. Te. Miss,' I stutter, my first human utterance.

'Artemis!' she cries, gesticulating wildly. 'Yes!' She kneels and throws her arms wide. 'Artemis!'

There's a shout from the riverbank. A rising hubbub of voices, feet splashing in our direction. I turn on my heel and run up the mountain, run and run and do not stop until I am safe, the word ringing in my head the whole way.

Artemis. Artemis.

In the den, Arktos is waiting. She peels back her lips, flashes her fangs.

'So, you have returned,' she snarls. I rarely hear anger in my mother's voice, even more rarely anger directed at me. 'I told you to go.'

'I did,' I say. 'And have returned. I hated every moment.'

'It makes no difference. You must turn around and go straight back.'

I sit in the furthest corner and hug myself. 'No,' I grumble. 'This is my home.'

'There is nothing for you here.'

'There is everything!' I slap my hands over my ears. 'Why are you being so horrible?'

She rolls over, tucks her paws over her head and will not look at me, even when I start to cry. Her shoulders quake and, selfish beast that I am, it takes much longer than it should to realise she is also weeping.

'Daughter of my heart,' she says eventually. 'Listen to me.' She slumps, paws in her lap, snout drooping. 'I am old.' She heaves a sigh. 'Half my teeth are gone.'

'Then let me stay and be *your* mother. Let me find food for you, as you did for me.'

'It is too late.' She lifts an arm, grimacing with the effort. In her side is the broken stem of an arrow, the barb festering in the wound. 'I have carried it for two moons now. I hoped it would heal.'

'Mother!' I cry.

I grasp the shaft and draw out the arrowhead. It comes away sluggishly from sickened flesh. Arktos does not even whimper. I am still so much of a child I half-believe that if the means of death is drawn out, life will rush into the gap. There are no miracles. She lays her paw upon my breast and her warmth sinks through my skin and into my core.

'I should have told you the truth. I have been trying to spare you.' She closes her eyes. Tears mat the grey fur of her snout. 'Beloved daughter, this is why you must go. I am dying.'

'No!' I wail. 'You can't!'

We wrap our arms around each other, the naked and the furred, and together we mourn the ending of innocence. I bury my face in her pelt and inhale her rank odour, the most beautiful perfume on this earth; more lovely than wild roses. The light goes, the light returns, the light goes again. I do not let go of Arktos, not even when her great heart stops its pounding, nor when she grows cold beneath her shaggy coat.

Once more, the light returns. It is not sunlight, however, but a pale glow as of fireflies on a summer evening. The light blooms and swells, filling the den. From its heart appear two girls, smiling with such benevolence I stop weeping.

'Who are you?' I ask, wiping my nose.

We are your protectors, they say in voices sweeter than nightingales.

'Why did you not protect my mother?'

We are your protectors, they say again.

'I don't need you!' I sob. 'Go away!'

I snap the arrowhead from its shaft and draw back my arm to hurl it at them.

No, says one of the girls. *Keep it.*

'Never. It killed my mother.'

I make to toss the barb as far from me as possible. A force grips my wrist; gentle as a child, inexorable as rock. I am not permitted to rid myself of the hateful weapon, however much I wish.

I turn it in my palm. Three-winged, flared on each side, and rusty with my mother's blood. I do not want it; I cannot let it go. I puzzle over the riddle. Perhaps the three sides are lessons: to remember my mother Arktos, to beware human hunters who dealt her death-blow, and that life is precarious and can be snatched away in an eyeblink. I tear out a lock of hair and bind the arrowhead around my throat as a reminder of vengeance. For I will avenge my mother's death.

No, whisper the spirits. *Not vengeance. Power.*

With the words, the light winks out and takes them with it. A yearling cub pads to my side. I sniff him in greeting. He swings his head, lets loose a whimper that swells to a growl. The growl rises to a roar. He paws the earth around Arktos, gouging out a deep rut and together, we bury her. We stamp down the earth over her body and bellow until the mountain shakes with our grief.

When we are done, the cub bares his teeth. He will not harm me, at least not for a while. He is simply letting me know I lived here on sufferance while our mother ruled the clan. Her time is past and gone, and a new monarch will soon be crowned.

As Arktos predicted, I go down the mountain for the final time, my breath cut in half by harsh winds. The whole way, I hear the mourning wail of my sisters and brothers dinning in my ears.

THE FATES

Olympos

A Time out of Time

Atalanta is born into peril. Her birth is blighted by human agency, and therefore easier to wrangle to an advantage. When she freezes on the mountain, we send a bear to guard her and she survives what could have been immediate death. She does not merely survive, she thrives in the care of Arktos, her strange foster-mother.

A child may have many mothers. Born of Nyx, we are blessed with the most wonderful foster-mother in the shape of Themis. Of her, we have many wondrous tales to tell. She may not have birthed us, but we are her daughters all the same. Let no man say otherwise. Likewise, Atalanta has two mothers, the beastly more admirable than the human.

Meleager is also born into difficulty, bowed under his heavy fate and seething with hatred.

To be hated is one thing; we can bear that burden, having shouldered the weight of destiny for a million years. To have our plot uncovered is another: the slightest upset may be enough to disrupt the smooth running of its course. Zeus was not supposed to notice. He may not understand why Meleager is cursed – to him it is an opportunity for vindictive sport. But his interference has worked its damage, how grievous we do not yet know.

We watch from our starry stronghold, try to persuade ourselves that Zeus's mockery will work to our advantage and deflect attention from our true intent; hope he thinks us cruel rather than devious. If he discovers our plan is to grant free will to mortals and release them from the dominance of the Gods, his vengeance will be swift and merciless.

This, we have witnessed.

All men know of the clash between the Gods and the Titans. The chronicles teem with praise-songs to Zeus's glorious victory. Whatever historians declare, there is no glory in war and especially not in its aftermath. It is an ugly story. Zeus is not content to win. He reduces the entire race of Titans to ashes, hunts down their kinfolk and slays them all, to the tenth generation. One Titan alone escapes obliteration: Themis, spared by Zeus as an example of what happens to any creature harbouring rebellion. Yet the slaughter of the Titans will be as chaff, compared to the devastation if Zeus realises we intend to wrest power from his grasp and shiver it to sawdust.

Our strategy must succeed. There will be no second chance.

The Plan is safe as long as we don't think about it. Our very thoughts might snag in the fabric of Time and betray us. A slip of the tongue, an unguarded whisper, and Zeus might sense the disturbance. Humankind will be undone. We try to stifle the rattle of our minds, but however hard we try, we create ripples in the void, which swell into waves great enough to sweep to Olympos.

We have to stop thinking.

In our desperation, we turn to Themis, the last of the Titans. She has good reason to see the reign of the Gods brought to an end. We beseech her to take our memories and lock them away; beg her to smother us in complete forgetfulness. She sobs as she strips us to nothing. We wipe away her tears and reassure her it is the only way. To protect the world, we sacrifice all knowledge of who we are.

Themis carries us from our fastness in the heavens to earth. We live on the slopes of Mount Olympos, right under the nose of Zeus, the last place he will think of looking. She disguises us as children. We, the undying Moirai born of Nyx, are clothed in the bodies of three small girls. Around our little home she weaves a shelter of enchantment, to shield us from the watchful eye of the Gods.

Happiness has two faces: that of fond remembrance, and that of forgetting. Our story is the latter. We drowse, we dream, we lose hold of who we are. Our minds are as untroubled as damselflies who skip upon the surface of a pond and do not sink. There is nothing to trouble us, neither threat nor danger, for Themis has seen to that.

She becomes our beloved mother, and we become her beloved girls. Three sisters: Clotho, Lachesis and Atropos. As far as we are concerned, we are simple lasses helping their mother with the daily round of weaving. Every day, we spin and measure and cut the thread of destiny, thinking it is common thread. The aeons pass and we age not, neither do we grow or ripen. We are forever children, lotos-eaters in a cloud of unknowing and are content in our idyll.

The births of Atalanta and Meleager are touched with hazard, their childhoods with adversity. We – in all our mysterious immortality – live as children also. To discover how this is possible for beings from before the birth of Time, we must return to our own beginning. We have our own childhood of which to tell.

THE THREE SISTERS

Clotho, Lachesis and Atropos

Olympos

We are unremarkable children, living an unremarkable life on an unremarkable mountain. Why anyone should wish to attend to our tale, we cannot hazard a guess.

Our kingdom is a narrow patch of green, clinging to the mountainside. Our home is a ramshackle dwelling, noteworthy only to those who love it, which we do in abundance. The walls are wattle and daub, the roof thatched tight with rushes, and in our opinion far cosier than the dressed stone and tile of fine villas. The track threading up to our huddled hut is pockmarked with potholes and studded with rocks. A wise traveller goes slow and careful, lest they twist an ankle at every second step. That's if a winter landslide does not carry the path away completely.

The olive groves peter out a long way downhill from our door. Here, halfway to the clouds, the air is too brutal for their gentle ways. Our brook does not babble: it careers down the funnel of a gorge, foaming and flicking white crests as it tears along, furious at any rock that dares stand in its way.

Winter is ruthless and summer bakes the mud to stone. The rain, when it comes, hurls itself sideways, as does the wind, tanning our cheeks to the brown of wheat berries.

Here, only the toughest of creatures and plants survive and thrive: bracken and thyme, wild myrtle and tough tamarisks. We boast a few bent-backed crab apples. In the spring, wiry flowers venture their small blooms; in the autumn rowans dangle meagre clusters of vermilion berries. Our birds do not twitter and chirp melodious tunes: carrion crows scrape the morning with raucous cries; buzzards scour the land for prey, yellow talons hooked and ready. Above it all, stretching to the summit of Olympos, the deep and endless pine forest.

We live in peace, with the elements of earth and fire, wind and water. We are hardy lasses, toughened by frost, scorched by sun. We are not pampered folk who fritter away the days leaning on smooth elbows, fanning themselves and gazing into the haze of distance. Our hands are calloused and we are not afraid to get them dirty.

We love every inch of our rough-and-ready home, and would not have it any other way.

Our days follow an unerring pattern: we are up early each morning to feed the chickens and seek out hidden eggs. We tend to the goats, especially our billy-goat Kyrios; father to his flock and lord to his ladies. Goats are marvellously bad-tempered and sly-eyed. Their teeth are tougher than iron and they can chew their way through a wagon, wheels and all, and suffer not the slightest indigestion. Their hooves are of solid granite as are their heads and their constitutions. If we were not little girls, we should like to be goats.

We squeeze curds from whey and make tasty cheeses. In season, we castrate the wethers, haul kids out of the mires and thorn bushes they have an unerring talent for flinging themselves into. At summer's end, we seek out precious honeycombs and take a little, begging the bees' pardon. They sting us all the same, and we learn for any sweetness there is a price to pay. The question is always whether or not one is willing to pay it.

The land is unlovely. We are unlovely. Our mother Themis says the valley folk whisper about us, saying we can pull up a birch sapling by its roots and use it as a toothpick. They say we are savages who pluck eagles from the air and grind their bones to make our bread. That we are dangerous and proud, wilful and strange. They can say what they like. We are strong and healthy and the happiest folk under the unrelenting sun.

We almost forgot our mother. Themis of the raven hair, brows kissing above the bridge of her broad nose, the eye of a lioness, and heart of a lioness also. That every child should be blessed with such a mother! Each morning, while we are about our chores, she makes our breakfast. We are spurred on by the hiss of frying griddlecakes, which she tears into scraps and drizzles with buttermilk. Every night, she sings us to sleep. In between the twin poles of dawn and dusk, we spin and measure and snip.

On a morning like any other, Themis is up before dawn, rinsing fleece and combing out the knots. It is a day of rare springtime warmth, the wind bothering some other mountaintop. Tufts of grass are sending out fresh shoots, braving the first signs of the summer to come. The bushes are alive with small birds, eager to seek mates after winter. The distant peaks are touched with terracotta light, pale and thin, but with a promise of mercy.

We help Themis drag the loom outdoors, wrestling it under the lintel carefully so we don't knock its beams awry. For a lifeless thing, it is stubborn as an ass. We match it for stubbornness, and are victorious. Our sister Clotho takes a fistful of combed wool and wraps it around the distaff, clamping the handle under her arm.

'For whom do we weave today, Mother?' we ask.

'A butcher, a baker and a king on his throne,' sings Themis, as she does at the start of every day's work.

Clotho selects a clay spindle-whorl painted with wheat-sheaves and begins, hooking a scrap of wool onto the spindle and pinching a piece between forefinger and thumb. She pulls it out in a long thread, swinging the spindle-whorl so swiftly it is a blur. She tugs and teases, winding yarn around the stick.

When there is a plump ball of twine, Lachesis loops the warp thread onto the loom. She takes her stick of burnished pine, straight as the flight of a hawk and fletched with measuring-marks and, biting her lip in fierce concentration, she ties the threads securely with loom-weights. She draws the shuttle through, working the weft into place, twanging and plucking to test for proper tightness. She tunes each thread as meticulously as a kithara-player their instrument, cocking her ear and frowning until each sounds a harmonious note.

The sun rises, bathing us in warmth. We work nimbly and true. The shuttle flies fast as lightning and row by row the cloth grows and increases. When complete, it is time for the most dangerous task. The slightest misstep and the whole piece will come undone.

Although we have woven a hundred times and a hundred more, we hold our breath as Atropos ties off each thread, so deftly even the keenest eye cannot tell where one ends and the next begins. She fastens the final binding loop and with skilful fingers, wields the shears and cuts the cloth from the loom. Not one wisp hangs loose. We breathe free again.

'One of your best yet,' declares Themis.

We smile. The secret to our success is clear. We share this task as equals. Without Clotho to spin, there is no thread; without Lachesis to measure, there is no woven cloth; without Atropos to finish, the fabric will unravel into a disconnected heap the moment we lift it away. Themis folds it neatly, and we begin on the next. We gaze into each other's hearts in the way that needs neither word nor gesture. *We are happy*, we say without speaking.

At our side, Themis works on her own loom, a smaller affair she wedges between her knees. While we fashion plain and simple cloth, she creates fancy border-bands. The first has a pattern of lambs, gambolling upon a green ground.

'For a shepherd!' says Clotho.

87

She nods. The next is a design of crowns.

'A king!' says Atropos.

The guess is correct and Themis nods again, smiling as she finger-weaves a ribbon with a design of smiling babies.

'For a woman,' says Lachesis.

'Yes,' says Themis, biting off the thread. 'Motherhood is a woman's joy.'

'I don't want babies,' Clotho snorts.

'I'm not sure yet,' whispers Lachesis.

'I want three,' says Atropos firmly.

'Then you are like me, dear Atropos,' says Themis. 'I am the happiest of mothers, and you are the best of girls.'

A pregnant she-goat staggers to the water trough, huffing with the effort of the weight she carries. Kyrios stalks her, sniffing her rump until she kicks him away with a well-aimed hoof. Sulking, he turns his topaz eyes to us in complaint. We think of babies born in the spring, and how they've swum in their mother's wombs all winter, shivering. Themis works on a band decorated with spearheads.

'For a hunter!' we say.

'Women can be hunters,' says Clotho, bending her arm and flexing the little bicep, tough as a river pebble.

'Oh no,' breathes Lachesis. 'Ladies aren't allowed. They have babies.'

'Babies are lovely,' says Atropos. 'But they *are* the only pattern you make for women, Mother.'

Themis does not look up. 'It is the way of the world,' she says. 'And that is that.'

The spindle whirls, the shuttle cracks back and forth, the shears rasp.

'I don't care about the world,' says Clotho firmly. She twirls the distaff and pinches out a madder-dyed thread the colour of dried blood. 'When I grow up, I'm going to be a hunter.'

'Clotho!' gasps Lachesis.

Clotho ignores her. 'I shall run faster than a stag, faster than the hound in hot pursuit, faster than the wind itself. Every arrow I let loose shall fly straight to the target. I shall win the laurel crown at the Athenian Games.'

'No,' says Themis, voice threaded with sadness.

'Why not?' cries Clotho.

'It is the way—'

'I don't care a fig for the way of the world.'

'It is not only that. You are a spinner. It is your life's task.'

Clotho glowers. She hooks on a fresh tuft of wool and unwinds another length of crimson thread before she lets the spindle drop. 'For now, yes. When I am grown, it shall be a different matter.'

The spindle-whorl swings round and around. Themis opens her mouth, and thinks better of persisting with an argument neither can win. Clotho works in silence, yarn building up around the spindle-shank. She does not see our mother's frown. Perhaps she does not wish to. It is a grain of discord, nothing more. However, it burrows its way under our skin, like a speck of grit in an oyster. We tell ourselves than an oyster needs grit to bring forth pearls.

At the close of day, the loom is gathered safely in and propped against the wall to slumber before its busy day on the morrow. For our supper, Themis makes our favourite: river trout stuffed with wild mint, fried crisp. Afterwards we tend to the she-goat, who brings forth a pair of kids, their soft hides a patchwork of cream and charcoal. In the time it takes to scrape a pan clean, they have clambered to their feet and are butting at their mother's teats, tufted tails quivering in milky bliss. We are about to shake out the bed blanket and curl up on our pallets, when Themis speaks.

'Tonight, I have a special treat for my girls.' We are wide awake in an instant. 'Unless you are too tired,' she adds, with a crafty smile.

We shake our heads, pinning our cloaks around our shoulders. Hanging onto the hem of her robe, we follow her through the deepening dusk until we reach the rocky outcrop we call the Throne of Artemis. Below, the roar of the river is hushed to a whisper, muttering about its long slide to the sea and how many rocks it will churn up along the way.

We love our special night-time visits to this place. Our mother is the finest of storytellers and always serves a feast of fables. She puts her arms around us and together we watch the stars open their eyes. First is the Evening Star, sacred to Aphrodite and as lovely. Next to show his face is Sirius, the dog star. Themis points to the hazy cluster in the Great Bull.

'Look, the Seven Sisters,' she says, squeezing us tight. 'The beloved daughters of Atlas and Pleione. How many can you count?'

'I see eight!' says Atropos.

'Me too, I think,' says Lachesis.

'And I, nine!' says Clotho.

'You are lucky. It is a good omen to count more than seven.'

'Another story,' we ask, cuddling under her robe.

Themis swings her arm. 'Look there,' she says. 'The Scorpion brandishing his venomous sting, sent by Gaia to slay Orion. And there, the Great Bull: head down and snorting as he prepares to charge.'

'Was Orion a wicked man?' asks Lachesis.

'Yes, my darling. A great hunter, but a bad man.' Clotho squirms, but says nothing. 'So fiendish, he was slain by Artemis, who placed him in the heavens. There's his belt, buckled tight and binding the night sky together. His dogs are flying at the Great Bull; see how its hooves are pawing up the black earth.'

Above us unfolds the indigo ocean of night, rolling from horizon to horizon. Bats whirl and whip about our heads, snapping insects. The scent of distant cook-fires drifts up from the valley.

'Another story,' we demand.

'Can you see the dragon, curling all the way across the sky? That is Ladon, the serpent with a hundred heads. He guarded the golden apples of the Hesperides, until mighty Herakles slew him and stole the apples.'

To the music of crickets and night birds, Themis tells of lions and crabs, swans and dolphins, eagles and rams, until she comes to our favourite story of all.

'And greatest of all is Nyx, who is the Night herself. She stretches over the earth, holding the stars in place. She is above us always. When Helios rides his dazzling chariot across the sky, we cannot see her, but she is there. She is above the Gods and Goddesses, above the sun and moon. We call her Night, but she is greater by far. She is beyond light and dark. She is endless and undying. We come from her, mortals and immortals alike, and to her we shall return.' Themis kisses our upturned faces. 'She sees you and loves you. She watches over you and holds you dear.'

However much we wish to listen until dawn, we cannot stop ourselves from yawning. Themis takes our hands and we make our slow way down the trail. Atropos falls asleep and has to be carried. By the time we are home, we are all partway to slumber. Themis lays us softly on our beds and, as she does every night, rolls up our day's weaving and tucks it under her arm. It is her ritual, and never once has she skimped on her duty, however weary.

'I'll be back before you know it,' she says, tiptoeing out of the door.

Once upon a time we asked where she goes.

To place your day's weaving into the hands of its new and rightful owners, she replied.

Once upon a time we asked why her task is done at night.

Some things are best done in the dark, she replied.

Once upon a time we asked to go with her.

Some journeys must be made alone, she replied.

Once upon a time, we asked why.

Patience, she replied. *You must be patient.*

She said all these things so long ago it might have happened in a dream. Our mother slides around straight answers, and we must make do with what we are given. The more we press her, the further away she dances. All we know is that, every night, Themis gives away our day's weaving. And each day we spin and weave and snip and make more.

The last thing we hear is the swish of the door as she goes out into the night, and in moments we are gone into dreams of mighty warriors, locked in battle forever.

The following evening, a visitor knocks on our doorpost. Themis calls out a welcome and an odd guest rolls in: snub-nosed, shaggy hair not quite long enough to cover his pointed ears and walking with a jolting gait as though in possession of hooves. We inspect his feet, but all seems to be in order. He spies us observing him and quirks a bushy eyebrow.

'These are my girls,' says Themis, her voice sharp as a fresh-honed boning knife. 'Very precious, and not to be trifled with.'

'Indeed,' he booms. 'And what charming girls they are.' He sweeps off his straw hat and performs a luxurious bow. 'I am Simos,' he says. 'I count myself a lucky cove, for I am friend to the Lady Themis.'

We've never heard our mother described as a lady before. We look the strange gentleman up and down. He is wrapped in a voluminous cape, and when we offer to help him shrug it away, he shakes his head.

'A fellow must preserve his private decencies,' he says.

Beneath the cloak we spy a twitching disturbance around his backside. Clotho is boldest.

'Master Simos,' she says politely. 'Do you have a tail?'

He chuckles. 'Why, yes I do. All satyrs possess a tail, and right proud of it I am.' He turns to our mother and runs a hand through his unkempt curls. 'Lady Themis, your girls are admirable. I could gobble them up.'

Themis skewers him with a glance.

'But I shan't,' he giggles.

We nod, indicating our approval of her friend. Simos makes another courteous bow and his tail wags in the folds of his cloak. Other than beasts, we've never met anyone with a tail. We would love to see it, but do not wish to appear rude. He inclines his head at the door and clears his throat.

'Well, my chicks,' says Themis, and we declare she is blushing. 'No stories this evening. Master Simos and I have business to attend to.'

She kisses us and skips away with Simos, carefree as a lamb. Partway to the tree line, Simos doffs his cape and hurls it aside. We are keen-eyed as kites and at last we see his tail, swishing and glossy as that of a parade horse. It's nothing to the rod he carries before him, bouncing and quivering. We are not fools: we've seen Kyrios mount his ladies when the season is upon him, cross-eyed with lust. We hope Themis and Simos enjoy similar delight. Throughout the twilight hours, their joyous cries shake the treetops, from the mountain peak down into the valley.

When our mother returns at cock-crow, her cheeks are pink as plums. A cat licking butter from its whiskers would not look as pleased with itself. She places our breakfast bowls before us, humming the song about the shepherdess and her swain.

'Simos is a fine fellow,' she says. 'And most delectable in his ways.' She glances at us shyly. We've never seen her shy. 'Do you mind him calling for me, when the situation arises?'

'No!' we sing in chorus, hug her till she laughs. 'When you are happy, we are happy also.'

There are not many folk who can make a giantess purr like a basketful of kittens. Every few weeks, Simos pays his respects, a goatskin of wine slung over his shoulder. He brings us little gifts also: in autumn, bristly cones packed with pine-nuts; in winter, a dish of snow sweetened with honey; in spring a twig hopeful with tight buds; in summer a sheaf of eagle feathers.

At first glance, a person might only see his outlandish looks: gnarled features, cracked and dry skin, toenails hooked like a lion's. For all his wild appearance he is kindly and generous and most important of all, he makes Themis glow.

'We were given bodies so we might taste joy in each other. With Master Simos, I taste gluttonously,' she says, smacking her lips.

Each time Master Simos raps on the door, they dance away hand in hand. Our hearts are light, for we share in their happiness.

'Shall you marry Simos?' asks Clotho one morning, ever the forward one.

'Oh, marriage is not written in my destiny,' replies Themis, her throat flushed with nibbled kisses.

Lachesis ponders this a moment. 'Would you marry him if we weren't here?'

'Lachesis!' we hiss.

'But would you?' she quavers. 'Are we in your way?'

'Girls,' Themis declares, kissing each of us in turn. 'I love you more than I can put into words. Simos and I have a fine pattern to our pleasures. Your skill at weaving has taught you that when you hit on a good pattern, you neither fuss nor fiddle, because that's a sure-fire way to spoil it.'

'We love you, dearest Mother,' we murmur. 'More than the stars at night.'

'More than the moon.'

'More than the sun.'

'More than the salt on our meat,' says Atropos, winning the game.

Themis spreads her arms and gathers us into their safe haven. She could encompass the earth and everything in it: everything that crawls, flies and swims. She could wrestle the Gods themselves, toss them off their thrones and send them *bump bump bump*, all the way to the valley floor.

We sniff the pungent aroma of her robe. No queen swabbed with oil of jasmine and bathed in asses' milk could smell as enticing. We would not trade her for all the treasure in the land; would not exchange a single strand from her shock of frazzled curls for all the golden tresses of Aphrodite. She is our world.

*

96

When a life follows an unexceptional pattern, any peculiar occurrence stands out, as a jagged rock from a river.

One of our favourite pastimes, after we have finished weaving for the day, is to gather honeycomb from the forest. The bees hide their bounty in the topmost branches, but we are wise in their ways. On one such hunting expedition, Clotho, the most reckless of our trio, climbs a tree taller than any we have climbed before.

From the ground, we watch the strangest thing happen. When she reaches the treetop, she vanishes through something we can only describe as a gleaming hole in the air, till only her legs can be seen. She cries out and reappears, bouncing through the branches. When she lands there is an ugly crack.

We dash to her side. Her arm is bent back on itself, and blood is streaming from a deep gash. She stares upwards, breathing shallow, face ashen. We try to lift her and she screams. We don't know what to do. It will take too long to run and fetch Themis. We cannot go, we cannot stay. We watch, helpless, as our sister lies bleeding out onto the forest floor.

Another odd thing happens. The crimson flow slows to a trickle and begins to creep backwards. We tell ourselves we must be seeing things, but we are not. The blood continues to return to Clotho's arm and, very slowly, the edges of the wound close together. We are held in the grip of a terrific stillness, watching our sister's body knit itself together until all that remains is a red seam along her forearm. The colour is restored to her cheeks. She takes in a deep breath and her eyes grow clear.

'Clotho?'

She blinks. 'Hello,' she says.

She sits up and bends her arm back into its rightful position. We gawk at each other, unsure what to say. In the time it takes to drink a bowlful of milk, Clotho is restored to her rash self, gambolling down the trail towards our home and waving her arm as though it never happened.

We tell Themis and wait for the chiding we deserve. Instead of punishment, she presses her lips together and nods, then turns and goes back to her finger-weaving. We look at each other. We have avoided a stern telling-off, but lack any explanation for the bizarre incident. Our questions simmer until dusk, when they spill over.

'Why did I mend?' asks Clotho, as Themis is crumbling bread into milk for our supper.

'Would all three of us mend in the same way?' asks Lachesis.

'Yes,' mutters Themis.

'Goats do not mend when they fall into ravines,' says Atropos.

'Goats are not the same as girls,' replies Themis in the blunt tone of voice used when she does not want to answer any more questions.

'Oh, and Mother,' mumbles Clotho through a mouthful of bread and milk. 'I poked my head through a hole in the sky. It was . . .'

'Don't speak with your mouth full,' says Themis tartly.

There is more we dearly wish to know, but pressing Themis is as much use as trying to fold milk. At her gruff bidding, we are sent to fetch water from the trough in the yard. The sun is at the low point in its journey where the surface is transformed into a sheet of silver. We peer into the pool and see ourselves reflected. Three young lasses, unlined and unwrinkled, in the dimpled flush of girlhood.

Perhaps it is the play of light, but it seems we can see the ghost of a skull beneath the skin. Our eyes are windows to an unfamiliar room far away from this mountaintop. Despite appearances, we are old. Older than the mountain on which we stand. It makes no sense.

Kyrios butts us aside and plunges his bearded chops into the trough. The image shatters. We return to the house looking over our shoulders, convinced we'll find ourselves followed by three withered crones wearing our faces, in a chilling game of grandmother's footsteps.

Something inexplicable has happened, and in some way we cannot understand and Themis will not explain, we are not the same as other girls.

ZEUS

Mount Olympos

The Throne of the Gods

I have learned the hard way that mortals break too easily. After the messy business with Europa, I am forced to accept that human females are more amusing when not split in half. A subtle approach reaps its own rewards. Leda goes permanently cross-eyed squeezing out those huge eggs. As for Danaë, she fishes gold coins out of her parts for weeks. Apollo and I fall off our couches laughing.

The young bride Althea is ripe for the picking. An innocent lass, born into a kind household with sweet-mannered brothers and an honourable father. I do everything I can to warp men to my way of doing things, and it's not my fault if some slip the net. There she hovers, in the balance. If all goes well, she will slide into a life of bliss, perfect family gathered at her knee. How terribly dull. It takes only one hour of foolery in the company of Hera, and we tip Althea over like a skittle.

The greatest difficulty is to do it without giggling. Hera and I stand at the door of her birthing-chamber, pinching our noses against the offal-and-innards stench of females squeezing out their young. We intone the destiny The Fates have planned for her son, in every delicious, unpleasant detail.

Remember, pipes Hera. *This is the curse of The Fates.*

I save the best for last: *Your son will die when the log burns to ash.*

Althea swallows every word. We could have told her to stick her head in a cowpat and she'd have done it. The tears roll down our cheeks and Hera has to stuff her robe into her mouth to stop squawking with hilarity.

For decades, I savour every morsel of Althea's miserable life, and all blame laid at the door of The Moirai. Year after year, I twist the knife; make sure Althea never rests, never dares to smile. I warp and wrangle her into a one-woman nest of vipers, burdening her brat Meleager with a debt of guilt impossible to repay, one he'll hand down to his own progeny, on and on and on.

The instant the boy shows any sign of contentment, I give Althea an extra tweak and enjoy the hissing and spitting. Fear wrings out every last drop of happiness, reducing her to a superstitious bag of bones, the boy to a trembling, knock-kneed fool.

What an ingenious idea of mine, to use a destiny woven by The Fates to corrupt the entire life of a mortal and see it poison the life of her offspring also! Watching Althea and Meleager shake their fists at The Moirai adds salt to the dish. After the Titan war, those cowardly bitches ran away, tails between their legs. However hard I search, they elude me.

They won't outwit me forever. In the meantime, one consolation is to ensure mortals hate them.

The escapade puts me in a fine mood. I even find Olympian feasts less irksome. For a while, at least. Earthly years flit past and I drum my fingers. It occurs to me that Althea is too easy to terrify. I sigh. As always, in my search for amusement, I am unjustly thwarted.

I sit through night after night of carousing, boredom gnawing me like a host of fire-ants. On one evening indistinguishable from any other for dreariness, Dionysus is warbling an insipid praise-song in my honour and I'm wondering what he'd look like if I wiped the mocking smile from his face, skin and all. He reaches the end of his interminable poem, and takes a bow to applause that grows fainter and fainter when folk notice I am not clapping. He slinks to his couch in a sulk.

At that moment, there's a flurry at the outer door and Artemis strides in, breathless and flushed, twigs in her hair. Her sandals are scuffed, calves smeared with mud. If she stood in a stream, she'd dam the flow with muck. She strides to my couch.

'Lord Zeus, esteemed sire,' she blares, thumping her flat chest in a brusque salute. 'I am instructed to attend. I offer my respect.'

'Sit, Daughter,' I say, cheered to see my disobedient daughter made obedient for once. 'Sit and be merry.'

I hoist my goblet, splashing ambrosia into my beard. Artemis makes a low obeisance and I decide not to remind her bowing is for men and that, she is not. A spate of tittering erupts from Aphrodite and her cronies. Artemis raises an unplucked eyebrow. I do not care for the quirk of her lips, as though she finds us beneath her in some unaccountable fashion.

'Sit!' I repeat, with a tolerant smile. 'You must be weary after all your galloping about.' I waggle my hand. 'Stabbing and shooting and what-not.'

Hermes whispers to Eros and makes a vulgar gesture with his fingers. They splutter like schoolboys. Artemis perches on the edge of a table, splays her knees and leans on one elbow. A hamadryad peeps up her tunic, swoons with shock and has to be fanned by a bevy of fellow-sprites. Unaware or uncaring, Artemis shoves a grubby finger into her mouth and digs between her teeth.

'Dearest niece,' coos Hera, proffering a goblet. 'Take a cup with your affectionate aunt.'

'My affectionate aunt,' echoes Artemis with precise courtesy.

She takes a sip, sets the cup down and picks at a scab on her elbow. Before she can hoist up her tunic and scratch her backside, I step in.

'Daughter,' I say merrily. 'You are most kind to attend.'

'I was commanded,' she replies, regarding me with an infuriating blankness of expression.

I cannot fault her manner, though I know it for insolence. There's a flickering of laughter along the lower divinities. If Artemis stays any longer, she'll start arm-wrestling her uncles and brothers, glugging flagons of nectar and shaking the rafters with belches. It is positively stomach-turning. I can't remember who advised me to demand compliance from my errant daughter, but when I remember they will lose their head.

'The moon is high, dearest niece,' says Hera. 'Haven't you got a hunt to attend to?'

'Yes,' I agree, grateful to my crafty wife. 'A deer that needs skewering? A Maenad to stir to madness, perhaps?'

Artemis bows and saunters away, whistling. The place seems emptier, the lights lower.

'Music!' I yell. 'Strike up a tune, you louts! Make it lively!'

The yodelling and plucking cannot entirely drown out what sounds like a woman's laughter echoing along the corridor.

Hera shakes her head with great sadness. 'My heart aches,' she sighs. 'Such a stringy creature. If she made an effort, she could pass for homely. Almost.'

'Who?' I snap. 'Oh, Artemis. I'd forgotten she was here.'

'I am not name-calling. I am too courteous to stoop to such a thing,' she continues, flicking her gaze at Eros and Apollo, who are still sniggering. 'It is my greatest fault.'

'Sweet wife,' I say, pinching her chin.

'My king,' she breathes, pretty as a handful of rose petals. 'Oh, I didn't tell you. I have seen the funniest thing.'

I grunt a reply. Another swig of ambrosia, and Artemis is put out of mind. Still, it rankles.

'Look,' Hera continues, poking a hole in the clouds with her finger. 'It's terribly droll. The Titan Themis has taken three human cubs under her wing.'

'Who cares?' I grunt. 'I do not.'

'She's hidden them inside a silly little cocoon, like the dull-winged moth she is.'

'What of it?' I snort.

'Oh, nothing,' says Hera carelessly, munching on a peeled grape.

It's a long while since I thought of Themis. Last of her race, I spared her as a warning: a reminder of my absolute dominance over the earth and everyone in it. I've regretted it ever since for I've never possessed the sense of fulfilment expected. I wish I'd extinguished her along with the rest of her hulking tribe. Knowing that harpy is out there, living and breathing, is a thorn in my divine flesh. My fingers itch with thunderbolts. I could throw a volley right this moment, and sear her to cinders.

No one knows I nurture this wrath, least of all Hera. My wife may think she's clever, but no one is as clever as Zeus. I permit myself a moment of smug satisfaction. Hera continues to peer down from her throne, absorbed.

'Themis loves them so tenderly.' She sucks her teeth with a delicate popping sound. 'Aren't mortals sweet.'

'Where?' I growl, shoving her out of the way to get a better look.

Hera picks herself off the floor gracefully, patting her golden circlet into position. She surveys the length and breadth of the feasting-hall, but no one is foolish enough to laugh. She settles herself and arranges her gown about her in perfect folds.

'Did Themis ask permission to keep pets?'

'No.'

'She did not?' gasps Hera in disbelief, stretching her eyes wide at the Titan's insult. 'And yet, I declare she parades them for the world to see.'

'How dare she!' I cry. 'I spared her life. I, merciful and benevolent Zeus!'

'You are tender-hearted, my lord,' she says.

'I am,' I agree.

'Such a shame little girls are so delicate,' Hera titters, patting her hands together and blowing on her fingers. 'I hear they are particularly sensitive to cold.'

She reaches behind her and grabs hold of the river-nymph who has been wafting her with an ostrich-feather fan. Holding the wriggling creature at arm's length, Hera exhales a stream of frigid air into its face, coating it in frost. The nymph gasps, turning blue and stiff. Icicles hang off its chin. Hera releases her grip and the nymph falls, frozen to the marrow and solid as a stone. There's a loud cracking, like the ice on a winter pond.

'Yes!' I roar. 'A fine idea. I'll show them what it means to displease Zeus.'

'Take me with you,' murmurs Hera, breath warm and humid on the back of my neck. 'Let me watch.'

THE FATES

Mount Olympos

A Time out of Time

We guide Meleager and Atalanta through the struggles of their growing years.

Meleager continues to churn with hatred for The Fates, and we cannot blame him. We yearn to undo his misery, unpeel its plague-ridden blanket and set him free, but his destiny is a vital piece in our stratagem to release humankind from the chains of Fate. We do what we can to nourish the roots of his spirit, urging him to escape the torture-garden of his home. Most of all, we send him a beacon in the shape of Atalanta.

Atalanta has grown into a wild and courageous woman. Through her childhood, we nudge her away from scorpions and precipices, for human cubs are as careless as goats when it comes to falling into ravines. Now, she has been forced to leave the rough paradise of her mountain fastness and live with human strangers.

From inauspicious beginnings great things may come. Meleager and Atalanta are forged of stern stuff. They are not content to moan and grizzle. Neither of them twiddle their thumbs, waiting for good luck to tumble into their laps. They wrestle bad luck into better.

They will need every scrap for the battles that are to come.

We keep our vigil, and we pray. Yes, even The Fates pray. Even though we were created before prayer, we are not so ancient that we surrender hope. We have made a promise to protect Meleager and Atalanta, and, whatever the myths say, we are women of our word.

MELEAGER

Calydon

I strive to love Toxeus; by all the Gods I swear this to be true.

It is for the elder brother to set an honourable example, and I try my damndest. I hold hard to optimism, remembering the motto that a spoiled child often grows out of the spoiling. In the case of my brother, my faith is misplaced. If Toxeus had merely been petted, perhaps things might have turned out differently. While his mind is still as malleable as river-clay, Althea moulds it into a warped shape and over the years, it sets hard.

One afternoon, I find him strutting around the courtyard and ordering the house-slaves to kiss his foot.

'Come now, Brother,' I say carefully, so as not to set him off. 'A noble fellow does not abase his slaves.'

He deals me a withering sneer. 'You dare speak of nobility, you son of a cur?'

'Toxeus,' I say, lowering my voice. 'Have a care. You insult our mother. And my father also.'

'Your father?' he snorts. 'A mere mortal.'

'As is yours, Toxeus.'

'Your sire may be mortal.' He tips up his chin, plants his fists on his hips. 'I am the son of Apollo.'

I press my lips together to prevent the laughter from escaping. Do I say, *No you're not?* I have no idea if he truly believes this claptrap, or whether he merely wishes to.

'That's taken the wind out of your black sails, hasn't it?' he says, tossing his head.

'Come now, Brother,' I plead.

'Don't soil my ears with that word,' he says, voice bitter as wormwood. 'You are not worthy to tie up the strap on my sandal. I am the new Herakles. I am the son of a God. I am—'

'Toxeus . . .'

He runs a hand through his boyish locks, determined not to be distracted from the flow of poetic rapture. 'Mother told me everything. Her beauty captured the eye of Apollo. Out of all mortal women, he chose her to bear his son.'

'Toxeus . . .' I bite my lip. This is not the time to remark that the Gods seize any mortal they choose: man or woman, willing or unwilling. My deluded brother is still warming to his theme.

'On the day of my conception, Apollo stepped down from Olympos and entered Althea's chamber. He could have filled the house with unbearable radiance, could have revealed himself to her in all his glory. But because Althea is a faithful and virtuous wife, he took the form of Therios, my base cuckold of a sire. Oh, how handsome the God appeared!' Toxeus warbles, eyes shining. 'His limbs were gold, his teeth were pearls, his loins were ivory! Far more beautiful than Therios. Which is how Althea knew.'

Toxeus pauses and spits. His aim is poor and the glob lands on his toe. He's so wrapped up in his story he ignores it.

I sigh. 'Toxeus,' I try again. It is like trying to staunch a flood with a feather.

'She knew!' he squeaks. 'Knew she lay with a God. Knew she was possessed by divinity. She felt her womb quicken with the seed of an immortal, not the sort of slurry that resulted in you.'

At last, he grinds to the end of the fable. He's wearing the inane smirk he's worn for as long as I remember. I understand its root, now. He has been fed the lie he can do as he pleases, acting honourably or dishonourably according to his whim. He is not subject to the laws governing men, because he is more than a man.

Althea must have been spinning this web of phantasy since he was at the breast, repeating it when he took his first steps, when he lisped his first word, and when he first poked me in the eye and hid behind her skirts, whining, *Meleager started it.*

My birth was cursed by The Fates. Perhaps Althea wanted Toxeus's birth to be blessed, and her brain cooked up the ridiculous idea that he's the son of Apollo. Not that I've ever seen the smallest sign of divine behaviour. It has puffed him up, as when rough boys stick a straw into a toad's back end and inflate it with sticky breath. Oh, my poor buffoon of a brother.

'Toxeus, I beg you to listen. We are born of the same mother. Let there be no separation between us.' I hold out my hand. 'Come. Let us be brothers in spirit.'

I swear his expression softens. His eyes glitter, close to weeping. Perhaps he too is worn out by our mother's babbling. Perhaps he too seeks firm ground on which to plant his feet and regain his balance. I taste hope that we might be true brothers, leaning on each other to weather the storms of boyhood. Toxeus holds out his hand. I can almost reach him.

I smile, to encourage untried kindness from its hiding place. It is my error. The expression is wiped from his face fast as water off a sailor's back. He snatches away his hand as though I'm offering a dead rat.

'You almost had me fooled,' he says, voice querulous. 'You're laughing at me,' he cries, snuffing the faint flame of sweetness. His eyes are flint-dry.

'Brother,' I murmur, hoping to calm him. 'Brother.'

'I am not your brother,' he says, voice throttled with need and pain.

'Oh, Toxeus,' I say kindly.

'Toxeus, Toxeus!' he snaps. 'Shut up. You sound like a parrot.'

There's a silence, and I realise he's waiting. For me to bend the knee, clasp my hands in wonderment, worship and admire.

'You are a bloody fool,' I growl, and turn away.

It is a mistake. It sets us further apart, and this time there will be no master mason skilled enough to bridge the gap.

Toxeus changes from an annoyance into a dangerous enemy. It is not long before I discover just how dangerous.

My boyhood continues as a battlefield, beset by enemies. I find respite in the strengthening of the flesh, and it is my salvation. I stop praying for Plexippus to step into the family and create a lasting peace. Instead, I take my future into my own hands. At the age of seven, I am exiled from the women's quarters as happens to all lads my age. I bend the knee to Therios and beg a tutor to train me in the arts of the warrior. He smiles, for the first and only time I recall.

As fast as I am able, I compel my body to transform itself from boy to man. Before cock-crow, I am running and lifting weights. I heft a man's bow by age eight, bend it by age ten, pierce the heart of the target with every arrow by age eleven. I eat with a passion, piling on muscle so I may cloak my frame in its protective aegis. Anything to aid me to withstand the schemes and falsehoods of Toxeus, the tirades and fault-finding of Althea.

Therios goes one better, packing me off to his estate in Parthenion the summer of my thirteenth year. Perhaps he seeks respite from a stepson who reminds him all too keenly of his turbulent wife. I care not: it is a happy time in a beleaguered life. Parthenion is famed for its abundant game, and I plunge myself with gusto into the pinnacle of all manly crafts: hunting. I join a gang of older youths, and at first they tease and call me Little Pup, but it doesn't take long for my skill with bow and spear to change their minds. They praise me as their lucky charm, for whenever I run with them, we bring in the greatest bag.

It is on one of these excursions I see her.

I wander off, desperate to bring down my first boar alone. Barely the size of a piglet myself, I possess the overreaching ambition of a lad longing to prove himself. I'm passing a steep slab of bare rock when an odd sensation compels me to halt. I ignore it, and push on. I get two paces before I am forced to stop.

'There's not so much as a rabbit here,' I say to emptiness. 'It's naked granite with not a scrap of cover.'

Except I am not speaking to myself. The air to my right gathers itself into the shape of a door. It shimmers with a peculiar radiance, rippling like water, except it is water standing upright. Through it step two smiling maidens. I've heard of divine beings travelling from their realm into ours, but thought it the invention of storytellers.

This is no invention. I fall to my knees.

'Oh, blessed Goddesses!' I croak. 'How have I offended you?'

They laugh soundlessly, and point up the rock face.

'I must scramble up?'

They nod, and, as suddenly as they arrive, whisk themselves away. I try to make sense of the vision. I should have eaten a better breakfast. Perhaps the cheese was rancid, the bread infested with ergot. While I'm goggling, the same force as before deals my backside a mighty kick. Not needing to be told twice, I scramble up the slope and peer over the summit.

At first sight, they look like a brace of bear-cubs, wrestling in the dirt. My heart leaps and I breathe a quick prayer of thanks to the spirits who urged me to this unlikely spot. No mere boar for Meleager: I shall bring back a bear.

As quietly as possible, I notch an arrow. As I take the sighting, I realise my mistake. One bear-cub, yes. Its playmate is a girl, as human as am I: arms, legs, hands, feet and all. I lower the bow.

I watch them gambol, girl and bear. I think of the fame and glory within my grasp: hardened hunters pressing neat wine between my lips, lifting me on their shoulders and praising Meleager, the lad who captured the Bear-Girl of Mount Parthenion. I imagine hanging a necklet of bear's teeth around my throat, strung on a thong woven of her hair; imagine myself as an old man, spinning tales to my grandsons of how I hogtied and dragged her into camp.

I see it all flashing before my eyes, swift as a mountain brook.

I am entranced. She is naked and yet her innocence clothes her more modestly than a matron. A day ago, I would have slain the bear without a second thought and counted myself victor. Watching them together, I am struck with shame: how arrogant to think myself above the beasts, and that I may dispose of them with as little care as my brother Toxeus breaking a toy.

An invisible hand runs itself along my spine, and I shiver. This girl-child, growling and rolling in the dust, is the most wondrous thing I've ever seen: grubby, scratched and entirely free. The Moirai dealt her a blow as dreadful as mine, for

I've heard the hearthside horror stories of unwanted girls tossed out and left to die. Despite her terrible fate, she has twisted tragedy into freedom and, from where I am spying, happiness. Compared to me she is braver and more resilient by a hundredfold.

The Gods have granted me a vision of resolve. I am decided. From this day on, I will strive to match this lass for courage. I shall take the reins of Fate into my own hands. I may not be able to escape my destiny, but I will be my own master.

Thank you, I breathe.

The girl cocks her head as though she can hear; she snuffs the air once, twice. Perhaps she doesn't know I'm there; perhaps she does and can tell I'm a harmless boy. Either way, she goes back to her game of tickling and tumbling.

I creep away, kicking over my tracks. I reach a stream and make a big show of stamping in the muddy bank, slathering myself all over. When I return to the hunter's camp, I complain how I spotted not so much as a pigeon and fell into a mire to boot. I bear their chaffing, and when they declare we shall find better game in the opposite direction, I smile.

From that day on I hunt as a changed man, with respect for my fellow-creatures. I only see the wonderful Bear-Girl for a handful of moments, less than the time it takes to eat a piece of bread. The memory nourishes far more than bread alone. Whenever I am laid low by my mother's wild manipulations and Toxeus's schemes, I think of her, thriving on a mountain with beasts for kin. She is a bright light shining into my darkness.

The months speed by. I hope the proverb *Out of Sight is Out of Mind* proves its worth and Therios forgets me. It is not to be. As autumn chills the morning air, I am recalled to Calydon and sail with black sails hoisted in my heart.

At home, all is as crazed as before. Althea continues to swing back and forth like the waxen mammets on the Mother-Tree. In the morning, she pets me, warbling how I'm her darling and how she'll guard the log with her life. Come the afternoon, she slumps on her couch, arm across her face and sobbing that I care nothing for her woes and she may as well toss the log into the hearth and have done with it.

I say, *No, beloved Mother* and *Yes, beloved Mother*. I know she doesn't intend to act on the threats. She sings a tune I'm so used to it washes over me like a river over its rocky bed.

Toxeus is a different matter. If anything, he is more underhand than before. He gobbles our mother's stories of The Fates' prophecy and adds them to his store of weapons. The first time I come upon him stabbing the casket-lock with a hairpin, I land him a clout that sends him bowling into the corner. He is a fluster of arms and legs, clutching his cheek and gawping like a landed trout. No words; only a moist popping of his lips. The soaring of my spirit suggests I should do this far more often. I wait for him to clamber to his feet and run to Althea in a storm of weeping.

'I hate you,' he hisses.

'Tell me something I don't know,' I say, blowing on my knuckles.

'Just you wait,' he says. 'Any lock can be picked. I'll find a way in.'

'No you won't,' I snort, less confidently.

'Try me.'

'If you do, Althea will have your hide for a door-curtain. She'll string a girdle out of your guts,' I say, tittering at the appealing picture.

Toxeus stands up as gracefully as he is able. Although years my junior, we are the same height.

'So she may,' he says casually, and skewers me with a look. 'But you'll be dead by then, won't you? She'll get over it, faster than you think. She'll still have me and we both know who she loves the best.'

'You're lying.'

'Am I?' He brushes the creases from his tunic. 'Let's face it, Meleager. Her chief emotion will be one of relief.'

'No,' I breathe.

'If I were you, dearest half-brother, I'd be a lot nicer to me. Or else.'

Toxeus swaggers away, nose in the air. He is such a practised liar I'd go hatless if he said it was raining. For the first time, I believe every word he says.

Althea's favourite hairpins go missing and are found bent and twisted. House-slaves are flogged. Meat skewers vanish from the kitchen and it is the turn of kitchen-slaves to howl their blamelessness. The lock holds its own, surrounded by a ring of gouges from Toxeus's furious attempts to break it. The crowning moment is when Althea accuses me of the damage,

Toxeus giggling behind her back. She does not listen when I ask why on earth I'd do such a dangerous thing.

It gives me an idea. Sooner or later, Toxeus will find a way into the casket. I have to be a step ahead. My training has already drilled me in the strategy that the best form of defence is attack, and so I take a direct approach.

I don't bother trying to pick the lock. The following afternoon, I wait until Althea is sleeping away the sweltering hours. As usual, she's swigged a draught of the poppy philtre she thinks no one knows about, and is snoring fit to shake the plaster off the walls. I bow to her body-slaves, who drift back into their own grateful slumber, these hours being a peaceful respite for them also. I step to her couch and unhook the key from her girdle. It turns in the lock without a squeak, the mechanism oiled and obedient. I slip my fingertips under the edge of the lid and push.

It won't budge. I flex my biceps, clench my jaw and try again. Nothing happens. The lid is as heavy as a temple lintel. Althea must have the assistance of giants to shift it. Hope drains out of me as wine through a sieve. I am so close, and yet so far. My eyes sting and in the glitter of tears, I see the same two maidens who guided me to the Bear-Girl. I stare at them and wonder if my hour has come; if my desire to see into the chest has angered the Gods, and they are about to convey me to the Underworld.

We are here to help, dear Meleager, they say. *Trust.*

It is the second time I've been visited by these messengers from beyond this world. I can do nothing but obey.

They kneel beside me and, together, we put our shoulders to the task. With a tremendous shove, the lid is open.

I've heard about the fabled log since before I can remember. As is the way of oft-told tales, it has grown in the telling and I'm expecting to find a hefty oaken branch the size of a roof beam. It is on the small side: a common lump of wood, one end blackened with charcoal. A trapped scent of long-doused fire rises to my nostrils, and I think of the wil o' the wisps that arose from Pandora's casket, releasing evil into the world. It is up to me to find the ghost of hope hidden here.

I glance over my shoulder to thank my helpers, but they have gone, leaving the green ghosts one sees after staring into a flame. I turn back. Surely nothing this ordinary can wield the power of life and death. I lean in and poke it with my finger, anticipating a resonating ache in my body. Nothing. I poke again, more roughly. Still nothing. I jab and jab, the log rocking back and forth. It's wood, that's all.

I. Have. Lived. In. Fear. For. Nothing.

Then it happens. An unseen blade rams its point between my ribs. I clutch my side, winded and gasping. Over and over I'm stabbed, once for each shove I dealt the log.

I thought I knew fear: Althea's threats, Toxeus's tyranny, the time I jumped off the roof and thought I'd broken my ankle, the stick wielded by my mathematics master with which he endeavours to beat a better understanding of the abacus into my back. Compared to this, my childish anxieties are as teardrops in the sea.

This is true terror. Althea's fables are not hot air. The prophecy of my fate is real, and rooted in a deep and dreadful enchantment. I am its target, as sure as if I daubed a crimson circle over my heart. If – no, *when* – Toxeus succeeds in plundering the chest, my life is over. What remains of it stretches before me, a wilderness unmarked by joy. I have to guard the log as carefully as my mother, if not more so. I can never leave home. My dreams of escape go up in smoke, much as this hunk of wood almost did, all those years ago. I am done for.

Unless.

The prophecy is that I will die when the brand is consumed. Completely. I examine it closely. The untouched end is frayed from a clumsy axe-stroke. I tug at a splinter and unpeel it. Once more, I'm wrenched with pain, worse than ripping off a scab before it is ready. It will be the discomfort of a moment, I tell myself. I keep going, teeth gritted, flaying away a piece of my life. I don't stop tearing until the splinter rests in the palm of my hand. Silently, I close the strongbox and return the key to my snuffling mother. Clutching my destiny, I step from the women's quarters into the commencement of a new, brave life.

The following morning, before the household is fully awake and about its business, I slip from the house and walk to the town gate. If I step outside its bounds, I am running away. If I stay within, I am merely a boy taking the morning air and stretching his limbs in crisp coolness before heat hammers the day flat and breathless.

The watchman and I exchange a grunted greeting. He clears the night from his throat, his hacking cough startling a flock of pigeons into a flap. They soar, wheeling in frenetic circles. A kite swoops out of nowhere, grabs one in its talons, and vanishes as swiftly. The pigeons flutter to the earth, and do not seem to notice one of their clan has been taken. Maybe they do not care. They peck at nothing, regarding me with unblinking eyes, not bothering to get out of the watchman's way as he lumbers off-duty in search of breakfast.

I go to the harbourside and beg a boatman for a scrap of leather. I make a little pouch with the help of a sail-needle curved like a gorgon's claw, sew the splinter within and tie it around my throat. I make a solemn promise, swearing an oath upon my own life. My existence may be as worthless as a pigeon's at this moment. It will not always be.

That evening, Toxeus sidles up to me and threatens to unlock the casket that very night. I shrug and say, *Do your worst.* He can tell I'm no longer gripped by fear. Like all torturers, he knows there's no sport in a horse that won't run. He will find other ways to make the days a misery. But a spell has been drained of its power.

I continue to train. Each morning I rise, marshal my spirits and tell myself I am one day closer to release from the gaol of home. I keep my head down and plod through year after raw, dank year.

Through it all I nurture vengeance against The Fates. Not satisfied with warping my mother's spirit, they twisted my brother Toxeus into a fool with delusions of Godhead, who amuses himself with fratricide as though it is a game of pitch-and-toss.

At last the day comes when I can call myself a man. I take what is mine, and shake off the cloying dust of my childhood. Wearing the precious splinter around my throat, I leave without a backward glance and sail for Parthenion, the site of my greatest boyhood happiness.

I grasp every opportunity and wrest it to my benefit. As a potter kneads a lump of clay into an elegant amphora, I shape myself anew. When I am fired and sturdy, I fill myself with the wine of honour, both on the battlefield and in the barracks.

My boyhood taught me the corrupting influence of envy, hatred and guilt, and these I shun, with every grain of my being. I deal with all men – I dare to say women also – with a clean heart and clean conscience. Nor am I some milksop paragon, hiding from the heat of the action. I take my fair share of blows to the flesh.

Five years pass and I'm scarred as the walnut trees peasants flog each autumn to fatten the crop. In ten years, my nose is broken, my right ear swollen as a bulb of garlic. I am unhandsome, crack-toothed and happy. I do not see my Bear-Girl again, but carry her in my heart; magnificent and indomitable; a shining example of resilience against an unfair fate.

Perhaps if I'd stayed, I might have calmed Toxeus and stilled my mother's lunacy. Perhaps if I'd not been so hungry for escape, things might not have turned out so badly. A man cannot know his future. Even if I'd been vouchsafed the secrets of mine, I wonder if I'd have taken a single step in a different direction. On the whole, I think not. What is, is.

My life will be redeemed. It will also be utterly destroyed.

ATALANTA

Parthenion

Arktos may have been confident my proper home is amongst men, but I am not convinced. When I come down from the mountain on the day of her death, dogs bark, cats arch their backs and hiss. Children dangle out of windows, mothers cover their daughter's eyes and men gawk, lower lips drooping to their navels.

They are alien creatures, and naivety is my protection. For all I know, this is common behaviour when a new neighbour strolls into town. My only schooling is in the etiquette of bears. I growl and scratch myself without any embarrassment, unmindful of the crowd following in my footsteps.

The first stone falls wide, in the way of first stones. The second is closer. The third strikes the back of my leg. If not for the young woman who darts through the crowd and plants herself in front of me, waving her arms, things might turn out woefully.

'Artemis!' she cries, throwing a cape around my nakedness. I recognise the dimpled lass who saw me by the river. 'Stop! It is Artemis!'

The long sleeves of her robe flap like dove's wings. She points at the arrowhead around my neck, babbling at break-neck speed. The only word I pick out of the tangle is *Artemis*. Whatever she does say, the urgency of her protestations makes the villagers lay down their stones. Indeed, many of them bow their heads and kneel. I grunt thanks to the young woman, who smiles.

'Antiklea,' she says, pointing to herself.

I manage it after many attempts. My errors make her laugh and it is a blissful sound in this stone-throwing, clothes-wearing world into which I've been exiled. She points at me, nods. It is clearly my turn.

I have no human name. Arktos called me *daughter*, *child*, *beloved* and all manner of pet names. I growl *daughter*, in the language of bears. Antiklea frowns and tries to repeat the sound. It is as difficult for her to speak my tongue as it is for me to speak hers. She smiles again.

'I shall call you Gift of Artemis,' she says. 'For you are our gift.'

She takes my hand. I never felt anything so tender. My palm is calloused from the rough-and-tumble ways of bears and I'm worried I will rub her raw. She seems cheerful enough, grinning and chattering as she leads me through the streets. I follow, trusting as a chick its mother hen. We are accompanied by village folk, who gossip in our wake.

Antiklea leads us through a maze of houses, all of which look exactly the same. I hold tight. Without her, I'd never find my way out and wander forever. By and by, the dense cluster of buildings becomes a dwindling straggle of smaller huts, and I wonder if she's going to lead me into the wilderness and deposit me there. She comes to a halt before a cottage surrounded with beds of carefully tended vegetables and sweet-smelling herbs.

At her shouted greeting, an old woman emerges, carrying a digging-stick. Her face is deeply lined. She regards me from under hooded eyelids, eyes black as dragon-glass and as unnerving. She is followed by a graceful gentleman with a chin as smooth as a pebble. With a great deal of back-and-forth and repetition of the word *Artemis*, I am motioned to sit.

Antiklea points at the old woman. 'Hiereya,' she says. 'She is a friend. Hiereya.'

I repeat the sound and make a fist of it, much to the crone's amusement.

Next, Antiklea points to the man. 'Pappas,' she says. 'Also a friend.'

I manage his name more easily. Hiereya disappears behind the hut and returns with a dish brimming with lentil broth. I don't need to be asked twice and tip the entire bowlful down my gullet. I let out a belch of satisfaction the trio find very droll.

At nightfall, Antiklea bids us farewell, and I make to follow. She repeats the word *Father* many times with a sad shaking of her head. It is clear I am to stay here. I watch her return to the village, pricked with my own sadness. Hiereya brings her goats indoors. She climbs a ladder to the space beneath the roof and beckons me to follow. I gaze longingly at the forested slopes in the distance. She shrugs. I remain outdoors, curled up in her vegetable patch.

In the middle of the night, I hear the snuffling of human voices. One of Hiereya's geese honks a warning and the two-legged wolves take to their heels. I dart into the house, shin up the ladder fast as a weasel, and dive under the blanket. It is nothing to compare with the warm fur of Arktos, and I startle in and out of sleep, ears pricking at strange sounds. At some point before dawn, I wake myself whimpering. Hiereya curves her arm around me, shushing my tears.

Grudgingly, I learn human ways. When I arrive, I am armed with a single word: *Artemis*. Each time I speak it, the villagers' eyes flicker and they back away, bowing and mumbling. When I learn its meaning I understand why. They think I'm sent by the Goddess. I don't know what they'd say if I reveal I was sent by a bear. I keep that secret to myself.

I wear clothes, although I refuse to dress as the village matrons, swaddled tight as butterfly cocoons. I submit to their dainty eating habits, picking food from a bowl with clean fingers rather than shoving my face into the dish and slurping it into my mouth. I study their language. Gradually, the mess of disconnected twittering untangles into words: bread, milk, meat. Man, woman, girl. Stand, walk, run. *Run* is my favourite.

The villagers find me funny and frightening at the same time. I prompt a lot of laughter with my clownish misunderstandings. I take no offence: I laugh just as loud at their ridiculous habits. What I think of as a simple task is beyond their ken. Not one of them can flip a fish out of a stream with their thumb, nor sniff the difference between a tasty mushroom and a deadly toadstool. Wherever I go, I am gawked at, groped and prodded. It is mostly good-natured and they are too weak to do any harm, not even the larger males. I return one poke, and the raw-boned youth who dealt it goes spinning head over heels and crashes into a wall, much to the delight of his fellows. After that, they mostly make do with staring.

I help Hiereya: milk goats, fetch honey and fruit from the forest, fish from the river. She takes good care of me. Rangy and tall, in her I see a woman who has spent much of her life running also. She reminds me of a hare – long-limbed and alert – but a hare with the heart and sinew of a wolf.

Antiklea is my guide, and I look forward to my lessons. I delight in her company more than her teachings, if I'm honest. She shows me how to crush walnuts, rub the oil into my palms and rake sticky fingers through my hair. I believe she is determined to render my tresses as shimmering and smooth as her own. It is impossible. My hair – if it deserves the name – is clumped into long wadded strands, thick as snakes. Hers is braided into a heavy coil, fragrant with mysterious fragrance. I find myself wishing to be close to her, so I can breathe her in. I sneak sideways glances whenever we are together: the lilt of her walk, both determined and elegant at one and the same time, the sway and loll of her generous hips.

Every few days, stalls are set up in the centre of the village, and Antiklea and I take our time admiring the delicacies: loaves, cheeses, vegetables and fruit. One morning, I select a glossy apple, chew a tasty chunk out of its middle, and receive a slap for my trouble. I have no notion why I'm being shouted at. Antiklea laughs at my confusion.

'The apples are here,' I say. 'This kind woman has saved me the bother of climbing a tree and picking one.'

'You must pay for it.'

'Pay?'

'Give her something of equal worth. An exchange.'

It makes a garbled kind of sense. Later that afternoon, I return to the village square and present the apple-seller with a chunk of honeycomb, wrapped in leaves. Her eyes widen in astonishment and she grabs the prize before I change my mind.

'Take as much as you want!' she cries. 'Figs, apples, olives. Keep bringing honey and what is mine is yours.'

I add the title Honey-Thief to my growing list of names: Fleet-of-Foot, Gift of Artemis.

I've been amongst the humans a handful of months when he finds me.

I'm seated in my usual place on the riverbank. I spend a lot of time there, upstream of the women laundering their clothes. It is a favoured spot, away from the tugging and patting and ogling. I watch the water tumble down into the cramped valley, carrying fresh mountain air with it. In my imagination I hear the rumbling voices of bears in its flow. I know it is not true, for I have been banished from my Paradise. Still in mourning for Arktos, the fancy gives me comfort.

A man sidles alongside and grabs my right breast with one hand, shoving the other between my legs. I recognise him as the gangling youth I tossed aside like a plum-stone. I wonder if this is how human males go about their mating rituals. I am not interested, and push him away. He sniggers unpleasantly and grasps me again, a good deal more roughly. I shove back equally firmly and he goes flying.

'Bitch,' he snarls, wiping his lip, which is bleeding.

I dig my heels into the mud, spread my arms wide and hiss a fair warning. He ignores it and approaches me afresh. I shake my head and the snake-locks swing to and fro. He stands stock-still. His cheeks grow pale as old milk, his mouth falls open and he moans, *gor-gun*. I shake my head again and growl. He takes to his heels and runs, yelling words I do not understand.

'He said *gor-gun*,' I tell Antiklea, later.

'Gorgon. I can see why.' She points at my twisted and matted locks.

'What does it mean?'

'A gorgon is a woman with snakes in her hair, so monstrous one glance turns anyone to stone.'

I snort. 'You're not turning to stone and I'm looking right at you.'

Antiklea giggles and her dimples appear, so pretty I want to kiss them. She regards me shyly.

'Remember when I first saw you beside the river, all those months ago? I thought you were Artemis.'

I laugh at the happy memory.

'There is a reason I sprang to that conclusion,' she says. 'I am a Sister of Artemis, one of the women who dedicate their lives to the Goddess.' She lowers her gaze, blushing. 'We are few but we are strong in resolve. Will you join us?'

I clasp her hand. Her dimples flash once more and this time I do kiss them. She returns the embrace with relish. It is the beginning of many such embraces, each more passionate than the last.

I become a Sister of Artemis. At the full of every moon, the Goddess calls and women gather to celebrate the flow of our monthly blood. Behind closed doors, the villagers whisper nonsense about how we devour men in our sacred rites. In faith, if they witnessed our ceremonies, I believe they would find them very disappointing. We drink and eat, and tell stories around the fire. We comb and braid each other's hair, snipping away the curls of beloved companions and twisting them into bracelets. I wear a band of Antiklea's hair around my wrist, where the blood beats. Each pulse reminds me of her affection.

Of course, not every woman joins our congregation. There are those who refuse to hear our songs; bolt their shutters so not even the smallest flicker of our torches disturbs their sight. Women who swear they see nothing, hear nothing, know nothing and wish it to stay that way.

Women who declare their only happiness is to be subject to their husbands, sit indoors and spin, and birth a child every ten months, eleven at the most. Women who do not speak a word unless permitted. Who bear every hardship, endure the concubines their husbands parade before them. Who swear women are inferior, nearer to the beasts. Who swear this is the rightful order of the world.

However loud the grumbling, no one dares disrupt the worship of the Goddess by preventing our meetings. They make do with slander. Behind our backs, they call us wild and dangerous Maenads. They can say whatever they wish: a hundred filthy names, and we brush them off easy as water off a kingfisher's back.

At the following monthly ceremony, Hiereya presents me with a bow.

'No,' I say, flinching away. 'It is the weapon that murdered my mother.'

'It is the gift of the Goddess,' croaks the old priestess.

I shake my head. 'Forgive me, honoured grandmother,' I say. 'I cannot. It is hideous to my sight.'

Hiereya does not withdraw the bow. 'Do not shrink from destiny,' she says.

I look at the women, their faces bright with encouragement. Antiklea nods, hers the brightest of all. As I hesitate, the shadows at the edge of the clearing waver. I watch as they gather themselves into the shape of a door, its outline glowing with faint green light. Through it step the two girls who comforted me when Arktos died. They float across the clearing, bare feet not quite touching the earth. They must be messengers sent by the Goddess.

'Oh, blessed Artemis!' I cry.

No one else has noticed their presence. They approach and stand one to each side of Hiereya. All three, the mortal and the divine, point to the bow and then at the arrowhead hanging round my neck.

Hiereya speaks. 'When you came to us, you were wearing a triple-lobed arrowhead. It is the sigil of Artemis.'

'Artemis!' echo the women.

Once more, Hiereya thrusts the bow towards me. The shimmering nymphs nod. The night presses close. Blood whistles in my ears. The Goddess herself is sending me a sign. I shall not disobey. I cannot. I step forward. The moment I touch the bow, my hand moulds to it as though we are part of each other. A thrill of fire and ice courses up my arm, setting my body aflame. I gasp at the unexpected sensation.

Yes, say the girls, and vanish, leaving me with a mingled sensation of protection and power.

'Yes,' echoes Hiereya. 'Now you understand.'

I do. From that moment on, my life has purpose. I belong to Artemis, who has sent two spirits to guide me. I can think of no greater blessing. I take to archery as though I have been awaiting its discipline all my life. Though undeniably a woman, I am equal in skill to any man. They give me a new name, one that is up to the task of encompassing my contradictions: I am Equal-in-Weight.

I am Atalanta.

MELEAGER

Parthenion

Parthenion is as happy a home as Calydon was miserable. The only nuisance is the sudden interest Therios takes, after ignoring me my entire boyhood. Leaving Althea in Calydon, he has moved his household to the estate in Parthenion, it being too far to hear her complaints. Every month, he sends word requesting my attendance and every month I refuse. However, I am an obedient stepson. Before I veer into offence, I accept his invitation. As soon as courtesy permits, I plan to leave discreetly.

However, it becomes clear Therios has no intention of letting me escape. As a renowned man-at-arms, I am of use to him, and he finds one excuse after another to quell my wanderlust. The land surrounding Therios's estate is famed for rich hunting. Thinking to avail myself of pleasurable activity whilst submitting to my stepfather's bidding, I supply myself with a spear, arrows for my bow, and seek out a hunting party in a nearby hostelry. I stand the company to wine, and while they empty an amphora, imbibe their gossip. In addition to a merry evening in the company of fine rustic fellows, I discover intelligence of a good place to hunt.

The next morning, I am deep in cover while the larks are still snoring, a scrip filled with bread and cheese slung across my breast. I kiss the amulet around my throat and fortune smiles upon me in the shape of a large stag. He is a noble creature, mighty antlers branched into sixteen tines, his call a sonorous bell. I follow my challenger, tracking him for three days and never resting more than the time it takes to plunge my head into a stream, or chew on a half-loaf.

I run him down far from the path, where he is drinking from a pool and crowned with a haze of hovering flies. I skirt the clearing and hide behind a tree, gripping the shaft of my spear. He tips up his muzzle and flares his nostrils. Even though I stand in the lee of the wind, he knows I am there. He knows why, also. I carry death in my fist, yet he regards me with dignified serenity. I am a child in the presence of the king of the forest. He lowers his head, and swings his massive antlers from side to side, the years hanging heavy upon his shoulders.

I draw back my arm. My spear flies true, whistling in flight. The stag does not flinch, not by a hairsbreadth. Lifting his chin for the last time, he watches his destiny approach. The blow is clean. He staggers forwards, forelegs folding in two. I'm at his side in the time it takes to speak my name. I kneel and wrap my arms about his neck, not to throttle, but to feel his failing heart beat against mine. I need this intimacy. I crave it. We lie close as lovers.

'Thank you,' I whisper into his ear, not as an enemy, but as a grateful friend.

I continue to murmur, comforting him from this world into the next. Perhaps I am comforting myself also. Gradually, he stops kicking. I feel him grow calm, beast and man together in a strange embrace, as we pant out the exertion of the chase. Shadows shift and lengthen in the westering sun, and still we lie, entwined and peaceful. Whisperings continue to spill from my lips until I fall into a drowse.

I hear a sound, no louder than the rustle of a leaf. After three days trailing this gallant creature, I swear I could hear an ant tiptoe past. I quiver with a peculiar anticipation and wonder if my guardian maidens are about to visit. A woman steps into the clearing, and at first I think Artemis herself has descended from Olympos.

She is long-limbed and lithe as a pine marten. Her hair is a bundle of snake-locks bound up in a topknot, skin pricked with a lifetime of scratches, both fresh and long-healed. Her tunic is hitched well above the knee and hangs off one shoulder, revealing breasts that are mere whispers of flesh. I've known women short and tall, buxom and slim as laths, yet have never seen anything like her. She is wonderful.

The stag senses the distraction and, despite its exhaustion, lashes out with its hooves.

'Help?' I say, with an imploring look.

I expect her to leap forward with a savage cry and dispatch the animal with a single thrust of her knife. I expect her to exult at the spurting of heart's-blood, the keening despair of the beast. No such thing happens. She stretches out along the stag's right flank, lays her cheek against him, and begins talking quietly into his ear. We look at each other over the long ridge of his muzzle.

'This stag has kept me on my toes for days,' she says. 'I began by tracking him, but for the past day I have been tracking you.'

'You have? I did not know.'

She grins. 'Of course. You would only know if I wished it.' The buck drags in a hurtling breath, and she shushes him gently. 'My mother Arktos taught me the holiness of all life. To kill cleanly and with respect. I never met a human who lives by this principle also.'

I grunt a gruff thank you, and together we speak a valediction.

'Oh worthy opponent,' I say. 'You have tested me . . . have tested us,' I add, correcting myself.

She smiles. 'Great adversary,' she says. 'We shall humbly partake of your flesh, your strength and your wisdom.'

'Most honourable foe, we salute you.'

The creature snorts. It is fancy, but I believe I hear assent. I unsheathe my knife and dispatch the stag with a swift and merciful cut. He lets out a sigh of such sweet release I declare I sigh also. His eye rolls up and shows the white, tongue lolling between his jaws. It is over.

When we are sure all life has fled, my companion dips a forefinger into the blood and swipes her brow. With a gesture imbued with tenderness and piety, she makes the same mark upon me. My skin quivers at the touch of her hand. I clear my throat and, to hide my embarrassment, begin to divide the carcase equally, gutting and jointing.

'Well now,' I bluster. 'I must introduce myself. I am Meleager, son of Oeneus of Calydon.'

She grins, revealing chipped teeth. 'Well met, Meleager. I am Atalanta, daughter of Arktos and Sister of Artemis.' I watch as she sacrifices the lights to the Goddess. They crisp and crackle, giving off the savoury perfume that confirms our offering has been accepted. 'My experience of human hunters is dire,' she continues, wiping her hands upon her tunic. 'I expect nothing from men. You have confounded my expectations.'

I mumble thanks.

'No one other than you has witnessed the good death I give my quarry.'

'Aye,' I say. 'When I hunt, it is a meeting of equals. I hunt to test myself.'

'Yes! I push myself to the utmost.'

'Every sinew, every shred of my strength.'

'Not to display trophies for men to admire and envy.' We smile at each other. 'What say you? Let us shake hands and be merry.'

She thrusts out her hand and I take it with a great good will. Her grip is so firm I daresay she can crush walnuts between forefinger and thumb.

'Will you eat with me?' I ask.

'I am always hungry, never more so than after the chase!' she declares.

Together, we gather kindling and make a fire. She watches as I heat a flat stone in the hottest part, flip it over with a stout stick and lay strips of liver upon it.

'I never thought of that,' she says, sniffing the pungent aroma with relish.

'An old campaigner's trick.' I produce a thumb-sized pouch from inside my bag, take a pinch of the contents and rub it into the sizzling meat. When satisfied, I spear a piece on the point of my knife. 'Here. Eat while it's still hot and tender.'

Atalanta needs no second invitation, stuffing the morsel into her mouth. She chews once, twice. Her eyes grow wide, and she pulls the meat back out again, staring at it as if expecting to see flames.

'What did you put on it?' she gasps. 'It is not salt.'

I smile, chewing happily. I know the searing sensation of old, but this is her first taste. 'You're right about that. Go on, give it a chance.'

She looks at me askance, but tries again. She screws up her face, waiting for pain. After a moment, the blaze on her tongue melts into delicious warmth. I watch as her features soften.

'I've never tasted anything like it,' she says. 'Painful and pleasurable at the same time.'

I laugh. 'I got it off a Persian sailor, who said he got it from a Bactrian, who said he got it from a land east of the sunrise.' I wave the little leather bag before tucking it away. 'Twaddle of course, designed to make me cough up more than its weight in silver.'

'Sailors have the best stories,' she says, fanning her mouth with her hand.

'You don't know the half of it. When I was a boy, I lived for old tars' tales. There was this one fellow, Pelagos was his name. He could talk the leg off a donkey. Here's one of his many inventions: a beast with legs thick as temple columns, and a serpent for a nose. Have you ever heard the like?'

'A fine story!' she agrees. 'What sturdy lad does not thrill at the creak of rigging and tang of salt air, whose blood does not rush through his veins when he hears the groaning of the sails, lashed tight?'

I smile. Atalanta has me to the very letter. 'I was that lad. My mother was forever chastising me for wasting time in the company of seamen. She warned me they were pox-ridden rogues who kidnapped small boys and dragged them away to sea. I couldn't imagine anything more wonderful.'

We lick fat from our fingers. After three nights of hard bread and stale cheese, the meal is finer than the feasts of ambrosia so beloved by the Gods. The meat makes me dizzy with satisfaction. From head to heel, my body sings with the gluttonous bliss that follows privation.

Atalanta belches. She glances sidelong, ducks her head and fidgets, drawing in the dirt with her finger. I realise she is waiting for me to snigger or to deliver a lofty lecture about how belching is not proper deportment for a woman, and neither is hunting for that matter.

'Good appetite,' I say and let out a resounding belch also.

She raises her head and blesses me with a smile of surpassing radiance. She is beautiful, even with grease smeared all over her lips.

'Good appetite,' she replies through a mouthful. 'So, Meleager of Calydon,' she says, regarding me thoughtfully. 'You are a long way from home. I have heard Calydon is a rich and fruitful land.'

'True enough. Yet I could not wait to leave. Such are the ways of restless youth,' I say mildly.

She laughs, and I hear an old grief tucked into the lightness. 'I did not want to leave my home. My mother had to force me out.' She tears off another chunk of meat. 'By her fur and paws, I would not trade a morsel of this. It is the most delectable thing I've ever eaten.'

'Fur and paws?' I say. It comes out as a squeak.

'Aye,' she replies, digging in the embers with a stick. 'At my birth, my human father Iasus decided he did not wish for a daughter, and so he threw me away like a bundle of soiled rags. My true mother was a bear.'

'A . . . bear?' A shiver runs through me, as if a bucket of well water has been tipped over my head. Atalanta is my Bear-Girl. There can be none other. My destiny is a mess of dreadful prophecies. How is it possible that I am blessed with this wonderful good fortune? I am Meleager, unlucky, through and through. 'You were raised here, on Mount Parthenion,' I say slowly. 'With bears.'

'Yes! How did you . . .'

'Oh, I must have heard tell,' I stutter.

I root about in the embers also. I can hardly tell her I've adored her since a lad. She turns her marvellous smile upon me.

'Then my fame has travelled.'

My mind reels, tying my tongue into a knot. Atalanta chatters merrily of this and that, stories I cannot recall due to the racket of my thoughts. After we've eaten our fill and more – for I am loath to quit this precious spot – we walk to the nearby village. Atalanta leads me to a humble cottage and introduces me to Hiereya and Pappas. They invite me to stay for victuals, and we talk until the stars appear. The wine is sour, the bread tough as a brick. I never feasted so well, nor so joyously.

I cannot prevent my hungry gaze from sliding sideways to Atalanta. I have been in her company for the space of an afternoon, barely the day's midpoint to dusk. Men have fallen in love in a quarter of the time. I have also been in her company since I was a lost and lonely boy.

My luck is turning. I have met the radiant star who shone hopeful light into my terrible childhood. We are fated to be together. Nothing could be clearer. With Atalanta come into my life, nothing can go wrong. I shall count the days till I see her again. There is a sailor's adage that the darkest storm-cloud is lined with silver. I shall find this Lord Iasus, offer my suit and demand her hand in marriage.

ATALANTA

Parthenion

In dreams, my little guardians whisper Meleager's name.

Yes, they say, taking my hand and placing it in his. *This, Atalanta.*

They entwine us in a glimmering thread, crown us with laurels, show a fire from which I pluck him at the last moment. I dream such a parcel of fancies I wonder if I'm eating too much cheese at supper. Whatever the case, my thoughts do find themselves straying to Meleager. When we are together, my spirit chimes in harmony with his. When apart, the thread woven by my two protectors draws us together again. It is unexpected and strange. My affection for Antiklea grows in accord with nature, from seed to shoot to budding flower. This connection to Meleager is sweet, but sudden.

All the same, I look forward to hunting expeditions with relish, hoping our paths will cross. When they do, it is barely a surprise and we fall easily into each other's company.

I continue to abide with Hiereya and Pappas. They live together so cheerfully, I wonder if they are a mated pair, not that I've seen any evidence. When I enquire one evening, Pappas laughs.

'To the world outside this hut, we live as husband and wife. In truth, we live as brother and sister.' He runs an elegant hand through his meticulously combed hair. 'It acts as a shield for us both.'

I nod. I understand the safety that comes from being Gift of Artemis, when one is different to others.

Hiereya chuckles. 'A woman living a solitary life ruffles many cock feathers, the more so if she is merry.' She pokes at the fire, and the logs collapse with a relaxed sigh. 'I set a dangerous example to womenfolk. Widows eye me longingly, pondering the contentment they might taste now they've shrugged off the burden of a husband. Young girls dare to dream they might not be parcelled off into a marriage.' Hiereya gazes into the embers, a strained smile playing around the corner of her mouth. 'I am too dangerous to remain unmolested. And so Pappas and I have come to an arrangement.'

Pappas takes her hand and kisses the gnarled knuckles. The veins on the back of her hands are thick as ropes.

'It is a fair exchange,' he says. 'I protect Hiereya, and she protects me. For I am a priest and devotee of Kybele. A eunuch.'

I look blank. The word means nothing.

He clutches his groin. 'I lack the parts that distinguish man from woman. I tread the narrow path between both and neither.' He wears the same wistful smile as Hiereya.

'When a person is deemed confusing, it is a short step to injury.' He laughs bitterly. 'My priesthood acts as a safeguard. But winter nights can be perilous. Dark deeds can be done under a cloak of secrecy, and I do not wish to wake up one morning and find that I am dead.'

Time passes, in its slippery fashion. My fame carries on the wings of rumour, which all men know spreads more swiftly than a brush fire in summer. The tales grow until they say I can shoot a sparrow with one eye shut, hear the slither of a snake from fifty paces and bring down a stag with a flick of my little finger. If that were not enough of a feat, they say I can carry the carcase with as little effort as a handful of goose-down.

There is a glimmer of truth in the gossip. Enough to reach the ear of my human father, Iasus. Of course, I know he must abide somewhere. It never occurs to me I shall ever meet him. I learn all I can, and the more I learn, the less I like. Iasus is an important fellow, son of Lycurgus and Lord of Arcadia. Killer of his firstborn daughter, or so he thought. I survived. More than that, I thrived. I am strong and clever and now, I am famous. I pique his interest, and he sends a messenger.

The villagers turn out to see the stranger, for we don't get many of them, let alone on a horse with an embroidered saddlecloth. They follow him all the way to Hiereya's cottage, clacking loud as magpies. I hear them coming from half a league away, and am ready. Hiereya and Pappas stand to the left and right of me, hands folded neatly.

'Hail Atalanta, daughter of Iasus!' cries the messenger, sliding to the ground and pressing his right fist to his breast, all in one liquid movement.

I decide this is neither the time nor the place to sneer how, if I am daughter to anyone, it is to Arktos. I take my time finishing my breakfast, licking the last scrap from the bowl. The visitor curls his lip. Curls it even more when I wipe my hand across my mouth. Pappas sets out a stool and invites him to sit. The messenger peers down his nose at our lowly furnishings.

'I shall stand,' he says, snipping off the words briskly.

Pappas and Hiereya bustle away, snickering.

'Iasus sends greeting!' roars the messenger, so everyone in the neighbouring valley can hear. The horse tosses its head, flapping the damp velvet of its lips. 'Attend his court, and be welcome.'

I incline my head a fraction. The horse paws the dirt with its hoof and snorts.

'Attend,' repeats the messenger.

'Now?' I ask.

'Yes,' he says tersely. 'You are to return with me.'

For years, Iasus thought I was dead. Nor, I'll wager, did he give my demise a passing thought. Of a sudden, he is in a rush to clap eyes on me. While the horse is being watered and the messenger offered wine and bread for his trouble, I prepare for the journey. It does not take long: bow and quiver, my strongest sandals and Pappas as chaperone, which is such a joke we have to repress fits of giggles.

147

Hiereya takes my hand. 'Be careful, Atalanta. You are untutored in the ways of men.'

'What better way to learn? I am curious to see what he is like, this man who claims me as his daughter.'

'Hurry back,' she frets, throwing a sharp look at Pappas, who is selecting which scarf to wear. 'Don't let Pappas drink too much. Be wary of curiosity.'

'What harm can there be in curiosity?' I say, cheerily. 'When it is satisfied, I shall return.'

'Just be on your guard, that is all.'

'Do not worry, Grandmother Hiereya.'

The messenger seems perplexed I do not possess a herd of stallions from which to choose a pair for Pappas and myself. We saddle up the mule and borrow an ass from the baker, with firm promises to have it back by the time he needs it for the next delivery of loaves. We make a comical procession. I take the mule, and even though a hefty beast, my toes scuff in the dirt. Pappas brings up the rear, whacking the donkey. The messenger leads the way, nose in the air and pretending he is master and we are his servants.

Compared to the village, the town is fit for a king. The streets are wide enough for Pappas and I to ride alongside each other, the flagstones artfully arranged so that water and refuse gather into a central gutter, to be washed away by the rains. The houses present plastered walls to the street and I brush my hand against the surface, flat as a pond. Small windows are set high up, shuttered to keep the sun's glare out, and the women in. I peep into courtyards planted with bay and laurel. The scent of basil and rosemary drifts into my nostrils.

The whole place is an assault upon the senses. We are led past food stalls laden with roasting vegetables, skewered meat, loaves and cakes. A man dunks a ladle into a steaming pot set into the counter and scoops out a spoonful of meaty broth. He plonks it into a bowl, whereupon it is slurped up by a hungry customer. My mouth waters.

'Is there a festival?' I say to Pappas.

'No, dear friend,' he replies. 'Welcome to the everyday life of a town.'

What a life it is. Folk throng the streets, thick as trees in a coppice. Women with rouged cheeks lounge in doorways and click their tongues at male passers-by. A boy shoves past, bowling a hoop and shouting for us to get out of his way. Men crouch in a circle around a cockfight, punching the air and squawking encouragement.

Butchers screech *Get it before it reeks!* A food vendor clangs a spoon against a copper tray, squawking *Fresh gruel! Nice and hot!* Bakers slap breadcakes together, showering flour. Fruit sellers hawk dates all the way from Libya. Lads dash back and forth, offering their services as porters. Everything is the finest, the freshest, the most succulent. I am dizzy with choice.

'I don't know how anyone decides what to buy,' I say to Pappas.

'This is whetting my appetite,' he replies, rubbing his hand around his stomach. 'I hope your father lays on a good dinner. I do hope there'll be quail.'

'With your appetite, I don't know how you manage to stay so slender,' I say, smiling.

He taps the side of his head. 'Salacious thoughts,' he says. 'They devour more energy than a discus-thrower at the games.'

He grins, and a smile tugs the corner of my mouth. I am learning humour, and at the feet of a master. I blow him a merry kiss.

'Oh, the gossip!' he chuckles, touching his cheek. 'The town will be buzzing with the tale of the Eunuch and the Bear-Woman!'

The messenger twists in his saddle and scowls. We stifle our laughter. A stately matron totters by, followed by a lithe Persian swatting a flywhisk around her ears. He and Pappas share a look of brotherly recognition and I am granted access to their private world, both tender and angry. A moment only, and they resume their careful masks.

One way there is no difference between town and village is the gawping. Doorways and windows glint with eyes, come to stare at the marvel. My ears brim with whispers like the soughing of wind through branches, and even though too faint to pick out words, I know what they are saying. *A woman more like a man. No, wait – a woman more like a bear, shaggy mane hanging halfway down her back.*

By the time we reach the house of Iasus, there is hardly any need to announce my arrival. All the same, a steward awaits us at the gate. He has the bearing of a Macedonian, with crisp raven hair and sharp eyes to match. He surveys us as we dismount from our less-than-noble steeds.

'Hail!' he growls, thumping a staff thick as a pike.

He pierces me with the sort of look that makes men wring their hands and knock their knees together.

'Hail!' I reply, without doing either.

'Enter the house of Lord Iasus,' he says with a condescending sniff.

I've been amongst humans for long enough to note the absence of the word *welcome*. I stand up straight, kirtle hitched to the knee, and sweep my gaze around the courtyard. To left and right grow oleander bushes, fragrancing the air, and by some wondrous machinery of hidden pipes a water-fountain is playing a tinkling melody.

I take in the fine oaken doors, flung open to permit tantalising glimpses into sumptuous rooms. The window shutters are decorated with vines, carved with such artistry I could pluck a grape. The floor is a mosaic marvel worked with sea creatures that seem to splash and swim. A bitter thought sinks its fangs into my soul. Iasus is wealthy beyond Croesus. He could have kept a dozen daughters, and yet he cast me out. I must have disgusted him. I shove the thought away and face my father.

His house may be striking; he is not. He appears from one of the side-rooms, flanked by two Ethiopians wielding brass-tipped staves. He pauses beside the fountain and approaches no further.

See. He is repulsed, hisses the snake in my breast. *He cannot bear to stand any closer to his monstrous daughter.*

The truth is less dramatic. Iasus is so short, he'd have to climb onto a footstool to look me in the eye. How this rabbit

151

sired a giantess of a daughter I have no notion. However, I am not here to strut about like a fighting cock. There are more subtle ways to shame a man. Making a courteous bow, I sink to one knee.

'Lord Iasus,' I cry, my voice ringing off the roof-tiles. 'Atalanta salutes you.'

He does not bid me stand, for that would defeat the object. Iasus knows what I'm doing, and knows that I know also. He snaps his fingers and the steward presents him with a tablet, the sort used by scribes.

'Before the witnesses gathered here, I acknowledge you as Daughter,' he cries, pressing his seal-ring into the wax. 'You may now address me as Father.'

Deep in my gut, the angry serpent uncoils and twists. *Never*, it hisses. *This cur tossed you onto a mountain to perish. How can you think of soiling your lips with that word?*

Pappas lays a restraining hand upon my arm. I look down to see my hands clenched in iron fists, the veins rigid. I swallow the pent-up roar building in my chest.

'Atalanta is overcome with emotion, Lord Iasus,' says Pappas, his voice the most charming it has ever been.

Iasus's face undergoes a convulsion. 'And who are you to touch your mistress, slave?' he sneers.

I recover myself quickly. 'Pappas is a priest of Holy Kybele and my valued confidante and counsellor,' I say as courteously as I'm able.

Pappas steeples his fingers and tilts his head graciously. Iasus looks like he just bit into a rotten plum.

'You listen to a eunuch?' he squawks.

'May all-seeing Kybele heap her blessings upon this house,' trills Pappas, drawing loops in the air with his fingers.

The steward mumbles a speedy incantation to mollify the Goddess, and Iasus is sufficiently canny to tamp down the spark of anger and mutter thanks. The silence that follows is not comfortable. His gaze flits to the walls, the windows, anywhere but at his daughter. He has greeted me, recognised my legal status as his offspring. Mountainsides at birth are an irrelevance. I am alive now, and that is all that matters.

Before he can prise open my jaws and inspect my teeth like a prize mare, a woman appears from one of the legion of doorways, accompanied by an Egyptian house-slave wafting a fan. When she steps into the full blare of the sun, the bleached linen of her gown is so dazzling I have to screw up my eyes. For all that, I have the oddest sensation she is dark-clad as a mourner. She glides forwards, the dolphins in the mosaic floor carrying her upon their backs. She looks at Iasus, she looks at me.

'The Lady Klymene,' says Iasus, snapping off the words like twigs. 'Your mother.'

I get to my feet and bow. 'Lady Klymene. I offer respectful greetings.'

Pappas does flowery things with his hands, clearly enjoying himself. 'And may the bountiful mercies of Kybele rain down upon your head, Mistress,' he tweets.

Klymene slides him a look. 'I thank you,' she says, her voice the soft brushing of leaves. She turns to me. 'I hear the people call you Atalanta.'

I incline my head. All this nodding and bowing is giving me a crick in my neck. As soon as we are away, I shall beg Pappas to rub away the ache.

'Yes, yes, we've established that,' says Iasus, jiggling his hands. 'I have business to attend to. You shall remain,' he adds, pointing at me. 'You and your mother have plenty to discuss.'

'My lord,' purrs Klymene, her face betraying nothing.

Iasus marches away, hands clasped behind his back. 'You will attend the feast!' he cries. 'You and your eunuch. At your *father's* invitation.'

The steward closes the wax tablet with a click. 'My Lady,' he says to Klymene. 'Daughter of Iasus,' he says to me, and skitters after his master.

Klymene and I size each other up. The air is so dense I could cut it with a knife. She is slim as a willow and as tall, wearing heavy earrings and a necklace in the Cretan style. She has the bearing of a queen unwillingly wedded to a tree-stump. I examine her features: there's something in the turn of her chin, the cheekbones. The likeness may be as well-hidden as a hare in a covert, but I see it and she does also. Klymene is the woman who birthed me. There is no doubt.

When the men's voices have faded to nothing, a tremendous weariness overcomes her. She sags, growing a hand-span shorter. Her smooth cheeks are suddenly wrinkled and deep grooves run from the corners of her mouth. She looks ten years older.

'Nefer,' she whispers, gesturing to her slave, a young woman with eyes a lover could lose himself in. The lass produces a footstool, seemingly out of thin air. Klymene sinks onto it. 'Thank you, dearest,' she murmurs, caressing the girl's hand and resuming her examination of me. 'The people may call you Atalanta. When you were born I called you . . .' She heaves a sigh. 'I did not call you anything. I was not permitted to hold you long enough for naming.'

Perhaps Klymene expects me to fall at her feet crying *Mama*. Perhaps she expects a tearful reunion. I have no notion what she wants, if anything. I have no idea what I want from her either.

'I have borne Iasus three sons,' she says.

An unspoken question swirls between us: *And how many daughters, mistress?*

She flinches, as though I asked it. 'I shall not concern you with their names,' she adds. Her expression is brittle. An imprudent word and she will shatter like ice on a mountain pond in midwinter. 'Daughter. Your father is not a bad man.'

Disagreement roils in my belly. It is a lie and we both know it. 'He is only interested in me because I am famous.'

'Hear me out, Daughter. I loved you.'

I can restrain myself no longer. 'Love?' I cry. 'Then why did you not fight to keep me? You could have refused to let go! You could have—'

'Atalanta,' murmurs Pappas, leaning close and patting my shoulder. I jerk away, roughly.

155

Klymene closes her eyes and opens them again with exceeding slowness. Just as slowly, she rises from the stool, straight as a column of smoke on a windless day. She rearranges a fold of her gown and fixes me with a glance. In her eyes, fire smoulders. A long while ago it might have scorched a man to ashes. A fire that warns, *Do not underestimate my power. I sleep but am not extinguished.* She places her hand upon my wrist. For a slender woman, her grip is like an iron manacle.

'Are you so dim-witted to imagine I had a choice?' she hisses. 'Do I look like a woman with a gay and untroubled heart?'

Without meaning to, I shake my head and mumble *No.*

'They call you Fleet-of-Foot, Equal-in-Weight. Equal in weight to a man perhaps. Are you equal in weight to a woman?'

'Of course I am,' I say, mustering my pride.

She cuts me off with an angry chop of her hand. 'We have all heard of your running and hunting and slaying. Do you have the strength to bear the yoke of womanhood?'

I am shaken to my sandals, but will not be undone. 'I choose not to abide by the rules forced upon women, Lady Klymene.'

'Choose?' she growls. 'I wonder if it is simply that you are not up to the task. I've yet to meet a man who is.'

'I am a woman.'

'Prove it,' she hisses. 'Bring forth a child. Clutch her to your breast. Weep with agony as she is torn away while the milk is bursting from your nipples. Then tell me you're a woman.'

For a moment, her mask drops and I peer into the shuttered room of her life. I see the brightness of her childhood: the laughing, leapfrog time before she knows she is a girl; before she discovers it matters; before she learns her sex will govern and oppress every moment of her existence. I see the day she is ordered to put away her toys and clamp on the chains of womanhood, heavier with each year. The void of her marriage to Iasus. The yearly round of births, of which I am only notable for being the first.

I see her learn the pointlessness of weeping, the pointlessness of hope. I see her brightness shrivel. The years of her life are a labyrinth of prison cells, each smaller and darker than the last. I see her close one door after another, retreating into the smallest cave of herself and cradling the ember of what was once Klymene.

'Lady Klymene . . .' I begin.

She sears me with a glance. 'Do not dare to pity me.'

She does not raise her voice, nor does she have to. Her voice is that of Gaia herself, rumbling so deep in the belly of the earth her tremors are felt rather than heard. There is a lump in my throat. I swallow. Klymene smooths a crease from her spotless chiton. Nefer picks up the hem and they turn to go.

'The feast,' says Klymene, over her shoulder. 'You will attend. You and your . . . counsellor.'

She disappears into her mysterious room, taking half the air with her. Pappas and I look at each other.

157

'You're going to get us gutted,' he says. 'And I for one am rather attached to my innards.'

We stand idle and ignored for what feels like an hour, though it is probably only the time it takes to eat a crust of bread. Eventually, a troop of house-slaves show us to a vestibule lined with benches and we are given wine that's been watered to within an inch of its life.

'I hope they serve stronger tonight,' says Pappas, pulling a face. 'I need to get very, very drunk.'

Despite my irritation I can't fail to be impressed by the sumptuous feast Iasus lays on. There's more food than I've seen in a year and an ocean of wine, which cheers Pappas immensely. I wonder if Iasus regards this as a homecoming. If so, more fool him.

Wherever I look there are singers and entertainers. A bevy of handsome Cretan lads shake their oiled ringlets and perform acrobatic feats, leaping so high it seems they are flying. Pappas and I are entranced by the spectacle. If the Gods themselves were in attendance, they would be open-mouthed also.

Considering how proud I am of my talent for observation, it takes far longer than it should to notice Iasus's behaviour. He is lolling on a couch at the head of the hall, surrounded by a group of men of a similar age, heads together. Every now and then, Iasus takes a swig from his goblet and points in my direction. The men follow the line of his finger, talking, pointing, looking. Talking, pointing, looking.

I nudge Pappas. 'Look at them,' I snigger. 'Gawping at me like yokels with straw in their hair.'

Pappas raises an eyebrow. 'Atalanta, they're anything but. Surely you know what's going on?'

'Iasus is apologising for the way he treated me.'

'Dear heavens above,' sighs Pappas. 'You are dim as a bear. They are suitors.'

'What? And bears are anything but dim.'

'Suitors, you idiot.'

I snort. 'I'm not getting married.'

Pappas lays down the quail he's been stripping of meat. He wipes his mouth, smearing a silvery trail of fat across his cheek.

'I wonder if this visit is a mistake,' he muses, tapping his chin with his thumb. 'Iasus has acknowledged you as his daughter.'

'What of it?'

'It's legal.' When he sees my blank incomprehension, he rolls his eyes. 'The wax seal. It's a short and slippery step to claiming you as his property.'

'I don't understand.'

'Of course you don't, dear bear,' he says. 'Oh, I'm the fool, dazzled by handsome dancers and succulent roasts. If you are his property . . .' He frowns. 'Let me explain it this way. Property is like this.' He slaps the cushion tucked under his arm. 'Or this.' He holds up the gnawed quail. 'It can be used thus.' He tears off a scrap. 'Or thus.'

159

He flings the carcase over his shoulder. One of the house-dogs slinks from the shadows, seizes it silently and vanishes.

'I'm not a spatchcocked bird.'

'No. You are far more valuable. To Iasus, that may be the only distinction.'

As it sinks in, I seethe. This feast is neither celebration nor homecoming. These men are not merely guests. Iasus is planning to auction me off to the highest bidder. As his newly-famous daughter, I have accrued a value I lacked at birth. After ignoring me for two dozen summers or thereabouts, Iasus is taking interest. My life during the years between is of no consequence. He is my sire. He planted me in Klymene's womb. I am his to dispose of, now as well as then.

'I may as well be a prize sow,' I growl. 'If that maggot thinks I'm going to agree to marriage, simper and curtsey and say *Yes, Papa* to his every command, he's a greater fool than he looks. If I find that wax tablet I'll break it over his head. We must go.'

Pappas lays a restraining hand on my arm. 'Not now. Brazen it out. I shall come up with a solution.'

He returns to the business of eating, spearing a chunk of lamb from the platter. Grunting an excuse, I storm off to cool my boiling blood. I find myself in a vineyard. It stretches as far as I can see, yet another reminder of Iasus's wealth and how he could have raised me without so much as a dent in his gold-hoard. I trudge up and down the rows, hands tucked in my armpits to prevent me from ripping up the plants by their roots. They've done nothing to hurt me and it's unfair to take out my ire upon them, however much I want to break something.

How dare my father – I still rankle at the word – parade me like a beast to be traded at market. How dare he swell with borrowed pride. Not at who I am, but at the ways I can enrich him further. Fame, gifts, prestige, connections: for these he is a man with an inexhaustible thirst. That I consider myself free of his governance has not occurred to him. Even if it did, I have no doubt he would find it hilarious. In my mind's eye I see him hugging his sides, squawking, *Free? That's the best joke I ever heard!*

After a fair amount of snarling and stamping, I come across a group of young men who've also escaped the feast and have set up an archery target. I spy Meleager in the throng and my mood improves straightway. At last, a man with an ounce of sense in the madness. I dash to his side and greet him warmly. He is as pleased to see me as I am him. He introduces me to the others and names are bandied about. They've all heard of me: Fleet-of-Foot, Sister of Artemis and so on. They slide admiring glances and, to my shame, I preen in the glow of their approval. I decide to forgive myself for feeling proud. It has been a difficult evening and is far from over.

Sport is the perfect tonic for a foul temper. We chaff each other good-naturedly, applauding good shots that strike close to the target, laughing at the arrows that go wide. I shouldn't show off, but can't help myself. Yard by yard, the butt is dragged further away, until only Meleager and myself remain in the competition.

161

He bends his bow, notches the arrow and makes a perfect shot to the very centre of the target. He is rewarded with the cheering and back-slapping he richly deserves.

'Well, then, Atalanta,' he says, face flushed with success. 'Do you concede the victory?'

I wink. 'I have one last shot, my friend,' I say. 'Let us see if I can come close.'

He makes a gracious bow. I fit the arrow to the bowstring and send it on its spinning journey. It splits Meleager's arrow-shaft down the middle.

'By the Gods!' says Meleager, beaming. 'I've never seen the like.' He clasps my arm. 'Hail Atalanta!' he cries, and his friends take up the cry.

'A toast to the Sister of Artemis!'

A flagon of wine pilfered from the feast is brought out from beneath someone's cloak, and we toast each other very merrily indeed. The night wears on and many of the archers return to the feast, leaving only Meleager. I've no desire to spend a moment longer in Iasus's company than is absolutely necessary. It is a far greater pleasure to sit with my friend, sharing the last of the wine.

'Please, go and join your companions,' I say, in case he is chaperoning me out of duty. 'Do not feel you have to keep me company.'

'I am very happy here,' he says.

'I am also,' I say, and we share a smile. I jerk my thumb in the direction of the feast. 'I could stand it no longer,' I continue. 'I feel like a steer paraded around a fair. Iasus seeks to marry me off.'

'Those grizzled greybeards?' Meleager takes a long draught of wine. 'You need not worry about them. I shall marry you.'

I laugh at his well-meant, if clumsy solution to the problem. 'You don't need to rescue me, my friend.'

'I'm not.' He tips the jug to his lips and drains it. 'It is my most fervent wish. I shall take you to wife.'

My heart sinks into my stomach. '*Take* me?'

'That came out askew. We shall be wed,' he says brightly, sweeping his arm and narrowly avoiding a blazing torch. 'My family is wealthy enough to satisfy Iasus's desire for gold.'

I groan and clap my hand over my eyes. He is not joking. He is sincere. 'Meleager, stop.'

'Married,' he declares, eyes gleaming. 'Man and wife.' He clasps my hand, kisses the scuffed knuckles. 'You're an arresting woman. We will have strong sons and striking daughters.'

I stare, taken aback at the gushing adulation. My guardians lean close and I hear them murmur *Yes*, as they do in my dreams.

'No!' I cry, and tug my hand from his grasp.

'No?' he gasps.

No? echo the spirits, ringing against the walls of my skull.

'But it's a wonderful idea.'

'It is not!'

His head droops, crestfallen. 'You feel nothing for me,' he whispers.

'On the contrary, Meleager, I feel a great deal.' I lay my hand upon my breast. 'A resonance plucking a chord deep within. I am with you when I am not.'

'As I do! We are fated . . .'

I hold up my hand. 'I cannot speak for The Moirai,' I say gently. 'Hear me out. There are a thousand ladies who dream of husband and children, and very lovely they are too. I am not one of those women. I am not a bird, to be thus caged. What I feel for you is not marriage.'

'What then?' he asks, his face a map of devastation.

Meleager displays an extensive number of battle scars. They are a disguise, behind which I spy a small boy whose spirit has been wounded more grievously than his body. I scrabble for kind words in the lumberyard of my lexicon, finding only sawn-off scraps unfit for the task. I take his hand. 'This simple feeling. I offer it to you with an open heart. Friendship.'

'Friendship,' he intones. With a dignity I could not match in a hundred years, he stands and bows. 'Then I shall take my leave, Atalanta, dear friend, as I am blest to call you.'

He walks away, stiff-shouldered, leaving me with a sense of abandonment I cannot explain. I get to my feet and drift aimlessly amongst lamplit statues. Bats fritter the shadows, hunting for insects. I can't face returning to the feast and its drunkenness and humiliation. Hiereya was right. I came here out of curiosity and have blundered into a lion's den, have wrenched open its jaws and thrust my head into its mouth. Worse, I have crushed one of the finest friendships I've found since my mother Arktos cast me out.

For the duration of the archery contest, I entertained a foolish dream that I might belong. For an hour, I felt at one with the world of men: accepted, praised. Like a fool, I believed they regarded me as their equal, and that I proved the truth of my name: Equal-in-Weight. It is an illusion. Shadow-puppets made with the fingers, dancing upon a wall. I will never belong.

A house-slave finds me wandering. He plucks a torch from a wrought-iron sconce and conducts me through a warren of corridors to the rooms Iasus has set aside for myself and Pappas. The furnishings are extravagant: walls frescoed with birds and flowers, a sleeping-couch with plump cushions, a lamp of fretted copper. It is a prison. Beautifully appointed, but a prison. I slump onto the couch, hands dangling between my knees. This is not my home, nor ever can be.

Pappas glides in without knocking. 'I wondered where you'd got to,' he says merrily. 'Behaving yourself, I hope.'

He sees my woebegone expression and seats himself beside me. He carries the scent of spices and expensive wine.

'Oh, Pappas, what am I to do? I am a hind, cornered by hunters. Meleager has proposed marriage. For all I know, Iasus will have me married off by morning. I am trapped.'

'Are you?'

'Iasus is my father.'

'He doesn't look like it. Why not tell him he's mistaken?'

'I cannot stand before the world and lie. You have seen Klymene. It is the truth.'

Pappas presses his lips together. 'Ah, the truth,' he sighs. 'And if you tell the truth, Iasus will use it as a chain to bind you to him.'

'Yes!'

'Ask yourself. Does Iasus deserve the truth?'

'I do not understand.'

'You are under no obligation to share the gift of truth with those who would use it to snatch away your freedom.' I gaze on him in wonder. He pats my shoulder. 'Now, sleep. I shall consult the Goddess Kybele. She has never failed me yet.'

My life is in the hands of a tipsy eunuch. I prepare to toss and turn all night. In the contrary way of slumber, I fall straightway into a deep sleep. In dreams, the veil between worlds is very thin, and I'm not surprised to see my two guardians approach. As before, they reach out to me. I hope they will bestow the strength I lack. Instead, they wail, *Why? Why? Why?*

The following morning, I'm woken at cock-crow by Pappas hammering on the door. I think he intends for us to creep away like thieves before the household is awake, but it is nothing of the sort. For an hour, he schools me in the art of my own deliverance. When he deems me ready, we stand in the courtyard. Pappas seems taller than usual and I realise how impressive he can look when he sets his mind to it. Before long, Iasus comes bustling out of a side door, fastening his tunic. I raise my hand in a respectful salute.

'Iasus, son of Lycurgus!' I cry. 'All men speak of your generosity. The great Homer himself would struggle to find

166

suitable words. What better example of your munificence than to acknowledge me as your daughter. I express my humble, heartfelt thanks.'

I watch him simper, mightily pleased with himself.

'Surely there is no greater accolade than to say before the world, *I am daughter of Iasus*. My heart leaps at the thought.' I pause. 'But,' I say. 'I am not worthy to accept this gift. I cannot betray your trust. To take advantage of your open-handedness would be neither honourable nor lawful.'

His expression shifts. Whatever he is expecting, it is not this.

'The truth is, I am not your daughter.'

He opens his mouth to protest. I am faster.

'You have told the world how, twenty-five years ago, you exposed a female infant on Mount Parthenion. Yes, I was abandoned there. But who can be sure of the year? I may be twenty-five years old, I may be twenty.' I smile sweetly. 'Bears do not keep a tally. Who knows how many girl-children were tossed onto the mountainside around that time? I may be that unfortunate child, I may not. I have no token with which to settle the matter one way or another: no seal-ring, no locket planted by a fond mother, not even a breech-clout to prove kinship.'

His face is flushing with angry blood. I perform a deep and courteous bow.

'And so, Lord Iasus, it is with the humblest of obeisances that I thank you for your benevolent desire for reparation.

However, I cannot bear false witness and pretend I am the child you abandoned. It is against the law. With a heavy heart, I state before this assembled company that I am not your daughter.'

Wisely, Pappas has made sure our mounts are saddled and ready. We show a clean pair of heels and hurry away, the sound of Iasus's frustrated bellowing ringing in our ears.

I pour out my complaints to Antiklea the following afternoon. We sit beneath the shade-tree outside Hiereya's cottage and I watch as she teases out her hair with an ivory comb set with knobs of ebony.

'Iasus planned to trade me like a heifer,' I scowl. 'It is outrageous.'

'Hmm,' she says, drawing the teeth of the comb through her curls and releasing a wave of sandalwood.

'He invited every wealthy man from here to Persepolis to inspect the goods. I was so furious I could have torn his cassia-wood doors off their hinges and hurled them into the next kingdom.'

'Hmm,' she repeats.

Late sunlight patches the ground with copper coins.

'The world has lost its wits. Even Meleager, who I count as a dear companion, proposed marriage.'

'If I were a man, I would do the same,' she says.

'As for Klymene,' I say. 'I could never call her Mother. It would sully the word.'

'Ah,' says Antiklea, her features calm as the sky at the end of autumn. All is quiet and serene, but I know that tucked beneath the horizon is the first storm of winter, flicking its tail in warning.

'It's all Klymene's fault,' I growl. 'When Iasus tore me from her arms, she could have refused to let go. She could have fought to keep me.'

Antiklea presses her lips together and lays down the comb. 'Could she?'

The galloping rush of my invective judders to a halt. 'Of course she could,' I bluster.

'How?'

'She could have said no.'

'Atalanta. Ask yourself truly. Think of all you've learnt about wives. When – I should say if – a wife dares say no to her husband, what weight does it carry?'

My thoughts canter in circles and come back to the same point each time.

'Well,' I say gruffly, picking at a fresh scab on my elbow. 'I still think . . .' I run out of arguments and stutter to a halt.

'You are angry.'

'Of course!' I roar. 'Are you telling me I should not be?'

'No. Only a fool would demand you brush off such grief and rage. But what sort of choice did Klymene have, truly?'

'Well, now you put it like that . . . But I still say . . .'

'Atalanta. There is none like you. I see you on a hilltop, wind flapping your cloak, wild-haired and tensed for battle or flight. No wall too high for you to scale, no river too treacherous to ford. Doing as you choose without a care for custom or gossip. We do not all possess your fearsome uniqueness.

Tell the truth, none of us come close. You live freely. Klymene does not.' A cloud passes over Antiklea's face. 'I do not.'

Her voice is soft. It reminds me of Klymene; of every woman I've met. Not one of them raises her voice above a murmur, save at the rites of Artemis, when we bellow to our heart's content.

'Antiklea . . .'

She holds up a hand, palm forward. 'I am not whining. I am lucky. My father is fond of his little princess, as he calls me. So fond, he has promised he'll not marry me to a man I dislike strongly. He says he'd prefer to see me settled happily. But marry me off, he will.'

She turns her face to mine. There is a strength in her I never noticed before. It was always there. I have simply been too wrapped up in my own selfish concerns to notice.

'Beloved,' I murmur, helplessly.

'Know this. There is no life of Atalanta awaiting me, nor any woman of my ken.'

'What about the Sisters of Artemis?' I say in a shrivelled voice.

'Oh, I shall continue to attend the rites. Only an unwise husband offends the Goddess by refusing her worship. I shall be let out on my leash each full of the moon. I shall embrace my sisters and howl my frustration at the stars. The following morning, I shall be reeled back in.'

'Antiklea, it is unfair.'

She skewers me with a look. I am humbled by her wisdom, far greater than anything I could approach.

'My dear, it is the best any of us can hope for.'

I clasp her hand and press it to my breast, so she can feel the pounding of my heart.

'Antiklea. Let us run away. Wait, listen. To the mountain. I know how to set traps, where to forage for roots and berries.'

'Atalanta, no.'

'Why not? We can be free.'

'You do not understand.'

I swallow the thistle in my throat. 'Antiklea, I love you.'

Very tenderly, she withdraws her hand. 'As I do you.'

'Then it is settled. We shall—'

'No. Love is not enough. It is never enough.'

In the window frame, a spider has woven her nest and it has hatched a hundred spiderlings. Tinier than grains of sand, they perch on the sill and send up plumes of silk. A puff of wind catches the lines and hoists the little creatures aloft. One by one they take flight and, on the breath of Aeolus, are borne up into the bosom of the clouds.

I imagine them carried far away, past the Pillars of Herakles and across the boundless ocean to a wiser land where mothers are heeded when they say *No*. Where daughters grow into women who live freely. Where women choose their husbands, or even more dangerously, no husband at all. Where a man like Iasus loves and honours his wife Klymene. Where they stand as equal-in-life. Where they are happy. Where Antiklea and I might be happy.

THE FATES

Olympos

A Time out of Time

We wrestle against the wish to interfere. It is in our power to compel Atalanta to wed Meleager, and ensure she is at his side at the appointed moment of his death so she can turn aside the hand of Hades. But to coerce a mortal against their will goes against everything we plan for humanity. We cannot soil the gift of Free Will by forcing Atalanta into a marriage she does not desire.

We never enwrapped ourselves so intimately in the life of a mortal. It is a revelation. Atalanta is so close, we can smell the blossom on a bough, taste the sweetness of fresh grapes, feel the ache of hunger in her belly. It is painful and yet desirable, exhilarating and desperate. If this is how mortals feel we wonder how they are not continually crying out with joy. We are the omnipotent Moirai and yet we lack the simple ecstasy of mortal life. A craving for which we are unprepared begins to bud and bloom. Oh, to share this tingling shiver!

In our idyll upon Olympos, we still believe we are little girls. We rise together, work together, sing our farmers' songs and sleep together at day's end. We are unaware that we have mislaid our memories. We do not know who we are, nor why we are important.

That is the nature of forgetting.

We conceal our glory and power from the world, and from ourselves also. We spin the thread of life in secret. We have no clue of the terrifying storm that is approaching. We have no idea Zeus is watching, his heart seething with hatred. We cannot know he is drawing back his arm, wielding a thunderbolt of ice. We are to find out soon enough.

We shall recover our memories, and soon.

That is the nature of remembering.

THE THREE SISTERS

Clotho, Lachesis and Atropos

Olympos

The sky empties itself for days on end, until we wonder if Persephone is spending an extra month in the Underworld, and spring has forgotten our mountain. Kyrios takes up position at the door, bleating plaintively. We work indoors, subdued by the endless downpour. We spin and weave and the shears swish, oiled and smooth. When Atropos declares that, at last, she can smell fine weather coming, we rejoice.

That evening, Themis peers into the barley-bin and announces she will go to market on the morrow. Market day prompts a great deal of activity. Themis will be up before dawn, pack strapped to her back and bidding us farewell with an admonition to be good. She will be back by nightfall and we'll crowd around, hoping her sack hides something that is not essential: a ribbon perhaps, or a little cake. One time she brought back a curious pebble with a stony shell fixed in its centre, telling us how it was from a time before we were born, when our mountain was at the bottom of the sea. Our mother tells the most extraordinary stories.

Never once has Themis allowed us to accompany her. She does not need our help, true, but we chafe against the confines of our nest and would test our wings. We speak a silent plan.

We shall go also.

After supper, we stand before our mother, arms folded.

'We are old enough to come to market,' says Atropos.

'We can help at the stall,' says Lachesis.

'We can help carry the load there and back,' adds Clotho.

'I will consider it,' replies Themis, wiping our bowls.

We glance at each other. This is one of her ways of saying *No*, hoping we'll forget we asked. We wish she did not look uneasy whenever we make a request to leave the narrow confines of our kingdom. It is as though she is anxious some awful misfortune is poised, waiting to pounce. We are not witless as chickens.

Once we are decided, we can think of nothing else. The next morning we are up at cock-light, sweeping out the old damp straw and strewing the floor with fresh. We pinch sprigs from the rosemary bush, bruise them between our palms, and sprinkle them also, scenting the room with a perfume fit for Demeter herself.

We milk the goats and fill the crocks without spilling a drop, collect droppings and spread them out to dry. We comb Kyrios and anoint his horns with butter, until he bleats approval. We gather kindling, feed the chickens, and find nine new eggs. We drag our mother's wooden comb through each other's tangled curls, and dress in our finest robes.

175

We mix batter for breakfast cakes and a dollop sizzles as we ladle it onto the griddle. Themis hauls herself from her pallet, scratching herself awake.

'Good morning, Mother!' we say gaily and flip the first cake, toasted brown as a wheat-berry.

'What's all this?' she yawns.

'We are making breakfast for you,' says Atropos.

'Aren't we clever?' asks Lachesis.

'We haven't burnt a thing,' adds Clotho.

She rubs her face. 'By the Gods, you're dressed in your festival robes. And you've combed your hair. You never comb your hair, not unless I wrestle you to the ground and sit on you.'

'That's because we want to look our best.'

'Aren't we good?'

'Oh yes, that too.'

Themis flares her nostrils. 'What have you done to my precious rosemary bush?' she groans.

'We only took the very tips,' says Lachesis.

'As you showed us,' adds Atropos.

'You are the finest teacher.'

'It's too early for this,' grunts Themis.

She plunges the dipper into the wine-pot and takes a swig, grimacing at the bitter brew.

'We have milked the goats.'

'And swept up the dung.'

'Look! The eggs are laid up in hay.'

We've never seen our mother look surprised. Of course, she feigns astonishment when we bring feast-day gifts of poppets

176

made of plaited grass, but that's because she loves us. This is true astonishment.

'You did all of this unasked? I need more wine.'

'Here, Mother,' says Clotho, proffering a cup.

'And a hot griddle cake.'

'To build yourself up for the day ahead.'

'It's good,' she says, taking a mouthful. 'No word of a lie.' It's only when the second cake is half-eaten that she pauses, and narrows her eyes. 'I'm awake now. What have you broken?'

'Nothing.'

'Not one egg.'

'Not even the water pot.'

'Enough. Something's afoot and I'll have it out of you if I have to fling you over the roof-ridge.'

We open our eyes wide in scandalised innocence. 'Us, Mother?'

She pokes in the last scrap of cake and wipes her fingers. 'Out with it.'

We can contain ourselves no longer. We rush at her, bury our noses in the folds of her wrapper.

'Take us to market with you!'

'We'll be so good!'

'We'll make you proud!'

Themis sighs. 'Going to market is not a game, my loves.'

'What have we forgotten to do?' wails Lachesis.

'Nothing. But the village is different to our mountain. The people of the valley are not hill folk, and are not always

kind to those who are. There are dangers you cannot understand.'

We search her face for answers. All we know is the safety
of our home.

'Please,' we beg.

'Perhaps it is time.' She chews her lip. 'Very well. A few
hours only. We cannot tarry. You understand?'

'We do, Mother!'

Themis bundles us up in our heaviest cloaks, muttering
about the world beyond being cold. We are puzzled, for a
mountainside is always colder than a vale, but we submit to
the swaddling. We load up and gambol down the mountain,
fresh as foals. Themis pauses at the roadside shrine, the furthest we are permitted to stray from our cottage. The wooden
God is wearing a chaplet of dried leaves. We weave him a
fresh crown, and sweep the dust from his feet. Themis spits
on the edge of her veil and washes his face.

'And now, we enter a different domain,' she says, scanning
the skies, as though in search of vultures.

'Don't worry, Mother,' says Atropos. 'The day is warm and
mild.'

Themis nods, but her brow retains its furrows. 'We must
be watchful, that is all.'

We take our first ever step past the shrine, and have the
oddest sensation of stepping through a door. We cannot see
or touch it, but it is there nonetheless. It is most strange. We
have no time to wonder for it becomes clear Themis is correct
about the weather. On the far side of the shrine, the wind

nips at our ears and our eyes sting with sharp drizzle. We tug our capes tight, grateful for our mother's fussing. When we reach the village, the odd turn in the weather is forgotten.

Every sight is thrilling, every sound. We gawp like hobble-de-hoys. The streets are crammed with buildings, slathered with plaster so white it hurts to gaze on them too long. Pots of herbs perch on each doorstep. Even the window shutters are a marvel of carved and latticed wood.

The market square is already busy. We are serenaded by the lowing of cattle, the squawking of hens, the barking of dogs, and traders yelling their wares. There's the splash of wine being poured, the sizzle and savour of chargrilled meat, the ripe and heady perfume of cheeses. Puddles of blood and offal shimmer in front of the butchers' stalls.

We pitch beneath a fig tree. Although in the full glare of the morning sun, the shadow will swing around, and by the afternoon we'll be smug and shaded. We spread out the cloth and arrange our cheeses and buttermilk. The first piece of Themis's border-cloth is sold before we've unrolled it completely. A cat-eyed matron plucks it from our hands so quickly we cry out a warning, imagining her a pick-purse. She is grandly dressed for a thief, in sandals that have been worn twice if they've been worn at all. The valley is so full of marvels, perhaps even their bandits are finely attired. Themis touches her hand to her breast and bobs her head.

'My daughters,' she says. 'Their first time to market. Simple country girls, my Lady, and unused to such beauty and bearing.'

179

'Get away with you,' replies the woman, clearly delighted at the compliment. She flourishes the cloth, which is still clenched in her fist. 'I'll take it.'

'Ah, you will,' says Themis.

The woman sucks her teeth. 'I trust you'll name a fair price.'

'Ah, I will,' says Themis.

'Your first sale of the day. I bring good fortune, do I not?'

'Ah, you do.'

We are entranced by the dance of words, as gripping as a hearthside tale. We screw up our toes with delight. In the end, a bargain is struck. Themis and the customer spit on their hands and slap them together, palm to palm, and the woman swaggers away.

'A good omen to begin the day's business,' says Themis. 'She'll flaunt that border-band and her friends will come running.'

'We think she was a queen,' we say, admiringly.

'Queen? Not her. A housekeeper to a fine man, who owns a quarter of the vineyards between here and the sea.'

'Housekeeper? No!'

'But her beautiful robe!'

'And sandals!'

Themis smiles. 'A bondswoman to a fine house receives excellent hand-me-downs.'

Our heads whirl with the colours, the sounds, and especially the scents. We are assailed by new aromas and cannot tell the half of them. Every time a matron walks by, an unknown perfume wafts from her gown. We learn a score of new names: spikenard, myrrh, cardamom, asafoetida and frankincense.

There is something lurking beneath. It is not dirtiness, for all of them are oiled and plucked. We know it is a foolish notion, but they smell unhappy. We must be mistaken. Compared to us, these ladies are as finely dressed as nymphs. We go barefoot and in homespun wool, our cheeks burnished brown as cedarwood. Surely they must be the happiest creatures to walk the earth. Anything else is unthinkable.

Our next customer is a girl, much of an age with us. She tugs her mother's hand and gazes at the border-bands, eyes hopeful and hungry. We understand her hunger: not merely for pretty things, but to possess something she can call her own. A treasure she can hold in her hand and say, *This is mine and no one else's.*

Her mother sighs, harried and in a hurry to get her shopping done while the day is cool. In her impatience, we perceive the work awaiting her at home: the flour she must sift, the bread she must bake, the cloth she must weave, the children she must feed and bathe and keep from hurting themselves. The husband she must please. The relaxation she can barely snatch.

'My lady,' we say sweetly. 'A moment of your time. Only a moment.'

Our voices cast a soothing glamour, and her shoulders relax a little. She smiles at her daughter.

'You may choose your favourite, Phoebe. But be quick.'

181

The girl's face is illuminated with delight. Biting her lower lip, she inspects the woven bands. Each is as beautiful as its neighbour and impossible to decide. We come to her aid.

'Perhaps this?' we suggest, indicating one with a design of birds in flight. 'The blue complements your eyes. The red, your lips.'

Her smile could not be broader. 'May I?' she asks her mother in the timid voice of a nestling, many moons from quitting the nest.

Her mother smooths a hand over the girl's head, and nods. We give them a fair price, far less than we should. Themis smiles too: she understands the need for happiness, however transient. The girl skips along, still young enough for childish glee. We watch them go, wrapped in kindness that lies lightly upon their shoulders. If it lasts the day, we are satisfied. The ribbon will last far longer.

A haughty maiden picks up a ribbon worked with crimson lambs, one of Themis's prettiest. She screws up her nose as though we are beneath her attention.

'I suppose it will suffice,' she sneers, flicking a finger at the piece. We hold our tongues, expressions calm as cream. 'I shall show good will by taking this rag off your hands.'

We smile, for we know the value and quality of the work. She names a price we would not spit on.

'Hmm,' we say, as though considering. Her eyes glitter. 'No,' we sigh, and shake our heads, aware of Themis watching closely.

'But I want it,' says the young lady.

We name a price ten times what she offered, thinking she'll toss her head and stalk off, nose in the air. She crumples slightly. Only a dip of her shoulder, but we do not miss it.

'Impossible,' she snaps.

'Such a pity,' sighs Clotho.

'Yes, a pity,' agrees Lachesis.

'Ah, well,' says Atropos and begins to roll up the band.

Another woman pauses at our stall. We shake it out again and spread it before her.

'Ah!' she exclaims, eyes gleaming. 'What delightful border-work.'

'Wait,' squeaks the first. 'I saw it before you.'

We watch them argue, and hold the ribbon out of reach, for they'll rip it in half if they get their greedy paws on it. We've seen Kyrios lock horns with rivals when in rut. This is no less fearsome, and as amusing. After a deal of hissing and swearing of oaths in the name of the Goddess, our first customer turns.

'I'll pay your price,' she spits.

The second grabs the last piece remaining, a design worked with flowers. Not as lovely as the piece with lambs, but better than anything she has already, we'll wager.

'I'll take this,' she growls, glaring at her opponent.

We scoop up the coins, more than we've ever seen. This must be how princes feel when they count out their money. Themis watches them stride away.

'Well, my loves. I have nothing to teach you in haggling, that's for sure.'

The remainder of the day is a blur. It seems we have barely set out our stall before it is time to pack up and return. The cheeses have been snatched up, the milk-crocks are drained and every one of Themis's border-bands has been sold. We set to purchasing our own provisions, beginning with meal for our griddle-cakes. The miller fills the measure to the brim and tips it into our sack. Lachesis takes it in her fist, jiggles it about.

'Thank you for the honest measure,' she says. She shakes the bag again, considering. 'Too honest, in fact.' She dips in her hand and scoops out a scrap of flour. 'You have given us extra.'

The miller laughs. 'That daughter of yours is a caution,' he says to Themis, beaming. 'Is she like this at home?'

'Better,' replies our mother proudly.

'You'd best marry a miller,' he says to Lachesis, winking. 'And I have three fine sons.' He waves away the proffered flour. 'Keep it. A little over for luck, that's my policy.'

He's still chuckling as we leave. A crowd of ladies are gathering at the quick news he's a miller who gives generous measure. One of his sons, a skinny lad dusted with flour, gives Lachesis a shy glance. His eyes are dark and sweet as fresh dates, and Lachesis returns the glance as bashfully.

'My little measurer,' says Themis, squeezing her cheek.

We buy salt and oil, and can't believe how swiftly our immense store of riches dwindles. There is a little left over, and Themis treats us to an almond cake, praising us for being the best traders a mother could hope for. The cake is soaked in wine and honey. We never tasted anything half so delicious.

Our journey back is lighter than the journey down. A troop of tipsy stragglers overtake us, having spent the afternoon – and most of their takings – in a wine shop. They wish us a hiccupping good evening before staggering away, bumping into each other and tittering.

Halfway up, we need all our breath for the steep climb, but the moment we step past the shrine, our journey is effortless. We skip along, thoughts tumbling over themselves. As always, Clotho is the one to begin.

'Mother. The valley people love your border-bands. They pay you well.'

'They do. That's why you can have an almond cake,' she replies, gaily.

We nod, giddy with the sweetness of the treat.

Atropos considers a moment. 'Every night, you take our weaving to the mountain,' she says.

'I do indeed,' says Themis, busying herself with the strap on the oil jug. 'And give it to its new and rightful owners. They are well pleased.'

'But they don't pay you,' says Clotho.

'No,' says Themis more carefully.

She continues to fiddle with the fastening. To us, it does not look in need of adjustment.

'Does that not mean our weaving is worthless?'

'No, Lachesis,' says Themis. 'It is priceless. A wonderful gift.'

'Do you throw our work away?' asks Lachesis. Our lips begin to tremble. We do not wish to cry, but it is proving difficult. 'If you do, you can tell us the truth. We will understand.'

'Enough,' says Themis. 'Stop asking questions to which you already know the answer.'

'We are simply curious, Mother.'

'Is it wrong to be curious?'

'About some matters, yes,' mutters Themis. 'I knew I shouldn't have taken you to market,' she adds under her breath, forgetting we have the hearing of bats.

'But, Mother . . .'

'I said no more chatter,' she snaps. 'We must get home.'

She marches on without another word. We scurry, to keep up. Themis has not exactly lied to us, but we sense as many holes in her truth as in a fishing net. We have a shoal of questions, but they will have to keep till we can cast the net again and catch her slippery answers. We arrive home, offload our packs.

'Are you too tired for stories?' asks Themis.

'Never!' we cry, full of hope that tales of the stars will rinse away the grit of the conversation.

'Good,' she replies, sounding relieved. 'Let us go to the Throne of Artemis.' As soon as we are settled, a shooting star pierces the night with a silver needle. 'Make a wish, my darlings,' says Themis. 'It's good luck.'

'I am still wishing to be a hunter,' says Clotho.

'You're not supposed to tell us your wishes, silly,' says Atropos.

'I don't care. Everyone knows, in any case.'

'No arguing,' says Themis. 'Time to begin.' She points into the northern sky. The moon is as thin as a fingernail paring. 'Look,' she says. 'Can you see that faint cluster of stars? It is Pandora. The Gods gave her a jar and told her to guard it carefully, and never peep inside. Of course, she burned with curiosity. She opened the jar and out flew all the evils of the world.'

'Why does it matter that Pandora was curious?' asks Clotho. 'I am curious.'

'The Gods didn't tell her the truth about the jar,' says Atropos, with a frown.

'It was a trick!' says Lachesis. 'It wasn't fair on Pandora.'

Themis does not reply. She points to the northeast. 'There is Andromeda. Daughter of Cassiopeia, she was punished for her mother's vanity. Chained to a rock and devoured by a terrible monster.'

'That's not fair either,' says Atropos.

'She didn't do anything!' cries Lachesis.

'Why do women have unhappy stories?' asks Clotho.

'Ah, but hers has a happy ending. At the last moment, she was rescued by Perseus. They were married and lived happily ever after.'

We are not convinced. Our mother's stories are changing their tune. Before, they danced freely, now they tread more heavily.

'I don't want to get married,' grumbles Clotho.

'Can we go home now?' asks Lachesis, voice plaintive.

'Not yet.'

Themis drones on, telling us of girls who were curious and were punished, girls who disobeyed their parents and were punished, girls who wanted to live freely and were punished. We've heard our mother's tales so many times they are as familiar as the lines on our palms. We can't understand why we never heard the barbs in Themis's voice, hooking us in; never noticed the unfair punishments. Our ears are ringing with miseries. At last, she comes to a halt.

'Thank you, Mother,' we say politely.

Never did we imagine we'd be grateful for the stories to end. Clinging to our mother's robe for safety, we trudge homeward. The descent takes far longer than the ascent and it is not because we are sleepy. The excitement of the trip to market raised our spirits high as hawks. Our wings are crumpling; the feathers slip away and we plummet.

After finishing our work, we curl up on our cots, kiss our mother's cheek and wish her a good night. As always, she rolls up our day's weavings, tucks them under her arm and heads out, fastening the door on its leather strap. Her footsteps fade into silence. We lie abed and amuse ourselves by making shadow puppets by the light of the oil lamp. Rabbits made of shadows dance across the walls. With a deft twist of her wrists, Clotho makes a new shape, one we've not seen before.

'She is a hunter,' says Clotho, before we can ask. 'She is carrying a bow.'

She crooks a finger and fires an arrow through the rabbits. Our hands flop, shot to the heart.

'Enough of your nonsense,' snaps Atropos. 'Women can't be hunters.'

Lachesis sniffles miserably. 'We cannot change the way of the world.'

Clotho licks her fingers and pinches out the flame. We lie in darkness, listening to the idiot whine of mosquitoes.

'I don't care what Mother says,' she hisses. 'No one is going to stop me. When I grow up, I am going to be a hunter.' We huddle under the blanket, pondering her determined words. 'And another thing, sisters,' she says. 'I've been thinking about our weaving.'

'Not again,' groans Atropos.

'Shh,' hisses Lachesis. 'Themis doesn't like your questions.'

'I don't care! I can't hold them in. I must speak or boil over.' There is a pause, deep as a well. Into it Clotho drops heavy words. 'I think Mother is hiding the truth. I think no one likes our work, and she tosses it into a ravine.'

'No, Clotho!'

'You are mistaken.'

'Am I?' she asks dejectedly.

'Our mother would not lie,' we say, wishing we were more certain.

'Mothers lie to protect their children from harsh truths,' says Clotho. 'They sing them to sleep with silly lullabies promising to fly them over the moon.'

'Those aren't lies. They're funny rhymes,' says Atropos.

Clotho pulls the blanket and rolls herself up in it, turning to the wall.

'Please don't worry, dearest sister,' says Lachesis.

'Themis loves us,' says Atropos. 'She has no reason to hide the truth.'

We wish we sounded convinced. A moth flaps into our faces, searching for light. The hut is clotted with darkness. We cannot see our hands in front of our faces.

'I think our mother is keeping a horrible secret,' Clotho whispers unhappily. 'Remember my arm? When I climbed that tree, I slipped through a sort of hole. It quivered like the invisible door we walked through at the roadside shrine. There is something surrounding our home, like a cloak. Why do we have to hide under a cloak? There is something wrong with me. With us.'

We lie awake. Dry-eyed and anxious, our fears circle like dogs who cannot settle. From a long way off, we hear a high-pitched scream. We know it for a fox, but cling to each other all the same. We wish our mother were here to tell us there is nothing to fear, not ever.

Atropos is trembling. 'I smell a change in the weather,' she says.

For the following few days we are on edge. One moment Themis is taciturn, the next she jollies us along, a brittleness to her humour. We are polite, tense and obedient. Gradually, the atmosphere softens and when Themis asks us to go and fetch firewood, we jump to obey. Atropos flares her nostrils and declares a fine and settled evening ahead. We trek to the tree line, branches littering our way, offering thanks to Daphne and her company of dryads for their generosity.

We have as much as we can carry in half the time we imagine, and pause to fill our skirts with pine nuts and mushrooms. Atropos sniffs each one, shaking her head at the poisonous and nodding at the tasty. Loaded with our prizes and bending under the weight of kindling, we turn homewards.

It comes out of nowhere.

We are within sight of the forest edge, close enough to see the glow of sunset speckling the path through the thinning trees. It towers to the treetops: a monster with the head of a lion, antlers of a stag, and the wings and talons of an eagle. It is blue-skinned, pale as the snow that grinds the peaks at the heart of the worst winter, its fangs long as icicles. If it stretched its wings they would cast a shadow across two mountains. A bitter chill grips our shoulders and shakes us so hard we drop our bundles.

'So, you are the brats beloved of Themis,' it growls, flicking its tail and felling a larch with a single swipe. 'Hera showed me where to find you.'

We try to say yes, but the word freezes on our lips. The beast sticks out a long black tongue and slathers its chops.

'You are so small,' it hisses, breath reeking of offal. It shoves its snout close. 'I can smell Themis's love. You are sticky with it.'

191

We nod again, shivering. It tips up its muzzle and howls a gale that blasts the trees to skeletons. Bark twists off the trunks, stripping them naked. Leaves curl, falling in a torrent of tiny ghosts.

'Am I not mighty?' it bellows. We nod frantically and wring our hands. 'Am I not terrifying?'

We fall to our knees, frozen to the marrow of our bones.

'Yes! Cower before me, and worship!'

We prostrate ourselves in the dirt. Anything to make it stop.

'How dare Themis defy me!' it cries, shaking the forest. 'See how I crush all who incur my wrath!'

It lifts its foot high, and brings it down upon our bodies. We ought to shatter into pieces. We are unbroken. We look at each other, our faces drawn tight with fear. It stamps again. We should be dead, and yet we live. Again and again the beast raises its foot and brings it down.

'I am Zeus!' it screams, hurling a bolt of lightning, which fizzles out in feeble sparks. 'Why don't you brats die?'

The screeching gets louder until we can't think for the noise. The monster whirls like a whipped top, faster and faster until it is a blur ablaze with the white heat of a smithy fire. Even though we cram our fingers in our ears, the shrieking pierces into our brains. With a final howl that rends the sky into shreds, it leaps upwards, bursting through the cover of leaves and leaving a tattered ring of scorched timbers. A scatter of stars peer through the hole.

We sprawl in beech-mast, halfway to being corpses laid in the grave. We are pale-lipped, wrapped in a deathlike numbness and unable to feel our toes or fingers. We remember how we once found a fawn on the mountainside in winter: a small creature, far from its dam. It was hard as stone, mouth open in its final bleat. All life was frozen out of it.

We shove the thought away. We are living, just. Somehow, we get to our feet. We are only a few paces from the borderline of the forest. Yesterday, we could cover the distance as swiftly as the shuttle flying across the loom. Today, our breath stands before us. When we breathe in, we inhale thorns.

Where we gather strength from, we do not know, but we manage to put one foot in front of the other. Rigid as dolls of wood and twine, we lurch forwards, pitching and tilting from side to side. Our clothing hangs in beggarly tatters. We have lost the pine nuts, the mushrooms and the firewood.

The instant we step out of the forest we are back in our warm, safe world. The sun is setting, the dregs of its heat swirling around us, yet unable to break through our wall of frost. We force ourselves on, tumbling down the well-worn track and shuddering like shades. Ahead, we see Themis racing towards us, face like thunder. We should have been home long ago.

'My beloved girls!' she cries, expression switching to joy. 'I came as soon as I—'

She is angry, but not with us. She sweeps us over her shoulder, weightless as the kindling we've dropped, and hastens homewards, muttering prayers she is not too late. As soon as she's hurled the door open, she lays us beside the hearth and builds up the fire. She thrusts in a fire-iron, riddles the embers until the tip smoulders, and plunges it into a bowl of wine with a scorching hiss. Our fingers are so stiff they cannot grasp the pot. Gently, she moulds our hands around the dish and slowly, warmth communicates through our flesh.

Our teeth chatter, wracked with spasms. Themis rubs our feet with oil scented with herbs, nags us to wiggle our toes. She bends our arms at the elbow, our legs at the knee. We cry out, howling with the pain, convinced we shall be snapped in two. She asks which parts of us are still asleep and which awake. When we point, she takes a birch-broom, wraps it in a rag and swats our drowsing limbs. As a drummer slaps a drum-skin, she smacks our skin from head to foot. She is gentle, but it hurts.

'Good,' she mutters, ignoring our tears. 'It must sting, to awaken the blood.'

One after the other, she pulls us upright. One after the other, we slump to the floor. Themis is relentless, forcing us to stand. She will not rest until we can circle the hearth, hobbling and weeping. Deep into the evening, our mother cajoles life back into us.

'It was a monster,' we stammer, when we are able to speak. 'We're not lying.'

'I know, my loves.'

'It said its name was Zeus,' whispers Lachesis.

'Zeus,' she growls. 'That misbegotten whelp of a graveyard cur.'

'Mother! Don't say that,' cries Atropos. 'He is king of the Gods.'

'He told us to cower. To worship him,' says Clotho.

'We did!' we roar in unison. 'We did!'

'He is . . .' says Themis. She does not finish her sentence. She takes a grim breath and smooths out her robe. 'He is powerful.'

'He stamped us with his foot.'

'But we didn't die.'

This does not make our mother as happy as we expect it to.

'Why didn't we die?' we ask.

'I got there just in time,' says Themis. 'I rescued you.'

'Mother, what will happen if Zeus returns and attacks us again?' asks Lachesis.

'I will never let any harm come to you. Never,' she says, her voice as threatening as a thunderhead looming over the horizon. Her eyes tell a different story.

The following day, Clotho is sullen and withdrawn, and refuses all attempts to cheer her up. When Themis pronounces that our weaving is done for the day, she dashes off.

'Leave me alone!' she cries when we follow.

'Don't be so horrid,' we sob, rubbing our eyes.

'We want to be with you.'

We trudge to the edge of the woods in a wretched procession. Clotho sets herself down upon a rock and crosses her arms. We try to squeeze alongside, but she keeps pushing us away. We have to find our own stony seat a few paces distant. We are telling Clotho how nasty she's being when Simos comes prancing through the trees, collecting fir-cones. He arranges himself between our rocky perches, and shrugs his cape around him.

'Good day, good day, good day,' he says to each of us in turn, grinning broadly. We sniffle a sorry reply.

'What! Tears on Olympos, and on a beautiful spring afternoon?' he declares.

We nod, weeping afresh.

'Dear me,' he says, waggling his ears.

Whistling off-key, he tugs at a handful of bindweed. We watch as he uproots an armful of stems and begins to weave a chaplet. He fashions three, adding pine cones, and places them on our heads. We venture a smile at Clotho, hoping it will make her merry again. She lifts the crown away.

'It is made of weeds and will wilt within the hour,' she whispers.

Our lower lips begin to tremble again.

'We don't want our crowns to die,' sobs Lachesis.

'We want to wear them forever,' says Atropos.

'You can, in a way,' says Simos, fashioning another from fresh weeds and balancing it upon his long ears. 'When the crown of this hour fades, all you need to do is make another.' He points to a sweet almond, afloat in a cloud of white blossom.

'But, Master Simos,' says Lachesis, in a small voice. 'What is the point of flowers when the Gods can destroy them with a breath?'

He yanks up a grass-stem and chews it thoughtfully. 'There is no point, other than taking enjoyment from their beauty today. As for tomorrow,' he says with a shrug. 'No one knows what the morrow may bring. Enjoy the delights of this hour.'

We consider his truths, as ancient as the oaks. Clotho fiddles with her crown.

'Happiness used to be easy,' she says. 'It is becoming more difficult with each passing day.' She lowers her head. 'There is something wrong with us,' she whispers.

'Goodness!' cries Simos. 'Not at all!'

Clotho holds up a finger. 'One: I broke my arm and as we watched, it healed.' She holds up another finger. 'Two: there is a strange glamour surrounding our home.' She unfolds another. 'Three: Zeus could not kill us,' she continues. 'Any other girls would be dead. There is more. It all comes to the same end. We are not like other girls. We are different.'

'Of course you are,' says Simos.

'We are?' we squeak in unison.

It's the first time we've heard the words spoken plain. We *are* different.

Simos rubs the back of his neck and scratches his stubby nose. 'Oh dear,' he mutters. 'Oh dear, oh dear. I have spoken out of turn. I fear Themis will berate me. I thought she . . . I thought you . . . Oh, my dears. I am sorry.'

'No, Master Simos,' says Clotho. 'Do not apologise. You have spoken the words we needed to hear.'

It is the confirmation of our suspicions. His revelation ought to make us weep. It has the opposite effect. The truth, even if unwelcome, wipes away fearful imaginings. When we trot down the track to our home, we are hand in hand again.

197

We are not precisely cheerful, but we are calm. We no longer feel as though we are going out of our minds.

We are different, and the knowledge no longer hurts. Things are sure to get better from this moment on.

ZEUS

Mount Olympos

The Throne of the Gods

It was supposed to be straightforward. Hera suggested I freeze the little brats, yet they would not be frozen. This is all her fault.

'You promised me amusement and diversion!' I scream. 'I am neither amused nor diverted.'

'Nor should you be, my lord Zeus,' says Hera mildly, taking a long draught of ambrosia.

'You said they were ordinary girls and I could kill them! You lied!'

Every deity apart from Hera cowers behind their supper-couches. A naiad crawls away on her belly, trying to get to safety. I blast her to a twig. Immortal creatures of all varieties prostrate themselves, tearing off scales, spines and hair in a frenzy of denial. Not my wife. She creases her pretty brows in confusion.

'I? Never,' she says, lip quivering.

'I should blast you to a twig too, and then you'd taste the reward for lies!'

Hera shrinks into the cushions, gnawing her knuckles and clearly in the grip of a compelling emotion.

'Oh, mighty Zeus,' she breathes, voice low and throbbing, eyes brimming with unshed tears.

'Oh, don't cry,' I say. 'I hate it when you cry.'

Hera nods meekly. She lifts a hand, to clasp it to her breast or reach out to me I cannot tell. The effort is too much and she lets it fall.

'My lord,' she whispers, close to swooning.

'Cheer up, I was only joking.'

Hera bites her lower lip. 'I am cheerful, my lord. I am your wife. The luckiest woman in all creation.'

'I'll make you happy,' I say, pinching her cheek and only leaving a small bruise. 'I can always put a smile on your face, can't I?'

She smiles bravely. 'You can, my lord and husband. You are incomparable.'

I have the perfect solution to make Hera merry again. She loves it when I dally with a mortal female. Such larks! Besides, a measure of jealousy never fails to restore the fire in her belly. I fly to earth and select Io: bashful, untouched and unplumbed. Perfect. When she refuses me – as some of the ungrateful bitches do, unaccountably – I plough her anyway. A flick of my finger and I turn her into a cow: dung-spattered and so broad she gets stuck in the door to her hovel, her whole family shrieking and shooing her away.

After I've had my fill of the hullabaloo, I carry her back to Olympos and place her at the centre of the feasting hall. She peers at us out of puddle-brown eyes and staggers backwards. I didn't think a beast of the field could look frightened, let alone confused, but Io achieves both, admirably. I thrust my face in hers.

'Boo,' I say.

Io starts lowing. The sound of her own voice terrifies her even more. 'Moo,' she bellows. 'Moo!'

It is hilarious.

'She doesn't know she's a cow!' squeaks Eros, stealing the words from my lips.

I ought to scorch his fat backside, but Aphrodite throws me a coquettish glance, and very disarming it is too. Besides, I am having far too much fun to chastise her son. There will be an opportunity later, and punishment has a special piquancy when dispensed with a cool head and cooler hand.

Astraea and Mnemosyne – bless their vain, primping souls – draw out mirrors of polished electrum and hoist them in Io's face. When she sees the bovine features gawping back, she panics. The feasting hall turns into a melee as Io stampedes between the couches, upending tables, and pursued by river-nymphs and tree spirits waving their arms and shovelling up her ordure. When the first naiad slips and falls into a pile of cow-dung, why, I think the merriment will bring the very walls of Olympos tumbling down.

Restored to my habitually charming disposition, I survey my subjects enjoying themselves under my benign and fatherly rule. Zeus is in his heaven, and all's well with the world.

Except for Themis and her exasperating, infuriating pets. I do not know who or what they are, and it rankles. I tap my fingers on the arm of my throne. They are neither muddy nymphs, nor limp and drooping dryads. I blasted them with ice, yet they did not freeze to death. I stamped upon them, and could not break their bodies. Any mortal would have been smashed to smithereens. I felt a surge of power emanating from them, deep as the river of iron that flows beneath the earth. More powerful, more deadly and more ancient than me. No. That is not possible.

Hera strokes my arm. 'How dare Themis conceal what is yours to demand,' she murmurs, as though my thoughts are writ plain on my face.

'Indeed. How dare she,' I mutter, shoving away Hera's hand.

'She deserves your wrath for her disobedience,' she says.

'She does.'

'You are merciful to those who do not merit mercy, my lord Zeus,' she says, glancing at Poseidon, who has finally managed to corner Io with a trident and is jabbing her out of the door.

'I am,' I say. 'It is a failing of mine.'

'My lord, you could never fail in anything.'

'True, true.'

Hera is correct. I have not failed. I am all-powerful. I am the king of the Gods. The brats are not ordinary mortals, and I want them destroyed. However, if I go chasing them with thunderbolts that fall like damp squibs, I shall run the risk of making a fool of myself. Again. It will not do. It will not do at all.

I shove Hera off her couch and laugh till I cry as she tumbles in an ungainly heap, squawking. That'll teach her for sending me on a wild goose chase. No. I have decided. I shall not concern myself with Themis and her strange girls, whatever they are. Let them play dress-up in the shapes of children. They are beneath the notice of Zeus, the mighty, the undefeated.

THE FATES

Mount Olympos

A Time out of Time

Not all wars are drawn up in battle order, with one host massed against the other, facing off across the wide and dusty plain of combat: cavalry to the left, foot soldiers to the right.

Each and every day there are wars fought on small battlefields. There, you will find no heroes in plumed helmets, breastplates flashing bright as the sun. There is heroism of a humbler sort; the rebellion that springs from standing up for oneself and saying, *This far and no further. I shall kneel not one moment longer.* The resistance and persistence needed to say, *I shall live my life freely and according to my passions.*

It is how Atalanta and Meleager face each day, each in their own fashion. They are not each other's enemy. Their foes are outside, laying siege to their sturdily constructed citadels of the self. In a world where men and women are corralled in separate pens, with high fences built between, Meleager and Atalanta stand as equals, with love as their prize.

On the battleground of his spirit, Meleager clings to rage against The Fates, keeping its blade keen as the sharpest sword. He never lets himself forget we cursed his life; never forgets he will be avenged. And yet, there is light in his darkness. The chief brightness is Atalanta. We see his hopes soar, only to be dashed. He wonders if her refusal of marriage is another twist of The Moirai's knife; wonders if that vile trinity guides him to Atalanta purely so they can laugh at him for daring to believe his life can get better. He does not know we are sitting beside him through the long and empty nights, cannot guess we are tending the guttering flame of his resolve.

Nor are we done with our fostering of Atalanta.

She too has entered the lists of human conflict. As a woman, she struggles against the fetters placed upon her sisters and herself. Having tasted freedom, she does not understand how to submit to the hobbling of female kindred. She does not seek confrontation – her overriding wish being to live in peace – yet enemies surround her and she must fight them off, a wasteful use of her time when life is so fleeting. Ill-wishers seek her out because she is clever; because she has never bowed her head; because she will not kneel. Her life is beset by aggressions and, unbeknownst to her, there are more to come.

We keep our promise. We cannot uproot the wickedness in mortal hearts, but we can stand shoulder to shoulder with Atalanta and Meleager through their travails. Their first meeting was not propitious, but a poor beginning does not always betoken a poor conclusion. They are learning that good fortune is equal to the effort put into its creation. The harder they strive, the luckier they become.

We grant them strength to endure. We have planted the seed. It is up to them to nurture its growth.

MELEAGER

Parthenion

I have been called a hero so often the word is like an old coin, worn smooth with the rubbing of the many hands through which it has passed. There is a face stamped upon it, but the features are vague. It could be anyone, and in the end is no one at all. Measure a man against a hero and he will always be found wanting. Hero: the notion is bandied about as though the world has a surfeit of these semi-divine beings. Men are men, with all their faults and failings. Heroes are impossible.

Here is my secret: whatever stories you may have heard, I am no hero at all.

Everyone talks about her. There is no escape. Whichever wine shop I frequent, I push back the door and she is the topic of conversation. Wherever I go, she is there in spirit rather than in person; her exploits praised, her achievements toasted.

Atalanta Fleet-of-Foot, the She-Bear, the strong-armed Gift of Artemis.

I feign the interest of one who is a stranger to her fame.

I prop my chin upon my fist and mutter, *Did she?* and *You don't say!* and *Go on!* I have a store of surprised nothings, one for each occasion and ready on my tongue. I pretend I've never met her, pretend I've not humiliated myself beyond any nightmare of shaming.

I toss back cup after cup of wine and cringe with mortified recollection. My drinking companions notice nothing amiss. As a boy I schooled myself in fakery, and my face can echo the opposite of my heart. I am a well-versed traitor to my feelings. No one knows the truth. No one follows me to my sleeping quarters, nor sees me draw the curtain around my bed. No one hears my nightly confession, my voice curdled with drink.

Meleager, you utter fool.

Atalanta offers friendship, and claims a deep connection. I cannot imagine her speaking anything but truth, but the doubts roil in my innards and hiss, *What a paltry thing is friendship. She is fobbing you off. Such are the fickle ways of females.*

Parthenion is also famed for its wine, and I swim in its russet sea. My miseries are strong swimmers and show no sign of drowning. After ten days of drunken devastation, I lose the fight. I pack my meagre belongings and book passage to slink back to Calydon, tail between my legs. The night before the voyage, I am woken in the small hours.

The wall opposite my bed seethes with an unearthly glow, more strange than any dream. A door appears where there is no door, and through it step the same two maidens I've seen before, carrying the light of the heavens around their bodies.

208

I can make no sense of their reappearance, but there's no reason why I should. The ways of immortals are far beyond my incomplete understanding.

'Oh, spirits of the air!' I cry. 'Have you come to laugh at Meleager?'

They smile, and in their faces is such kindness my throat closes up with smothered weeping.

No, brave Meleager, most fortunate of men.

'Fortunate?' I say bitterly. 'If you knew me, you would not use that word.'

Their expressions remain calm. *Again, we say fortunate Meleager. More than you shall ever know.*

'My birth was cursed by The Fates,' I growl. 'I curse them in return.'

They wince, as though my words are painful to them. *A cruel and unfair destiny*, they say. *As it is now your destiny to be loved by Atalanta.*

'Then you *are* come to taunt. It is a strange sort of love that will not be blessed by marriage.'

It is greater by far.

'What can possibly be greater than marriage?' I say, ashamed of the whine in my voice. I sound unnervingly like Toxeus.

A love strong enough to turn your destiny upon its head. A love stronger than Death itself.

'Nothing is stronger than Death!' I cry.

One more hunt, Meleager. Restore the blood to your veins.

With the words, they melt away. I leap from my bed to haul them back and demand they stop speaking in riddles.

The wall is a wall again, and I beat my fists uselessly against plaster and clay.

The disciplines of the body saved me when I was a boy. Hoping to restore myself to a semblance of manhood, I do as bidden and throw myself into a final hunt before quitting Parthenion for good. I rise early and tramp through the hinterland, choosing a part of the forest far from Atalanta's village. I used to look forward to our meetings; now I cannot think of anything worse. I wade through rivers up to the knee, climb slopes so precipitous I'm forced to go on hand and knee. I thrust myself through thorn and briar, driving the game before me as though in pursuit of peace. Which eludes me.

When I feel the spectral maidens tugging me in one direction, I stamp in the opposite, growling at them to leave me alone. Perhaps they trick me with a double bluff, because about mid-morning I hear a two-legged beast twenty paces to my rear. I am not in the mood for my seclusion to be disrupted.

'Who's there?' I snarl. 'Show yourself.'

Atalanta steps from the shadows. I groan inwardly, and no doubt outwardly also. I dread the thought of uncomfortable conversation. Indeed, I have ventured this far off the beaten track to escape any conversation at all.

'Ah,' she says.

'Ah,' I reply, blood flaring in my face.

'So,' she continues, arranging the arrows in her quiver. 'I am tracking a she-boar. You?'

'I am tracking . . . nothing,' I say, fiddling with the buckle on my satchel strap. Somehow it needs my full attention.

'She is too great for me to bring down alone,' she continues, inspecting her arrows for the tenth time. 'I could do with the assistance of a fine hunter.'

Finally, I meet her gaze. In her eyes I see a mirror of my own discomfort. The following hour is a dream of bliss. Together we stalk the boar, signing to left and right, finger to lips for silence, as though we've been hunting at each other's side our whole lives. We bring her down and dispatch her with honour. When we are done, I heft my spear and bid Atalanta a courteous farewell. She lays a hand upon my shoulder. An instant only, but a hint of power sizzles through my flesh.

'Please, Meleager. Tarry awhile. Let us eat together.'

I can refuse her nothing, and set to arranging stones for a fire-pit. The crackling of fat reminds me I am hungry. 'This will feed a battalion,' I say, glad to be talking about pork.

We distract ourselves in eating, talking of game and other safe matters.

'I will present the finest cuts of my share to my friend Antiklea's father,' says Atalanta. 'He despairs of his headstrong daughter and disapproves of her outlandish friend. He is convinced I am leading Antiklea astray. If only he guessed it is the other way around.' We laugh at the drollery, and the awkwardness between us loosens a little. 'And now you have met my human father,' she continues, wiping her lips, 'you can see why I speak so highly of my ursine mother.'

'Oh, when it comes to terrible parents, I out-top you by far!' I declare.

'Your parents?' she asks tentatively. 'Do they still live?'

'My sire Oeneus was gone when I was a stripling. Then my mother Althea was married off to Therios, who has an estate ...' I pause. 'Do you truly wish to know, or are you making polite conversation?'

She snorts, spraying crumbs. 'No chance of that. I am neither polite, nor skilled in the niceties of etiquette. It is just that every man I've met draws upon his lineage as an opportunity to puff himself up. You don't seem the sort of fellow who'll swear he sprang from the loins of Apollo or some such.'

I chuckle. 'Oh, I am mortal through and through. As for my mother, she is what you might call an *interesting* woman.'

Atalanta snorts again, and a piece of meat becomes wedged in her throat. I have to pound her between the shoulder blades before it dislodges. She spits it out, eyes streaming and snot running down her chin.

'You, too, are interesting, though not in the same way,' I say dryly.

We laugh till the tears flow, wiping our eyes and hugging our stomachs.

'Oh,' she says. 'I have not laughed like that for a very long time. You truly are not like any other hunter I have met. Human hunter, leastways.'

'There is nothing to compare with the excitement of a good chase,' I reply. 'The pounding of the heart, the sparkle of breath in the lungs.'

'The cramp from standing in a ridiculous position when you've sighted a deer,' she adds.

'The black eyes from running into low branches.'

'The bruises from tripping over your own feet.'

'See this scar?' I say, bending my arm. 'I earned that reeling in a pike. Damn thing had teeth like daggers.'

'That's nothing!' She points at a silvery line beneath her chin. 'I fell into a crevasse. Broad daylight too. I was distracted by a butterfly. Could have cracked my skull open.'

'What a pair of heroes we are,' I cackle.

Another knot of tension unties itself.

'I have Artemis to thank for preserving me,' she declares, touching the arrowhead tied around her throat. 'I am twenty-five summers in age and strong as a Molossian hound.' She stretches, cricks her neck. 'My life has barely begun.'

'Atalanta, hush,' I hiss. A shadow ripples across my mind, whispering of danger and death.

'Meleager, you look serious.'

'I am. The Fates are vicious. I speak from experience. It is unwise to tempt them. To them, we are of no more significance than knucklebones. They throw us up and watch us fall, laughing over the terrible destinies they have spun. When they tire, they sweep us from the board and seek new lives to despoil.'

'Ah, do not worry yourself. Look at me. I'm the size of a house and built as robustly. I have many years yet.'

At her words, I feel an unsettling, as when country folk talk of a goose walking across a grave. 'I hope so, with a full heart.'

A silence blooms. Not completely uncomfortable, but nevertheless tinged with unease. I poke at the fire idly.

'Meleager,' she says. 'You're grinding your teeth so hard you will crack your jaw.'

I tug at my amulet. 'It is because of The Fates I wear this. I am a victim of their spiteful meddling. My mother Althea was a troubled woman. At my birth, she overheard The Fates curse me with a spiteful, unjust destiny.'

'Meleager, you do not need to speak if the telling pains you.'

'You are the only person I *can* tell,' I say. I take a deep breath. 'I have never told this to anyone. My fate is tied to an enchanted hunk of wood. When it is consumed by fire, I shall die.'

She takes my hand and grips me tight. By the Gods, I never want her to let go.

'This amulet contains a splinter of that accursed log.' I sigh. 'I could have been a better son. If I'd stayed at home, I might have soothed my mother's turbulent mind. But I itched to be away; itched to live amongst warriors.'

'I have never heard you speak so openly, friend Meleager.'

'I should have done so long ago.' I straighten my shoulders from their slump and smile shyly. 'I have never had a friend to listen.'

Reaching the end of my speech, I stammer about speaking out of turn and look aside.

'Ah, Meleager. Don't be ashamed.'

I rub my stubbled chin. 'It is good to see you again, Atalanta,'

I mumble. 'It is also difficult. I cannot forget Iasus's feast. I spoke like a hare-brained fool.'

'Meleager, there is no need for apology.'

'I disagree. I wish I could blame it on the follies of youth. I cannot. I have a habit of charging in without thinking. I am impetuous, thinking with my sword-arm and not my head. If I'd used a grain of the sense I was born with, I'd have known a remarkable woman as yourself would not wish to be a soldier's wife. Or anyone else's.' I hold up my hand in a salute. 'No more clumsy wooing. You have my word. Thank you for not scorning me today.'

She elbows me in the ribs playfully. 'That I shall not do,' she says. She stands, and readies the packs. 'You may also remember that I offered friendship that night,' she says, kicking dust over the embers of the fire.

'I have not forgotten,' I say.

'Are you ready to accept?'

An attachment more profound than any I've ever known sounds its bell in my heart and I can do nothing but answer its clarion call. I swear by the Gods the maidens bend close and murmur, *Yes, Meleager. Say yes!* My expression gives Atalanta all the answer needed. I unsheathe my knife, make a nick in my thumb and squeeze a crimson bead of blood.

'My blood to your blood,' I say.

She pricks her thumb also, and clasps my hand. 'My oath to your oath.'

'Closer than brother to sister.'

'Than sister to brother.'

'None shall rend us asunder.'

'Never,' she breathes.

'This I pledge, sweet Atalanta. I shall never desert you, however dark the night, however fearsome the battle.'

'This I pledge also,' she replies, her voice resonant with passion.

We return to the city, swapping stories and as easy in each other's company as brother and sister. Easier, indeed.

The nature of rumour is to strap wings to its heels and fly faster than Hermes. There is gossip: salacious tales of how Meleager and Atalanta are seen coming down from the mountain, arm in arm. People love nothing more than to pick over spicy tidbits. They stretch their eyes wide and declare themselves appalled, pretending shock when in truth they are ravenous for more.

It is assumed that when a man and a woman are alone together for more than the time it takes to blink, they are engaged in rutting. To folk who think in that way, it is beyond the realms of possibility that Atalanta and I might be engaged in friendly conversation. A man and a woman talking? Never. The very notion is preposterous. We must be engaged in scandalous activity. And if that is what the villagers, the townsfolk and for all I know, the courts of Egypt and Persia are chattering about, let them chatter. Much good may it do them.

Atalanta and I fall into friendship with an ease that pours honey upon my bitterness. I barely need to seek her out, for the divine maidens guide my footsteps and I do not – cannot – resist. Whenever I go hunting, Atalanta is there, greeting me as though expected. We share the exhilaration of the chase and it matters little if we catch anything. I am pressed to visit the abode of Hiereya and Pappas so often it becomes a second home. Or perhaps the first, for beneath its sheltering eaves I experience more open-handed generosity than in the fine appointments of Therios's grand villa.

It is there I am introduced to Antiklea, a lass of such luscious form as to turn the head of any youth, though my eye is ever upon Atalanta. Antiklea observes me, and I feel my affection laid bare under her keen appraisal. She smiles with the indulgence of one who finds me unthreatening and rather amusing.

Men are slow at many things. I can hurl a spear and slap on a field-dressing as well as any fellow, but am a blundering dullard when it comes to matters of the heart. I look at Antiklea. I look at Atalanta, exchanging secret glances. I am still a fool, it seems. They are in love.

I mumble about a call of nature and take myself outside. Frogs are trilling a twilight melody and, in the distance, there is the shrilling of a goatherd as he bullies his brood into the byre. I yearn for Atalanta. There is no other word. In the past, I've known the heated ardour of the flesh, the cool fondness of filial duty. I have never tasted this variety of love, woven of trust, affection, respect and a deep sharing that reaches far into the realm of the spirit. Yes, I burn with desire, but I'm not a man to force a woman to change a firm *no* to a frightened *yes*, for the sake of lust.

I tell myself I am a fish let off the hook. Atalanta loves another, that is all. I am blessed with the finest friend a man could dream of. Friendship is a gift, I tell myself. The air stirs, startling me from contemplation. I turn to find Antiklea, following the line of my gaze to the stars. She seats herself and takes a sip from her cup.

'We both love the same woman,' she says, without preamble.

I thought Atalanta had tutored me in frankness, but Antiklea takes me completely off guard. I could demur, but she strikes me as the sort of woman who would laugh in my face.

'Aye,' I reply, simple and straightforward.

'Well spoken,' she says, with equal plainness. 'I'm glad you aren't a man to treat me as a simpleton.'

'No. To love Atalanta and be beloved in return demands otherwise.'

A smile brightens her stern features. 'True. Then we are agreed on love, that rarest of birds. I like you, Meleager, and can see why Atalanta does also.' She pauses for a mouthful of wine. 'More than liking. I sense the bond between you.'

'You are not jealous?'

She grins and her dimples flash. 'If Atalanta threw me over for you, my envy would be terrible to behold.' She leans close. 'You would lose a hand,' she whispers. 'Or some more vital appendage.'

I swallow. 'Oh.'

She giggles. 'Oh yes, Meleager, I like you very much!' She claps me on the shoulder. 'It seems to me we are engaged in a dance for three, when the world supposes a dance for two. This is a falsehood: men take mistresses in addition to their wives; the Sisters of Artemis retain their lady-loves when marriages are arranged.' She takes a measured sip. 'The difference in our arrangement is honesty. I shall not conceal my love for Atalanta for the sake of convention. What say you?'

I look at her in stark admiration. 'I say you are the wisest of us all, Antiklea.'

'True again,' replies Antiklea, with a nod of acquiescence. The moon raises herself above the village, bestowing her soft light. 'Meleager,' she continues quietly. 'Atalanta is troubled. She loves us both and it is tearing at her. She will not speak when I press, so I have ceased.'

Her voice is light, but I hear the hurt.

'The soldier in me concurs with your strategic retreat,' I reply. 'Though such a manoeuvre weighs heavy where the heart is concerned.'

'It does,' she says. 'For once I am at a loss.'

'All we can do is offer affection, without tugging neediness.' I thrust out my hand. 'To this I pledge.'

'With all my heart,' she says, clasping me tight.

'Can it possibly be that simple?'

'By the Goddess, I doubt it,' she replies. 'It is possibly the most difficult thing any of us shall attempt. However, where there is love, anything is possible. Even the impossible.'

My head reels. I'm not in the least surprised Atalanta loves this remarkable woman. I have an inkling I will, also. Atalanta is the spring at which we both quench our hearts' thirst, and I am resolved we shall not drain her dry with demands. I hope the love we share will forge a bond to defy the world and its interference. Hope Antiklea might become the wonderful sister I never had, and never dared to dream for.

Men are not supposed to regard women with awe: we honour our mothers, respect our wives, lust after our mistresses. But awe? Love free of envy? It is not only unusual, it is a challenge. I have never shied from challenges.

We return, smiling. Atalanta glows with pleasure to see us arm in arm, linked in amity. There must be some mistake about her being troubled. But with each moment, I am less sure. Doubt casts a damp on her, scoring deep lines at the corners of her mouth. The thread between us stretches and strains. Atalanta is in a tug of war. Neither with me nor Antiklea: with herself.

ATALANTA

Parthenion

Life amongst humans continues to exhaust me. My dearest
Meleager invites me to lodge in the city with his uncle
Plexippus and aunt Klytemnestra, but the prospect of living
in a metropolis with all its clamour and bustle is more than
I can countenance. The complexities of village life are sufficiently taxing to my spirit. I am often tempted to slip away at
the dark of the moon and take my chances with the beasts of
forest and mountain. Their ways I understand. Then I look
upon Antiklea's face and bask in the warmth of her love. She
is my lodestone and my northern star.

On sleepless nights, I am visited by my little protectors.
In dreams they step over the threshold to this world, and I
rush to embrace them. At first I was timid, for they are the
Goddess's messengers and I am a humble mortal, but they
welcome me into their arms. Always, they seem to be bursting
with an urgent message. Always, I am on the brink of understanding something of great importance when they shimmer
into nothing. It is most peculiar.

The days pass: I face each one, complete with its paradoxes. I run, and I hunt.

My spreading fame brings unexpected wealth. Visitors present gifts, which Pappas seizes with a gracious bow before embarrassment prompts me to decline. Our cottage becomes a little palace with a tiled roof and a paved courtyard to receive the stream of guests who wish to gaze upon the woman warrior.

I'm glad I can go some way to repaying Pappas and Hiereya's many kindnesses. Meleager accepts my gift of leather greaves with delighted thanks, clasping me to his breast. I would dearly love to give Antiklea a longbow as a present, although I'm wise enough to realise she would profess pleasure and never use it. I pay a goldsmith to fashion a pin in the shape of my lucky arrowhead, and it gladdens my heart when she wears it to fasten her gown.

One morning, I hear furtive voices at the courtyard gate. I step out and find a clutch of young lasses. They stare, part in fear and part in adoration. My glance might turn them to stone, or bless them with the power of flight.

For girls, they are dressed bizarrely: bare-legged to the knee, tunics hitched up around their waists and slung over the left shoulder, leaving the right breast bare. Not that any of them possess anything that could be called a breast. They mutter amongst themselves, shifting from sandaled foot to sandaled foot. It is as though I am looking at small versions of myself.

'Greeting, little sisters,' I say.

After more whispered conferring, one of them takes a step forward. She raises her hand in a salute. I reckon she's been practising, and a fine show she makes of it, too.

'Oh, Atalanta, Equal-of-Weight,' she intones gravely. 'Beloved of Artemis. Daughter of Arktos,' A companion hisses *Fleet-of-Foot* into her ear. 'I know,' she snaps tartly. 'Fleet-of-Foot, Incomparable Huntress.'

I incline my head. 'I thank you,' I reply, with equal solemnity.

They glance at each other, and there is a quantity of poking and muttering of *You. No, you.* The brave lass who spoke first rolls her eyes. Her hands may still be petal-soft, but she prickles with thorns. I like her a lot.

'Before you came to our village, we did not know a girl could live a life such as yours,' she continues. 'You have shown us a different way.'

Her friends nod passionately.

'We have decided to follow your example. We pledge and dedicate ourselves to Artemis.'

There is more nodding and agreement.

'Little sisters,' I begin. Their lives dash before my eyes. I see them lonely, spurned, spat upon. I see mothers weeping in confusion, fathers demanding they marry. 'It is not an easy life.'

She sticks out her chin, proud and unafraid. 'You have lived it. Would you take a different path, if the Gods gave you the choice?'

'No,' I say with a full heart. 'For all my struggles – and they have been as numerous as sand-grains in the sea – I would not barter one moment of my life if I were offered the crown of Egypt.'

'There you have it,' she says triumphantly.

A second girl, emboldened by her companion, steps forward and salutes me also. 'We know we are not like other girls. We know it will be hard. But we have you to remind ourselves it can be done.'

Few are able to run as free as Atalanta. I don't know whether to grieve for the hard road ahead of them, or gather them up like a mother hen sheltering her chicks beneath her wings. I clear my throat, which seems to be full of pebbles.

'Sit with us awhile,' says Hiereya, appearing with a loaded platter. 'There are dates and bread.'

I give her a grateful smile, and find my voice at last. 'Well now, little sisters. I must re-string my bow. Who would like to help me?'

Tales of my exploits grow in strangeness. One of the most famous – notorious is a more fitting word – is how I slay two centaurs. The reality is less fanciful and a great deal more odious. Legends of daring deeds have a tendency to smooth over an ugly truth. Storytellers create rousing diversions to amuse city-dwellers as they while away their evenings, lolling on cushions and gobbling figs. The closest those folk ever come to a centaur is a painting on a vase.

Here is the truth, told plain. Whatever people may say, my attackers are not centaurs. They are two mortal men.

From the day of my arrival in the human village, I make it abundantly clear that I have no interest in romantic dalliance. I do not shun the male sex, although there is little in them I find appealing. Either they're all fingers and thumbs, tripping over their tongues and feet, or are slick as eels with a mouthful of lies to entice silly girls. As for their greasy, groping elders, the less said, the better.

Despite my rebuffs, I am plagued by unwelcome attentions. When lads think no one is watching, they whisper at me from doorways, sucking their teeth and making lewd gestures with their fingers. It is most vexing. The word *No* is not a difficult word to understand. A well-aimed kick is usually enough to send them scattering. Some need more persuasion.

Two in particular – Rhoecus and Hylaios – are not content to jostle and paw. With dogged insistence, they stalk me as though I am prey, seeking out occasions when I am on my own. I am unconcerned; I am Atalanta. I fear neither man nor beast. Antiklea advises me to be on my guard, for they are well-known in the valley and for the wrong reasons.

'Fathers keep their daughters well away,' she tells me, massaging goose-grease into my hair. She is wondrously dextrous when it comes to untangling my unruly locks. 'They have molested friends of mine.'

'Why are they not punished?'

'Their fathers are important men.'

'What of it?' I cry.

225

'Dearest Atalanta,' she says. 'Your straight dealing is admirable. It saddens me you must learn the worst side of humanity along with the best. Hear this and be mindful: a rich man's son does as he wishes. There is one law for the wealthy and one for everyone else.' She runs her hands through my braids and with a deft twist, piles them on the crown of my head, securing the topknot with a scarlet band woven with stags. A delicious breeze cools the nape of my neck. 'There,' she says. 'I have tamed that mane of yours.'

I kiss her sticky knuckles. 'Thank you, my clever lion-tamer,' I murmur.

I do not have to wait long before I discover the truth of Antiklea's warning. Although fortunate to thrive under the protection of Artemis, a Goddess cannot spend all her time engaged with the needs of a single woman. There are days when I am left to my own devices. I meet my dear companion Meleager in the forest so often I grow careless, forgetting there are hunters who stalk different game.

On an afternoon like any other, I'm beside the river, gutting fish for supper. I toss the innards to a vixen who is hoping for any sweetmeats I can spare. The air is gentle, the river babbling its soft and meandering chatter. I hold a trout by the tail and scrape against the grain with my knife. The scales flutter like insect wings, and I am so distracted I do not notice the fox prick her ears and scuttle away.

They are upon me before I can cry out. A clout to the back of the head and next thing I know, I'm face down in the stream, spluttering. I lash out at the lunk who's shoving my nose underwater. Bend of the knee, kick, and I am released. I scramble up the bank, gasping for breath.

'It's a fierce one,' says Rhoecus, grabbing my ankle before I can escape.

With the word *it*, I am transformed into a thing, and things do not have to be treated like humans. *It*. A tiny word with the power to make me less than an animal.

'I like it when they struggle,' says Hylaios. 'It makes the meat tastier.'

'Get hold of it, Hylaios,' says Rhoecus.

At his command, Hylaios grasps my other ankle. I'm taken aback how easily I was caught off guard, and lash out, writhing fit to rival the Hydra. Rhoecus tilts his head on one side and grins, teeth gleaming.

'It should thank us for even looking at it,' he sneers.

'It's so ugly,' adds Hylaios. 'Smells, too. Maybe it's a man.'

Rhoecus wafts his hand before his nose. 'No, Hylaios. It's a woman. Only women stink like fish.'

'You're ours for the taking,' says Hylaios, rubbing at the bulge in his groin. 'Slut.'

They whicker like geldings, mauling me with clammy hands.

'Oh, stop taking rubbish,' I scoff, kicking and shoving, but unable to get free.

'Rubbish? Rubbish?' he whinnies. 'We'll show you rubbish.'

Rhoecus scowls. 'You ugly whore,' he spits.

We are far from the village. An army could rattle sword against shield and the keenest ear would be none the wiser.

On and on they go, telling me I want it, that all women do, however loud and long they say *No*. They boast how they're stallions from the waist down, for the Gods have bestowed them with the parts of horses. They brag how once they've had me, I'll be stretched so wide no other man will be able to satisfy me, and mating with me will be like waving a hay stalk in a temple.

They hoist up their tunics, displaying pizzles that seem much like those of regular human males. They're expecting me to beg for mercy, like every other girl they've grappled to the ground. Perhaps if they spent less time swaggering things might take a darker turn. Luckily for me, they are ignorant braggarts.

I take in a deep breath and roar. Arktos herself never made such a din. The tree at my back shakes loose a flock of birds. They wheel around our heads, diving close to Rhoecus and Hylaios and startling them into loosening their grip for the split-second I need to wriggle free. I jab my heel between Hylaios's thighs. With an agonised squeal, he clutches his jewels and rolls up tight as a hedgehog. While Rhoecus is distracted by his yelping friend, I run.

I crash through the bushes, scratching my arms to ribbons. Behind, I hear the thump of their pursuit, yammering what they'll do when they catch me, how there's no escape. Even I, Atalanta, who fear nothing – be it lion or evil spirit – am afraid.

'Artemis!' I cry. 'Look down upon your sister!'

Winded, I stumble to a halt and brace myself against a birch. As I catch my breath, my two sentinels step from their world. I send up a prayer of gratitude. The Goddess has heard and sent the help I need. Although my body screams at me to keep running, I force myself to stay put. The girls nod, and in their eyes I see a force beyond reckoning. Power floods through my limbs, twisting fear into a weapon.

My guardians take up position at my shoulder. With their guidance, I sharpen my terror into a point and turn it against my attackers. There, to the left, twenty paces away: I cannot see him, but know it is Rhoecus. I swing the bow from my shoulder, fit an arrow to the string and pause. The river of Time grows sluggish and comes to a halt. Blood stops dashing through my veins. A wasp dangles before my nose, wings unmoving. I hear the breath of every leaf, every blade of grass. The air is thick as honey. In the stillness, one of the girls steadies my arm. The other places her fingertip upon the bow and moves it a hairsbreadth to the right.

Now, they murmur, and I loose the arrow.

It flies with a grace so leisurely a man could see it coming and step out of its way. Rhoecus does neither. A shriek pierces the forest. Time speeds up and resumes its onward torrent. I notch a second arrow and the girls direct my aim towards Hylaios. I fire. There is more screaming.

I find Rhoecus first, sprawling in a thicket, my arrow stuck in his gut.

'You bitch,' he squeaks, spitting out slurs that'd make a *porne* blush, voice growing fainter until he runs out of filth. His eyes are soft and frightened, those of a weak boy. 'Help me,' he begs, breath ragged. 'I'll give you anything you want.' His hair is matted with sweat. 'Anything.'

'I see you,' I say.

And I do see him and all his kind. Taking what is not theirs. Choosing girls whose lives they deem less worthy. Rhoecus and Hylaios have mothers who pretend they do not hear the accusations. They have wealthy fathers who talk of high spirits and wild oats, and shrug off any lowly farmer who dares complain. For who will take the word of a ditch-slut, when set against a bright and shining son?

I brace my foot against his hip, twist the arrowhead and yank it out, dragging a knot of purple intestine. He will die, and it will be long and painful. Hylaios is dead by the time I find him, arrow in his throat, the earth drinking his lifeblood. He seems smaller in death, lips parted in a final insult. As I watch, a dung-beetle crawls out of his mouth. I wrench out the arrow, wipe the tip on his tunic and slam it back into my quiver.

Blades of sunlight are slicing through the canopy and smattering the forest floor with fragments of broken gold. I turn up my face and let loose a bellow. I've not forgotten the language of bears. It may be fancy, but I am sure I hear my animal kin take up the cry.

I hear a tiny sound and am on the alert. I'll not be caught out again. I scan the undergrowth, arrow notched and ready, every muscle poised for flight. The vixen is eyeing me from the bushes. She licks her chops, fangs glinting with saliva.

'Yes!' I moan. 'Feed on them! Call your brothers and sisters. Call the wolves, the bears, the lions. Let there be a feast!'

She nods.

I return to the river, staggering and bumping into trees like a drunkard. These glades, my home and harbour, no longer belong to me, nor I to them. I wade in, up to my waist. I wash and wash, plunge my head underwater, rub my arms with nettles. I have escaped uninjured. I am one of the lucky ones and yet I cannot rid myself of an unclean feeling. There is an inner dirt I cannot scrape away.

By the time I climb out of the water, the sun has gone down. My two guardians step from their world, take my hand and guide my dripping footsteps. Step after clumsy step, it dawns that I've killed two men and called beasts to devour them. I fought hard, reacting with instinct rather than sense, and did not have time to think about what was happening. The realisation forces itself upon me now.

I am a murderer.

I topple against an oak tree and hang on desperately, as though it's the only thing anchoring me to earth. A sob breaks from my throat. I'm racked with the horror of what I've done. What they would have done if I'd not succeeded. I had no choice. It does not alter the fact: they are dead and their blood is on my hands.

My spirit messengers work another miracle, for as I lurch from the forest, I meet Meleager, running towards me and crying my name. He leads me to the house of Hiereya and Pappas, where kind hands wrap a sheepskin around my shoulders. The scent gives comfort, and I stop shuddering.

'I found her coming from the forest,' groans Meleager. 'I should have been there earlier!'

Hiereya holds a cup of wine to my lips. I spill more than I swallow. Pappas chafes warmth into my feet and fingers. Slowly, I gather up my tattered wits. The walls swarm with shadows, leaping and twirling in the firelight. Even the scant mouthful of wine is giddying.

'I have been . . . they tried to . . .' I gabble. 'Kept saying they were stallions. Two of them. Dead.'

Why, I know not, but at the word *dead*, I begin to weep. Hiereya draws me into her arms and I sob confusion and rage into her chest. Antiklea barrels into the house, panting as though she's run a league. With the briefest of greetings to Hiereya and Pappas, she flies to my side and places a palm on my brow.

'Is she dying? She looks like she's dying. Tell me!' she cries.

'Atalanta is well, and unwell also,' says Hiereya, a sibyl speaking in riddles.

Antiklea tips my head from side to side, peering deep into my eyes. She squeezes my limbs, opens my mouth and tugs at my tongue before she is satisfied I am not partway to the underworld.

'She is unbroken,' murmurs Pappas.

Antiklea lets out a long, whistling exhalation, and presses a hungry kiss to my forehead.

'The forest,' says Meleager. 'An assault. The spirits told me . . .' he stammers, before hiccupping to a stop. He strokes my cheek. 'I should have run faster. I could have rescued you.'

'I rescued myself,' I croak.

His brow creases. 'Yes, Atalanta. I know. My desire to protect you springs not from arrogance, but from the love I bear.'

Meleager and Antiklea exchange a glance and even in my befuddled state I see a shared understanding. Pappas presses his lips into a grim line and taps his chin with his forefinger.

'Atalanta has been attacked by . . . animals,' he muses. 'Yes. We shall put it about that she was injured whilst slaying two centaurs, and is recovering from wounds.'

I hoist myself onto one elbow, and wince. 'Wait,' I wheeze. 'I knew them. They were Rhoecus and Hylaios.'

'They were centaurs,' says Pappas firmly. 'A centaur is a worthy opponent.'

'Worthy?' says Meleager. 'They were less than goat-droppings. Flyblown and stinking. They were . . .'

'*Centaurs*,' says Pappas, stretching his eyes wide.

'Pappas,' I say. 'I cannot . . .'

'I know, I know,' he says, wafting his hands. 'You are excessively opposed to falsehood. Well, they said they were horses. We are granting their wish, from the waist down in any case. Let the conceit be their undoing. It is fitting.'

Antiklea looks from Meleager to Hiereya to Pappas and back again. 'Pappas is right,' she says. 'We shall announce the news. Two monsters attacked Atalanta and she slew them. They were headed to the village. Who knows what damage they'd have wreaked if she'd not been victorious.'

I pluck the hem of Pappas's robe and press it to my brow. 'I ask forgiveness, Pappas. It is the fire in my blood.'

'Of course, my dear. You have rid the valley of two dangerous creatures. Your fame shall be even greater.'

He is correct. The news flies as fast as a falcon. The gossip on every tongue is that the centaurs must have been mighty beasts indeed, if they could lay Atalanta low. No one guesses my sickness is not of the body, but of the spirit. I exulted in the killing of Rhoecus and Hylaios. I did not honour them with the good death I'd grant a beast. Even though they were dishonourable, even though it was self-defence, I am riven with guilt.

A day passes, and another. On the third, an alarum is sounded. Word passes from mouth to mouth, ear to ear: Rhoecus and Hylaios – or what remains of them – have been found. The truth is bound to come out. No one can possibly believe I killed two centaurs. They must suspect I killed the two youths. Despite the calming words of Pappas, I wait for the fathers of the dead men to troop to my door, trailed by village elders armed with mattocks and hayforks, demanding my head as a blood-price.

They do not come. I decide to go to them, instead. On the day of the funerals, I head to the village square to await my fate. I will face my death with courage. Antiklea and Meleager insist on accompanying me, and although I make gruff noises about not wishing to take up their time, I am grateful.

Two small pyres are burning, there being little left to cremate. The square is crowded with women I do not recognise. They wear long indigo-dyed gowns, woollen wigs and their cheeks are daubed with green paint. I am reminded of a flock of ravens.

'I did not realise Rhoecus had so many friends,' I say.

'He didn't,' says Antiklea.

'All those women.'

'Them? They're professional mourners,' says Meleager. My incomprehension is clear. 'Rhoecus's father bought them in. He's paying them to cry.'

Antiklea grunts. 'The wealthier a man, the more women he can afford to screech at his funeral.'

The longer I live with humans, the less I understand. I stare into the flames, losing myself in the dancing flicker. The air shimmers, as it does when my guardians appear. Instead of their sweet comfort, I see two different pyres, far from here, stacked higher than the eaves of a house. A boar's head dripping upon an altar. The stink of burning flesh. A ship with black sails. I see Meleager, fleeing unbearable grief. I shake my head and the vision winks out. The sense of foreboding does not. Stumbling, my right arm is caught by Antiklea, my left by Meleager.

'Two pyres. Burning,' I mumble. I look into Meleager's eyes and in them see confusion. 'Not these two. From another time. I don't understand.' I grip his arm. 'Do not run away.'

'Run away?' he says. 'Never.'

'You must not,' I reply, seized with a terror I cannot fathom. 'Ever.'

He pats my hand. 'Do not fear. I gave you my promise.'

235

I have little leisure to catch my breath. A man calls my name, startling me out of my trance.

'Atalanta, Gift of Artemis! I am Plousios, father to Rhoecus.'

'My lord,' I say.

His face is blank as a temple keystone. Jaw set like granite, holding in the tumult of grief he cannot permit himself to show.

'My son,' he croaks, grimacing. 'Rhoecus . . .' He clears his throat. 'You slew two centaurs. Pappas has told us. Meleager made his pledge also, and he is an honourable man.'

He looks me over with what I think is distaste, but could be fear. With humans, it is invariably one of the two. I take a deep breath.

'My lord.'

'The same day my son and his comrade went missing.'

Now, he will come out with the truth. He will point his finger, call down the punishment of Gods and men. I shall be seized and slain. A life for a life. Indeed, to satisfy the family of Hylaios I ought to be executed and then brought back to life so I can be killed a second time. A strange thing happens. Something I could never have foreseen, not if I'd consulted a hundred scryers with a hundred copper mirrors.

'I offer thanks,' he says.

'My lord?'

Antiklea pinches the inside of my forearm. I'm too leathery for it to smart, but I know a warning to keep my lips sealed.

'Centaurs are well-known for their hideous strength,' he begins. 'Rhoecus and Hylaios were unwise to go into the forest unarmed. They made themselves easy prey for those fiends.' He is interrupted by a keening wail as a woman collapses in a heap of black rags. Plousios's head snaps in her direction. 'Wife!' he cries, as if calling a dog to heel. 'Attend me!'

The mourners help her to her feet. Their greasepaint is melting from standing in the sun, disguising their faces with a puzzle of green and brown blotches.

'It is quite clear in my mind,' continues Plousios, piercing his wife with a glare of command. 'The centaurs murdered my son.' He pauses, licks his lips. 'And Hylaios.'

'My lord.'

His gaze flicks away briefly. With a great deal of effort, he forces himself to look me in the eye. 'You brought down those two centaurs. You avenged the death of my son and his friend.' He pounds his fist against his chest. 'I owe you a debt of honour.'

We stare at each other, tongue-tied for completely opposing reasons.

'My Lord Plousios,' I say eventually.

He takes it for politeness, or deference. In fact, I have no notion how he takes it. Antiklea and Meleager steer me away, my legs stiff as knives. I walk straight into Rhoecus's mother, a dark kerchief pressed to her face.

'I beg pardon . . .' I mumble. 'Mistress.'

I don't know her name, and she shows no sign of entrusting me with it. To her kin, she exists in relation to the father who sired her, the man she married, the son she birthed. Her name is of no significance. And here I stand, Atalanta: free of father, brother, husband, son.

'You!' she hisses.

'Mistress?'

'My boy!' she squawks. 'My gentle, innocent boy!'

At the cry, the mourners resume their lamentation and outlandish dance, which involves sinking to the ground and rising, only to sink again. I have to get away. From the smell of roasting bones; from the ululating women, rending their garments and flailing inky wings. From this performance of woe, as unreal as a play, where the true faces are concealed behind wooden masks.

Rhoecus's mother tears her veil aside. Her eyes are dry. Oh, those eyes. I shall never forget them, burning with a revulsion that singes me where I stand. Without meaning to, I take a step backwards.

'My lady,' I say, recovering my composure.

In her glare I read the message plain. She knows precisely what her son was, and what business he and Hylaios were about. She knows and does not care. Not for me, nor for any other woman. We are fodder to the fire.

How dare you fight back, she says without words. *How dare you win.*

My mind fizzes, stutters. I will never be one with these people. I am alone.

No, I am not alone. The realisation floods my body as a draught of spring water after drought. I am borne up on the arms of my companions: beloved Antiklea, most astonishing of women, and dear Meleager: honourable, steadfast and beloved also. I feel the warmth of love's balm wash through me as a miracle, and stand tall again. Until a cold blade cuts through the enchantment.

Meleager, beloved? The answer rings clear: yes, I love him. I also love Antiklea. A woman with two lovers? It is an impossibility. A heart cannot be split in half. It is the worst kind of selfishness, and unfair. I cannot love them both. Yet, I am compelled.

Back and forth I go, until reason bends and breaks as an overburdened branch. My skull is a wasps' nest, buzzing with confusion, anger, guilt, and shame. I've witnessed the funerals of men murdered by my own hand; have seen a vision of what I fear is Meleager's pyre, and who can tell, maybe my own. I love against the laws of Gods and men. I am a disgrace.

I can tell no one.

I let myself be led away, helpless as though my eyes have been struck from my head. Somehow, we reach Hiereya's house. I lie down on my pallet and face the wall. Antiklea and Meleager take it for exhaustion, unable to guess I am ashamed to look them in the eye lest they spy the secret hiding there.

The light goes, the light returns, the light goes again. I eat, I drink, I sleep. I did not expect to fall in love with Meleager, thought Antiklea alone held the key to the private places of my heart. How can I explain to them? Indeed, how am I to explain it to myself? At odd hours, I see my little sentinels at the foot of the bed, hovering in a haze of light.

Love, they murmur. *Trust in love and it will guide you to your goal.*

A few days after, Pappas finds me at the riverbank, the place where Antiklea and I first met. It is a favoured spot when I am troubled.

'You are pacing, my dear,' he says. 'If you keep it up, you will wear a hole in the earth all the way to Hades.'

'I cannot rest, Father Pappas. I have been surprised by love. It has swung open the door to my heart and strolled in. I should feel joy, yet all I feel is shame.'

'Indeed?'

I lower my voice to a mumble. 'I love two when the world says I must love only one.'

'Are you hiding one lover from the other?'

'No! Not at all.'

'Then you are honest, and an honest love is a good one.'

'That's all very well for you to say. I am in torment,' I growl. 'I wish to make my life easy again. Tell me how to cast love out of my heart, Father Pappas.'

'Let me tell you my story to while away the time.'

'I do not want a story!' I cry. 'I want a simple answer.'

'Ah yes, simplicity. To my story,' he continues, ignoring my plea. He swipes dust from a convenient rock and arranges his robes about him. 'You will, of course, have heard gruesome accounts of boys taken captive in war and made eunuchs; of boys sold into slavery and gelded.'

'Yes, and how is that supposed to help?'

He clears his throat. 'My story is not one of those. I grew

240

up in an unexceptional village. No tragedy blighted my child-hood, no cruelty warped my mind. My father respected his wife, my mother honoured her husband. I had merry brothers and fiery sisters. It was all rather ordinary. And yet, I grew askew.'

He steals a sideways glance.

'Very well,' I snarl, tearing up tufts of grass and throwing them into the water. 'Go on.'

He coughs delicately. 'From before I can remember I knew I was – how shall I put it – different. Outwardly, nothing distinguished me from my tumble of brothers. My difference was invisible and yet the older I grew, the more I felt it radi-ating from my body, bright as the moon. I had no name for it, and lacking a name I was bewildered. All I knew was, I did not fit my skin.'

He pauses again. He peers inside his satchel and produces a small wineskin and two clay bowls. He fills one and hands it to me, before serving himself and taking a refined sip.

'Well?' I ask.

'Ah,' he says, as though only then noticing my presence. 'I had the outward tokens of manhood, but my daemon was another matter, chafing against the body into which I'd been born. I lived in the house of a stranger, both uncomfortable and ill-fitting. And then I heard of the priests of Kybele.'

I take a mouthful of wine and perch at his side. Pappas continues without waiting for me to prompt him.

'I heard how their attachment to the Goddess is so pas-sionate and all-consuming that whatever she commands, they give freely. I heard how she commands the sacrifice of their manly parts. It was as though a window-shutter was flung wide, letting the light of day into a room closed up for a lifetime. My daemon leapt in my breast and cried, *Yes!* I could see my way clear. I became Pappas, priest of Kybele. Neither man nor woman, and entirely myself.' He looks up. 'You have ceased your pacing. Good.'

I had not realised, but my breath is coming more easily, my heart pounding a slow and even drumbeat.

'Thank you, Pappas,' I say.

He flourishes his hand in an exquisite gesture. 'It is nothing, child. My fate was waiting for me patiently, and as soon as I discovered it, it fit me close as water. Perhaps loving Meleager and Antiklea is your destiny.' He smiles at my surprised expression. 'As is being loved by them in return.'

'It is unfair, surely. I choose to live on the boundary of what the world accepts, but I can hardly expect them to do the same.'

He swirls the dregs at the bottom of his cup. 'Perhaps you should leave the choice to them. Deciding what's best for another seems the unfair path, especially in love.'

It makes sense, but I cannot shake off the doubts. 'Pappas,' I continue. 'Isn't it selfish to keep two people all to myself? They only get half of me.'

He quirks a finely plucked eyebrow. 'How bright is a lamp?' he replies.

'I do not . . .'

'It lights a room,' he says, answering his odd question. 'If you light another lamp from the first, is its light dimmed in half?'

'No, of course not.'

Pappas empties the wineskin into my bowl. 'Perhaps love is a lamp. If we love more than one, do we not simply bless the world with more illumination?'

'Oh. Pappas, you are a fine physician.'

'I cannot cure you with words, my dear. I see you wary of engaging in a dance of intricate step and rhythm, for there are many chances of stumbling and tripping. You can live out your life at the outskirts, watching the dance of love play out, or you can rush in.'

'I can,' I say, cautiously. 'And if the world condemns me, then the world is wrong.'

He puts his arm around me. 'My dear Atalanta,' he says and raises his bowl in a toast. 'What a marvellous strange family we are, to be sure.'

We drain our cups. Pappas is correct. I have a choice: I can dash away, hands clapped over my ears and pretending I do not hear love's call. I can bolt my heart and deny the truth of my feelings. Or I can admit complexity into my life. I can admit that I love Meleager and Antiklea: differently, but equally. It is the only way I can describe it. I love Meleager with the spear of my spirit. I love Antiklea with the arrow of my heart.

I look up. The sky is a patchwork of small clouds, scattered like the white pebbles found in a fast-flowing stream. A day of fine weather.

'Father Pappas,' I say. 'My courage still fails me. I seek strength to take this dangerous step.'

'It shall be yours,' coos Pappas. 'Hiereya shall call your sisters together, and tell them Atalanta is in need of the guiding hand of Kybele and Artemis.' He slaps his knees and stands. 'We shall gather in the holy grove of the Goddess. There shall we make a ritual.'

That night, Antiklea and I walk to the sacred place, Hiereya leading the way. The forest is scented with pine, their needles cushiony underfoot. Croaking frogs provide our music. Pappas bears a pot of salt, a heavy sack, and embers from the hearth in a tiny basket made of birch bark. Shadows net my feet and it's all I can do not to trip. I cling to Antiklea and we tread in their footprints, holding to the faint glow from the fire-basket.

Our sisters are already in a clearing lit with small oil lamps. Voices rise and fall in waves, flowing back and forth. One by one the women embrace me, offering words of love and healing that wrap me in their spell. Antiklea gives me a kiss also, lingering upon my cheek.

Pappas walks in a ring, sprinkling salt and chanting. Hiereya draws four waxen tapers from the sack and nurtures them to flame. Around each, she pours a libation of wine and the soil drinks it thirstily. We seat ourselves, and at a sign from Hiereya, woman takes the hand of woman. Pappas places a circlet of ivy upon Hiereya's head and she raises her arms, encompassing the sky, the earth and everything in between.

'Oh, Sisters of Artemis, be present here this night,' she says.

'We honour the Goddess,' our voices murmur in response.

Pappas stretches his arms to the heavens also. 'From Chaos sprang Nyx, the night. From her sprang the earth and all things on it, without help from God or man.'

'Hail Chaos! Hail Nyx!'

Hiereya beckons, calling me forward. I obey, and stand in the centre of the circle. She turns to the north.

'Oh, Gaia, guardian of the north! Hear us! Bear us in your arms tonight.'

'Hail Gaia!'

She turns westwards. 'Oceanus! Drink our tears so we may stand tall and brave!'

'Hail Oceanus!'

'Hephaistos!' she calls to the south. 'Strengthen our hearts in your furnace! Help us to endure.'

'Hail Hephaistos!'

She turns east. 'Oh blessed Artemis!' she says. 'Unseen and mighty. Watch over us this night. Grant us your wisdom.'

'Hail Artemis!'

Hiereya slaps her palms together. 'The circle is cast,' she says. 'All who attend, do so in loving care for our sister Atalanta.'

A murmur rings around the glade. *Atalanta. Atalanta.*

Pappas places a boar's tusk into Hiereya's left hand, a pomegranate into the right.

'Oh, Attis!' he cries. 'Daemon of the mountain, consort of holy Kybele! We call upon you, self-wounder and spiller of your own blood, to heal up the breach in our beloved sister!'

245

'Hail Attis! Hail Kybele!'

Hiereya slices open the pomegranate and mashes it in her fist till juice flows to the elbow, red as blood. Holding it over my head, she drizzles liquid that runs down my cheeks, dripping off my chin onto my breasts. She rips the fruit apart and massages it into my scalp, the soles of my feet, my armpits and between my thighs, until every inch is covered and I wear a second, scarlet skin.

'Accept this as our offering! Let our sacrifice be pleasing to you.'

Pappas throws back his head and howls, fit to split the night in half. 'Sisters of Artemis!' he roars. 'Approach! Be the mouths of the Goddess! Grant healing!'

On all fours, and growling like my mother Arktos, the women crawl towards me. Beginning at my feet, they lick me clean. Each toe is sucked into the warm cave of one of their mouths. My anklebones, shins and knees are caressed with tongues warming to their task. My thighs, my stomach, the furze at the fork of my thighs, nothing is passed over. Up and around they go, climbing the trunk of my body.

The touch of their tongues draws me back to life, coaxing me from the dull nothing in which I have been drowning. They climb the ladder of my spine, nuzzling my ribs, my nipples, the column of my throat. The magick sparks me into fire. I am a flame at the heart of the forest. I am a torrent of stars, rushing into the mountain's deepest cleft. At the edge of the sacred circle, I see my two beloved watchers, nodding encouragement. I am healed. I take a shuddering breath.

'I live again!' I roar. 'Strength is restored!'

Cheering rings out. Hiereya opens the circle with the tusk and Pappas draws a goatskin of wine from his bag, winking. One woman produces a loaf, another cheese, another milk and dried meat. We make a feast and offer every scrap to the Goddess, who grants us the privilege of devouring it in her stead.

When we've eaten our fill, Procris takes Callisto by the hand with a knowing grin. They bow to Hiereya, who raises her hand in blessing and, smiling, they step between the trees. Three more, arms linked like the Graces themselves, step forward and are blessed in turn before slipping into the shadows. In pairs, in threes, in fours, women receive blessing and leave, gentle laughter drifting in their wake. As well as merriment, my keen ears catch sounds of pleasure, my nose the tang of salt.

Antiklea appears at my side, catching me unawares. When it comes to Antiklea, I am happy to be taken by surprise.

'It is the most secret rite of Artemis,' she says. 'To offer up the ecstasy of our bodies.'

I swallow. I have what feels like a pebble lodged in my throat. Her face, open and eager. Her eyes, bright with intent.

'Shall I bless the two of you?' asks Hiereya.

Pappas laughs. 'Oh, Atalanta. What shall I do with you?' he says kindly. 'Are you going to sit there till sun-up, gawking at Antiklea like a bumpkin?'

I shake my head, lay my hand upon Antiklea's shoulder.

She kisses my cracked knuckles. Once again, I have the odd sensation of Time moving slowly.

'Mother Hiereya, Father Pappas. Give us your blessing,' I croak.

'Yes, with all my heart,' says Antiklea.

The Goddess leans down from Olympos and plants a kiss upon our brows. I shiver with the delicious gift. Antiklea leads me, or perhaps I lead her. It hardly matters. We creep out of the grove to find our own secret spot. The moon rests on her side, leaning upon the mountainside and looking down upon us kindly. We go barely ten paces before Antiklea shoves me against a tree trunk.

'At last!' she whispers, pressing her mouth to mine. 'I thought we might never get around to enjoying our own kisses.'

I devour her with my gaze: I could stare all night and all day. As I think it, I am pricked with guilt. I am behaving no better than the village youths who gawp and paw. A moment ago I was made clean; now I am dirtied with self-doubt. I let out an anguished groan.

'Atalanta? What is amiss?'

I twist away, shutting my eyes tight. 'I was staring at you,' I say in a squeezed trickle of a voice.

'I should hope so too.'

'You don't understand. I was *ogling* you.'

'And?'

'I am no better than men on the street,' I mumble.

Antiklea shakes me. Not roughly, but enough to get my attention. 'You are nothing like them,' she growls. 'Nothing.'

'But I am staring at you. Salaciously. With . . . desire.'

'Look at me.'

'I can't. It's not right.'

'I said, look at me.' She tilts my chin so I have no choice but to face her, eye to eye. 'The way you gaze at me is completely different to those street-rats. Why? Simple.' She smiles. 'Because I *want* you to. I want you to find me beautiful. I want you to feel desire. There. It is said.'

'Oh.'

'Now. Look at me. I command it.'

Antiklea swirls around, the folds of her chiton clinging to the curves of her body. The fabric gathers itself in damp pleats around the swell of her succulent hips as though it loves the flesh it touches. She takes a sliding step to the left, jiggles her shoulders and her breasts shiver lusciously. She swings her head and her braid dangles in the crease between. I swallow, throat dry as a thistle. She pauses, plants a fist on one hip, mouth quirking in a wicked grin.

'You are a sorceress,' I squeak.

'Your sorceress,' she replies.

'You desire me,' I say, half question, half wonderment.

'Here is your answer,' she says, holding out her arms. 'Come. I have waited too long.'

We wrap ourselves around each other and collapse onto a heap of leaves.

'At least let me unbuckle my quiver and bow,' I say with a smile.

I shrug off my cloak and we spread ourselves upon it. My fears continue to nag that Antiklea will look upon my body with the same lip-pursing, nose-wrinkling distaste of other humans. I am wiry, my limbs tough and unyielding as the caulking ropes used to lash boats together. I'm so scratched and scarred from hunting there's barely a clear patch to be found.

Fear melts in the fire of our lovemaking. Kiss by kiss, touch by touch, Antiklea awakens my flesh. I thought I was stone through and through, thought it was impossible to soften. I never thought I could taste the quickening of skin on skin. Never thought I could learn my own moaning urgency, slow at first and growing ever more insistent, coiling into a knot and leaping into joy.

Glowing, I prop myself on my elbow beside Antiklea and drink her in. I work my fingers through her heavy plait, tease out the threads and unfold the ebony curtain of her hair, lifting skeins to my nose and inhaling her perfume. I swipe my tongue across her stomach, purse my lips and blow a stream of chilly air. Each tiny hair pricks upright as I conjure gooseflesh. I nibble my way over the luxuriant swell of her belly to the twin delights of her breasts, and browse on each nipple. She lets out a bubbling moan.

Antiklea is beautiful, her flesh generous and lush. Her contours ripple, a landscape of sumptuous hills and deep wooded valleys in which I wander at my leisure. When I discover a

spot that gives her a particular thrill, I pause, dawdling wick-
edly. I delight in her delight. There is no greater excitement
than listening to her gasps of excitement and encouragement,
as I lift her closer and closer to rapture. Not that either of
us is in any hurry.

Afterwards, she lies across my chest, tracing the curve of
my ear. 'Tell me how you love me,' she murmurs.

'Antiklea, my skills are of the body, not the tongue.'

'I don't know about that,' she says, grinning impishly.

'I mean words and you know it.'

'You are brave enough to leap across ravines. You can
cudgel a few words into obedience.'

I frown. 'My love for you is true as an arrow-shot: an anchor
that holds fast in a storm. In your arms, I quiver and gasp as
after a race up Mount Parthenion and back.'

She smiles a crafty smile. 'You are more skilled than Homer.
Now, I shall press you further. This fine man Meleager: who
and what is he to you? Dearest Atalanta. I have eyes to see.'

The truth is difficult. Not once have I shied from difficulty.
I shall not begin to do so now. Perhaps the ritual truly has
granted me wisdom, for words spring to my tongue.

'You are to my right hand,' I say. 'Meleager to my left.
Neither one of you higher or lower than the other. I experience a deep connection with Meleager and at the same time,
love you wholly. I meet you both on the bridge of my being.'

'A good answer,' she says, kissing the tip of my nose.

'You do not fear losing me to him?'

'You are a strange and marvellous creature, Atalanta. I

knew that the day I first saw you at the river. It is no surprise if our love is also strange and marvellous. You love me. It is all I need to know.'

I take her hand, uncurl her fingers and pour kisses into her palm.

'Beloved,' I say. 'Beloved now, and through all that is to come.'

Rain in the night wakes me. It patters softly on the forest floor, quenching the earth. Green shoots will awaken and sprout, and grow again. I cover Antiklea with my cloak, tip my face into the drizzle, taste its blessing. At last, I understand. I am a woman who will toe no ordered line. I can do the same with my heart. At last, I let love into my life, wholly and without fear.

I honour the advice of Pappas and Hiereya and lend the story of Rhoecus and Hylaios the conclusion it deserves. That night around the ritual fire, and the ones following, I call them centaurs. The tale travels down the mountain and into the neighbouring valley and beyond. In the way of stories, it gathers speed. It runs like a river to every door, growing in the telling until Rhoecus and Hylaios are no longer mortal men; they never were. They are centaurs, grotesque and terrible to behold.

And I slew them, for their outrage.

I am now Atalanta, slayer of centaurs. I am famous. I am feared.

THE FATES

Olympos

A Time out of Time

We continue to stand watch over Atalanta and Meleager, relishing the piquant exhilaration of mortality. Each moment bestows fresh pleasure.

When Atalanta runs, we feel the wind tug her hair, the thrum of blood in her veins. We dance to the rhythm of her heels pounding the earth. She runs until her limbs cry for rest; keeps running and breaks through the pain. No, that is not quite right. Pain and ecstasy melt into one.

We watch as she falls in love: with Antiklea, with Meleager, with life itself. Love. By All-Mother Nyx, we are unprepared for love. We think we have drunk deep of mortal sensation until we experience its wonder; a fire that races around the heavens, from the icy wastes of the outermost planets to the heart of the sun. There is no turning aside its lance. No quenching its flame.

It is so all-consuming, we are fearful it might endanger The Plan.

We think again and realise, love *is* The Plan. Atalanta and

Meleager share a bond more profound than marriage's friable transaction, and have sealed it with blood. Love is the key to unlock the shackles of destiny. We need its power to carry The Plan to fruition. Without it, we cannot succeed. With love, everything is possible. Even our impossible scheme.

And what of us, we three sisters, living as children upon our mountain?

Our lives as children are almost done. We are stumbling towards the truth of who we are. Our memories are too powerful to remain hidden forever, even though we are the ones who demanded Themis bury them deep. We grasp at threads, half-hopeful and half-fearful that one will lead to the answer. Slowly, very slowly, we are returning.

It is not to be an easy journey.

THE THREE SISTERS

Clotho, Lachesis and Atropos

Olympos

Sisters share everything, especially their terrors. We follow Themis wherever she goes, clinging to her robe. Behind every bush we conjure a brigand, within each dark cloud a fresh disaster. The slightest wisp of a chilly breeze sends us skittering into a corner. Themis diverts the stream of our anxious questions. Although she pretends nothing is wrong, she too is watchful. Our agitation intensifies.

A month passes and another. The oil jar runs low. The level of meal in the barley bin drops. As stores diminish, our panic rises. One morning, we peep inside the bin and find bare scrapings. Themis announces she must go to market, and we lift the roof with sobbing.

'Don't leave us!' we wail. 'Let us come with you.'

'Not after the last time,' she replies. 'It is too dangerous. We are being watched.'

'We know! If you go, we'll be carried off by a monster!'

'It'll freeze us to pillars of ice!'

There is a difference between pretending alarm and the

real thing. We know it and Themis does also. With little more than a brisk nod, we are permitted to accompany her. We race about in a flurry of preparation and set off before dawn, glad to leave our fears behind for one day. Or so we think. Perhaps Themis should have refused outright; perhaps it is time for us to discover the truth.

When we pass through the invisible door at the roadside shrine, we huddle close to Themis, jumping at each rustle and squeak. But we are still children, and the ordinary beauties of the morning work their soothing charm. We laugh at the rock-rabbits bobbing away at our approach; admire each flower showing its face in the midst of sedge and bracken. We note the bushes astir with the chittering of birds, and lay bets on which of us will be the first to see the rays of the sun warming the peaks. By the time we reach the market we are some way to being restored to our carefree selves.

We rejoice at the press of bodies, the tussling to and fro of setting up stalls, the shouts of *Hot cakes! Fresh hot cakes!* There's the ear-splitting whine of a knife-grinder's wheel, a peddler with ribbons dangling from his hat brim, the clanging of a blacksmith hammering iron. A bullock's head sways over a butcher's stall, keeping time with the thump of a cleaver through bone. Blood pools in the gutter, and a mangy yellow dog with its tail between its legs slurps it hastily before it is chased off.

The sun warms our faces, behaving as the sun is supposed to. The earth is solid and reassuring beneath our feet. There is nothing to fear. These past two months we have been jumping at our own shadows, nothing more. We unwrap the bread we brought for our breakfast and when we brush away the crumbs, we brush away the last remnant of worry and taste release from the fright freezing our minds.

'All is well,' says Themis, hopefully. 'Let us pray it remains so.'

We nod ardently, and spread out our wares: Themis's woven ribbons, crocks of sweet buttermilk and soft rounds of goat's cheese, nested in straw. No sooner have we settled ourselves comfortably than customers crowd round, running Themis's border-bands between their fingers and declaring they've never seen the like, not ever. It must be flattery, for Themis comes here every few weeks. That, or their memories have as many holes as a sieve.

At midday, Themis treats us to a snack of salted liver, chopped into pieces and grilled over charcoal. It is so delicious it could make a cat weep, and we suck our fingers, unwilling to waste a single shred. While we are licking our lips, an old woman totters past. One gnarled hand clenches a stick, the other grips the arm of a young woman. They pause.

'Come on, Nonna,' says the lass, talking in the loud and babyish way used for someone hard of hearing. 'No dilly-dallying.'

'Don't shout, child,' snaps the old woman. 'I'm not deaf.'

'But, Grandmother . . .' moans the young woman, rolling her eyes.

'A moment will make no difference. What are you in such a hurry for, anyway?' She peers at Themis's woven bands and champs toothless gums. Her eyes are clouded and silvery as her hair.

'Good day, little Grandmother,' says Themis politely.

The crone squints at Themis, squints at us. 'I know you,' she murmurs.

'Do you like the border-bands?' asks Clotho.

'Aren't they beautiful?' says Lachesis.

'We'll give you the best price,' says Atropos.

The old woman flaps a hand in irritation. 'Look,' she says.

She twitches a fold of her robe and reveals the hem. It is edged with a patterned band of birds in flight, worked in blue and red. It is not any ribbon; it is the very one we sold to the little girl Phoebe when we came to market two moons ago. We'd know it anywhere. Themis never weaves exactly the same design twice, one of the many reasons her work is so prized. But the band bordering the crone's robe is almost as ancient as the woman herself. It can't be Themis's work. We must be wrong. And yet we are not. We don't understand.

'See,' she croaks. 'I bought this from you. It was—'

Themis interrupts. 'Perhaps you'd like to sample this fine goat's cheese?' she says, voice strident.

The old woman swats away the words, clinging to her line of thought. 'It was a market day. I remember . . .'

'Or this delicious buttermilk,' brays Themis, loud as a donkey. 'Churned fresh this morning!'

'I was a little girl,' she perseveres. Her jaws work side to side and we think of Kyrios chewing the cud. She points at us. 'You were little girls. You still are.'

'Come now, Nonna,' growls her granddaughter, yanking her arm. Not roughly but enough to make the old woman totter. 'You're bothering these nice ladies.'

'I thought . . . I was sure . . .' She falters, losing her grip on the thread of memory. Her shoulders slump.

Her granddaughter turns to Themis and twirls a finger at the side of her head in the sign for befuddled wits. 'I'm sorry, ladies. She's at that age, you know? She gets very confused.' She turns to her grandmother. 'Don't you, Nonna Phoebe?'

It is a common name; nonetheless we startle. A chill slithers down the back of our necks, despite the sweltering heat.

Clotho clears her throat. 'Your grandmother's robe,' she whispers. 'That's lovely border-work.'

'Oh! She never wears anything else, even though it's falling apart. She's had it since before I was born, before my mother was born also. Swears it was woven by fairies!' she hoots. 'Don't you, Nonna Phoebe?' she yells into the old woman's ear. 'Shall we get you a new one?'

Grandmother Phoebe shakes her head. We watch as she is steered away, clutching her robe tight in case anyone tries to take her beloved border-band from her. We turn to Themis.

'Mother? Grandmother Phoebe . . .'

'. . . is wearing your woven ribbon.'

Themis shrugs. 'You are mistaken,' she grunts, looking the other way. 'We must go.'

'But it's barely . . .' says Lachesis.

'Now. I said we must not linger.'

The hurried bustle of packing cannot smother our misgivings. We recognised the border-work. It was made by Themis two moons ago. We are *not* mistaken. We have always believed our mother would never lie, and are no longer sure. If we are no longer sure of that, we are no longer sure of anything.

Themis rushes to purchase oil and grain and we shoulder the loads without a grumble. As we pass the last house on the way out of the village, an upper window creaks open. A woman peers out, clutching her veil around her mouth. Her face is as pale as milk left too long. She frowns like a sparrowhawk, watching our sauntering stride.

'Good day, my lady!' we cry.

Rather than returning the greeting, she makes the sign of the horns with her fingers and slams the shutter. We know we are different to the people of the valley; all mountain folk are. We are prepared for scorn. This is unexpected: fear and mistrust. We do not understand this, either.

Menace haunts the homeward trail. We trip over roots and limp along, rubbing the ache out of elbows and knees. The straps of our packs chafe against our shoulders. The air has an odd, brackish smell. Flocks of birds rise up, squalling and screeching. Themis is on her guard and only breathes easy when we pass the roadside shrine.

That evening, we sit up late, watching the lamp. The flame bucks and bends in the draught that creeps through gaps in the thatch. Lachesis measures the hours it burns, and when Atropos announces that the oil is almost exhausted, Clotho fetches a fresh dipper from the pot.

'Girls,' says Themis in the kindly yet firm way that brooks no disobedience. 'Do not refill the lamp. The oil must last until the next trip to the market.'

'When will that be, Mother?' asks Clotho, a sharp edge to the question.

'A few weeks,' replies Themis, not looking up from the band she is finishing off by lamplight, woven with a pattern of frisking goats. A casual observer might think it the same as one of her other designs, but we can tell the subtle differences.

'Or a few years?' says Lachesis, voice so brittle it would shatter at a clumsy touch.

'Weeks,' says Themis softly.

Atropos licks her fingers and snuffs the wick. 'Years,' she mutters.

Our shoulders droop, the fight drained from us like wine from a cracked pitcher. We clap our hands to our faces and sob. At last, Themis raises her head and comes to us. It is a scant three paces, but seems far further. We huddle together, a mother and her little girls. The same as every other family on the earth, we tell ourselves.

We make excuses and go to our beds, trying to amuse ourselves by making shadow puppets upon the wall. However hard we twist our fingers into the happy and harmless shapes of rabbits, they take on outlandish forms. In the end we hide our hands beneath the blanket. Only when Themis leaves the hut on her nightly journey do we release the questions tangled in our throats.

261

'Grandmother Phoebe had the same name as the little girl,' says Clotho.

'Lots of girls are called Phoebe,' whispers Lachesis.

'But only one has Themis's birds sewn to the border of her robe.'

'Another weaver copied the pattern,' says Atropos.

'Mother's work is unmistakeable.'

Our minds turn over the conundrum. It rolls and tumbles without finding purchase on a solution. Clotho breaks the uneasy silence.

'What if it was the same Phoebe?'

'It can't have been,' we sneer.

'But what if it was?'

'It would mean the little Phoebe aged sixty years in the space of two months,' says Atropos. 'Which is impossible and you know it.'

Clotho's thoughts clatter as loud as beads on an abacus. 'Maybe . . .' she tries again.

'Maybe what?' we snap.

'Maybe,' Clotho continues, undaunted. 'Maybe the years pass swiftly in the valley and slowly on the mountain.'

'That's a silly idea,' we snort.

'Think about it. In the valley, decades have passed. On our mountain, a few weeks. Maybe the problem is not with Phoebe. Maybe it is with us.'

A bleak chill descends upon the hut, sliding through the chinks in the daub-and-wattle. It digs in its talons, and we shiver till our teeth rattle. We wonder if it is the monster returning to finish us off, but it is our fear, grinding us to ice. Not one of us speaks. If we do, there will be no other way to go than further into the fearsome territory of admitting we are touched with oddness.

Perhaps Time flows around us in a rushing onward stream, carrying everyone else from youth to old age and death. Perhaps we are not part of that natural order. We stand on the riverbank, watching the world flood by. We thought we could shrug off the memory of the ice-monster; thought we had discovered a form of contentment wherein we were resigned to the truth of our strangeness. It was a brief respite. The old fear reawakens. We are banished, we are exiled. We are all wrong.

The following day, Atropos sticks her head out of the door, sniffs the air and predicts rain coming in from the west. We set up the loom indoors and sure enough, by the time Lachesis is tying on the third loom weight, it is drizzling. We congratulate our sister for her keen nose for the weather. We busy ourselves in our work, determined to put aside horrible thoughts.

By our midday bread and cheese, the rain is coming down in sheets. Kyrios is slumped in the yard, shaggy pelt dripping and up to his ankles in mud. He bleats mournfully, hoping we'll let him in. The spindle-whorl swings; the shuttle flies swift as a plover; the shears rasp. Until the thread snaps. The thread never snaps. Clotho could spin yarn from straw if she put her mind to it. She mutters an oath, hooks on a fresh wad of fleece, pinches it between forefinger and thumb, and twirls the spindle-whorl. It holds an instant, and breaks a second time.

'Clotho, take a deep breath,' says our mother, gently.

'I am breathing!'

Two snapped threads become three, then four, until there are more broken than unbroken. Clotho picks at the heap of teased fleece in her lap.

'I cannot spin,' she says, miserably.

She is not the only one to struggle. Lachesis ties on the loom-weights, but they drag the warp off-kilter. Her measuring rod keeps slipping from her fingers. And however many times Atropos takes the whetstone to the shears, the blades remain blunt and will not cut clean.

Through all our botching and breaking, Themis calmly weaves her patterns: shields for a soldier, wine bowls for a wealthy man, babies for the women. She tries to cheer us up by singing the song of the man who slept under the hill a hundred years.

'He struck the rock with his staff,' sings Themis.

'*She* struck the rock with *her* staff,' says Clotho, changing the words.

'The hillside opened and he stepped in.'

'*She* stepped in,' cries Clotho.

The duel continues, Clotho chanting *she* whenever Themis says *he*.

'Have it your way,' says Themis eventually. 'It makes no difference.'

'It does to me,' says Clotho, and the thread snaps again. 'Can't you even let me have a song to make my own?'

'No good can come from daydreaming of things that cannot be. I do not want you to be unhappy. We are happy together on our mountain, are we not?' she asks anxiously.

It is unlike our mother to ask a question in need of a comforting answer. We think of all the times we run to her with grazed knees and how she bathes the scratch and kisses away the tears. Her question is a wound, and it seems we must be mother to Themis and salve her aches and pains.

'We are happy,' says Clotho. 'This is not about happiness. It is about us. Everything that was simple yesterday is impossible today. The ground tilts beneath our feet.'

'Mother,' we say in unison. 'What is wrong with us?'

'There is nothing wrong with you.'

'You know that's not true. We are not like other girls,' says Clotho. 'We spin, we measure, we snip. Every day is the same. Which is the riddle. The same for us, but not for the people of the valley. We have witnessed it, even if we do not understand. Phoebe has grown from a child to a crone, and we have remained young.'

'Why don't we grow, Mother?' asks Atropos.

'Shouldn't we be old, like Phoebe?'

'My darlings,' says Themis, shushing us, but we will not be shushed. Not this time.

'Mother, what are we?' asks Lachesis. 'Children, or some kind of monster?'

'You are not monsters.' Themis bites her lip, considering. 'You are not children, either.'

'Then what are we?' growls Clotho.

'Who are we?'

'We are frightened,' sobs Lachesis. 'We are lost.'

Themis lets out a long breath. 'I know. You are old enough to understand. By the sun and the moon, it has always been so.'

'Yes, Mother,' we say. 'There has been too much silence.'

'It has weighed heavy upon us.'

'You have kept secrets and we need to know them.'

Her jaws work from side to side, chewing the gristle of a tough confession. 'First, believe that I love you and will shield you with my life.'

We nod. Of this we have never been in any doubt. We feel it in the marrow of our bones, at the beginning and end of every breath. We clasp her hand and cover it with kisses.

'I have been protecting you.'

We do not ask from who or what. She will tell us in her own good time.

'You live in a paradise under my protection. Whilst here, you are safe,' she continues. Her words quiver, like the leaden air before a storm. 'I have doled out morsels of truth. It is no longer enough.' She blows her nose on a fold of her gown. 'I hoped for a longer delay. But you deserve – need – to know who and what you are.'

'Mother,' says Atropos softly. 'Are we not common goat-girls?'

She heaves a deep breath. 'No, my loves, you are not. You are much more. More than queen, dryad or wood-nymph.' She lowers her voice to a burr soft as a feather. 'More than the Gods themselves.'

We stretch our eyes. No one is higher than the Gods. There ought to be a crack of thunder. The lamp ought to gutter, snuffed out by a blast of angry air. The crickets buzz on, the heat of the night a steady hum.

'Before the Gods were, you are.'

'We still do not understand,' we say.

Themis surveys us, weighing our expressions as carefully as a goodwife weighs fine-milled flour for festival cakes. We hang in the balance of her gaze. At last, she comes to a decision.

'Of course not,' she says. 'Words are not enough.' She rises. 'Come with me. I shall take you to the Throne of Artemis. I shall show you why I go there each night, and you will understand.'

'The Throne of Artemis?' asks Clotho. 'I don't want to hear more stories of unhappy women. I have heard enough.'

'I have too, Mother,' agrees Lachesis, timidly.

'Quite the contrary,' says Themis. 'We are far beyond fables. What I am going to tell you is no story.'

We climb the familiar track. As we ascend, Helios dips his brow behind the mountain and the day cools into dusk. In the sea of the sky, stars begin to surface from the deeps. We seat ourselves on the rocky spur thrusting out from the mountain, and peer down into the crevasse. Its sides are packed with thorn bushes that dive into darkness.

We sit in silence and wait for Themis to begin. Not out of obedience, but a hunger to learn. The moon-Goddess Selene peeps over the treetops and leans close to listen, her face gentle.

'Things are changing and we must change also,' says Themis. 'I should have guessed your memories would be too strong to remain hidden for ever. It is not right that you should be frightened and confused. The truth can be concealed no longer. It is time.'

The moon rises higher, climbing across the sky. Themis tells us of the Great War fought between the Gods and the Titans; tells how the Gods were victorious and she was the only Titan to survive. How Zeus enthroned himself upon Olympos, hurling thunderbolts at anyone daring to disagree with his commands. He sits there still, calling himself Most Powerful, Mightiest of All, the Great and Fearsome Lord of Thunder.

'And yet,' says Themis, 'Zeus burns with jealousy. For there exists a power greater than his: The Moirai.'

She tells us of The Fates: three sisters born of Nyx before Time began. Tells us of their power, to spin and measure and sever the thread of mortal destiny. For aeons they weave. Mortals outgrow their cradle, and the need for The Moirai's protection. Once, destinies were nurturing; now they stunt mortal growth and keep them hobbled.

A plan forms in the minds of the endless Moirai: to surrender their immortal power, and give free will to mortals. To do this, a single man – Meleager – is cursed with an unjust and cruel fate. All that needs to happen is for him to dodge the moment of his death. The power of The Fates will be broken, and humankind will live free of destiny and the interference of the Gods. For ever.

Themis pauses.

'Mother,' we ask. 'This is a stirring story. How does it affect us?'

'Dearest girls, you are those three sisters. You are The Moirai. You spin and measure and snip the thread of human life.'

The forest stirs with a susurration of leaves, sounding like the blades of shears being sharpened on the wheel.

'But we are not immortal, Mother.'

'We have no great powers.'

'Listen, and I shall explain the heart of it. Zeus must not uncover our strategy, or he will make sure it fails. He is not the sort to surrender his might willingly. So I hid you – The Fates – where Zeus would not find you. I concealed you in the bodies of little girls and bore you to the slopes of Mount Olympos.'

'We don't remember.'

She bows her head. 'You pleaded with me to blur your memories, in order to assure the success of our scheme. At your command, I hid your secrets even from yourselves. Perhaps I wronged you.'

'No, Mother!' we cry. 'You hid our plan from Zeus. You protected us.'

She wraps us in her arms, embracing us passionately. 'Yes. It has been my life's work.'

The evening thickens into night. We neither hunger, nor thirst. The scent of oleander creeps up from the valley. A graveyard dog yips far away. Familiar sounds and scents, but tonight they prick us strangely, as though new and untasted. Themis lights a lantern and moths quest about the flame.

'Words cannot encompass your marvellous nature,' she says. 'They can sometimes get in the way.' She points to the Milky River arching over our heads. 'From this crag we can see this single river of stars. There are more such rivers, further than our eyes can see. There are torrents of starlight, so many even the Gods have lost count. We are made of stardust, and to stardust we shall return.'

The stars look down, winking in agreement.

'Since I first took you into my care, I have brought your weaving here each night.'

'What of our weaving, Mother?' asks Atropos. 'We have always believed it common cloth.'

'It is anything but.' Themis unrolls our day's work and shakes it out: plain homespun wool without decoration or fancy stitch-work. 'I will show you how wonderful you are. Look.'

We hold our breath. The stars twinkle, the moon gazes down, hollow-cheeked. A shooting star dashes overhead, running a slipstitch through the night. Nothing happens. We breathe out. Just as we are opening our mouths to ask what we're supposed to be seeing, it begins. A thread works loose, the tip unlooping itself inch by inch. As it uncurls, it kindles into flame.

'Our cloth has caught fire!' gasps Lachesis in horror. 'Stop it, Mother!'

'Wait,' purrs Themis.

It is unlike any fire we've seen before. The thread burns without being consumed, and we watch as it winds upwards, zigzagging this way and that. It is a flickering ribbon of light, dancing above our heads in what we can only describe as delight.

'It looks happy,' says Clotho.

'It is,' says Themis. 'This is the final piece of your puzzle. You are watching the ecstasy of a single mortal birth.'

As we watch, a second tendril wriggles out, twirling and coiling like a tiny golden serpent. Another pulls itself free, and another, each one ablaze with unearthly radiance. They rise and twist, braiding themselves together in a circle that grows wider and wider. More and more threads join the gathering, showering sparks in a rainbow – gold to red to green to indigo.

'You see?' says Themis. 'You weave the very thread of existence. Without you, there is neither birth nor death.'

We watch the skeins weave and unweave in a dazzling frenzy, rushing like a fiery river in spate. And, as suddenly, the dance comes to a halt. The ribbons pause and then fly apart, dashing away in all directions: north, south, east and west.

'There they go,' says Themis. 'Fast as a thought, each is flying to its rightful owner. Some threads are short, some long. Each is a new life, hastening to be born into mortal flesh. Across the world, babies are taking their first breath. In Hyperborea, where ice cracks underfoot all year round, they receive the gift of life; in the endless western desert of the Egyptians also. Further and further away, to lands I cannot name. My beloved girls. This is your miracle, to weave the destiny of mortals.'

'Mother,' whispers Atropos. 'Our work today was rough and ugly.'

'The thread kept breaking,' adds Clotho.

Themis laughs. 'Even your worst weaving is good enough. Not all lives are slick and easy. Some are troubled with knots and tangles. Every mortal knows times of difficulty, when life seems threadbare and barely worth the living. Each day has its cares, each day its gifts. The lives you wove today will have more trials than most.'

'We are sorry!' cries Lachesis. 'We did not mean to spoil their lives.'

'They are not spoiled. Think of it this way: imagine a courageous warrior, the bravest of his troop, forever in the thick of every skirmish. He is wounded, and healed; wounded and healed. He is the most beloved of his army of lovers and dies an honourable death, venerated by all his clan.'

Themis stands and spreads her arms. As heat rises in a shimmer over a pot, she rises, her feet leaving the ground. We watch, mouths agape, as she stretches to the heavens. The crown of her head brushes the dome of the sky, face dark as a thunderhead, tresses streaming like the beams of the sun.

She is storm and sunshine rolled into one. Her right hand grasps the sunset, her left the sunrise. One foot is planted in the encircling ocean, the other in the deserts of Babylon. She draws in a breath.

'I am Themis, the last of the Titans,' she says, voice quaking the earth.

We stare at her, wreathed in glory. We have never seen her like this, never heard her speak so stunningly.

'Mother, you are astonishing,' we breathe.

'Know this, my beloved girls,' she roars. 'My power is as a grain of sand when set against yours. When the earth was without form, in fire and darkness, you were born of Nyx. When life took its first gasping breath, you were there to spin and measure and snip the thread of destiny. You are the never-ending Moirai. Join me,' says Themis, reaching down to gather us into her arms.

At the tips of our fingers, we feel a tingling. Neither heat nor cold, it is a quivering thrill running up our arms and through our bodies, filling us to bursting. We look at each other and our spirits spark into understanding. Our feet leave the confines of earth and we ascend into the night.

'Sisters, we are beautiful!' we cry.

Violet sparks shoot from our fingers. Our skin is aglow, our hair a plume of fire flowing upwards to the heavens. We float, we ripple, we gleam. Hands joined, we dance around the mountaintop. We are whirlpools of wondrous radiance, spinning life and casting its net across the earth. We reach up and cup the moon; a little higher and pluck stars to string like

273

pearls around our throats. We laugh and meteors drizzle from our lips. We are day and night, sun and stars and moon rolled together. We are three in one. We swirl in the space between worlds. We are beyond the ways to describe ourselves, and so we let go of trying.

'We are The Fates!' we cry.

The earth joins in our hymn, all four winds singing through the jagged crags. Our voices no longer sound like those of little girls. We do not sound like women, either. We have the voices of immortals.

ZEUS

Mount Olympos

The Throne of the Gods

So, this is Themis's great secret. She has been sheltering The Fates behind her skirts. Does she take me for a dolt? Does she think I am not watching? I am Zeus: I see the fall of every sparrow, the flight of every dragonfly, the curl and crisp of each leaf in autumn.

I thought her brats were mere children, easy to obliterate. If there were any justice in the world they would have been, but the devious bodies with which Themis has clothed them are rags of light and shade, knitted into a simulacrum through which my thunderbolts pass. How dare Themis defy me.

Indeed, how dare Hera defy me. This is her fault. She's the one who sent me careering after a trio of girls, a task so far beneath me as to insult my majesty. She's the one who tricked me into trying to dispatch The Moirai. I have never been so humiliated.

'What can I do?' I cry, pounding my fists together. 'Can no one rid me of these vexatious Fates!'

275

There is a pause in the revelry, as though a sculptor carved my fellow Gods from marble: Aphrodite on her bloated backside away to the right, Apollo to the left, goblet partway to his pretty lips.

'How dare everyone ignore your plea,' twitters Hera, stripping the meat off a bone with the daintiest of bites. 'They deserve your wrath for their unhelpfulness.'

'Do they?' I growl, turning on her. She has the audacity to smile. 'Do they?' I say, louder.

That wipes the smirk off her conceited face. She slides to her knees, down where she belongs. Hermes crawls to the foot of my throne, and joins her there.

'Surely your thunderbolts would work against The Fates, sire,' he suggests, grovelling.

'Do you think I haven't tried?'

Poseidon prostrates himself. 'I beg forgiveness, my lord. My oceanic storms are as nothing against The Moirai.'

'My gales also,' whines Aeolus, bowing low.

'I am not interested in what won't work. I want to know what will.'

There's a nervous muttering. A dryad tries to creep away and I aim a small shaft of lightning at her. She limps from the feasting hall, dripping green blood.

'Drooling idiots!' I roar. 'Every last one of you!'

An ivory statue of Ares rattles off its plinth and shatters into toothpicks. I am watched by twitchy immortals, poised for what I'll do next. I know they'd love to see me lose control and reduce every tree-spirit to wood pulp. I've heard them slavering over my grisly punishment of Prometheus, tittering over Tantalus jumping for grapes he'll never reach. My wrath is always amusing as long as it is aimed at someone else.

'The Fates were created, therefore they can be uncreated,' I cry. 'There has to be a solution!'

'There is none.' The voice rings out, clear as the tolling of a bell. All heads turn. Hades stands at the far end of the hall, silhouetted against the door. 'The Moirai are true immortals,' he continues, smiling his hangman's smile.

'What's that supposed to mean?' I snap.

Hades sighs as though addressing a simpleton. 'They cannot be killed because they existed before life itself. Before the Gods were, they are. After the Gods, they will endure.'

A silence wraps itself around Olympos, holding us in its thrall.

'What do you mean, *after* the Gods?' I ask. 'Be careful how you answer.'

Hades shrugs. 'I am Lord of Death, dear brother,' he says. 'You cannot kill that which is already deceased.' He arranges his robes, flicking a speck of dust from one shoulder. 'We Gods live a long time. Long enough to watch an empire or two rise and fall. Three, perhaps. But we will die.'

A wine bowl falls from Dionysus's grasp and rolls clanking across the crystal floor. Stifled sobs break out. Hades surveys the ashen faces and grins. I did not know he had so many teeth.

'You've never visited my realm, have you?' he says. 'It is not as pretty as Olympos and the wine is on the muddy side.

But be assured; one day I shall feast you all in the Underworld. For eternity.'

Swinging his mantle, he sweeps away, leaving the banqueting hall swollen with a dank and humid fear. No one is in the mood for feasting and the party dwindles and dissipates. It is not fair. I should live forever, not The Fates. Whatever my brother says, I am not done yet. A solution will present itself and when it does, I shall be ready.

Hera strokes my arm. 'Why not consult the Oracle?' she says. I raise my hand but she does not flinch, gazing at me with a serene expression. 'A silly notion I'm sure, but they do blether on about destiny and so forth. They might know something.'

I lower my fist, pat her rosy cheek.

'Besides,' she adds. 'It would be just like the conniving Fates to keep the secret of their own destruction from mighty Zeus.'

'Ah, Hera,' I say. 'That's better. Only you understand me.'

It is the journey of an instant from Olympos to Parnassus. One small step, and I am there. Everyone knows the sibyls play their trickiest word-games on kings, so I disguise myself as a shepherd, bow-legged and scabby.

I drape a reeking goatskin about my loins, wedge crumbs of barley bread between my teeth and join the queue of mortals. Their pitiful questions throb between my ears: *Will this bloody flux never cease its flow? How can I make Diomedes love me? What must I do to bear a son? Who is placing a murrain on my flock?* On and on goes the tiresome gabbling. I itch with suppressed lightning. With one flick of my little finger I could reduce the entire stinking company to cinders.

Patience, I counsel myself. It is not easy.

The line winds up the hill to a building of white stone, scrubbed to a dazzling gleam. I pretend to be impressed, swipe my straw hat from my head and fidget with the brim in true peasant fashion. However, play-acting is tedious work. With a breath I transport myself to the head of the queue and step up to the portico.

A priest directs me to stand beside a draped doorway and speak my piece. I knock him aside, tear the curtain off its hooks and clump down a flight of steps. The priest squeaks that no one is permitted to approach the lady, so I silence him for ever.

I enter the cave of the Oracle, an unadorned box chiselled into the body of the mountain. A thousand years of footsteps have burnished the flagstones to the sheen of a bronze mirror. The frigid breath of Gaia creeps down the back of my neck.

There is no heaped gold, no fine statuary. Nothing but a tripod on skeleton legs, seething with a choke of laurel fumes. On a tall chair hovering over the fug is a woman, gown pulled over her head and hooded as a crow. The light from the weakling fire of the brazier picks out the features of a crone: the blade of a chin, yellowed teeth. Cracked and grimy feet dangle from the bottom of her robe, her toenails long and curving in on themselves.

'I have a question,' I say.

She neither stirs nor replies, her face deep in curdled shadow.

'You shall answer,' I continue, louder.

She continues to show no awareness of my presence. I feel myself bristle.

'How dare you not acknowledge divinity, you old baggage!'

'I answer to Apollo,' she says quietly, and tosses back her veil.

A shock of fox-red hair streams around her shoulders, the apples of her cheeks plump and unbitten. Her mouth is soft and dimpled, except for silvery lines of scar tissue running from the corner of her lips. She cannot be more than thirteen summers old.

'Tell me how to destroy The Fates,' I command.

'You know the answer to this question,' she says. 'The Moirai are endless. Before the Gods were, they are.'

I punch the wall and the mountain shivers. 'I am asking again. I demand a better prophecy.'

'It is not prophecy if you will only accept the answer you crave.'

'Then I will consult every oracle under the sun!'

She waves away my words, sprinkles shredded leaves onto the charcoal and takes a gulp of the bitter smoke. 'And receive the same reply.'

'Obey me,' I say. 'I demand it.'

Her shoulders jolt and jar; she begins to rock to and fro, emitting unearthly sounds. Sounds that existed before the birth of words. Sounds that existed before me. She gags, retches.

'Mother!' she bellows, the moan of a labouring beast. In a paroxysm, she stretches her jaws and deafens the cavern with a scream. The scars at the corners of her mouth tear afresh. 'Oh, Mother!'

Blood drips onto her breast and still she howls, eyes rolling until only the white is visible.

'Tell me!' I cry, stamping my foot. Rubble trickles from the ceiling. 'I want my answer!'

Her shrieking snaps off. The cave rings with silence. 'The God speaks,' she whispers, gazing around in a daze of wonderment. 'No. Not Apollo. It is the Mother herself.'

'The Mother, Apollo, I care not. Stop babbling and give me what I came for!'

She touches her lips, examining the blood on her fingertip as though bemused to find it there. 'The Fates,' she says. 'The world is on tiptoe.'

'Speak straight! I demand the truth!'

Slowly, she turns her gaze in my direction. 'Thunder does not desire the truth,' she says with a shrug. 'It seeks destruction.'

She hoists her skirts, climbs down from her perch and totters away. I gallop after, wrap my hands around her neck and shake her like the toy she is. Her face is tranquil. She does not fight, does not cry for help. A howl starts deep in my bowels and bursts out in a clap of thunder.

'Tell me how to grind The Fates to dust!' I wail, hating the desperation in my voice, hating that she can hear it too, hating her for reducing me to a craven beggar.

'They will do that for themselves.'

'What? Never. You're saying this to save your flea-bitten hide.'

I squeeze my thumbs into her throat. Scarlet foam bubbles from her mouth. Her lips move but no sound comes out. I release the stranglehold and she draws in a hurtling breath.

'I cannot lie,' she wheezes, hawking up a gobbet of bile. 'The Mother compels me.'

'The Fates will destroy *themselves*?'

She coughs, gathers herself. 'Surrender their power,' she says. 'Return to the stars. You need do nothing. It is their intention. For aeons now, they have . . .'

I toss her aside. 'I have won!' I crow. 'The Fates will be wiped from the earth and the heavens! I am Zeus! Supreme and unchallenged! There will be no other to compare!'

The Oracle sprawls in a heap of rags, wittering about a lump of burning wood sealing the end of the Gods, of corridors filled with our shattered statues bleached white as bone and gawped at by mobs of mortals. I silence the drivel with a twist of her wizened neck, summon lightning and sear her bones to ash.

I charge back to Olympos, blazing a trail of triumph. When The Fates return to the stars, I'll show mortals what it means to bend beneath my yoke. I rake my fingernails through earth's flesh and hurl clods the size of temples at any creature that gets in my way. I uproot mountains, raze forests; flatten shepherds and sheep, turn lakes into mudflats, cornfields into dung heaps. I topple ancient trees like splinters. My hymn of conquest maddens cattle into stampedes; swine hurl themselves off crags.

'I am Zeus!' I scream. 'I am invincible! I shall outlive The Fates! I am immortal!'

THE THREE SISTERS

Clotho, Lachesis and Atropos

Olympos

We have one final secret to divulge.

We have recovered our memories. We are the undying Moirai: we wear the bodies of children. We spin homely fleece: it is the thread of life. We live in a humble cottage: we dance in the space between stars. We are insignificant girls who trip and graze their knees: we are ageless, boundless, endless. We are Other, entirely so.

For the moment, we are safe. Zeus has visited the Oracle, but listened to only half the prophecy. He has not guessed our true intention. At least, this is what we hope.

'Oh, Mother!' we say. 'We are sorry we demanded to know the truth about ourselves. Our curiosity has endangered everything!'

'Not at all,' says Themis. 'We must work quickly, that is all. Your thoughts are already beginning to snag in the fabric of the cosmos. If we delay, the disturbance could alert the Gods.' She pauses. 'Our plan must change. I hoped we might simply guide Meleager away from his death. It is no longer enough. One of you must go to earth and ensure his safe deliverance.'

'To earth?' We look at each other. 'How?'

'As a mortal. You cannot be as one of The Moirai. Otherwise, Zeus will sniff you out. You must be stripped of every trace of immortality to have a chance of success.'

The silence swells with unspoken questions.

'Themis,' says Clotho. 'There is something you are not telling us.'

'Yes. Once born into a mortal body, you cannot return to Olympos.'

'Never?' gasps Lachesis.

'Never. Once the task is accomplished and Meleager's death delayed, you will live out a span of mortal years. Your teeth will ache, your belly will gripe, your bones will break. You will know sickness, age, and death.' Themis plants her hands on her hips. 'It is a fearsome undertaking. Who shall it be?'

The hesitation is brief, less than a breath drawn in and released.

'I will go,' declares Clotho, stepping forward.

We should not be surprised by our brave and headstrong sister.

'Think carefully, child of my heart,' says Themis. 'As a mortal, you will face danger from your first breath.'

'I understand,' says Clotho, warming us with her generous smile. 'It is the only way to be sure. There is too much at stake to trust to chance. I will prevent Meleager from keeping his appointment with death.'

'You must. If we fail, Zeus will be Lord of all, forever. A selfish, devouring, vindictive master. With nothing and no one to rein in his power, he will reduce the earth to rubble.'

Themis hands Clotho her distaff, to spin her own destiny.

'I shall measure the thread, dearest sister,' says Lachesis, holding up the ivory wand.

'And I shall grant you a long life,' adds Atropos.

Clotho grins and shakes her head. 'No,' she says. 'I shall be born without a fate. It is only right I take the first step and lead the way, stumbling, unplanned and free.'

'Of course,' says our mother. 'There is no other way. You have your instructions, Clotho. Find this man Meleager and guard him well.'

She presents Meleager's thread. Woven a thousand years ago, it is as brutal as the moment it was spun.

'Here,' says Atropos, pointing to the tip, dripping with vicious fire. 'The moment of his death: a burning brand, consumed in flames.'

'Delay him,' commands Themis. 'Pull the log from the hearth. Get him drunk. Go dancing. Anything. An instant's hold-up is all that's needed to fulfil The Plan.'

Clotho nods, her jaw set firm.

'We want to help!' cry Lachesis and Atropos.

'Oh, you shall,' says Themis. 'You shall watch over them both and guide their footsteps. Retain the appearance of little girls, for your true appearance would stretch a mortal mind to breaking.'

'Mother,' says Clotho. 'I shall wait for the stars to align. Tell me when, for I am ready.'

'There is no need for conjuration, Daughter. The Moirai are outside Time. You shall be born the same year as Meleager. As he grows, so shall you.'

We embrace, Lachesis and Atropos promising to be guardian spirits and never sleep, not for an instant.

'Your mortal life begins now,' says Themis.

I unknot, unstitch, unravel from the trinity of Clotho, Lachesis and Atropos. No longer *We*, I become an *I*. I am myself. The flame of life ignites in my breast and rushes through my being. I laugh out loud with the keen, sharp joy of it. I am alive!

Like a comet I blaze through the void, radiance sizzling through my veins. Like the threads we send across the heavens to find their new owners, I burn, yet am not consumed. I am fire and air; I am earth and rain. There is nothing to stop me. I unleash myself across the heavens, unfettered and exulting. I am a brilliant thread spinning out of eternity and into the count of mortal days.

I plummet past the stars and planets, diving towards earth, closer and closer. As I tumble I dress myself in bone, flesh and skin. My body is in uproar, a surging agony that fills me to breaking point. I scream, but the torment goes on, an ordeal that purges me of immortality and leaves me flayed, raw and howling.

This is the price of mortality.

It is Themis speaking, or Nyx, I am too lost in anguish to tell. I can bear it no longer. I've changed my mind. I am a fool. Who would choose this misery? I open my mouth to beg for mercy, words gathering on the tip of my tongue, when the torture ceases, snuffed out swiftly as a candle flame. I gasp at the shock of release, breathe my last immortal breath, and plunge into a baby at the moment of her birth.

My mother Klymene claps me to her breast. I seize her nipple with a ravening hunger. How do mortals bear it, I think, this endless famine of the self? How are they able to put one breath in front of the other, when they suffer this tearing of the insides?

I wail, and suck; wail and suck some more. I weep for the loneliness of being human, stripped to a naked nothing. My need and want is a howling ache so vast it blots out memory. I lose everything. I forget my name, forget Lachesis and Atropos, forget Themis. Forget my power. Forget it all in the agony of becoming girl.

My mother Klymene also screams as I am torn from her arms. She fights to hang on, but her husband Iasus is stronger. I am borne away and tossed onto a mountainside, where I am left to shriek in outer darkness.

By the Goddess Artemis! cries Klymene. *Protect my daughter! Through the mercy of The Fates, let her live!*

The mystery is unfolded: our sister Clotho is Atalanta.

Horrified, we watch her taken from Klymene. On Mount Parthenion, we send Arktos and pray for mercy. We only breathe easy when Arktos takes our sister into her shaggy arms; we clap our hands with joy and relief when Clotho seizes her new mother's nipple and sucks with the lust for life she will need. We lean close. The baby looks at us with blank eyes.

'Mother, wait,' whispers Lachesis. 'Something is wrong.'

We sift gently through the little mind, gentle as thistledown. Nothing. She is a waxen tablet, blank and uninscribed.

'She has forgotten,' says Atropos. 'Why she's been born, who she is, what she must do. Everything is gone.'

'I am a fool,' cries Themis. 'I should have anticipated the shock of childbirth upon an immortal.'

'How will she find Meleager?'

'She does not know her purpose. Does not even know her name.'

Themis smiles. 'You shall watch over her every footstep.'

And so we do our part, stepping through the gateway between worlds. We protect Meleager and Atalanta through dangerous childhoods and beyond. We guide them to each other, and nurture affection. Perhaps it is for the best she has forgotten she is Clotho. The Moirai are anathema to Meleager: his hatred burns with a passion so intense it would scorch away any chance of closeness. If our sister were to reveal her identity, he would send her away.

From the day of her birth into mortal flesh, we do not leave her side. She is a breath away, and less. A world away, and more. As Atalanta, she grows strong and wayward. As if our sister could be anything else! We steer her away from dangers, of which there are plenty, always at her shoulder.

We whisper in her dreams: *Be strong, sister, be strong*. When we reach out, she feels the ghost of our breath brush her cheek, sees us glimmering at the corner of her eye. We smile, and wave. In her expression, we see no recognition. But we see affection.

As she grows, we yearn with her yearnings, rejoice in her rejoicings. We taste her joys and sorrows; share the soaring of her heart when she is near Antiklea and Meleager. We revel in the scent of night-gathered herbs, the damp crumbling of earth between her fingers, the bursting of a ripe plum upon her tongue. We are not envious: we love our sister and delight in her every delight. We are wistful, rather. We stroke each other's hair, tease out each other's braids; trace the curve of chin and cheek, the plump curl of lips. Our girl-selves are smoke and fog when set against the sensations experienced by our sister's mortal body.

The longer we watch, the more we understand. Clotho was always the quickest to see to the heart of any problem. After all, she is the one who untangles the cat's cradle of eternity and spins it into the thread of life. As a mortal, she caresses the spark of life passing through her fingers and takes a pinch of stardust for herself.

We can't believe we've been so slow to see that Clotho is showing us what is possible. We imagine what it might be like to join her; what we might also experience if we were permitted to choose mortality for ourselves. In our hearts we plant a small seed of determination.

Our story has come full circle. We are back where we began, in Calydon, on the eve of the hunt for the monstrous boar. It is time for our stratagem to enter its final working-out. Meleager's hour is close. Only Atalanta can avert the coming evil, and save the world through the indomitable force of love. The Plan is in motion. There is no stopping it. We can do nothing more.

For the moment, all is well. Atalanta and Meleager hum with the excited anticipation of a testing chase upon the morrow. We stand sentinel a little longer. In a handful of hours, their lives will be changed for ever. Their lives and those of every mortal, born and yet unborn.

The hunt begins.

Time Is

ATALANTA

Calydon

The clanging of the temple bell knocks away sleep. Meleager's nose is rammed in my ear, and my legs are wrapped around his waist. We spring apart in a blushing fluster.

'Well now,' he coughs, adjusting his kilt.

'Well indeed,' I harrumph, counting the arrows in my quiver.

I tally them upwards of ten times and the number is the same at each counting, before I dare slide a look at Meleager. He is busy rasping a whetstone along the blade of his sword.

'Good morning, comrade Atalanta,' he says, grinning shyly.

'And to you, comrade Meleager.'

We burst out laughing, and clasp each other's hands.

'Are we fools to be abashed as maidens?' he snorts.

'Perhaps,' I say. 'Though I do not feel foolish.'

'Nor I. Hungry, however.'

I take in an appraising sniff. 'I smell bread baking.'

We make our way back to the camp. Judging by the livid smudges under their eyes, our fellow-hunters slept as lightly as Meleager and myself. Not that any one of us is whining. Excitement and anticipation thrum through our veins. We wolf down bread and cheese, drink twice-watered wine and chaff each other heartily for having groggy heads. The early morning air is sharp and cool with mountain dew.

Meleager's brother Toxeus arrives, twirling his cape. His Kushite slave assists him with buckling his quiver over one shoulder, and presents him with a spear as thick as my arm. Toxeus brandishes it flamboyantly, showing off oiled biceps.

'You sluggards!' he roars. 'Leave off your guzzling. We have a boar to hunt!'

Once again, I battle the urge to kick him into the nearest well. I don't believe he's here without a fine breakfast inside him. I distract myself by stamping down the embers of the fire and kicking over the ashes. Plexippus is last to arrive, patting his curls into place. I did not pay it much attention before, but he puts a lot of effort into appearing younger than his years. His beard and browline are stained with dye, the wrinkles around his eyes disguised with kohl.

'Ah, Uncle,' says Toxeus tartly. 'We have been chewing our knuckles, fearing your knees would not be up to the task ahead. Now you are here and we can breathe again.'

Plexippus smiles: unable or unwilling to distinguish flattery from sarcasm, I cannot say. I groan. If Toxeus upsets the steady progress of the day, I truly will kick him, and hard. Meleager pats my shoulder.

'Fear not. Toxeus is a fine hunter, even if he is maddening in other matters.'

Once more Meleager reads my thoughts, cleverly as an augur reads the flight of birds. We make our final preparations. I'm fastening a sandal-strap when I realise the encampment has fallen quiet. It is a silence I recognise: I am being stared at. I finish what I'm doing and take my time about it before I straighten up. Just as I thought, some of the men are muttering and casting glances in my direction. I meet their gaze. As is ever the case, they will not meet mine, looking everywhere else but at my face. I am so very tired of this behaviour. I know full well what's going to happen next.

The one named Kepheus is first to speak. 'You are a woman,' he grunts, demonstrating remarkable powers of observation.

A second coughs into his fist. 'I shall not – cannot – hunt alongside a woman. It is unlucky.'

There's a rumble of agreement. The roster of blackguards I'm planning to toss into a well is growing fast. Very slowly, I slip off my quiver and bow and lay them on the ground. Meleager steps forward.

'Unlucky?' he snarls.

'Yes,' says Kepheus. 'It is written—'

Meleager cuts him off. 'This is ridiculous. You've had all night to complain, and are choosing this moment to make your objections?'

'We spoke of it yesterday evening,' continues Kepheus, striving for bravado and falling a long way short. 'When you were . . .'

He pauses. Toxeus joins the fray. '. . . Amusing yourself in some other fashion,' he drawls, examining his fingernails.

A couple of the younger men snigger. A growl gathers itself in Meleager's chest and they shut up immediately.

'Many things are written,' says Meleager, his tongue dripping bile. 'It is also written that piss tastes of figs.' He grabs a cup and holds it at his groin. 'Who's the first in line for some delicious fig juice, eh?' There's a bout of throat-clearing and foot-shuffling. 'I thought not,' he says, tossing the cup aside. 'It is also written that roasted mule excrement will turn grey hair black.' He glances at Plexippus, who is concentrating on a pebble between his toes. 'Have you tried that, Uncle?'

'Yes,' mutters Plexippus.

'Did it work?'

'No, of course not.'

'Of course not,' echoes Meleager. 'Yet, it is written.'

Kepheus clears his throat. 'We are many, Meleager. She is one. We do not need her.'

I hear hopeful mumbling.

'You think not?' snarls Meleager. 'Were you snoring below decks when we sailed up the Evenus? Did you not see the devastation? You have all witnessed what the boar has done. We need every single bow, every single spear.'

'But she is dedicated to Artemis,' says a man whose name I neither know, nor can be bothered to discover. 'And it was Artemis who sent the boar,' he continues, pointing at me.

'What better way to test the truth of it,' declares Meleager. 'Than by welcoming a sister of the Goddess into our ranks?

If Artemis is truly angry, she will strike Atalanta down for blasphemy. If not, her arrows will fly true.'

The muttering shifts back and forth: agreement, disagreement; agreement, disagreement.

Toxeus interrupts. 'Talk, talk, talk,' he says, tapping thumb and forefinger together. 'I'm up to my eyeballs with it. You lot could talk the hind leg off a goat. By the Gods, let Atalanta join us so we can get started.'

Meleager steps forward and thrusts out his hand. I clasp it warmly. Another joins him, and another, till we are linked as one. Toxeus does not precisely speak for me, but does not speak against me either. Perhaps I shan't have to shove him off a cliff after all. I retrieve my bow and quiver.

Kleitos and a priest bustle into the clearing, bowing and touching their foreheads. The priest is festooned in an embroidered robe, his beard braided and knotted with great care. The scent of a standoff still hangs in the air, and they glance about nervously.

'Well met and a good greeting to you, Kleitos,' says Meleager. 'We are ready, are we not, comrades?'

There's a ragged cheer.

'Are we not, comrades?' he asks again, louder.

This time, the bellowed response is enough to startle the crows out of the trees. They veer away, flapping and cawing. The priest raises his hands and speaks an impassioned blessing, his faith in us desperate and touching.

It has begun.

The forest is thick with deep cover. I can barely see two paces distant. We fight our way through, making slow headway. The boar could be lurking anywhere in the endless tangle of twigs and branches that snatch at our hair and slash our faces with stinging blows. Ancaeus is the first to come upon the beast's droppings. Peleus points out a tree with the tell-tale scuffmarks of its tusks on the bark. Before long, we pick up the spoor. The splayed imprint of its hoof is unmistakeable, but three times the size of any boar I've seen previously. Of the beast itself there is no sign.

It has wiles as sharp as its teeth. Every time we get close enough to pick up its scent, it slips deeper into the brush. We are forever finding ourselves facing east, morning sun dazzling our eyes. Whenever we try to flush out the beast, it drives us deeper into the dense tangle of undergrowth, thorns pricking our arms and backs so thickly we look like hedgehogs. I feel we are not the pursuers but the pursued. I'm wondering if we are going to be led in circles till nightfall, when an exultant cry rings out and the hounds start baying.

The boar! Here!

The shout runs like wildfire through the trees. While the men yell to one another at the full stretch of their lungs, I hang back and hearken to the sounds between and beneath their fierce outcry. The stifled chirp of a bird, a swishing of leaves, and there to my left: the muffled panting of a great beast.

Once again, it has sent the hunters in the wrong direction. I take slow and furtive steps until I get a clear sighting of this cunning adversary. I've never seen a boar the like. The size of my mother Arktos, and as dangerous. Slimy froth speckles his shoulders and he drools blood-flecked foam. The bristles cresting his spine are thick as a thorn bush, his tiny eyes sunk deep into the skull and burning like coals. As he catches my scent, he opens his jaws wide, displaying tusks as long as my forearm. When he squeals, the noise rips the day in half.

Hunters charge through the bushes, drawn by the sound. They make more of a racket than the animal itself, ruining any chance of a stealthy approach. The boar bursts from the covert. A spear flies, although it misses its target by a league. Half a dozen men thump into the clearing, Ancaeus swinging a two-headed axe. The boar lowers its head, eyes glinting with ancient rage. It paws the ground, churning up the earth.

'Ancaeus,' I hiss. 'Get out of its way!'

'I am Ancaeus, son of Eurytos!' he cries. 'I'll chop off its head and feed its liver to the—'

The boar charges, gores him in the stomach and tosses him aside like a broken doll.

'Help me!' he yowls, staring at his belly. It is slashed open, spilling a skein of red and purple intestine. 'Gods! Gods!' he squeals, and falls backwards.

The boar skids to a halt and turns as neatly as a temple dancer. It stampedes into the crowd of men who've dashed to help Ancaeus, and skewers two of them like so much chargrilled meat.

The world descends into chaos. Everyone's feet are in the way of everyone else's. Hunters run a few paces, only to turn and run back, tripping over weapons and plummeting into the path of the boar. Some scurry to the trees, clambering onto low branches to escape the next assault. Hounds race in all directions, yipping and barking. The forest floor is churned up with the thrashing and heaving of man and beast. A storm of arrows whips through the air. There's a shriek as one finds a human target. The stink of loosened bowels.

'Stop!' I cry. 'You are shooting at your comrades!'

No one is listening. Even if they are, no one can hear me above the din.

Meleager appears at my side. 'We must press on,' he whispers.

I nod. We leave the shrieking rabble who seem to have forgotten why they're here. We tiptoe past tree-trunks splashed with scarlet spray, human or animal I cannot tell. Everywhere, the drifting reek of blood. Meleager points a finger to himself and off to the right. I take the left hand path.

I sight the boar at the heart of a thicket. Its tusks gleam in the paling afternoon light seeping through gaps in the canopy. I heft my spear, feel its weight balance perfectly in my grasp. I am motionless as a rock. Nothing stirs, not as much as one hair on my head. The boar matches me for stillness, both of us caught up in a strange, frozen moment. Birds fall silent. The forest holds its breath.

As though waiting for this precise opportunity, my two protectors appear. One measures the distance between the boar and myself; the other whispers, *Now. Finish it.*

I let loose my spear. It flies straight into the eye of the boar. The spell is broken and there is a frenzied eruption of sound:

the beast howling in its death-agony, hunters screeching in the distance, and my exultant shout: *A hit! A hit!*

A flurry of arrows are fired in my direction. Luckily all of them fall short. Before I end up stuck with a stray dart, I close the distance between myself and the boar. I prod it with my toe. Nothing. It stretches on its side, completely motionless. My javelin is lodged deep. An hour ago, it was the size of a mountain. In death, it has shrunk to little more than a large pig. Ordinary blood oozes from the wound, not unearthly ichor. Sunlight glimmers through the branches, dappling its hide. The hunt is over and done.

'Thank you, most blessed guardians,' I murmur.

Perhaps I imagine their lips upon my cheek, perhaps it is simply the breeze. Bracing a foot against the boar's flank, I grasp the spear-shaft.

I should have known it would have a final trick to play. I was sure it was dead. I heard it shriek, saw it crumple. With a squeal of triumph, it springs to its feet, swinging its head. I hang on, flung about like a fishing-skiff in a gale. Bellowing, it gallops into the bushes in an effort to dislodge me. I cling to it as passionately as I clung to my mother Arktos when I was a starving babe. We plunge though thorns and briars, till I'm flayed to rival Marsyas.

'Lay down!' I cry. 'Let me give you the good death you deserve!'

When I fastened my sandal-strap this morning, I imagined a dignified scene: Meleager and myself kneeling beside the dying creature, speaking words of kindness to ease its departure from this life. I imagined our prayers reaching the ear of Artemis, imagined her bending down from her sacred grove and bestowing her blessing.

This is an ugly death, and I can do nothing to make it better. Tears stream into my mouth. I hang on, slippery with shared blood. Just when I think we will perish together and continue this race in the Underworld, it trips on a root and slams into the trunk of a massive fir, dousing us in a downpour of needles. It tries to struggle upright again, but the battle is over. Before I can gabble the smallest prayer of farewell, it is gone. I wrap my arms around its neck, and sob into its bristly mane. A swoon drags me into its undertow and I float out on the current, lost to the world.

MELEAGER

Calydon

Guided by the racket, I find Atalanta crushed between the hulk of the boar and the bole of an ancient fir. I shoulder the animal aside and haul her out. She's as limp as wet bread, and as dead as the beast. I clutch her to my chest, heart swelling with a grief I did not know a man could possess. I thought I'd stamped out all tenderness when I was a lad; thought I'd made of myself a cold and impassive soldier.

Indeed, I was that man, until Atalanta unlatched the door to my spirit and breathed life into my cinder of a heart. I let the tears flow; tears banked up for half my life. Behind me, I hear a clumsy hubbub: Toxeus and Plexippus have been sticking close as gulls to a fishing boat, hoping for gleanings. I don't bother to turn. This final moment is mine and no one shall steal it away.

'Oh, look. Meleager is blubbing,' drawls Toxeus.

'Sweet words, dear Nephew. Sweet words,' says Plexippus, scratching his head. 'Atalanta was a worthy hunter, and deserves a fitting valediction.' He clears his throat. 'Atalanta, Fleet-of-Foot!' he warbles. 'Atalanta! Equal—'

'Do hush up, Uncle,' snaps Toxeus. 'You're no bard.'

Their bickering swings back and forth, like a child's game of pat-the-ball. I bury my face in Atalanta's hair. With a jolt that shakes us both, she draws in a rattling gasp and starts coughing.

'Atalanta!' I cry.

Her eyelids flutter. I cradle her over my shoulder in the way I've seen women calm spluttering infants. Gradually she stops choking; gradually, her eyes grow clear. Her lips make the shape of my name, soundless.

'I am here,' I say, placing a finger over her battered mouth. 'There'll be time for talk later.' I turn to Plexippus. 'Wine, now! I've never known you to be without.'

I snatch the proffered goatskin and grunt a quick *thank you*. As I'm coaxing Atalanta to take a little, more men crash into the clearing, spears hefted and ready to strike. Now he has an audience, Toxeus sets back his shoulders, plants a foot on the animal and throws out his arm in the manner of an orator.

'So dies the dread boar of Calydon!' he crows, poking the tip of his spear into the beast. 'See! I have killed it.'

'Poppycock,' I say. 'Atalanta got in the killing shot and you know it.'

'Come now, Nephew. It is already dead,' says Plexippus, trying to sound stern and failing.

'Shut up,' he hisses. 'I am Toxeus, hero of the hour.'

The hunters survey the scene: Atalanta half-living and half-dead, three men arguing like fishwives, and the slain boar. They see Atalanta's spear, thrust deep into its skull. They see Toxeus's spear, barely causing a scratch.

Atalanta hoists herself onto one elbow and grimaces with the pain. 'No!' she groans. 'It is mine, by right.'

'Not if I say it isn't,' says Toxeus.

Hunters shift from foot to foot, embarrassed by the show.

'Then grant me a prayer,' she wheezes. 'A prayer over this worthy foe before we hack him into pieces. Then you can take the head, the feet, the tusks, the lot. I don't care.'

'Yes, a prayer,' says Plexippus, hastily. 'Atalanta speaks well. It is right to do so.'

Toxeus screws up his face as though chewing wormwood. He flounces to the edge of the clearing and plants himself on a hummock, swearing he'd rather eat his own vomit than pray over a dead pig. With one hand under each of her armpits, Plexippus and I raise Atalanta into a sitting position. We gather in a bruised congregation and make what meagre leave-taking as we are able. No one can remember any prayers, and Toxeus's complaints of how he's sore and thirsty make pious words impossible. The instant we're done, he leaps up, produces a long dagger and starts sawing off the trotters.

'By all that is sacred,' I say. 'Can't you leave well alone?'

'I demand the feet,' whines Toxeus. 'And the tusks. And the head.'

'No,' I say. 'It is Atalanta's prize, by rights.'

More men arrive, and watch the ignoble pantomime open-mouthed. Kepheus speaks up.

'Meleager speaks truly, Toxeus. That's Atalanta's spear. It was there first. She made the kill. To her go the spoils.'

Toxeus rounds on him. 'Who asked you, gutter-brat?'

Peleus and Telamon step forward, a brace of fellows as bulky as a siege engine. They gather their hands into fists. Toxeus blanches. Plexippus holds up a palm in a gesture of peace-making.

'Comrades, comrades,' he says. 'My nephew spoke in the heat of exertion.' Exertion my eye, I think. He's not even broken a sweat. 'Didn't you, Toxeus?' adds Plexippus, opening his eyes wide in a warning.

Toxeus twists his lips into an insincere smile. 'By the Gods, Peleus, it was a joke. Don't take on so.'

Peleus and Telamon step down.

'I'll not waste breath on a man dressed for a night at the theatre rather than a hunt,' says Peleus, throwing Toxeus a look of chilly disdain. 'Meleager, if your brother knows what's good for him, he'll curb his tongue. Out of respect for you I shall leave him with his head attached to his neck.'

'And I've had my fill of this unseemly bickering,' says Telamon, wiping his brow with the back of his hand. 'I've seen finer manners displayed in a harbourside whorehouse.'

They turn to go.

'Peleus,' I call after him. 'By your good grace, carry Atalanta to a doctor.'

'That I shall, Meleager,' he says. He glances from one of us to the other and spits. 'We'll see you back in camp.'

They hoist Atalanta into their arms and carry her away. Many follow them, muttering excuses. I don't blame them. The boar is slain and the victors are tussling like dogs over a bone. The audience dwindle to three, then two, and finally we are left to our sorry selves. As soon as all onlookers are out of sight and hearing, Toxeus resumes hacking at the carcase. I grab his arm and yank him aside.

'For the last time, Toxeus, leave it be,' I say. 'It is Atalanta's.'

'Don't tell me what I can and can't do!' he bawls, voice rising to a squeak.

'Listen to me, Nephew,' coos Plexippus. 'Give the lass her due. I've never seen the like and neither have you.'

'What's she going to do to stop us?' says Toxeus. 'She's not here. She's halfway to Hades. With luck, the Gods will finish the job before we're back in camp.'

I draw back my arm and deal Toxeus a punch that sends him bowling head over heels into a thorn bush.

'How dare you!' he howls. 'I'll . . . Ow! Plexippus, get me out of this damned bush so I can kill Meleager.'

I throw Plexippus a look of entreaty. It is in vain. He may have been able to calm the boy, but the man is beyond anyone's reach.

'I am son of Apollo!' squalls Toxeus, clambering out of the undergrowth.

'Not again with that cock and bull story,' I say. 'You're laughable.'

'I demand the hide,' bleats Toxeus, picking spines out of his backside. 'You're not giving it to a bloody woman.'

'How often have I got to say this before it sinks in to that thick skull of yours?' I say. 'She dealt the first blow.'

'And I the last.'

'It was dead by then. Flat on its back with its trotters in the air.'

'Lies! Son of a—'

'Have a care, Brother,' I say. 'Or you shall insult our esteemed mother.'

'Uncle!' Toxeus shrieks, face flaring with furious blood.

'Lads, lads,' purrs Plexippus. 'Meleager, for the love of all that is holy, award him the hide. Give him something. Anything. He's your brother.'

'No.'

'Please, Meleager. Or we'll never hear the end of it.'

'For once, Uncle, no.'

'I'll take the whole boar if I want,' shrills Toxeus, waving his knife wildly. 'You can't stop me!'

'For the first time in your life you're not going to get your own way by whining,' I say. 'Be a man, and don't just wear the appearance of one.'

The boar's head is massing with flies, blue-black and glittering. There is a lull, like the leaden pause before a storm breaks. Toxeus is the one to start it. No, that is untrue. The commencement of our suffering was many years ago. It is too late to reach back and weave a happier fate for the two of us.

The Gods alone know how many prayers I have offered up. I've learnt to my cost that the Gods do not care.

With a squeal of thwarted fury, Toxeus lunges, brandishing his dagger. If I weren't so quick on my feet, he would finish me then and there. I'm a soldier, and soldiers spend their lives on their toes. With the lightning reactions of an old campaigner, I leap sideways before the blade can get in its sly blow. Toxeus is unprepared for my swift reaction and follows the force of the thrust, tumbling forwards and planting facedown in the dirt.

I stretch out a hand. 'Toxeus,' I say warmly. 'Stop, I beg you. Let us . . .'

He scrambles to his feet, fast as a rat, and stabs at me. Once again I dance out of reach. I grab his arm and squeeze until his fingers grow limp and the dagger falls to the ground.

'You're hurting me!' he yowls.

'Lads, lads!' bleats Plexippus.

'Call him to heel, Uncle,' I hiss. 'He won't listen to me.'

Toxeus struggles to free himself from my grip, screaming and yelling. He calls on the Gods to strike me down, calls me a by-blow of a slut, a misbegotten cur, a filthy whoreson, a whole host of vulgar slurs of the sort boys toss at each other. I draw back my free hand and smack him across the chops. He sucks in a shocked breath, clutches his cheek. I think he may burst into tears. The silence holds for the time it takes to swallow a mouthful of wine.

'Struck by my own brother!' he wails. 'Let the Gods witness how cruelly I am treated!'

311

'Cruelly treated? You just tried to kill me!'

'Lads, lads,' repeats Plexippus, waggling his hands.

I round on my uncle. 'And for the love of the Gods, stop quacking like a duck and do something useful!'

I'm only distracted for an instant. In that instant, Toxeus deals me a kick between the legs. Searing agony shoots an arrow from my ballocks to my brain. I let go of him and collapse, grasping my aching groin. While I'm down, he kicks me again, springs across the clearing and retrieves his knife. Through a dizzying haze of nausea, I see Plexippus stretch out a hand.

'Easy now, Nephew,' he says softy, curling his fingers. 'Give your uncle Plexippus the knife.'

'Shut up, you old goat!' squeaks Toxeus.

He swings the blade wildly and slices through Plexippus's raised wrist. Blood fountains across the clearing, the alarming bright red of poppies. Plexippus gawps at the spray, pulsing to the rhythm of his heartbeat. His jaw goes slack, mouth flops open.

'I . . .' he gasps.

He sinks to his knees, clutching his wrist. Gore streams through his fingers. Toxeus stands there, wearing the smirk of nasty victory I recognise from boyhood. I want to pound his nose till it breaks, but there's not a moment to waste.

I hobble to my uncle's side. His breath is shuddering in and out, his gaze locked to the weakening flow of heart's-blood. Frantically, I search for something I can make into a tourniquet. I'm wearing a leather kilt. My cloak is back at the camp. Toxeus's cape is uncreased and neatly pinned. I grasp the hem, tear off a strip and bind it around Plexippus's arm.

'Hey!' squeaks Toxeus. 'That cloak cost me a king's ransom!'

'It cost you nothing,' I mutter, twisting the band tight. 'I'll wager you fluttered your eyelashes at Althea and she bought it for you. Nothing too expensive for her dearest sweetling.'

Toxeus mutters an oath I'm too busy to hear. Plexippus turns watery eyes to mine and shakes his head. Black dye is leaking from his brow and beard, drizzling down his chest. The bleeding has ebbed to a trickle. His skin is grey, his lips pale.

'Bless you, Meleager,' he whispers. 'May all the Gods exalt your name.'

He pitches forwards, lets out a rattling wheeze and is gone.

'Uncle!' I cry. I turn on Toxeus. 'You did this!'

Toxeus blinks. For the first time in both of our sorry lives, I have him on the back foot. He glances left and right. There's no one to come to his rescue, no one to whom he can whinge.

'Me?' he says, voice wavering. I watch his expression shift from fear to malice. 'Not a chance. You're the one covered in our uncle's blood.' His voice strengthens as he grows in devious confidence. 'You're the one clutching his body. Like a murderer.' He licks his lips. 'I'll tell everyone you did it.'

'As if they'll believe you. You're holding the knife, you idiot.'

Toxeus startles, as though only that moment noticing the weapon in his hand. I think he'll throw it away. Fool that he is, he charges at me a third time, snarling. A third time, I

313

reach up and grab his flailing arm. He somersaults in a clumsy arc. Head over heels he goes and lands on the dagger, heavy as a sack of barley. I dash to his side and roll him over. The knife is plunged into his chest, up to the hilt. We are nose to nose, eye to eye.

'Toxeus,' I say, covering his stupid, deluded face with kisses. 'Brother. I swear I did not mean . . . You should have let go.'

A crimson flower is blossoming on his spotless tunic. His eyes grow dim and distant. He draws in a shallow breath.

'I hate you,' he gasps. 'Hate. You.'

ATALANTA

Calydon

I surface from the well of oblivion to find myself in the hands of a physician who is slathering my wounds with unguent. He is kindly, unlike many a sawbones, and possesses the skills of a man well-versed in patching up warriors on a battlefield. I submit to his deft prodding. When I grunt thanks, he grunts in return.

'The others,' I wheeze. 'Meleager?'

'He has not returned,' he replies, bending my leg to test for fractures.

I float in and out on a tide of consciousness. In the place between sleeping and waking, I dream I am upon Olympos. I see a weaver's cottage, hear the singing of children and recognise the voices of my guardian spirits. They race from the hut and dash to my side, crying, *Sister! Hurry!* I reach out my arms to embrace them, when a shout goes up and I startle awake, flat on my back in the hospital tent.

The alarum is sounded again and without thinking, I'm on my feet. I yelp with pain and fall back onto the pallet. I try again, wincing. Pain is of no importance. All my thoughts are of Meleager. He pulled me from under the boar. He nursed me with wine. He was arguing with his brother. I struggle to my feet and stagger to the tent-opening, hanging onto the flap. A man, one of the beaters I think, bursts out of the trees and into the camp.

'Dead!' he screams. 'The boar! Meleager! Gods! They are dead!'

His words are so scrambled I can't work out who or what is dead. I sieve through my scattered thoughts, trying to recall what happened, but my last memory is of being borne away. Unbidden, the awful vision of two funeral pyres returns. My heart is gripped in ice. No. It cannot be Meleager. He cannot be dead.

I hear more voices, also mangled and unclear. Using a snapped spear-shaft as a makeshift crutch, I make my way gingerly out of the tent. Men dash left to right, without pausing to answer my questions. I hobble to the man who brought the first message. He is half-sitting and half-fallen by a pile of discarded spears.

'What of Meleager?' I croak, grabbing his arm.

He blinks rapidly. I am unsure if he can see me. 'I cannot. It is too terrible,' he babbles. 'Oh, Meleager!'

I squeeze tight. Blood wells up where my nails dig into his flesh. He is so far gone into shock that he does not notice.

'Meleager,' I growl. 'Tell me now. Does he live?'

My answer steps from the shadows of the forest. It is Meleager, although not the beloved friend I saw less than an hour ago. While I've been sprawled on my backside being pampered by a doctor, a cruel God has plunged to earth and stolen Meleager away. In his place stands a ruin of a man. His eyes peer out of dark pits, his cheeks have shrivelled to the bone, his jaw is slack. From the matted hair on his head to the torn soles of his sandals he's clothed in blood, tight and shining as a second skin.

He raises an arm. It flaps woodenly, as though a puppet master is tugging a string.

'My uncle, Plexippus.' He swallows, licking cracked lips. 'My brother, Toxeus.' He speaks with the uncertainty of a lad learning his letters and clumsy with long words. 'They are . . .'

The unspoken end of the sentence is revealed as a group of hunters, bows slung across their backs, carry two bodies into the clearing. Meleager stands still as a statue daubed in red ochre, and watches as the corpses are laid upon the ground.

'Lay your cloaks beneath them!' he shouts.

The command breaks the spell. Half a dozen cloaks are spread. Meleager falls to his knees.

'Toxeus!' he wails. 'Hear me! Your brother Meleager weeps for you!' He wipes his nose on the back of his hand. 'Plexippus!' he cries. 'Hear me! Your nephew Meleager weeps for you!'

No man cries a refrain. No beast or bird stirs. The shades of Toxeus and Plexippus are already a long way off. The silence thickens. After the time it takes to drink a large cup of wine, Meleager says, *Burn them.*

The slaying of the boar ought to be the greatest celebration in the history of Aetolia. It takes six men to carry the hide up the sanctuary steps, as many acolytes to arrange it upon the altar. They prop the severed head on top, where it sits, masked by blowflies that sip from the corner of its eyes. Temple incense hovers, dense as autumn fog. The priests pour libations and chant noisy thanks and prayers. They roar my name, but when they get to Meleager's, they stammer like whipped boys. He is a kin-slayer.

I can't listen to the muddle of gratitude and fear. I climb down the sanctuary steps into the public square, where a crowd of men are building funeral pyres for all the slain hunters, including Toxeus and Plexippus. They shout instructions and commands, busying themselves with tasks in order to take their minds off what Meleager has done. As long as they keep moving, as long as they keep blaring, *More wood! No, here, you fool!* then all will be well and they can escape unpleasant thoughts. I do not wish to be here when they run out of things to do. If I am honest, I do not wish to be here at all.

Meleager and I are bruised and battered, but breathing. My vision was clearly of the pyres of Toxeus and Plexippus. I ought to feel relief, but prickle with unease. I must find Meleager, must hear his version of the matter from his lips.

Trying to speak to him is like trying to catch the wind in a fishing net. He will not meet my eye. Every time I get close, he sinks back like a shade. I wonder if he is avoiding me, or is simply lost in a daze of grief. I believe I could jump up and down, shouting his name and waving, and he'd totter past, unseeing and unhearing. Men shrink from his touch, fearful of being infected with the taint of death he wears like a mantle.

The bodies of the dead are laid atop the stacked logs, Toxeus and Plexippus on the highest heap. The scent of pine and myrrh is unable to disguise the quick ripeness of decay. Priests wave their hands and warble incantations over the corpses. They may be the same priests, they may be different. Every man looks the same. The only one in the length and breadth of Calydon who stands out is Meleager. Prayers drone like the buzzing of crickets. I have had a bellyful of priests today. I've had a bellyful of everything.

I want to scream, *Can't you see what ails Meleager? Will no one shake his hand, call him brother, and draw him from the wilderness of the mind in which he is wandering?* No one moves. No one offers comfort. We are helpless as prisoners, each of us locked in a separate cell, unable to find release.

Twilight falls, and I'm grateful for the concealing darkness. Meleager steps forward, weeping openly, and thrusts the first torch deep into Toxeus's pyre. One after the other, we toss firebrands. The timber has been drenched in pitch and burns fast and fierce. Smoke belches in a heavy cloud, unable or unwilling to rise to the heavens. I can bear it no longer. I plough through the smog to Meleager's side and stand close, not daring to touch, but close enough to feel his warmth. We stare into the flames.

'I have sent word to my mother,' he says. He speaks stiffly, as to an audience, not a lover.

'Meleager?'

'I must comfort her.'

'What of your own comfort?' From what he's told me of Althea, it's unlikely he'll receive a drop of kindness from that quarter.

His head twitches. 'For all his faults, Toxeus was my brother. I give him full honours, as he deserves.'

'You are generous, Meleager. A good man.'

'Am I?'

At last, he looks me in the eye. The Goddess help me, I wish he did not. His expression is so haunted it is an agony to hold his gaze.

'I have killed my brother,' he whispers.

'He ran onto his own knife when trying to kill you!' I hiss.

'I am to blame.'

'He killed Plexippus!'

'Wasted lives,' he murmurs.

'Not wasted, Meleager. The hunt was . . .'

'Do not say glorious. By all the Gods, do not say that.'

I clutch his forearm, which is still coated in dried blood. He observes my hand coldly. A few hours ago, the touch would have resounded with urgent music. Now, there is no quickening. The doors of our bodies and spirits are closed to each other. I have lost the sweet Meleager whose love I tasted only last night.

He blinks. 'I must go,' he croaks.

'Once, you promised never to run from me. You are fleeing now.'

His shoulders sag with an unbearable weariness. 'I am not. I could never do such a thing. I am running from myself.'

'But I must speak to you . . .'

'No, you must not. There will be time, but the time is not now. Soon.'

'Meleager, I—'

He lurches away and I lack the strength to follow.

As though waiting for permission to release its pent-up fury, the rain begins. The pyres fizzle, but burn on into the night. When the funeral feast begins, I creep away. I can't sit through the celebrations, watching Meleager grim as a spectre. I shall leave him to drink away the keen edge of his misery and we will talk on the morrow.

I climb to the Holy of Holies to pray for comfort. Out of the downpour, the air is perfectly still. If I dropped a feather it would drift to the ground in a straight line.

'Oh Holy Artemis,' I say to the emptiness. 'The boar is dead. Meleager is saved. My vision of the pyres was of Toxeus and Plexippus. Yet I am troubled, and seek your guidance.'

The air begins to quiver, a vibration stirring the shadows. To the eye of the body, the sanctuary is empty. To the eye of the spirit, it swells from floor to ceiling with the presence of the Goddess. I never felt the boundary between her world and mine to be so fragile.

I gather up my courage. 'Blessed Artemis,' I whisper. 'I beg of you, grant peace to Meleager.'

A shimmering pearlescence dances around the altar and my messengers appear, bobbing upon the air as a fishing skiff upon a gentle sea.

'Thank you, oh Goddess!' I say, relieved that my kindly guardians are close. With their support and succour I shall be able to endure this miserable night.

Sister! they cry.

'Why do you call me sister?' I reply. 'I have no sisters.'

By way of answer, they step forward and lay their hands upon me. I am filled with wrenching fire that turns my bones to ash.

'Stop,' I beg. 'I cannot . . .'

They will not release me.

We wished to spare you, they say. *We can do so no longer.*

With their words, my immortal self sweeps into my frail mortal body. The gates of memory burst open and a flood of remembrance breaks upon me in a cascade, threatening to drown all that is Atalanta. I grit my teeth and keep her afloat in the deluge of understanding: I am Clotho of The Moirai. I spin the thread of mortal destiny. The two guardians are my sisters Lachesis and Atropos. Lachesis measures the thread I spin, and Atropos cuts it with her shears. I am endless and undying. I am older than the Gods. And Meleager hates me, for cursing him with a cruel fate.

'Sisters,' I wheeze. 'Stop. It is too much . . .'

Beloved sister. There is no time to waste. You must find Meleager.

'And tell him I am Clotho of The Fates? I cannot. I am

322

afraid. His hatred for we three sisters is fierce enough to reduce our love to ashes.'

Do not doubt the power of love. Please, sister. Find him.

'He is grieving.'

The vision!

'It was of other men. There is no need for alarm.'

There was more in your vision! A ship with black sails. It is not for Toxeus and Plexippus. It is Meleager's. He is sailing to his mother. To his death.

'No!' I cry. 'He promised not to run away!'

You must hurry! they cry. *Go now. You cannot save him. And yet you are the only one who will.*

I have no time to work out the riddle. I rush from the Holy of Holies to the temple precinct, where the pyres are smoking. The sound of the funeral feast is a muted rumble of snores and half-hearted song. I shiver, despite my cloak, and turn my gaze upwards. Night is giving way to morning. But I was in the temple for moments, surely.

The sky tells a different story, shot through with the crimson flashes of approaching dawn. Wisps of pinkish cloud are combed into long fluffy strands, as a spinner teases out the wool before hooking it onto the distaff. I tell myself the heavens are touched by the hand of Artemis herself, though a nagging caution reminds me a red sky at this hour is an ill omen. I dash down the steps and run straight into Kleitos. He can't have slept either, the shadows around his eyes dark as pitch.

'Your reward!' he bleats, hoisting a leather satchel. 'I've been looking for you everywhere! The feast . . .'

323

'I've been praying,' I say, trying to untangle myself from his grasp without seeming rude.

'The Goddess!' he squeaks. 'She blesses us?'

'Yes, Kleitos. All is forgiven.' He drops to his knees and sobs like a child. I shake his shoulder gently. 'Lord Kleitos. I must find Meleager.'

'Oh,' he says, clambering to his feet and drying his eyes on his sleeve. 'He went in the night.'

'He's *gone?*'

'He left a message.' Kleitos clears his throat. 'I regret my harsh words. Grief is a poor master of my tongue and I hope you can find it in your generous heart to forgive me. It is a short journey to my mother's house. I must tell her. I shall be gone a day only. When I return, we shall not be parted.'

My stomach sinks to my sandals. His mother. The half-burned log. The Fate we wove, so carefully and so cruelly. Meleager promised to wait. He *promised*. Why did I believe him? I close my eyes, but the glare of the rising sun follows, searing green and orange ghosts upon the back of my eyelids. When I open them, Kleitos is forcing my share of the bounty upon me, and the only way I can escape is to accept.

Meleager has a head start.

I run faster than I've ever done, but no one can outrun time, especially not when burdened by a bag clanking with coins. At the jetty, I rouse a bleary-eyed steersman, who wakes promptly when he sees the heap of gold I tip at his feet. The barge drags itself downriver at a slug's pace and I have to swallow my desperation so as not to scream at the crew. I may be Clotho of The Moirai, but I am sealed in mortal flesh: the mightiest power in the cosmos at the whim of a river-captain.

A day ago, these fields were abandoned. The sun is barely over the ridge of the hills, but already the land is thronged with farmers reclaiming their wounded meadows. We crawl past a wheat-field that was a mound of stinking straw and is already half cleared. Men are raking the rotted and mouldy stalks aside, forking them into heaps and setting them on fire. Filthy smoke rises, reminding me uncomfortably of the pyres.

Women and girls, skirts bundled to the knee, follow their menfolk, sifting through bare earth. Or at least, it seems bare. With a more careful glance, I realise they are seeking out seedlings, sprung from fallen grain. They cry out cheerfully at each tiny discovery, pressing dirt around the fragile roots. One lass peers at me through draggled curls and waves, her body illuminated with joy. She couldn't be happier if she found a pot full of silver. I straighten my spine and think how swiftly our mother Gaia renews herself, and with only the slightest encouragement.

My captain yells that he is carrying Atalanta herself, the slayer of the boar. Folk watch wide-eyed, leaning on hay rakes. If they've heard about Meleager and the deaths of Toxeus and Plexippus, it's clear they care little for the family feuds of unknown men. The boar is slain, the land is healing and that's all they need to know.

I wish I shared their indifference.

At last, the barge reaches the harbour. Fast or slow has made not one whit of difference. I could have ridden piggyback on

Hermes or hitched a ride in Hera's chariot. I am too late. Meleager's ship has sailed, the billowing black sails a memory. I stare at the horizon, a dark and empty line dividing sea from sky. The words of my sisters ring in my head.

You cannot save him. And yet you are the only one who will.

I am not finished yet. I find the swiftest ship in port and offer half the remainder of my reward for passage round the cape; promise the captain the entire sackful if he can get me there before Meleager docks. He does his lusty best, and we fly over the wave-tips, borne on the shoulders of Poseidon. We do not outrace Meleager, but we come close. At the harbour, I'm told he only berthed two hours before.

Hurry, my sisters are urging.

Everyone knows the name of Althea, and clucks sympathetically at the mention of her name. I follow the harbour-master's pointing finger and race up the cliff path, blessing the vitality of my mortal body. In all my years, I never ran so urgent a race. I have the constitution of a charging horse, but even I am panting when I reach the summit. I fly to Althea's cottage and burst in without knocking.

'Stop!' I cry.

My world stops turning.

ZEUS

Mount Olympos

The Throne of the Gods

Just when it seems I will never find a solution, the idiot Fates play into my hands. The Oracle reveals their secret: they are going to surrender their immortality. I need do nothing to bring about their fall.

'How clever you are,' murmurs Hera, 'to plant such a clever idea in their heads.'

Hera is correct. It is exactly what I must have done. There is no other conceivable reason why immortals would choose to shrug off their tremendous power. I am in a fine mood. Even Dionysus's awful poetry cannot put me out of joint. Hera rubs her thigh against mine.

'Beloved husband,' she coos. 'I have scented out a new diversion for you. Look. Upon earth. A mortal named Atalanta.'

I wave the words aside.

'My lord. There is something about her. She smells different.'

'Aye, she does that!' crows Eros, holding his nose. 'Like a she-goat in season!'

'Her face is no better,' Ares chips in. 'If I had a goat with a face as ugly as hers, I'd teach it to walk backwards!'

Hera ignores the ribald laughter. 'My lord Zeus,' she continues. 'About Atalanta. I think you should . . .'

'Should?' I hiss, a warning the stupid woman ignores.

'I have been observing this Atalanta and there is something different . . .'

I slam my goblet onto the table. 'Away with your empty opinions!' I cry. 'Since the Oracle gave the good news, I have no interest in unwashed females. Mortal women are too revolting to touch with the smallest of my divine fingers.'

'My lord, I—'

'I?' I roar. 'I? This is the heart of the matter, is it not? Hera, Hera, Hera. I, I, I. Everything is about you and your desires. Oh my lord,' I wheedle, imitating her maddening drone. 'Toy with this female. Toy with that female. Smite Themis's brats. On and on and no peace until I do your bidding. I, Lord of Olympos, at his nagging wife's beck and call.'

'But this Atalanta makes the man Meleager happy. I thought you wanted him miserable.'

'Don't tell me what I want and don't want!'

'But what about taunting him with his cruel and unfair destiny?'

'What of it? When he dies, it will be her turn to be miserable. You see? Everyone will be miserable. Success.'

'I only suggest—'

'Again, that word I. The last time I listened to your suggestions, I made a fool of myself.' I hear the sound of stifled

328

giggles. If it is Apollo, I swear I shall reduce him to a smear of ashes, son or no son. I glare at the company. Stony-faced, every last cowardly blackguard. I point at Hera. 'Yes. I, Zeus, King of the Gods, made a laughing-stock by my esteemed spouse.'

'In that case, with your permission, I shall seek out this Atalanta and—'

I round on her. 'And what?' I say. 'Take over my settling of scores? Usurp my power? That's just what you'd like, isn't it?'

'My king, no!'

It's not often I see true fear in Hera's eyes. It is delicious and I want more. I grab her by the artfully tailored curls piled atop her head. 'You shall obey me,' I hiss, dragging her to the floor. 'You shall sit here and hold your tongue, or I shall cut it out and serve it to you in a pastry.'

That shuts her up. I glare at my immortal kindred, licking their lips in anticipation.

'You lot too. Not another word. Unless you wish to find yourself keeping Scylla and Charybdis company!'

Hera spends the evening worming her way back into my affections, dabbing her eyes and sobbing delicately, surrounded by a flock of cooing sycophants. I shall not give in and be entangled in her web. Not while everyone is watching over the brim of their cups.

I grin. I possess knowledge far more suited to my power than the obliteration of a guttersnipe mortal. The Fates are stepping down from immortality. Perfect! I could not destroy the endless Moirai, but the moment they shrug off their might – well, that is a different matter. I shall crush them as easily as an insignificant spider.

Hera sidles alongside, pressing her generous breasts against my spine. She has her advantages, all things considered.

'How shall you crush The Fates, mighty Zeus?' she asks, as though she's been eavesdropping on my thoughts. Her breathing is shallow and hurried, little puffs of air she sucks through pursed lips. 'Tell me.'

'They will die in agony.'

'Oh, good,' she says, clapping her hands together. 'I can almost hear their shrieks of terror.'

'There is more,' I say, patting her arm. 'I am not finished yet. I shall incinerate them into a smouldering heap.'

'Oh yes,' she murmurs, a flush creeping across her perfect breasts. 'Is there more? I do hope there is more.'

'I shall toss their ashes to the four winds.'

'Oh, husband,' says Hera avidly, squeezing out her words in excited gasps. 'You have the most thrillingly inventive schemes. Go on.'

I am warming to my theme. 'They will be portrayed as vile harridans, wrinkled and foul, breasts dangling to their knees.'

'So clever!' Hera breathes, her gaze rapt. 'More.'

'They will be named unnatural, fearsome, hags.'

'More.'

'They shall be reviled through the ages.'

'More!'

'Mortals will spit on their name.'

'Yes! Oh by the Gods, yes!' she cries and falls back upon her cushions, spent.

'Ah, Hera,' I say fondly. 'There is none to match your wildness. It is why I took you to wife.'

'Oh, my king,' she says huskily. 'My whole being flutters at the memory of that day.'

'The others mean nothing: dryads, nereids, mortals. Nothing compares to you.'

'You do me too much honour,' she purrs, a little moan at the back of her throat. 'I kneel before you.'

I crook a finger and chuck her under the chin. 'Little wife,' I say fondly. She really is adorable. 'You no longer need to kneel.'

She peers up through lowered eyelashes. 'Do I not, my lord?' she asks coyly, and runs a fingernail along the inside of my thigh.

MELEAGER

Calydon

Althea will hear the news from my lips first. I commandeer the fastest ship and when I disembark, take to my heels so as to outrace gossip of my arrival in a ship with black sails. Toxeus and Plexippus are dead. Even if not by my hand, I am surely guilty.

Therios tired of Althea a long time ago, and packed her off to a deserted crag on the outskirts of the town. One husband dead, another distant. I climb the track threading up the headland to her eyrie, and am staggering and breathless by the time I reach the crest. A north-easterly is blowing sharply enough to pierce my cloak with its claws. Scrubby tamarisks crouch, heads down against the gale. In my ears, the insistent keening of gulls.

Her cottage perches on the cliff-top overlooking the harbour, door swaying on its leather hinge. I have rushed here faster than the winds, and now am unsure whether to call her name or turn around and walk away. Unsure how to begin the most difficult conversation of my life.

Mother, your brother Plexippus is dead. Your beloved son Toxeus is dead. I slew him. I am your eldest son Meleager, and I am a murderer.

'Come in if you're coming in.'

Althea's voice floats through the door, shrill as a seabird. I duck my head and step under the lintel into the shadowed room that is her kingdom. It takes a moment for my eyes to adjust to the darkness. A stamped dirt floor, a bronze lamp on spindly legs, a brassbound wooden chest. A hearth in the centre, a hole in the roof to let out the smoke.

'A palace, is it not?' she snips. 'Secluded, inaccessible, and cheap. One room, one chair, one footstool. One body servant, and one old retainer to observe the niceties. What more does a woman need? A generous man, my husband Therios,' she spits. An emerald fly thumps against the wall, searching for a way out. 'He says the bracing air is good for my health.'

'Mother, I must speak.'

She continues as though I'm not there. 'Ah yes. My esteemed spouse banished me to this paradise when I became too public a source of entertainment for our neighbours, and the supply of sons dried up after Toxeus.'

It's a complaint I've heard a myriad times. Althea is a storyteller with few examples in her store. She clutches her chiton about her bony frame, head swaying side to side. The Gods forgive me, I think of a cow with the staggers.

'My lovely Toxeus,' she mutters. 'Now, there's a son who loves his mother.'

'I have news of Toxeus.'

She continues to ignore me. 'I suppose you'll be wanting wine and bread. There is none. My slave is away fetching the meagre rations Therios deigns to bestow,' she says, with a languid flap of the hand. She sniffs, wipes her nose on her arm. 'I suppose you can sit. If you wish it.'

'Mother.'

'I am that woman, it is true,' she says, chewing the inside of her cheek. 'Yes, Therios is so generous to his cast-off wife that he sends a basket of leftovers every day. Oh fortunate Althea!'

'Listen to me, for the love of the Gods!'

She tilts her face to mine. I open my mouth and close it, unable to speak. In the end I close my eyes so I do not have to look at her as I impart the news for which I travelled here. I think it will take me until nightfall to explain, but the words slip quickly from my tongue. It is done in less time than it takes to drain a small flagon of wine.

When I open my eyes again, Althea is staring at me in such a vacant fashion I'm not sure she's heard a word. The moment swings a plumb-line, slow and leaden. She drags in a guttering breath and throws herself at me, screeching like one of the Furies.

'You've taken my beloved Toxeus!' she howls, pounding my breast with puny fists. 'He was all I had!'

I snort, bitterly. 'And yet your eldest son stands before you.'

Once again, she cannot, or will not, hear. 'You have destroyed my life!' she squalls.

'No, you have done that for yourself.'

She stumbles across the floor of the room, wrenches open

the chest. Inside is the half-burned log. She has kept it all these years. For some reason, I thought it might have got lost in one of her voyages from household to household, husband to husband.

'See?' she says. 'I have kept this safe your whole life. I, your mother, have saved you from the jaws of death. And now it is in my power to send you into them.'

Despite myself, my hand creeps to the little pouch I wear around my neck. No. I shall not join Althea in her tangled web of superstition.

'Again, with the same old threat. You never act upon it. Empty words, Mother.'

'Empty words?' she shrieks. 'It is the curse of The Fates: *When the log burns away, the boy will die.*'

For years and years Althea has sung this tune. For years and years we've gone round and round in this barren, endless dance. I have had enough.

'Do it, then!' I bellow. 'It's a lump of bloody wood!'

Althea stands stiff as a grave slab, her only movement an erratic blinking. As I watch, she tosses the log into the fire. A small flame licks the unburned portion and finds it tasty. I am battle-hardened, but nothing prepares me for the torrent of agony that sweeps in, wrenching a cry from deep in my throat. A force greater than an oaken club knocks me to my knees; knocks me again onto all fours.

'Yes!' shrills Althea. 'Down, like the dog you are!'

'Mother, no,' I gasp, dragging myself towards the hearth, and it comes to me that I'm crawling towards the same

335

burning brand as Althea did on the night of my birth, and as desperately.

'I want you dead,' she whines. 'If you'd never been born, I'd have been happy.'

Larger flames leap, devouring the log in a burst of fire. It sinks into embers, fades to grey and winks out. It has taken scant moments, barely enough time to fasten a buckle. Another wave of pain crashes over my head. I do not die, but I venture perilously close to the brink.

Wearing the life-preserving splinter around my neck, I made the mistake of slipping into a lazy complacency, imagining the log had somehow lost its power. Now it has gone, I am stripped bare, hanging on by grace of a whisper of wood no bigger than a nail paring. I fight harder and harder, until I manage to hoist myself onto one knee.

'I have faced worse enemies,' I wheeze, a lie fooling nobody.

'No!' cries Althea. Her jaw hangs slack. 'The prophecy. You should be dead! Where is my curse!'

She starts to pound the remains of the log with her fists, sending up a cascade of sparks. I pull her away and she pummels me, her hands burned and bloody.

'Stop,' I say. 'You're hurting yourself.'

She claws at my face, screeching like an owl. 'I gave you life!' she babbles. 'It's mine to take or give. You killed Toxeus. You should be dead, not him.' Her talons snag around the little pouch. She tugs: the thong snaps. I grab for it, but in my weakened state she is able to hold it out

of reach. 'What's this?' she snorts. 'The esteemed warrior
Meleager wears a charm?'

'It contains a sliver of that log,' I say. 'As a boy, I tired of
your wheedling, so I stole a piece. I carried it for luck. To be
master of my Fate. This is my life, not yours.'

She stares at the amulet. The bronze sheen of leather worn
next to the skin for a score of summers. Her features sharpen;
her eyes flash, greedy and ravening.

'You *cheated*,' she hisses.

She tears at the pouch to get at the bit of wood, but the
stitching is old and tough. At that moment, the wall beside
Althea begins to glimmer, and from within appear the two
divine girls.

No! they cry.

Althea's head twitches. She can see them also. 'Demons!'
she squawks.

'Mother, calm yourself. These are guardians come to offer
help.'

'The prophecy must be fulfilled,' she mutters, gnawing
through the stitches and spitting shreds of ancient leather.
The splinter tumbles into her palm. She glowers at me, face
ghastly with triumph.

No! cry the girls, reaching out but unable to touch.

I do what they cannot and grapple Althea, pawing for the
splinter in her hand. 'Mother,' I beg. 'Listen. Please.'

She holds her arm away from me, clutching the splint so
tightly it digs into her flesh. Blood wells through her fingers.

'The prophecy. Your birth.' Her head wobbles, disconnected sounds bubbling from her lips. 'The Fates,' she says, pointing at the spirits.

'The Fates are three dread crones, Mother. These are two messengers sent by the Goddess in the form of children.'

I swear I hear the cracking of her spirit, though I suppose it is only the fire. She totters and falls, a tree axed at the root. I catch her, clasp her to my breast. She is frail as a bundle of twigs, her little frame consumed by shaking. I hang on tight, for fear she will fly into pieces. She takes in shallow gulps of air, her eyes blank and unseeing, skin clammy. With a final shudder so violent I am almost thrown off, she lets out a rattling wheeze and sinks into a deathly faint.

I press my face into her withered breasts and weep. Weep for the woman she might have been. For the grandchildren she might have dandled on her knee, the husbands who might have loved her. I mourn for every bitter, wasted moment of her unlived life. Driven out of her mind by The Fates. If she'd been left in peace, who knows what joys she might have tasted. But as the proverb goes, if wishes were horses, beggars would ride.

Althea takes in a guttering breath and her eyes snap open. She lives!

'Mother!'

Slippery as a weasel, she wriggles from my grasp. Her arm jerks out, the spillikin still pinched between forefinger and thumb. She holds it over the hearth. When I was a child,

Toxeus held a little wooden horse of mine above the fire, waiting for me to plead for mercy. I refused, and watched dry-eyed as he dropped it into the flames. I felt no terror then. I do now. The key to my life is in my mother's grasp.

'Don't,' I whisper, wringing my hands in desperation. 'By the Gods, Mother, I love you.'

'And I loathe you,' she hisses, face a mask of hatred.

Several things happen at once. The spirits wail, *Mercy!* The door bursts open and Atalanta falls through, panting like a war-charger.

'Meleager!' she yells.

Sister! cry the spirits, adding to the madness.

Althea's head snaps around. 'You want this?' she sneers, waving the splinter.

Atalanta springs forward. I am rooted to the spot, entranced as if under a spell.

'Too late,' Althea spits.

Until the last moment, part of me does not believe she will do it. Her hand snaps open. The splinter falls, drifting into the embers. It flares briefly, sending up a curl of orange flame. Atalanta thrusts her hand into the fire, scrabbling in the cinders. The flame sinks, and dies.

I topple like a felled bull.

'No!' wails Atalanta, dashing to my side and hugging me tight. 'He cannot die. He must not. Meleager, my love!'

The last thing I hear is my mother's voice. It sounds as though she is swept up in the squalling cackle of lunacy, but no. She is sobbing.

'My son! My beloved Meleager! Oh Gods! What have I done!'

I lose myself. The world dims and does not brighten again. I fall into the darkness, and there is no returning.

THE FATES

Olympos

A Time out of Time

Meleager is dead. He dies at the precise instant foretold in his destiny. He was but a half-day journey from Althea and the working-out of his fate. All Atalanta had to do was delay him by an hour, a moment. We are not blaming her. It is our fault, our most grievous fault.

We have failed. The Gods are watching now.

Zeus has won. There will be no freedom for humankind. They are doomed to stagger under the yoke of the Gods forever. It will be even worse than when we wove the fate of mortals. At least we were fair, and urged mortals to strive. Zeus will crush any sign of growth. He will grind mortals into mindless, craven puppets. Anyone who dares to raise their brow from the dirt and question his commands will be annihilated.

We hold the severed thread of Meleager's life in our hands, and we grieve. Legend says The Fates never shed a tear, but it is untrue. We cannot staunch the torrent of misery. There will be no second chance.

341

'Mother,' we sob. 'What can we do?'

'Nothing. It is finished.'

'We must do something.'

'Impossible,' says Themis. 'Meleager has crossed the river of Lethe and is in the Underworld.'

'Then we must turn back the wheel of Time!' cries Atropos.

Themis gathers us into her arms. 'He is gone. No man returns from Hades.'

'But we are The Fates! We are powerful!'

'Clotho spun the thread. Lachesis, you measured it. Atropos, you cut it. There is nothing you can do.'

'Make it possible. Spin him a new thread.'

'I do not spin the thread of life. Only Clotho can do that.'

We look at each other and share a soundless exclamation. *Yes, Clotho! She can save him!* We peer at Meleager's thread, exhausted and listless. If Clotho can spin the thread of life, who's to say she cannot wrangle new life into the old? Perhaps she can do what we cannot. Maybe it is imagination, maybe it is the force of our desire, but we are sure the end is glowing, faint and feeble as an ember in the ash of an abandoned hearth.

'Meleager,' we whisper, and breathe upon the tip to nurse the tiny flicker. 'We are holding you in the light.'

ATALANTA

Parthenion

I return to Hiereya and Pappas, there being nowhere else to go. The days slide past in a nightmare of nothingness. Meleager's fate has run its course. He is dead. I was supposed to be there on time to avert it. I have failed. The Plan has failed. I will live out a pointless, empty life and I will die. I think I will never sleep again, but am more exhausted than I thought it possible for a body to feel. For three nights I dream, and it is the same each night.

I stand on the corpse-road to Mount Tainaron, the Gate to the Underworld. The spectres of countless men and women trudge past, fluttering like smoke. Every grave stele I've seen shows the departed in the prime of life, unmarked and lovely. In my nightmare I am surrounded by a flock of hideous spectres: soldiers cradling spilled entrails; grey-skinned victims of river-fever; the staved, the pox-ridden, the stinking.

'Take me with you,' I beg, grabbing at a man who is trailing his shattered leg as a child drags a broken toy.

He neither shakes me off nor jostles me out of the way.

To him, I am as insubstantial as the breeze. I cling to a woman and my arms swim through her. She shuffles onwards, her eyes sunken pools that reflect the sky. Then, in the distance, I see him: Meleager. He shines bright as a new-forged blade in the midst of the stream of tarnished ghosts.

'Meleager!' I shout, leaping up and down and waving. 'My friend! I am here!'

He cannot hear me, pressed from all sides by phantoms, who are nudging him towards the gate. I have to reach him. I plough through the mob, and in the way of dreams, my feet are stuck fast in a sucking quagmire. The more frenzied my attempts to run, the slower I go.

'Meleager!' I scream. 'Can't you see where you're headed? Turn around, my love. Turn around!'

I flail my arms, drowning in the sticky glue of the un-dead and yelling, *Come back! Come back!* Meleager does not turn. I watch the speck of his head grow smaller and smaller until he is engulfed in the mouth of the Underworld. And I wake, panting and desolate.

I should cry out my devastation; should rend my clothes and honour Meleager with grief. I am cold and unreachable as granite. The barque of Time lets loose its moorings, the hours float in and out and I float with them. I do not resist when Pappas massages oil into my injured muscles, nor when Hiereya slathers me with poultices that make me smell like a dung heap. The villagers bring gifts that render me tongue-tied with gratitude: little pots of unguent, a dish of green olives, a waxen amulet to ward off the green festering of flesh.

Antiklea visits every day. She sucks her teeth at my straw-filled mattress and fetches a heap of down-filled cushions, which she spends a lot of time plumping up and arranging. I let myself be arranged. Slowly, my bones and body meld together until I begin to take on the appearance of Atalanta once more. The wounds of my spirit are another matter. I am Clotho of The Fates yet spend my days bundled up as a widow in her dotage, sipping broth. My immortality is a memory, like that of pain. The reasoning mind knows there was pain, but the stabbing intensity is at a remove.

'I grieve with you, beloved,' Antiklea says one afternoon. 'Meleager was half of your heart.'

She has always been able to see into the place where I keep my secrets, even those secrets hidden from myself. She begins to untangle my hair with her favourite comb, the one set with knobs of ebony. Sunlight patches the floor with red and gold, and I lose myself in the distracting glitter.

'The warp and weft of my spirit are fraying.'

'Yes. You are very far away,' she says, kissing me. 'I see you in a land beyond farthest Thule, where it is colder than the peak of Parthenion in winter. I see you lost, snow-blind and stumbling.'

She touches a fingertip to my cheek, catching tears I'm not aware I am shedding.

'I am lost,' I croak. 'I want to find my way back to you. I do not know how.'

'Atalanta. I will neither demand nor beg you to return. But when you are ready, I shall be waiting.'

My mind slithers with questions. What is a name that means Equal-in-Weight when I could not save Meleager? What sort of friend am I that I cannot undo the wrong done to him by Althea? I pause. The words of my sisters ring in my memory.

You cannot save him. And yet you are the only one who will.

At the time, I did not understand. I do, now. Don't know why I didn't think of it before. I am no ordinary mortal. I am Atalanta and also Clotho. I am an impossibility, therefore I shall do the impossible. I shall disrupt the power of Death itself. By breaking an even greater law than Fate, I shall send such a raging tide through the cosmos as to shake Olympos into sand and rubble.

The Plan shall not fail.

For the past few nights I have had one foot in the land of the dead. Now, the rest of me shall follow. I shall tread the road to Mount Tainaron, stride through the gates of the Underworld and stride back out again.

It cannot be done, whisper my sisters.

It must. Death is more powerful than Fate, and love is more powerful than Death. I shall return with Meleager, or I shall not return at all.

I carry only a wineskin, bow and quiver, and the clothes on my back. Although it feels far longer, it is the journey of a handful of days. Rearing up from the sea are pale, beetling cliffs tormented by the screeching of seabirds. The only boatswain I can persuade to row me within a bowshot of Mount Tainaron does not pause long enough to ship oars. By the time I'm wading ashore through the shallows, he's paddling away. I reflect how my most common view of boats is of them leaving.

I know the path well, having dreamed it for three nights. Even if I did not, it is impossible to ignore the endless procession winding up the hill. As in my dream, the world's dead are gathering, heads lowered and trudging like cattle returning to the byre at the close of a weary day.

Unlike my dream, I am cautious. Impetuous Atalanta would barge to the front of the line, firing arrows left and right. Impetuous Atalanta would swear to fight a hundred champions to save Meleager. Impetuous Atalanta would be detected and denied entrance.

I learnt craftiness from my mother Arktos. She taught me how to wait till dawn, when bees are at their drowsiest, before swiping a hunk of honeycomb. I do not hurl myself at the ghosts, demanding to be let through. I slump my shoulders and join the troop, matching their sleepwalker gait. No one chases me away or tells me I have no business to be there. One shuffling step after the other, we trudge towards our destination.

Herakles entered by this road, as did Orpheus. Both of them returned. Orpheus brought Euridike, but he looked back and lost her. I will not look back. Persephone returned but for only half the year because she ate six pomegranate seeds. I will not touch a bite, and pray Meleager has not eaten the food of the dead, or else he is as lost as Persephone.

Ahead, the mouth of the cave gapes, swallowing all. For the first time in my life, my courage fails. A chill prickles the nape of my neck and I step off the path. This is no dream from which I can awake. What form of lunacy makes me imagine I can save Meleager?

I can outrun a deer, shoot an arrow to the furthest target, but neither are of any use against the terrors of the Underworld. I am a mortal female. I lack the strength of Herakles, and unlike Orpheus, I cannot coax a single bewitching note out of a lyre. I must turn around. No one will criticise me. They think I'm a madwoman as it is. I can return, live out my life in the service of Artemis, and grow fat on tales of how I killed the Calydonian boar.

As if in response, my sisters appear. They wring their hands, hope and desperation writ clear on their faces. *Be strong, sister*, they say.

If I return without trying, there is no point in returning at all. My neighbours may not look down on me, but I shall forever look down on myself. I grit my teeth. As a mortal, I have lived a courageous and fortunate life. If my luck is to run out, I think wryly, this is the most convenient place on earth to do my dying.

Hurry, they murmur. *Beloved sister, make haste!*

With them at my side, I can do anything. I rejoin the march of the dead. We enter the cave, the way worn smoother than finest marble. The roof arches high and stirs with roosting bats, stretching leathery wings in preparation for their nightly flight. I realise I'm the only one with face upturned, so I tuck my chin into my chest, and sneak glances to see if the slip has been noticed.

No distractions, Sister, if you would secure your prize, they whisper. *Distractions will see you tumbling into a ravine.*

I rub the scar on my chin. I ought to have learnt that lesson by now. Luck smiles. There are no shouts of *Seize her!* No finger pointing at the living stranger amongst the dead. Down and down we go, not steep enough to slide, but I take care where I place my feet. I smell it before I see it: a gagging stench of stagnant water. My stomach pitches and rolls as we reach the river Lethe.

The ground is boggy and it is hard to know where land ends and river begins. Mud sucks at my sandals, releasing them with an unwilling slurp. Unmindful of the stink, the shades tramp towards the flat-bottomed barge waiting to carry them over.

A few paces, and I find myself face to face with Charon. His eyes twinkle in the scrubby marshland of his face. They are an unnerving azure, as though the Gods granted him a portion of the sky before confining him below the earth. I slip onboard and crouch at the stern, hoping not to attract attention.

'So, I have a live one,' he grumbles, plonking himself beside me and leaning on the gunwale.

'Aye,' I say, there being little point in denial.

'There's no accounting for mortals,' he mutters. His passengers gather at the prow, elbowing each other to get to the best spot. The boat tilts and yaws to starboard. 'Keep steady there!' cries Charon. I can't tell if he is addressing them or his living guest. He peers at me from the alarming blue eyes

349

that seem to see all, know all. 'Never worked out why they're so keen. They have an eternity awaiting them below.'

Charon's words resonate through my mind. I think of the sweetness of life: the gift of each day when I walk the earth and savour its wonders: the love of Antiklea, the bond with Meleager, my blood singing a praise-song when I run to the mountain.

He hawks, spits off the bow. 'So. Think yourself another Orpheus?'

'I have no lyre,' I say. 'And I'm as far from being a musician as is the bottom of the sea from the topmost peak of Olympos.'

His lips contort. He is smiling, and mightily unversed in it, going by the look on his face. I take it as a cue to continue.

'If I played a lyre, all the cats in the world would cease their yowling and concede to me the victor's crown for the most ghastly din.'

The smile stretches, cracks into a grin. The cargo of souls shuffles restlessly, complaining about why we aren't moving.

'Hold your horses,' croaks Charon. 'You're not in a hurry to be anywhere.'

The restless hum dissipates.

'No lyre,' I say. 'But I do have wine.' I slip the goatskin from my shoulder. His eyes flash. 'It is cheerless to drink alone. Perhaps you will do me the honour of sharing a draught?'

His hand snakes out, snatches the wineskin and pulls out the stopper. He tilts it to his lips with the blissful desperation of a hungry infant at the teat. The muscles in his throat dance as he gulps. He wrings out his beard, licking drops from his fingers.

'By the Gods, that is good. I don't suppose you have more?'

'No,' I say. He watches wistfully as I take a modest sip, barely enough to wet my lips. 'But I have drunk my fill. You finish it.'

The wineskin is in his fist before I've finished the sentence. He stoppers it carefully, clutching it close as a miser his purse.

'You'll be wanting a favour in return,' he says with a hiccup.

He may be tipsy, but he's not addled. I won't insult him with falsehood. I point at the far bank.

'Take me, and bring me back. I shall have a companion.'

He squints his eyes. 'From over there? You *are* another Orpheus.'

'Ah, but he failed at the last moment and returned alone. I shall not.'

For reply, Charon nods. He stretches out a hand. I clasp it and we shake on the bargain. It is like holding a fine-planed piece of oak. With a cry of *Hold hard*, he shoves the skiff from the shore and it glides into the stream. The current is slothful, more sludge than water, clinging to the sides as though loath to grant us passage.

'Who is this lost soul to you?'

I consider my answer. 'Friend. Brother. Lover. He did not abandon me when I was in need, and I shall not abandon him.'

Charon grunts. He lifts the pole and digs it into the sediment, punting us forwards. 'Your way will not be easy.'

'None of my life has been easy, from my first breath to the one I take now.'

Bubbles rise from the slurry. They pop, belching sulphur.

'You are determined,' he says, regarding me evenly from his piercing eyes. It is like being weighed up and judged by the sky. 'Good. You'll need it.' He scratches his backside. 'Now, that Orpheus. Came strutting in like he owned the place. Very fond of himself. You know the sort: forever twiddling their hair.' He pats the wineskin with a protective gesture and lowers his voice to a conspiratorial murmur. 'Between you and me, I reckon he looked back at Euridike on purpose.'

The barge sways lethargically. As soon as the prow noses the bank, the phantoms leap to the shore, eager to disembark. I am the last to leave.

'You're a queer one,' says Charon. 'But finer company than anyone since Herakles. I rather hope I do see you again.'

He shoves the pole into the bank and pushes off. I draw a coin from the pouch around my neck. He waves it away, chuckling.

'Everyone gives me gold,' he cries, already halfway across. 'As if I have anything to spend it on!' His laughter drifts across the river. 'Hearken!' he adds. 'I'll throw in a bit of advice: Fill the bowl first, loosen the collar second.'

Musing on his strange words, I follow the trail of the dead. We trek through a huge cavern, its walls bristling with spikes as sharp as spearheads. I am compelled to touch, and am surprised to find they are stone, not bronze. Swathes of the same strange rock hang from the roof, dripping with moisture. An outcrop the shape of a horse's head arches from the wall to my left, a lion springs from the right. It is as though two living beasts peered into the face of a Gorgon and never stirred again. The stone is wrought into every shape: a waterfall, frozen and unmoving; fluted columns a temple priest would be proud of; vast staircases that lead up and curve around before descending again. I stumble on, open-mouthed. Shadows dance around the cavern and amongst them I see my sister sentinels.

No time for gawping, they chide me, fiercely. *Hurry. You are running out of time.*

They are right. Wool-gathering will keep me from my goal. The procession squeezes through a narrow defile and we enter a new cave, also leaping and juddering with shadows. Looming higher than them all is Cerberus, the guardian hound of Hades. He towers above, spine writhing with snakes, and flexing the whip of his tail with a ferocious crack.

As the phantoms pass by, he lowers each of his three muzzles in turn to sniff. When satisfied, he growls, *Move on, move on.* I nibble the inside of my cheek and try to look as dead as possible. The queue edges forwards. Cerberus sniffs and growls, *Move on*; sniffs and growls, *Move on* until I stand before him. He lunges forwards to the end of his leash. I leap out of his way.

'No!' he roars, claws scrabbling just out of reach. 'Turn back!'

'I mean no harm,' I cry.

'You do not belong here!' he bellows.

'Nor did Herakles. Nor did Orpheus.'

He creaks open his huge jaws and howls, the sound loud as thunder. I fall to my knees, hands clamped over my ears. Spectres flood past, bumping against me. On and on Cerberus wails, and it comes to me it is not anger. It is agony. He swings his heads to left and right, pulling on the brutal chain that pins him to the rock. With each plunge, old scabs tear open. Still he hurtles to the end of the chain, tearing his flesh and drenching his shoulders in blood.

There is no way past. I think of Charon's words: *Fill the bowl first, loosen the collar second.* It made no sense then and makes no sense now. I pause. The underworld is the opposite of the upper world: death where there is life, darkness where there is light. A topsy-turvy land. To understand, perhaps I need to go against everything I have learnt.

I look about. The water-trough is empty. Of course! Cerberus is thirsty. The problem is clear: fallen branches and leaves have blocked the stream flowing into the cave. While Cerberus barks and whines, I climb up to the ledge, lean against the nearest log and shove. Nothing. I shove again, straining every muscle until I feel it give. I scoop out muck until fresh water pours into the tank. I turn to find Cerberus licking cracked lips. I stand at a safe distance as he shoves in his snouts and drinks deep.

Very slowly, I approach. He can kill me with a single bite, if he chooses. I stretch onto tiptoe and loosen his iron collar.

It has rusted into his neck so deeply the white of bone shows at the heart of the gash. The poor creature has been driven mad with pain.

As he quenches his ancient thirst, he slobbers thick ropes of saliva into the tank. It sparks an idea. I'm reminded of the soldiers' trick of letting a dog lick their wounds to aid healing. If the spittle of a one-headed dog can heal wounds, how much more powerful is the spittle of an enchanted three-headed beast. I unfurl my cloak and dip it in the trough, lay it around his neck as a poultice. He lets out a sigh of gratitude.

'I thank you for your kindness,' he whimpers. 'I shall reward you with advice. As you go forwards, you shall face your third and most dangerous challenge. Hear my words: Hold your nerve, whoever you see.'

I thank him, making sure he has plenty to drink before I continue. The walls of the cave close in and the roof leans down until my head brushes against it. First I have to crouch, then I am compelled to go on all fours, then I have to flatten myself onto my stomach and wriggle. I think of the grim journey an infant makes from the dark waters of the womb into the dry, harsh light of the world. I am making that journey in reverse, crawling back into the womb of Gaia.

I am pressed from all sides, and knock the back of my skull whenever I raise my head to work out where I'm going. In the end, I give up the attempt. The way is black as pitch in any case. I go slowly as a snail, if not slower, digging in my elbows and edging onwards. And then I get stuck. My chin is pressed into the dirt. When I breathe, I snort mud. The muscles of my arms scream with exertion. I can't move forward, I can't move backwards.

My body trembles. It builds and builds until I am quaking so violently I'm going to fly apart at the seams. I can't go on. Fright is draining every last scrap of energy. I am drowning in terror. I choke. Can't get enough air into my lungs. Can't breathe. Panic rises. A whine spirals up my throat and breaks free. I'm going to die.

Just when I need them, my sisters speak.

We are with you always, they say. *You can do this. You are more powerful than you can guess.*

I summon all my nerve. Yes. I am Atalanta.

I can grovel here until I truly join the dead, or I can continue what I came here for. I have circumvented Charon, I have passed Cerberus unharmed. In order to see this mission through to the end, I must do that most difficult of things: trust. Trust that the boatman of the dead has not lied. Trust that Cerberus has not sent me to my doom. If there were enough space to breathe, I would laugh.

Gradually, the panic subsides. Gradually, I breathe again. Inch by excruciating inch, I shift forwards. I start to wonder if I'm going to crawl forever, when the walls relent their squeezing. Little by little the way eases. I prop myself on my elbow, get onto my knees. I shuffle along until, abruptly, the roof flies away and I'm able to stand.

I'm in another cavern, which is flickering with an eerie radiance, silvery as moonlight. Cerberus warned me of a fearsome adversary and I'm on the lookout. Each muscle is taut, my bow gripped, an arrow notched and ready. All I can hear is my ragged breathing and the percussion of water dripping.

All around, the walls are painted with beasts: horses toss tufted manes, deer stretch their legs in flight, and bulls leap across the face of the living rock. Some creatures are bizarre: there is one with a snout longer than its tail, tusks curved over its head; another has a thin neck longer than its legs, its hide spotted like that of a leopard.

Around them in a constellation, thick as stars in the night sky, are the prints of little hands. So many, it would take a year to count. Small and neat-fingered, they are the hands of girls. I think of them, venturing into the belly of the Great Mother at the dawn of time, pressing their hands to the rock and daubing the walls with ochre the colour of oxblood.

I startle at a faint sound. Fool, I think, to have been distracted. I heft my bow.

'I know you are there,' I growl. 'You placed these pretty pictures here to throw me off my guard. You did a good job, too. Show yourself.'

The shadows shrivel away and a man slides forwards, of such grace and beauty I let out a gasp. I press my lips together. Careful, Atalanta, I counsel myself. You have been warned of a treacherous and cunning foe. He towers above me, lithe as a whip, his cloak a cascade of indigo darkness around his shoulders. He spreads his arms and smiles.

'Child,' he murmurs, gentle as sleep. 'Come to rest. Come to safety.'

His words plumb the core of my being. As Atalanta, I have been fighting all my life, from my first yelping breath. As Clotho, I spun the thread of Fate without ceasing, a million years and more. I am so very tired. Here stands the Sovereign of Death himself, inviting me to cease from striving. I grit my teeth and dig my toes into the dirt.

'My Lord Hades,' I say, and hold my nerve.

'Hush, child,' he murmurs. 'You can lay down your weapons.'

I ache to fly into his arms. I never fought so hard. The boar hunt was nothing set against this yearning to let loose the reins of life.

'My lord,' I say with a firmness I do not entirely feel. 'I am Atalanta. I have never laid down my bow, and shall not do so today.'

'Well met, brave Atalanta,' he says, voice sweet as milk straight from the teat. He narrows his eyes and sucks in a whistling breath. 'Well now. I declare I detect a pinch of Clotho also.'

I bow my head. I am too wary to be hoodwinked into letting down my guard, even for a God. He laughs, the sound of an ancient door creaking open for the first time in many years.

'You have passed the final test, Atalanta.' he says. 'The game is done. Truly. You are my hearth-guest, and very far from home. For what reason?'

'I have travelled here to claim my friend Meleager,' I growl. 'I demand it.'

'Ah, of course,' he says. 'The Fates' secret stratagem! The law of Death broken, the power of destiny cast down, free will given to mortals, etcetera. Have I missed anything?'

'You *know*?'

'Goodness me, yes,' he replies, with the susurration of a nest of snakes. 'Ah. I almost forgot. The power of the Gods winnowed to chaff.'

I wait for him to blast me into the wall of the cavern. He smiles, elegant hands folded over each other.

'You are not going to stop me?'

'No my child, I am not. Don't look so surprised. The chance to see my ghastly brother and his equally ghastly kin cast upon the winds? I wish I'd hatched The Plan myself. What sport!'

'You're a God. You will lose your power also.'

He laughs again, a tremor that rattles the bones of the earth. 'Oh, you are a darling child. I've not laughed so long in an age. I rarely have such . . . *lively* visitors. The Underworld can be frightfully glum.'

'But, my Lord Hades . . .'

'My dear, the power of the Gods may be broken, but I shall still be Lord of Death. My kingdom shall be unaffected. Busier, even. I promised the Gods they would join me. Never knew how I'd bring it to pass, and you have dropped it into my lap. I could kiss you. However, being embraced by the Lord of the Dead is inadvisable.' He laughs again. 'Come. You have won.'

'If I have won, give me my prize.'

'He is already here.'

Meleager steps from the darkness, as blank-faced as the last time I saw him. I have seen so much that is unreal and fear this is another phantasy, the cruellest yet.

'Trickery, my lord?'

'No. It is your friend,' says Hades. 'He has ventured deep into my kingdom and has forgotten himself, as all the dead forget. With each step towards life, he will recover a morsel of what was Meleager.'

At the sound of his name, Meleager blinks. He curls his hands into fists and rubs his eyes. I touch his arm. He is still warm. He lives.

'You are . . .' he gulps, blinking.

'Atalanta.'

He clasps my arm.

'Come now, children,' chides Hades. 'There is no time for a tearful reunion. Atalanta, bravest of women. You have proved yourself mighty as Herakles. Now you must prove yourself wiser than Orpheus. Do not look back until you have cleared the Tainaron Gate.'

'I shall be wise.'

'Be wiser than wise.' Hades clears his throat. 'Help me, Atalanta!' he cries, in the voice of Meleager. I gawp. 'Now you know what you are up against. My ghouls are as proprietary as eagles and as averse to releasing their prey.'

'My lord, I cannot thank . . .'

'Enough, enough. Off you go,' he says, wagging his hand. His cape drips shadows that curl around our ankles. 'Hurry. Ignore the pleading.'

'I will.'

He leans forward, pecks me lightly upon the cheek. I smell scorched flesh as he brands me with his lips.

'Go well, Atalanta,' he whispers. 'Go *now*.'

Further talk is unnecessary. The glow is beginning to fade from the walls and the shades are gathering themselves for pursuit. I grab Meleager's hand, and we run as only those escaping Death can comprehend. With each step, light turns to darkness at our heels. We race through the hall of painted beasts, the walls quivering with leaping bulls and galloping horses.

Help me, Atalanta! cries the voice of Meleager that is not Meleager. *Turn around, for pity's sake!*

I set my jaw and keep my eyes forward. Faster and faster we go, shadows panting hungrily at our backs.

Help me or I am lost! howl the deceiver spirits.

I ignore them. It is a final trap, and those are the easiest to fall into. A seasoned hunter knows it is when the beast is slain that the knife is most likely to slip and deliver a grievous wound. Meleager and I are not safe yet. I lead the way through the crushing tunnel, pursued by ravening gloom.

At last, we reach the cave of Cerberus. He barks in joyous recognition, his sores healed up. I throw my arms around all three of his shaggy necks, press my nose into his fur and murmur a prayer of thanks. He slathers me with his tongues, plants his enormous paws in the dirt and growls at the pursuing spectres, who shrink to a frightened halt, long enough for us to catch our breath. We stagger onwards, Cerberus guarding our safe passage.

At the riverbank, Charon is offloading a fresh cargo of souls. He waves merrily, gestures us onboard. I leap into the empty vessel and hear the thump of Meleager behind me. I must not turn to reassure myself he is onboard. Charon lifts the pole out of the sludge, shoves it in again and nudges us towards the living world. He lifts, he pushes. He lifts, he pushes, and all without the slightest sense of urgency. I clamp my hand over my mouth to stop myself crying out.

Inch by languid inch, Charon punts the boat through the slurry. The instant it touches the bank, I spring ashore. Shouting a hasty farewell, I battle my way through the crowd of dead fighting to climb aboard. I run, and run. I do not look back, not once. I keep running and do not pause, not until we're clear of the Tainaron Gate, not until we're a half-bowshot further. Not until I'm sure no demon can reach out and snatch us back.

We are out; out in the light.

The world dances and shimmers. I cannot see Meleager, cannot see anything in the glare. My heart sinks to my heels: I've been deceived by Hades. I am still in the Underworld and only imagine I've escaped. What a fool, to think I could venture to the very brink of life and then return.

It lasts a moment only. The dazzle subsides, and the things of this world gather into their recognisable selves. Sky separates itself from earth, an emerald blur becomes a tree, a grey mist becomes a rock. At my side, clutching his knees and panting with the effort of racing out of death and into life, is Meleager.

I hug him till he cries that I'll break his ribs if I'm not careful. I laugh also. I have done the impossible. I have plumbed Hades and brought out my beloved friend.

The Plan has not failed.

Around us the dead stream past, shrugged beneath their cloaks. The clouds hang low with rain and a frigid wind gusts in from the north-east. Crows cry their rough lamentation. To my mind, the weather has never been more favourable.

'I knew you would come,' says Meleager, gathering his breath.

'You did? I'm glad of it.'

'It was most strange. Then again, I could expect no less! Two magical girls appeared, as they have done all my life. They said their sister was on her way to save me.'

'Two girls? Beloved Meleager, those girls have protected me also.'

'You see them too?' he gasps. 'Thank the Gods. I wondered if I was going down the same path as my mother.'

'Never. They are Lachesis and Atropos, sent to protect us both through all our adversities.'

'The Moirai?' he says, brow creasing. 'But I was cursed by those hags.' He eyes me warily. 'They called you sister.'

'Yes, my dear Meleager. It is a tangled tale. I am unsure where to begin, for I only discovered the truth for myself a few days ago.' I rub my temples. 'A few days! The hunt seems a lifetime past.' I take a breath. 'I am Atalanta,' I whisper. 'It is not all I am. I am also Clotho of The Fates.'

'You are Atalanta and Clotho? I do not . . .' he mumbles, blinking. 'Am I still dead?'

I hug him until his trembling subsides and his breathing smooths into calmness.

'It is a long story,' I murmur. 'We have our lives to tell it.'

The words are only half-released when a gentle tremor runs through the ground. Even the dead pause in their unceasing march. All creation stands on tiptoe. The dust-motes at our feet begin to dance and pebbles roll about.

Meleager shivers. 'Is it an earthquake?'

'It is beginning.'

His eyes beg the question. Before I can answer, the air buckles and warps, gathering into the shape of a door. Through it, we see my sister-guides beckoning, familiar as always. I clasp Meleager's hand and lead him towards the light. He digs in his heels.

'Atalanta. I cannot. I have had my fill of other worlds.'

'Trust me,' I say.

Fear melts from his face. We step through and into a weaver's cottage, a loom propped against the wall. My sisters draw us towards them, faces radiant with bliss.

'Welcome, Sister!' they sing, pulling me into a dance. 'Welcome Meleager!'

The thatched roof is busy with the tenancy of insects. A cooking pot is wedged in the embers of the hearth, bubbling with rabbit stew and savoury with the aroma of sage and rosemary. I have never been here, and yet I have lived here longer than ten lifetimes.

Meleager looks about him, gawping. 'Is this the abode of The Moirai? I imagined a palace.'

'It is not as it seems,' says Lachesis.

She swipes a hand through the air and the room shivers, like the reflection in a quiet pond when stirred with the fingers.

'A comforting illusion,' adds Atropos. 'Our immortal forms are too fantastic for mortal minds to encompass.'

A giantess steps out of the shadows, her head brushing the roof beams. 'Welcome, Meleager!' she booms. 'Welcome, Atalanta!'

'Themis!' I cry, flying into her arms and covering her face with kisses.

One by one, they kneel.

'We offer our gratitude, honoured Meleager, most courageous of men,' says Lachesis. 'For the sake of humankind, you suffered the lash of a pitiless destiny.'

'And you, brave Atalanta,' says Atropos. 'You gave up your immortality to stand at Meleager's side. You descended into the Underworld and challenged Hades himself to ensure the success of our stratagem. We thank you.'

'Thank you both,' says Themis. 'Together you have fulfilled our plan, to grant free will to mortals.'

Meleager looks from smiling face to smiling face. 'I truly am dreaming,' he gulps. 'I am still in the Underworld.'

'This is no dream,' says Themis, getting to her feet. 'We

thought it right to bring you here and offer thanks for every one of your sacrifices.'

Meleager takes my hand. 'My whole life, I craved this moment. A hundred times I dreamed of coming face to face with The Fates and repaying them for the wreckage of so many lives. In my dreams I grabbed the three harridans by the scruff of their scraggy necks and ground them into the dirt until they begged for mercy. Now the moment has come, and I am at peace.' He bows to Themis, Lachesis and Atropos in turn. 'You have my thanks also. Mortal thanks, but wholehearted all the same.'

Themis smiles. 'We chose well. Now, beloved Atalanta and Meleager. Return to your lives with our blessing.'

There is a moment when the cosmos takes in a breath.

'What of us, Mother?' asks Lachesis.

'It is time for you to surrender your power and return to the stars,' says Themis. 'You shall melt into the void, sleep a million years, and a million more. Life will end and begin, end and begin. Creatures will rise from mud and sink, and rise again. You shall watch over them, motherly and kind.'

They exchange glances.

'We have watched our sister,' says Lachesis. 'Tasted her joy and sorrow, the sharp and the sweet.'

'We wish to go with her and Meleager,' says Atropos, firmly. 'I would rather live an eyeblink as a free mortal than an eternity as a star-being.'

Lachesis grasps Atropos's hand. 'I choose mortality also,' she declares, determination in her voice.

'Take heed, my girls,' says Themis. 'When the power of The Fates is gone from the world, it is gone forever. You cannot change your minds and return to Nyx if you find mortality not to your taste. To be mortal is not easy.'

Atropos sticks out her chin. 'Did you not teach us the easy path is never the best, nor the most contented?'

Themis's eyes twinkle as the stars themselves. 'Observing human life has taught you wisdom, my children.'

'You taught us wisdom, Mother.'

'I have done well, in that case.'

In all my uncountable years as Clotho, I never saw Themis so happy. Lachesis and Atropos take a deep breath and let go their hold on immortality. Perhaps I expect the change to be dramatic: to pulsate and throb in a riot of colour and excitement, as upon that night when we were transfigured upon the mountain. It is a slow and gentle release, so quiet I almost miss it. They are no longer The Fates, smothering and controlling the destiny of mortals. The power of The Fates, and of the Gods also, drains from the world.

Liberation ripples across the earth: soft as the rabbit breath of a newborn child, mighty as the rust-red torrents that pour down the mountain after winter rains. Each mortal takes their first breath of freedom: A young woman straightens her spine, bent from weaving; a man laid low by despair sees a glimmering of hope; a drunkard shoves aside his wineskin and crawls from the gutter of his life; a peasant girl declares, *I will learn to read.*

367

The aftershock is still echoing when we hear it: a distant rumble approaching with the lumbering din of war-horses. The walls shudder, dust and splinters raining down upon our heads. The roof is torn away like the lid of a patch-wood box. We look up and see him, unmistakeable in all his gaudy magnificence.

Zeus.

He leans close, licking his lips.

'Ha! I have you now! I've been waiting for this moment. Look at you!' he crows. 'Daughters of Nyx, reduced to mortal mud and spittle. You are dirt beneath my foot. I shall grind you with my heel! I'll rip you all to shreds! Him as well!' he cackles, pointing at Meleager. 'No one can stop me. I shall crush you like—'

'Do it then,' we say. 'Stop boasting how you'll do this or that. Get on with it.'

He blinks, mouth open, but recovers quickly. 'You dare defy me?'

'We do.'

He tips back his head and bellows triumph. A thunderbolt materialises in his fist, a lance of penetrating flame that hums with the urge to be released. He draws back his arm and lets it loose. It lands with the force of a damp crust of bread. We stand unharmed.

'No!' he cries, and throws a second volley, which spatters at our feet. 'What's happening? What have you done to me?'

Bolt after bolt falls short, sizzling into cinders that barely singe the ground. Zeus hurls daggers of divine fire, javelins of ice. We feel nothing, fear nothing. He cannot harm us.

'Give me back my power!' he wails, and tosses another impotent bolt. 'You are puny mortals. Why won't you die? The Oracle said you were surrendering your power.'

'The Oracle spoke truth. You only listened to half of it.'

'Yes, we are no longer The Fates,' we say. 'We no longer decide the destiny of mortals. Humanity is free.'

'Free? Free? What difference does it make?'

'Mortals are not only free of us interfering in their lives,' we say. 'They are also free of the tyranny of the Gods. It is over, Zeus. Your temples are crumbling. Your power is gone.'

'No, no, no!' he screams.

'You have never understood freedom,' says Themis. 'Terror can only govern for so long before it collapses under its own weight. Give up, little brother.'

'Never! I am Ever-Living Zeus!'

He hurls another shower of lightning at Meleager. It is gentle as a beam of evening sunlight.

Themis laughs. 'You can stamp and sulk and toss your thunderbolts but they lack divine power. You are a ghost of yourself, Zeus. You shall fade. You are fading already.'

'Themis!' he roars, shoving his face close to hers. 'This is all your fault, you raddled old sow. When I slaughtered your kindred, I thought my greatest vengeance was to let you live and watch helplessly as I gutted your existence of every pleasure.' He rubs his palms together, sparking storms. 'My thunderbolts may be powerless against free mortals, but they will work on you.' He eyes glitter venom. 'I should have done this aeons ago.'

He hefts a spear of quivering light, hurls it at our mother and pierces her through the heart. She crumples, falls. We rush to her side.

'My girls,' she whispers, blood bubbling between her lips.

We turn on Zeus. 'Coward!' we cry.

'You are mortal,' he sneers. 'Taste mortal grief. I hope it chokes you. I am still king of the Gods. There will always be men I can force to worship me. You have not heard the last of Zeus!'

Roaring with laughter, he flies away, smaller and smaller until he is nothing but a fly-speck. We turn to Themis. The wound is fatal. We know it, and so does she. She tries to raise herself and falls back, exhausted unto death.

'Mother!' we cry. 'Don't leave us!'

'Do not weep for me. I am returning to Nyx, the Mother of all. While there is a sky above you, I shall never be wholly gone.'

'Themis,' we say, smiling on her with such balm it could bring a soul back from the dead. But Themis is gone too far even for our efforts. 'You are more dear to us than we have power to say.'

We kiss her battered forehead. It is what she did for us, when we were girls. The child is become the mother.

Themis lifts a hand, and lets it fall. 'Go, my beloved children. Go, my son Meleager. Go with my blessing. Quickly. The enchantment cannot hold.'

Her eyes glaze, she lets out a final breath, and enters her other life. We pray it is kind. The hut is disintegrating, shafts of unearthly radiance tearing rents in the walls. The loom, the distaff and the shears melt away as the glamour evaporates.

'This was a wonderful home.'

'We were happy here.'

'Happy as carefree children.'

I hug my sisters to my breast. They have always been my sisters, even when I believed they were spirits dancing in my dreams. Together with Meleager, we run to the roadside shrine. The protective shield surrounding our little kingdom is almost gone.

'It is time for our new adventure,' I say. 'Our lives will be our own, to make of what we will.'

'It will be difficult.'

'Harsh and unforgiving.'

'It will be joyous.'

'It will be life.'

Sister takes the hand of sister. We smile at Meleager and take his hand also.

'I have seen The Fates,' he says. 'I have seen the last of the Titans. I have seen Zeus himself.' He grins ruefully. 'No one will believe me.'

'I will,' I say, and kiss him fiercely. His face is the sun, rising into joy.

We approach the threshold, radiant with possibility. We take a breath, close our eyes, count *1, 2, 3* and leap.

Time To Come

ZEUS

Olympos

The Throne of the Gods

So, The Fates think I am beaten? They think I am gone because my temples have fallen into ruin? Fools, if they imagine for one moment I am rendered incapable because they've surrendered their immortal powers and handed over free will to humankind. They have thwarted me for now, but not forever. I shall bide my time.

How little they understand mortals. There will always be those who yearn to believe. Men are so needy, so desperate for something to worship. The Gods may be dead, but see how they are lost without us. Mortals do not want to be free. They hunger for divine authority, lacking it in themselves.

What need have I for shrines of granite, which can be abandoned to the swallowing sands? My temples shall be built in the human heart. Millions of invisible altars, where men offer dripping sacrifices of envy, lust and greed. Where there is anger, you shall find me stoking the fires of violence. Where there is war, I shall urge men to greater atrocity.

I hunger. I thirst. I feed and fatten on terror, hatred and

despair. Every filthy human feeling is my meat and drink, and I am never sated. Mortals will tremble. I shall make them slay their own children to prove their adoration. Anyone who speaks one word against me, I shall crush their tongues with bricks. I shall show no mercy, yet all will call me merciful.

Yes, I shall have the final word. When history comes to be written – and it shall be written to my liking, for I am the greatest of the Gods – it will portray The Fates as doddering and venomous, spinning and weaving, measuring and snipping, because after all, that is all women are good for.

History shall say precisely what I tell it to. It shall say Themis was my wife and The Fates my children or sisters, I care not as long as they are under my control. Meleager shall be a drunken roisterer, remembered for the number of virgins he deflowered. As for Atalanta, History will marry her off. Of course, I shall permit her a modicum of youthful gallivanting with bow and arrow, so that men may enjoy her pretty breasts bouncing as she canters through sylvan glades, but wed she will be: to Meleager, Hippomenes or some other fellow, it does not matter. Anything else is unthinkable.

The Sisters of Artemis shall be written as corrupt slayers of beast and man, frenzied and horrible to behold. I shall toss their names into the ash-bucket of forgetting and good riddance. No more Mother Goddess. No more power. I shall bury the knowledge so deep no one will ever be able to dig it up.

Hera's suggestion to wreck a single mortal's life lacked ambition. Dear, silly wife and her fluffy female brain. I shall hammer my stories into the world. I shall warp history itself, for centuries. Millennia! I rub my hands, sparking glee.

I am going to have so much fun.

I, Zeus, with my hundred names, shall be feared and adored. To the uttermost reaches of the earth, when men sing praise, it shall be in my name alone. I shall wipe out the memory of other Gods, pound their statues into dust and plough them into the muck. I shall pluck out their names and replace them with my own.

I will never die. I am Zeus. I am a jealous God, and men shall have no other God but me.

THE FATES

Olympos

A Time out of Time

In the way of the best tales, our ending is simply another beginning.

Let Zeus rant and rave and spit his bile. His lightning bolts are little more than toys hurled out of a cradle. We have heard his tantrums a hundred times, and the tune never changes. He rages, he storms, and like a storm, he blows himself out.

His power is split to its core. He is a clay pot, filled with dried peas and shaken to amuse a child. His temples are fallen and visited by foxes. Curious travellers trace the remnants of his name carved upon tumbled walls, and wonder how men were once so credulous they worshipped the weather. When dark clouds churn and lightning pierces the sky, it is the working of nature, not a divine command.

The earth is better off without immortals: no thunderbolts, no chariots, no wing-heeled messengers bringing dire news to the sound of golden trumpets. No miracles at all, save that of men and women carving out a little space in a rough and unruly world.

We are no longer The Fates. We lay down spindle and distaff, dismantle the loom, and weave the fabric of destiny no longer. We are the female Prometheus. He brought the gift of fire to humankind: we offer Free Will, which is a fire all of its own. We pass the flame into mortal hearts. If they refuse to step into its light, we cannot force them to do so. If there are some who wish to shackle themselves to a destiny, it shall be one of their own devising. They can call it what they wish: fate, fortune, the whim of the Gods. We have no part in it.

Men call this the Age of Iron. They mourn for a Golden Age when The Fates decreed and mortals obeyed; when we spun, and measured, and snipped. A never-never Time when immortals strolled through a green and pleasant Arcadia; when heroes grappled monsters and rescued swooning damsels; when Herakles flexed his meaty thews and ripped lions in twain.

Folk forget it was also the epoch when the Gods plundered and stole, ravaged and rained vengeance upon any mortal who dared raise their face from the dirt. No, we do not grieve for this so-called Golden Age, neither do we weep. A glittering age, perhaps, but all that glitters is not gold.

Humans are treading their own path, standing and stumbling by turns. They are forging their own fortune, the bad and the good. Crafting lives of their own free will. They are choosing to burn or to build, to hate or to love. We leave them with the wish that they choose wisely and live in joy.

The Egyptians have a saying: *Speak a man's name and he lives forever.*

We have already lived forever. We, who watched the planets form from the dust of stars; we who clasped the strong arms of spiral galaxies and swirled across the dancing-floor of the heavens. Now, we shall live once and briefly. We wake to each morning granted us, and give thanks for every one.

We are mortal and we are happy. Such bliss is dangerous. The rumours rush around the feasting-halls of Olympos, and the immortals look upon us wistfully. The first to sneak away is a dryad, her absence overlooked or unnoticed. Another follows, stepping down to join us upon earth. The trickle swells into a flood as the heavens empty out. God after God, Goddess after Goddess quits the dragging tedium. They choose mortality with its joy and pain, leaving their couches to gather holy dust.

We step through the door between worlds and into exploration. Who knows where we shall go, the people we shall become. Never before, in all our uncountable years, have we not known what tomorrow will hold. If a soothsayer offered us a glimpse into the secrets of our future, we would refuse. We tread our own path and build our lives one step, one breath and one moment at a time. We sleep and wake, in the full knowledge we shall one day sleep without waking.

Yes, the winds of the world are sharp and gust through our lives. We weather the storms with a great good will, with no inkling what we shall discover. But oh, it shall be unexpected and wonderful.

ATALANTA

Parthenion

What more to tell?

So many adventures, I could fill a years' worth of evenings recounting the tales. Enough. An end to wild stories, for now.

I live simply, with Antiklea and Meleager.

I do not care if the world disapproves of our arrangement. I have never lived my life to please others, and have no intention of beginning. I love Antiklea; I love Meleager. My love is unbounded, knowing neither barrier nor impediment. Antiklea is a woman, Meleager a man. As for that, I have been called both, and neither. I see no obstacle. My love surpasses the happenstance of sex. Love is a joyous dance and I am the dancer. Male, female. Does it matter overmuch, if there is love?

If we love contrary to the world's rules – and we do – so be it. Kingdoms rise and kingdoms fall, and what is deemed improper behaviour in one is commended in the next. Perhaps this world will come around to our peaceable way of living. Perhaps I will live to see it, perhaps not. Either way, no scowling busybody shall stop us living as we choose. I divert my energies into kindness and affection. For what is greater than love, and sweeter than life?

With delight and pride, I recall the day my dearest Antiklea stands up to her father and refuses marriage. She is ablaze with the fire of her will, dawn to dusk. She credits me with teaching her the strength. As if I could teach Antiklea anything. She is a skilled healer. Her poultices and philtres against ague and fever are famous, and bring visitors from across the land to our door.

Meleager grows ever more grizzled. His limbs are scratched and scored, his legs bowed. Too old for battle, he trains youths in the arts of combat. I stand at his side and teach the art of the bow. My eye is true as ever, my aim also.

Our living arrangements prompt gossip, but folk know full well their sons will find no better teachers. All a lad need do is say he was a pupil of Meleager and Atalanta, and a shrewd captain hires him on the spot. There is always war. Each year brings a new feud, for kings are petulant boys, every last one of them. Soldiers are trained by Meleager and myself; they fight, are wounded, and Antiklea patches them up.

As for my sisters, they could live distant in time as well as space, but we have always loved each other's company. Lachesis marries a miller and invents a weighing-scale so accurate customers flock to her door for fair measure. Millers from three kingdoms away pay for the right to make a copy of the device. Atropos chooses the body of a man, and earns fame as the firmest and fairest law-giver in Parthenion, his judgements satisfying all parties.

Once a year, on the night marking the accomplishment of our plan, we climb Mount Parthenion. High as the flight of falcons there is a rocky outcrop shaped like a throne, or so our fancy suggests. We pour a libation of wine, sit together and watch the stars prick their tiny lights across the vault of the sky. Once upon a very strange time, we listened to Themis telling stories.

'Look,' I say, pointing to the Pleiades. 'The Seven Sisters, beloved daughters of the Titan Atlas and nymph Pleione. How many can you count?'

'I see eight!' says Atropos.

'Me too, I think,' says Lachesis.

I hug them tight. 'It is a good omen to count more than seven.'

As I grow older, memories brighten my days. I remember my mother Arktos. She nourished me on strong milk and I grew up free of the falsehood that girls are timid, so I became brave. I grew up free of the falsehood that girls are feeble, so I became brawny. I grew up free of the falsehood that girls are weak-minded, so I became clever. I grew up free of the falsehood that girls are inferior, so I became Equal-in-Weight.

I became Atalanta.

I have honed muscle of body and spirit and if not beautiful, well, I don't squander valuable time mourning that state of affairs. I live in the house of my body, and know its undecorated rooms well. There is no other woman like me. No. Strike that proud remark. There are legions of women like me.

I have been told that no one will listen to my story, that no one has the slightest interest in what a woman has to say, and that female words are as the squabbling of sparrows, empty and meaningless.

I have been told that women are naturally subservient and meek; naturally foolish and prone to error and therefore it is for our own good that man leads and woman follows. Have been told it is the decree of the Gods; that it is the way things have always been done and there's nothing I can do to change it.

I save my breath when I hear this twaddle. There is no advantage to be gained in setting out clear and logical arguments to the contrary, of which there are a multitude. I have learned it is a waste of time to reason with those who've already made up their minds. As my beloved Antiklea says, it's as much use as playing *petteia* with a chicken: it will strut across the board and knock over the pieces before defecating and flapping away.

I am a dangerous woman. My name is one of the few to endure. I began with my breath and nothing else. From that nothing, I built myself. I stepped out of shadow and into the torch light of legend, which is flickering and unreliable. I paused awhile, a wil o' the wisp in the hinterland of history.

I am remembered because I refused. I lived against the grain. I lived on the wrong side of opinion, but on the right side of a good yarn. My stories are true on the inside, where it matters. The outside is a cloth, embroidered with pretty patterns. Believe what you will, and discard the rest.

As for the Sisters of Artemis, history describes our rites as bloodstained lechery. We are painted as women driven mad with wine and unnatural passions, defiling ourselves with goats and stags. Whirling into a frenzy and tearing beasts apart with our bare hands, plunging our faces into the entrails and slabbering our bodies in gore, our ululating howls shredding the heavens into splinters.

It makes for a colourful fiction, salacious and lip-smacking. A cautionary tale told to frighten boys into mistrust of their wives and sisters; told to scare girls into treading the narrow path of miserable existence, barely daring to draw breath without a man's say-so.

And yet.

Despite all attempts to make us monstrous, to each generation are born girls who dare to dream; who dare to step off the narrow path and discover worlds they never guessed. The road is never easy for these girls, as I have discovered. It is a journey beset with trials and buffeted with fearsome storms.

I recall the first ones who visited me, declaring themselves Sisters of Artemis, and vowing to lead an Amazon life. Girls like them still come to our door. Not in great number, but enough to plant hope. Shyly they approach, these marvellous young women. Shyly, they peer through their eyelashes. Shyly they ask, *Were you really suckled by a bear? Did you really slay the Calydonian boar? Can you really outrun any man?*

I invite them to sit awhile. They count my battle scars, and we drink buttermilk and eat a little bread. When their questions are answered, and their bashfulness laid to rest by my kindly answers, they get around to revealing the true reason for their visit.

Will you teach us? they say. *Will you teach us to be like you?*

They ask why they are so at odds with the world's demands. They are anxious, convinced they've enraged a God, or labour under a curse. I tell them gently, *there is nothing wrong with you*. The fault is with a world that only deals in absolutes: day and night, up and down, black and white. A world that insists men act one way and women the other. A world that forgets we are all created of the same clay, and into us our mother Nyx breathes the same breath of life.

They do not believe me at first, not because they do not wish to, but because it is hard to change rigid ideas, however great the desire. Little by little, I watch self-belief bud and flower as they accept themselves in all their marvellous variety. Some choose the bow, some the marriage bed. Some choose both, some neither. The most important thing is they choose their own path, rather than having it chosen for them.

And oh, the exhilaration of living versus existing! The joy of meeting sisters along the way, forging a family of treasured kith and kin linked by the powerful ties of choice, not blood.

Once, I said to Meleager that I have many years to live. I have skated close to making that an empty boast, and have learned my lesson. I know my existence will be the briefest of glimmerings, a flame that burns a moment between the twin darknesses of birth and death. The flicker of a small star and then . . . gone. One more year, ten or twenty, I have no idea. Yes, one day I shall die. I am not frightened of Death, nor am I in any hurry to greet Hades a second time. Without life, death has no meaning. Without death, there is no meaning to life.

As the years pass, I marvel at the crinkling of skin in the crook of my elbow, the spots on the back of my hands, as though I spilled wine thereon. I kiss each wrinkle dancing at the corner of Antiklea's smiling mouth; I kiss the salt-and-pepper in Meleager's beard. Age brings a lessening of antagonism. My silvered hair grants me a measure of respect I lacked as a young woman warrior, when half the world spat on my heels, and the other half refused to believe in my existence.

Antiklea teases me that Praxiteles is angling for a patron to commission a statue of me and I fear she is only half-joking. Knowing that fellow, I shall be carved svelte and winsome. Once an artwork is wrought, people tend to believe in its perfect appearance and no longer bother with the rough and ready model herself.

Sometimes, a far-off look creeps into Meleager's eye. We sit, I take his hand and listen to him speak of the Underworld, until his face clears and he lays down that fearsome weight of remembrance for another day. I know there are things he cannot, will not say. He knows the next time he crosses the river Lethe there will be no returning.

Where he goes, I shall follow. Where Antiklea goes, I shall follow also. At the going down of life's sun the three of us shall meet on the riverbank, together and inseparable. We shall be just as loving in Death.

Acknowledgements

With gratitude to the creative team at Quercus, for this opportunity: especially Emma Capron, Gaby Puleston-Vaudrey, Celine Kelly and Cassie Browne.

Thank you – always – to my wonderful agent, Charlotte Robertson.

To Tom and Rachel Ashton (& assorted livestock), who welcomed me into their forest home near Athens, Georgia; gifting me with generous space and time to write.

And for every library that sheltered and nurtured the child who loved nothing more than hiding in a corner with a book of Greek myths.

Rosie Garland has a passion for language nurtured by public libraries. She writes fiction and poetry, and sings with post-punk band The March Violets. Her debut novel *The Palace of Curiosities* won the Mslexia Novel Competition and was longlisted for the Desmond Elliott Prize. Subsequent publications have been widely recommended by *The Times*, *The Guardian* and *The Sunday Times*. In 2023, she was made a Fellow of The Royal Society of Literature. *The Fates* sees Rosie take her writing in an exciting new direction.